Newearth Progeny

A. K. Frailey

Hardcover Edition

ISBN of Hardcover: 979-8-9998241-1-0

Website
https://akfrailey.com/

A. K. Frailey Books

THE WRITINGS OF A. K. FRAILEY

Books for the Mind and Spirit

https://akfrailey.com/

Contemporary Literary Fiction

OLDTOWN Fly, Sparrow, Fly

OLDTOWN Brothers Born

Historical Science Fiction Novels

OldEarth ARAM Encounter

OldEarth Ishtar Encounter

OldEarth Neb Encounter

OldEarth Georgios Encounter

OldEarth Melchior Encounter

Science Fiction Novels

Homestead

Last of Her Kind

Newearth Justine Awakens

Newearth A Hero's Crime

Newearth Progeny

Newearth Relevance

Short Stories

It Might Have Been—And Other Short Stories 2nd Edition

One Day at a Time and Other Stories

Encounter Science Fiction Short Stories & Novella 2nd Edition

Inspirational Non-Fiction

My Road Goes Ever On—Spiritual Being, Human Journey 2nd Edition

My Road Goes Ever On—A Timeless Journey

The Road Goes Ever On—A Christian Journey Through The Lord of the Rings

Children's Book

The Adventures of Tally-Ho

Wise Home

Wise Home on Lily Pad Pond

Poetry

Hope's Embrace & Other Poems 2nd Edition

Prologue

Who Wasn't

—Waukee—

Tuesday, August 22nd

Clare, wearing a long nightshirt, stood in her living room before an antique bookshelf, holding a family photo of herself as a baby in her mother's arms. Her dad leaned over her mom's left shoulder, a grand smile on his face. Everyone was smiling…even baby Clare. *We were happy then.*

With a sigh, Clare replaced the photo and tried to clear her mind. She ran her fingers along the edge of the shelf and stopped on a fat album made in the OldEarth style.

*OldEarth…*she could practically smell the rich humas of the bygone era. Generations ago, the dim past where nameless humans suffered catastrophic infertility. *It had been their fault, right?*

Maybe not. So many opinions written over the decades, few to explain what really happened. Certainly, everyone was clear on one point—calamitous wars set off a cascade of planetary destruction, nearly dooming the population. Only the intervention of Luxonians, Light Beings, had brought healing to remnant humanity. Cerulean's brilliant blue eyes rose in her mind. *The best of the best.*

Dragging her thoughts back to the present, she tapped the album, a gift from Bala who, besides being her partner in the Human Services Division, was also an all-knowing advisor when it came to matters of the soul. She never asked, but he offered various proverbial insights whenever the mood struck, which was much too frequently for Clare's taste. What he didn't know, his wife, Kendra filled in. Such insight could be handy—at times.

Her heart constricting with old losses, Clare snatched the album into her arms and cradled it as she paced to the couch and plopped down with a huff.

Flipping through pages of family and friends, her life passed before her eyes. Herself as a baby, her mother forever young and vivacious. Dad almost always smiling. Her little school pals, her fellow trainees... Her first Human Services assignment in the South West Island District. Oh, Jay McKenny and the Adul Brothers! Such clear-eyed professionals who took everything so seriously. Of course, Ms. Jan, her first boss, cranky and viciously insensitive, but the woman knew how to get all the right forms filled out on time. Her last big dinner celebration with Mom and Dad…

Then blank pages. Nothing more.

Pain rippled through Clare's body, nearly bursting through her chest. A poisonous meal that should never have happened. Her parents dead amid heart-wrenching questions she could never answer.

Blasted aliens!

Protecting humanity was her only solace through the dark days. Dependable friends helped, of course—Cerulean and Bala—but also terrifying enemies haunted her sleep. *No! Stop it!* A deep cleansing breath. *I've put all that behind me; I don't need to think about it anymore. I have a good job, good friends...*

She shook her head, trying to banish rising panic. It wasn't *who was* in the album. It was *who wasn't.*

No brother.

No sister.

No husband.

No lover.

No child of her own…

"By the Divide! Stop it!"

Her cat, Jillian, a stray found scrounging in the neighbor's compost heap, wandered in from the kitchen, ignored the outburst, and meowed a long complaint. It rubbed itself against her ankles.

"I wasn't talking to you, cat." Clare slapped the album shut, stood, and pounded back to the shelf. She shoved her memories, along with the book, back into place. With a quick pat, she retreated from the shadowed past and comforted the animal. "I fed you plenty, and you're getting fat. So out you go! I've got work to do…you go round up a mouse or two and earn your keep."

With efficient motions and fixing her mind on the workday ahead, Clare hurried to her bedroom and tied her shoulder-length hair into a ponytail. She tugged off her baggy nightshirt, replacing it with more professional attire: dark blue dress pants with a white, short-sleeved button-up blouse. She snapped her datapad onto her wrist, opened the side door, suffered the blast of late summer heat, and ushered the cat into the backyard. Then she turned her face toward the center of town.

Despite the early morning heat, her lethargic soul stirred with invigorating possibilities. *The future—that's what matters.* She had important affairs to attend to. Bala had said something about a child abduction case. Or was it a porn ring? Surely, not more drug smuggling. *Whatever.* Once they met at the Breakfastnook Café in Vandi, he'd fill her in.

Her stomach growled. As she marched down the Waukee sidewalk, ignoring the storm clouds looming on the horizon on this humid August morning, autoskimmers glided up and down the road, while a couple of imposing Interventionalists loitered on the corner. A lady directed her poodle into William's Veterinary Clinic, sidestepping a pair of Bhuaci girls strolling toward the new Waukee Middle School. A Cresta, manager of the local farm implements, seed, and fertilizer emporium, eyed Clare, his tentacles clasped complacently over his rotund middle, as he stood under the shade of a colorful banner advertising “Fruitful Farms.”

Crossing the street, an Ingot, her bio-mechanical suit well-tailored to her womanly form, clasped the hand of a small Ingot child…a rare sight indeed! Clare stopped on the corner and watched the duo make it safely across the small-town intersection and head toward the park.

Strange. Don't think I've ever seen an Ingot child before. But they must exist...just hardly ever out in public. Or are there so few because they live so long?

Shoving the puzzling thought aside, Clare ordered an autoskimmer and directed it to Vandi. She'd feel like her old self again once she reached the Breakfastnook Café and enjoyed a wholesome breakfast.

Her partner's long history of losing track of time set her heart racing. The skinny, awkward guy loved to deflect his lack of promptness with the absurdity that at least he looked like a Greek God but that only made her laugh, not forget the time.

Bala, you had better not be late!

Chapter One

Never Would Have Predicted That

—Vandi Township—

Clare breezed into the Breakfastnook Café—the door chimes tinkling merrily—as if she owned the place. Though she hadn't invested in the establishment, per se, the ties that bound her to the family-style establishment were far stronger than any legal contract.

The sight of Faye, her Bhuaci shape-shifting friend and occasional accomplice, added bounce to her step as she headed to the bright red booth. She stared down at the petite child-like figure. Though Faye could morph into an eight-foot Sectine lizard at the snap of her fingers, she preferred the unassuming form of an elfin youth and always dressed in soft pastel fabrics. "Almost didn't recognize you without Taug. Where's he at?"

With a twinkle in her eyes, Faye patted the seat next to her. "I told him to get his work done early because I've got a surprise waiting for him at home."

Uncertain as to where this conversation might lead her, Clare plopped down onto the plastic bench and hummed low. "Hmmm…so you…?" Honestly, she wasn't sure what to ask. A shape shifting Bhuaci and a water-based alien twice her size formed an interesting, even baffling, couple. They couldn't live as lovers but their mutual devotion endured nonetheless.

Sensitive to the needs of others, Faye glanced about and wiggled her fingers discreetly at the owner as he stepped into the dining room. She pointed to Clare meaningfully.

Riko, a slim Uanyi wearing his usual white uniform over his rubbery exoskeleton, swept his gaze across the bustling establishment and grinned. His bulky breathing mask had been replaced with a slim tube that entered one nostril, though his crab-like mandibles hadn't changed one iota. The heavy kitchen door swung backward in his wake. Locking onto Faye, Riko's enormous eyes lit up, and he bustled over.

Clare couldn't help but smile. *It's as if we're his favorite customers.* A deep current of well-being competed with tumultuous hunger pains. "Hiya, Riko."

Beaming, Riko stopped beside the table. "What'll you ladies have this fine morning?"

Faye laughed. "I already asked Wendell for my usual, but Clare just got here."

As if deciding the fate of the universe, Clare squinted at the ceiling and tapped her fingers on the table. "Pancakes with your scrumptious protein topping…fruit salad…coffee…and that yogurt cup you make so colorful."

Riko bowed. He never needed notes. Whatever else those big eyes and mandibles did, they didn't take up his brain space. "Wendell is in the back helping cook with a little refrigeration issue." He shrugged. "Hard to get parts for some of the original equipment. But if there's one thing I like to say about the place, we're as authentic OldEarth as they come."

Covering a slight choke, Faye slurped from her water glass.

Clare stared deadpan at Riko. "Though *you're* not from OldEarth stock."

Riko's grin didn't waver as he slapped a hand over his chest, presumably in an attempt to make a sincere pledge. "But my refrigeration unit most certainly is!"

Faye's chuckle turned into a gasp. She nudged Clare in the ribs. "Look at that, will you!"

Clare glanced around, trying to get up to speed. Then she followed Faye's fixed gaze.

Riko's hands were thicker than humans, but he had the

fingers of an artist, long and slender. On the fourth and shining in glorious brilliance, a ring shot light rays across the room.

Clare leaned in. "What's that you've got, Riko? I'd almost think it was…but it couldn't be…" She pulled her gaze away from the flashing diamond to his face. "Is it?"

A pink flush colored Riko's normally pale face. "It's just an exchange—an exchange ring with Jayla. We pledged to make a pledge…in a year's time."

With a snorted laugh, Clare slapped the table. "Like *I* always say, make all the pledges you want, just don't lie to me." Love relationships were not on her short list. People were too unpredictable and aliens were almost always suspect.

Wendell, an Ingot youth with less of the bulky techno armor than most of his kind, stepped forward with a tray and laid a bowl of creamy cereal before Faye, and then set two drinks beside the water—orange juice and dark green tea.

Faye nodded with a pleased smile. "Perfect, Wendell. You're an expert server these days." She patted Clare's arm. "I need to freshen up a moment, that'll give Riko a chance to get your order ready."

In quick comprehension, Clare slid out of the booth and took her place on the opposite side while Faye bustled to the lady's room.

Riko hurried toward the kitchen.

Wendell yanked a bottle of disinfectant and a cloth from his multi-purpose belt and started cleaning the table across from the booth.

Before she could stop herself, Clare blurted out the question she'd always wanted to ask. "Where's your family, Wendell?"

His eyes wide, Wendell straightened and stared back at Clare. "Family?"

Uneasy feelings suddenly riding roughshod over her

momentary happiness, Clare shrugged, as if the matter was self-evident. "You know, your DNA matches…father, mother, siblings?"

Wendell blinked, apparently stunned into silence by ignorance personified.

Irritation rose and Clare plucked her shirt sleeves to match exactly. *Why am I pushing this?* The detective spirit inside her couldn't be stopped; she had to dig deeper. "It's not important or anything. I was just curious. You never talk about your family or where you came from. I know that Ingots do weird things…raise their young in laboratories so that they can get used to all the tech implants, but still, surely, they have records of your people. Right?"

Without the standard Ingot headgear, Wendell's placid face was an open book. Dejection was written all over it. "I was discarded. No good. No people. No one claim me but an old woman. A human. She took unwanted babies and saved us before we died in trash heap."

Swallowing back a sour taste, Clare pushed the ugly image aside and appraised the youth before her. He was good-looking, as Ingots go. Not as tall as most, but solid and well-proportioned. Most of his body was encased in techno armor, which, according to Ingot's reasoning, made him not only stronger but more perceptive as well. Though she'd seen little evidence of that in most Ingots. Except for Wendell. His perceptive abilities went well beyond the norm.

Riko bustled in from the kitchen, balancing a heavy-laden tray. Her breakfast, undoubtedly.

Frustration rose as Clare leaned back with a sigh.

Despite being from completely different races, Riko had practically adopted Wendell, teaching him fine cooking skills and how to manage a café. He even sent food home—to share with "mom."

Clare perked up at the thought of a new line of

questioning. “You’ve mentioned your mom before; I know you have.”

With quick nods, Wendell seemed eager to agree. “Yes. She call me her son and tell me to call her mom. A kind woman, old but strong, she accept broken children. We share food and home as family. But no DNA.” He sighed. “My race reject me. Humans, some others, accept me. Orphans know only friends, not family.” He glanced aside at Riko and a spark between pride and gratitude shone in his eyes. “I belong here. Friends be family.”

His pale face turning a light shade of pink, Riko maneuvered between the tables like the expert he was. Grinning, he stopped at the booth and unloaded Clare’s breakfast. Like a father reminding a son of his duty, he glanced from Wendell to the unwashed table and tilted his head meaningfully.

His good nature as strong as ever, Wendell returned to his work with all the zeal of a kid who knows that a piece of pie awaits in the kitchen.

With a head shake, Clare tried to refocus on the breakfast set before her. *I don’t even know why I’m interrogating the guy.*

Riko propped the empty tray on his hip and smiled as Faye bustled back into her seat. “Everything good?” Assured that it was, he refocused on his other customers and turned away. “I’ll leave you two to your gossip and plans for the day.”

Shivering with delight, Faye scooped up the first bite of her cereal and called after him, “It’s wonderful. Thank you!”

Unenthusiastically, Clare poured syrup on her stack of pancakes and then cut into it with her fork. All hunger fled. She glanced at Wendell as he moved to the next table, repeating the pattern: spray, wipe up and down, then a quick swipe around the edge. As if being pushed by an inner demon, she cleared her throat and leaned in his direction. “So, you’re adopted, right? The woman who claimed you actually adopted you?"

Her eyes narrowed, Faye peered at Clare, her spoon frozen halfway to her mouth.

Wendell turned, his gaze bouncing between Faye and Clare. "No. Not legal. She claim unwanted, and no one stop her." He shrugged. "Same with human unwanted." A pained look rippled over his face. "Cresta kill their unwanted before birth. Luxonians have few, so they want all."

"And Sectine? What do they do?" In full-blown detective mode, Clare pushed for more. *Questions need answers!* A growing urge to understand herself as well as her world demanded to know what happened to the babies of Newearth.

"They fight in wars and die. Lots of little ones hatch but few live." He shrugged. "No orphanage, no me."

Frowning, Faye laid her spoon next to her bowl, her gaze following the conversation, now centered on Clare. "What's going on?"

Clare shrugged and stabbed a piece of pancake floating in syrup. She took a bite and chewed slowly. Taking her time, she wiped her lips and glanced from Wendell, who had moved to a table across the room, to her friend, whose brows had risen to peak heights. "Just curious. Bala has a case involving kids…babies…something. Anyway, I always wondered—a professional and personal interest. I'd like to adopt someday. Maybe there's another Wendell out there who would appreciate a mom like me."

Faye shook her head and took a slurp from her orange juice. Daintily applying a napkin, she freshened her face. "Parenting is never easy. Look at what Justine has gone through."

Gulping her scalding hot coffee, Clare nearly gasped, but then she quickly tore into her fruit salad. She talked between rapid chews. "Justine is a human-android given a daughter by the same Eternal who created her! Hardly call that a fair comparison. Kendra is human; she manages to do quite nicely, and she has seven!"

Wearing the cool demeanor of the Dalai Lama, Faye nodded slowly. "With Bala's help and her own amazing good sense, Kendra accomplishes more in a day than the average saint. But she gave birth to her children one at a time and knows how to manage them. Adoption, especially from a different race, is a challenge beyond the scope of most."

"So, you think I'm not up to it? That I couldn't have done right by Wendell or any other orphan?"

Faye took another calming sip of tea. "I'm not saying that. I'm just trying to state the obvious. There is a reason why kids should be raised by their own kind. No one understands their particular needs better."

Flummoxed by Faye's reasonable reason, Clare demolished her pancake stack with ruthless determination. Yogurt cup emptied, fruit salad obliterated, and her coffee swigged, Clare wiped her mouth with her napkin and checked her datapad. "Where are you, Bala? You should have been here half an hour ago." She huffed.

Faye shoved her empty dishes aside and rested her head on her hand, a relaxed pose that didn't deceive Clare for a moment. "Why are you so upset? What's happened?"

"I'm not upset, and nothing has happened. I told you; Bala is on a case involving children, and it got me thinking. Just wondering if it would be possible for me to adopt an orphan. I like Wendell, and it'd be rather nice to have a kid of my own. To claim the unwanted. To make a difference in someone's life." An embarrassed flush heated her face. "I'm jealous of his mom, maybe."

"She's dead."

Clare swallowed a lump in her throat, her stomach clenching. "What?"

"He doesn't talk about it, but the poor woman was worn to a rag and died a few months ago. He takes the extra food home and eats alone now, so far as I can tell."

Clare glanced up. Riko bustled around the café like a proud proprietor, chatting and laughing with the customers. "Does Riko know?"

"Of course. He's the one who told me. He knew the woman…made burial arrangements and helped to get the last little ones settled. Though Wendell still checks in on them. Soft heart inside that hard shell he wears."

Strangely deflated, Clare leaned back and let her gaze wander the room.

Faye scooted out of the booth and slung the strap of a colorful cloth bag over her shoulder. "I still have a little shopping to do before Taug comes for dinner, so I better hurry on."

"What're you having?"

"Oh, a new recipe, a seafood delight I copied from a famous Cresta cooking show."

"Is that your surprise, then, a seafood dinner?"

"Oh, no, I was given a new game with the most astonishing figurines; I can hardly wait to play. There are twenty figures, but I have only identified fourteen of them. I don't know who the rest will be."

Squinting, Clare tried to follow Faye's thought process. "Can't you just make them up?"

Scandalized, Faye flapped her hands, her eyes wide with astonishment. "But each one represents someone real: you, me and Taug, Bala and Kendra, Riko and his girlfriend Jayla, Wendell, Cerulean and his Luxonian friends—Roux and Sterling. Even our human-androids are included—Justine, Max, and Zara. There are seven more people coming into our lives. I can hardly wait to meet them."

Despite a strong dislike for games, Clare leaned forward,

her interest caught. "What is this? You pretend to act like us, pantomime or something?"

Faye patted Clare's arm. "Not at all. We just predict your future and see if it comes true." A quick goodbye hug and she was off.

Clare exhaled a long breath as Faye practically bounced through the diner, tossing smiles to Riko and Wendell, and then sauntered out the door.

A vibration drew Clare's attention. She tapped her datapad and read a message from Bala. *Finally!*

"Help! I'm about to commit murder, and I need you to talk me out of it.

Ingot Services in Aram County.

Meet me at the Spare Parts Shop, asap."

Ingot Services? Spare parts shop? Clare glanced up, ignoring the ceiling, glaring toward the Heavenly spheres. *You trying to tell me something or confuse the heck out of me? Well, whatever else, you'll have to save me from wringing Bala's neck.*

Tapping on her datapad, she transferred the whole breakfast tab to her account and slid out of the comfortable booth. She looked around and realized how much she cherished Newearth. Riko and Wendell worked shoulder to shoulder, carrying trays to waiting customers with all the dignity of co-workers who were good friends besides. Neither of them had had easy lives before coming to Newearth. She sucked in a cleansing breath as Wendell's words rang in her ears. *I belong here. Friends be family.*

Her life may not be perfect and questions still needed answers, but happiness wasn't a complete stranger. *Considering my history, I never would have predicted that.*

Chapter Two

In All Honesty

—Louie City—

Bala insisted that his stomach stay put even though, as he stood in the middle of the dingy Ingot shop, the sights all around him depicted the most nauseating wares that he had ever seen.

Left of the front door, a transparent freezer unit displayed organs in thematic groups—hearts, livers, lungs, eyes, and even a variety of skin types. On the right, a bank of three screens competed for attention. The large central one depicted assorted human, Ingot, and Cresta limbs spread across steel tables and arranged in size from tiny baby limbs to enormous giant-sized. In the center of the room, a long screen reached from floor to ceiling, offering a dizzying array of bagged blood types. In the right corner, a bank of sperm tubes jutted from wall slots with dominant male characteristics highlighted in orange.

Most unsettling, the entire back wall peered into tiny, specialized embryotic pools where fetuses of numerous species floated in various stages of development.

The Ingot dealer, Saran, slouched in a swivel chair before the main computer bank, flinging dirty looks at Bala and sneaking glances at his personal message screen. A sign in block letters—a large one above the door—announced the shop's purpose of existence. **"Spare Parts—Buy, Sell & Trade"**

Bala set his jaw and hoped that Clare would hurry up. He kept his dustbuster leveled at the sedate Ingot but knew he'd have a hard time firing. Much as he hated what he saw before him and the frequent abuses he'd discovered in his ten years as a detective for Human Services, he'd never actually killed anyone, and he didn't want to start now.

Clare bustled into the shop out of breath and grim-faced. A green light flashed the word CUSTOMER on the back wall.

Saran jumped to his feet, his eyes shifting nervously.

Bala waved one hand, keeping the dustbuster level with the other. "Don't worry; you're not about to lose a sale. Sit down, Saran, and tell me and Detective Clare what's going here."

Saran flopped down on his chair and shrugged helplessly. Apparently, he'd never been asked a question before and hadn't a clue how to respond.

Clare wandered to the middle of the room, her head swiveling and her jaw dropping. "Bothmal! Inside the darkest prison system in the universe, I've never seen anything…like this."

Resting his head on one hand, Saran leaned on his desk, a grin glinting from his eyes. "I should hope not. We're a one-of-a-kind business here on Newearth. Ingots specialize in trade, so it's a natural fit. But few managers can handle the delicate nature of our wares and the sensitive needs of our customers."

The dustbuster being superfluous with Clare present, Bala slid it into its safety on his belt. He perched on the edge of Saran's desk, while Clare continued her appraisal and then leaned in close. "Delicate and sensitive—that's you all over. But just so we're clear, do you have a license to practice medicine? Are you associated with a hospital or any medical agency that supplies your goods and matches them with the appropriate customer? Who performs the medical procedures when your spare parts are…adopted?"

Twirling in his chair like a bored child, Saran reached a lazy finger to his personal computer and tapped a single key.

Bala's stomach sank. *He knew we were coming...he's been ready for us all along.*

A sharp intake of breath and Clare turned on her heel, away from the bank of fetuses. She bent double, breathing oddly at each gasp, which wasn't normal by any standards.

Bala rushed over and gripped her arm, steadying her before she fell in a limp heap on the brown tiled floor. "Hang on, Clare. Here—" He rushed over and yanked Saran out of his chair and dragged it next to Clare, then directed her onto its firm base. "Sit down and catch your breath a second." He glared at Saran, who didn't appear unduly disturbed by Clare's helpless situation.

"If I aimed my dustbuster at your middle, maybe you'd take this whole thing a little more seriously, eh?"

Satisfyingly, a trace of fear flashed through Saran's eyes.

Clare exhaled a long cleansing breath and staggered to her feet. "Stop, Bala. I'm okay. Just the…well…I ate breakfast too fast before I hurried over. And that wall of…" With a grimace, she straightened and then stomped to Saran's desk. She leaned in and began scrolling through the open document.

Bala nudged up close so he could see.

Pages rolled before their eyes: Official Inter-Alien Alliance Permit for Trading on Newearth, fourteen hospital donation resources accompanied by permits to receive discarded biomaterial, and at least fifty physician services offering plastic surgery, reconstructive surgery, and enhancement services, with contact information and available hours listed on the right. Clare's head dropped to her chest in apparent defeat.

Disgusted, Bala ran his fingers through his hair and wondered if he ought to give up detective work and buy a farm. At least on a farm, animal behavior would be natural. A flicker out of the corner of his eye caught his attention; he turned.

One of the human fetuses jerked spasmodically and then quieted.

Horrified, Bala froze. *That could be one of my babies. It's someone's baby!*

A smile crossed Saran's face as he paced to the door and opened it wide. "It's all legal, so I'm not doing anything wrong. I'm distressed that you'd even thought so. But now that you're satisfied, I really must get back to work. Surely, you have real criminals to chase down, somewhere."

Unable to contain himself a second longer, Bala rushed forward, grabbed Saran by the collar, and shoved him against the wall. "Legal does not necessarily equal moral. This whole setup stinks, and I'm not going to rest until we shut you down."

With surprising strength, Saran yanked Bala's hands off of him. "What are you, a maniac? You'll make a lot of powerful people very angry. Why, a commander staying at Newearth Docking Bay was in here only last week picking out a baby girl who'll be raised for service in his fleet. Would you want to deprive a good officer of a loyal assistant and an otherwise worthless human a chance at a productive life?" Saran scowled, his mouth puckering into an ugly grunt. "You really think you know what's best for everyone, don't you? Your moral code stands high above the rest of us?"

Stunned beyond a rational response, Bala hesitated.

Taking advantage of the moment, Saran shoved Bala out the door and into the bright day.

Furious at his loss of composure, and his stomach tied in knots, Bala glanced at the bustling population on Louie City Main Street and sucked in a deep breath. He smoothed down his shirt sleeves, straightening himself.

Hidden from view behind the half-closed door, Clare murmured in a short conversation with Saran.

Saran responded in an unusually polite tone.

What the—? Bala reached for the door.

Clare stepped out, bumping into him. Then she swept past. "We're done here."

Stymied, Bala lifted his hands, a question on his lips, but Clare hustled away as if hounds nipped at her heels. He ran after her. "Hey, wait, hang on a minute. We need to talk."

Darting autoskimmers, flying airbuses, the roar of underground trains, and the bustle of hurrying pedestrians set a frenetic city pace. Clare didn't slow down one bit.

Irritation nearly overmastering him, Bala grabbed Clare's arm and pulled her to a full stop. "What was *that* all about?"

Jerking her arm free, Clare glanced impatiently at the sky, the spitting image of a teen girl being interrogated by her dad. "What?"

"That confab you just had with Frankenstein?"

"Frankenstein? Don't be silly. I just asked him where he gets his human and Ingot fetuses."

Bala folded his arms, his gaze locked onto Clare. He didn't even budge when a Cresta carrying a load of groceries squeezed by him.

Clare huffed. "The human fetuses were donated by women who didn't want them. And the Ingots were discards slotted for destruction."

His stomach churning to the point of meltdown, Bala felt exhaustion seep through his body. "You can't possibly think that Ingot shop is okay—can you?"

With an impatient sweep of her fingers through her hair, Clare's edgy, sarcastic tone might have impressed a rookie. "Well, they would've died otherwise. You think that's a good option? This way they have a chance."

Tears burned in Bala's eyes. "But not the *right* chance. Not the chance they *should* be given."

A shrug and Clare started off again. "A chance is a chance. No one expects perfection."

Bala stood rooted to the ground.

Looking over her shoulder, Clare stopped. "You know what your problem is, Bala?"

He didn't dare ask.

She turned back and pounded into his personal space. "You live in an idealized world. And you think we should all aim for that. Well, let me tell you, buddy, I've never known ideal. Just lots of hardcore reality. So, we'll keep our eye on Saran, but I'm not for shutting him down. He performs a worthy service. Someone has to save the lost."

Bala winced. "You can't save the lost, if you don't know where you're going. The ideal is a good goal."

Not even listening, Clare checked her datapad. "We're due at headquarters in an hour."

Bala strode to the corner and hailed an autoskimmer for two. He glanced at Clare and shook his head. Images of babies floating in murky tanks filled his mind, sickening his soul.

—Vandi Township—

Taug, a Crestonian scientist from the water-based planet Crestar, lounged on a comfy white couch in Faye's living room. Faye's dinner invite had pleased him, though her description of Clare's behavior at breakfast sent twinges down his spine. *Clare's always been an unpredictable human. Never know what's going on in that brain of hers.*

He refocused his attention on present reality. Pillowing the spiral shell protecting his brain sack with two tentacles, he leaned back to get comfortable and stared at the colorful board set up on the low oak table before him. He wasn't sure what he thought of this new game. Twenty figures in all but only fourteen were ranged across the board. The other seven stood on the sidelines like kids waiting their turn to play. He almost felt sorry for them.

Faye, dressed in a pastel pantsuit, bustled in with a tray loaded with goodies.

Two tall Nutra-Green drinks with frothy tops made his mouth pucker. He blew bubbles through his new breather helm in anticipation.

"Gosh, but that helm is noisy. However, I must say, I like the streamlined look. So much easier to see if you are smiling or frowning." Faye set the tray on a small table at the south end of the curved couch. "There! We should have everything we need." She pointed out each snack in turn. "Spicy squid, salted sardine bits, plankton and sea veggies, and assorted shell powders for a strong constitution." A mother offering her offspring a savory, nutritionally balanced diet could not have looked prouder.

Distracted by the sidelined seven, Taug couldn't resist changing the subject. "What about them? They look rather lonely and set off by themselves. Can't you let them play, too?"

Laughing, Faye snatched up one of the tall Nutra-Greens and placed it in his outstretched tentacle. "We have to find out who they are, first. These here"—she pointed to two figures, a short rotund Cresta male and a pixie-like female with a cloak thrown over her shoulders—"represent us. The human woman with a pouty expression is Clare, naturally. The loving couple is Bala and Kendra. Riko and Jayla are obviously the Uanyi figures, and Wendell is the only one with modified Ingot armor. Cerulean looks like a man but with lightened edges, while Roux and Sterling are clearly Luxonian—see how they glow? Though, Sterling looks quite faded, doesn't he? Max, as an android, is the most solid figure; no one could guess his human soul, while Justine looks too perfect to be human, though that's what she is, on the inside, at least. And her daughter, Zara—the unpredictable one—is the only child figure on the board."

"There are two little ones on the sidelines..." This fact had disturbed Taug no end, almost to the point of curbing his culinary enjoyment.

Faye squinted as she picked up the tiniest figure of all. "Yes. I mean, this isn't full-grown, whatever it is. She turned it in various directions, a frown building between her eyes. "I'm not even sure which side is up. I laid it on its side because I can't tell for certain." She refocused her attention on the other small figure. "But I do recognize this other one as a girl; strange that she has mismatched eyes and marbled skin, a mixed breed, perhaps. Who she belongs to—I can't imagine. And this one—" She placed the infant down and plucked an unknown, fully armored Ingot from the sidelines. "What would a militant Ingot want with our humble assembly?"

Taug sprinkled sardine bits into the breather helm and smiled as the salty flavor set his salivary glands into overdrive. "How do you know he's militant? There've been plenty of Ingots who, despite their techno armor, have lived peaceful lives."

Faye held the figure before her eyes, scowling. "No, this one has no kind spirit. He seems to have two natures since his back—" She gasped and started scratching the figure with her nail.

Alarmed, Taug nearly choked. "By the Divide, what are you doing?"

Peeling a tiny figure off the Ingot's back, a satisfied smile replaced Faye's frown. "It wasn't twenty figures; it's twenty-one!" She lifted the distinct figures in each hand. Raising her right, she clucked her tongue. "The armored Ingot has a nasty look, and this here—" She narrowly examined the figure in her left hand. "It's an Ingot, too, but scrawny, and I'd almost say witless. Its eyes convey only emptiness."

Harumphing, Taug brushed shell powder from his tentacles and decided that he'd had enough. He must focus on the matters at hand. Apparently, Faye was losing her reason, and he must lead her back to the land of logic and sense. He toddled over to the game board and considered each of the figures in turn. "Yes, I see. You've done a marvelous job finding figures that match us so well. Couldn't have done better myself." He viewed the unknown figures. "These seven are a mystery to be sure. Can't say I like the look of the big Ingot, but then, Ingots rarely impress me." He shrugged. "And the little guy seems harmless enough. Few have wits these days, so he'll fit right in." His gut tightened at the sight of the small figures, the tiny one and the odd little girl. An unnamed fear spread through him; he moved on quickly.

Set to the side, the last three were a puzzle. He lifted them, one by one, turning them all around. He shook his head and snorted. "I'd say they were human but yet not. Nothing I recognize. Crossbreeds, perhaps?" He peered at Faye awaiting her explanation.

Surprisingly, Faye's eyes widened in bewilderment. "I haven't a clue. They aren't *my* figures. I mean, they are mine now. They came from a hermit on Helm. He's known to be very holy, works miracles, they say."

Laughing, Taug set the figures down and returned to the food tray, his sense of humor, as well as his appetite, restored. "A holy hermit on Helm who makes games? How fun!"

Looking unusually solemn, Faye stood at the board and lined all the figures, known and unknown, at the baseline. "This isn't an ordinary game. We're supposed to figure out where each figure belongs in relationship to the others and what their real purpose is." She took a deep breath and intoned her words, "We are ready to begin." As she swept her hand over the left corner of the board, an exact replica of Faye's apartment appeared out of thin air.

Disturbed, Taug stood absolutely still.

Faye placed her and Taug's figures just as they were standing at that moment—before the game board. "Other sets will probably develop as we play. And we move the figures about as we learn events."

A cold chill worked its way over Taug's body. "I'm not sure I'm going to like this game."

Faye met his gaze and held it as if in a steel trap. "I didn't ask for it. The package arrived with the instructions that we were to play in absolute honesty and see if we could save humanity's soul."

Suddenly feeling parched, as if he'd been dropped into a desert without hope of ever seeing water again, Taug swallowed hard. "We don't even know all the players, and I haven't a clue about saving souls!"

"That's why we must play—to learn—and, above all, be honest."

Dread filled Taug as he stared at the figures. Honesty had never been his strong suit, and in this matter, he was definitely not alone.

Chapter Three

That's All

—Vandi Township—

Thursday, August 25th

Clare didn't mind irony. In fact, she enjoyed a good laugh, and ironic aspects of her work often gave her plenty to chuckle about. Today was no exception. Of course, this wasn't work, this was personal, but the irony of meeting the Ingot trader at Vandi Central Park two days after Bala nearly blasted him into oblivion brought a grim smile to her lips. The juxtaposition of an alien dedicated to technological implants in a place humans dedicated to native beauty formed a painful knot in her gut. *This should be amusing, so why do I feel like a mouse in a cat's paw?*

A late summer day, not too hot but pleasantly sunny and warm. Reports warned of powerful storms in both Ishtar County and along the Teal Island Chains, but rough weather was a part of life on this planet. *Nothing to get worked up about.* Not like the Newearth News reporter who seemed intent on scaring the watching audience into some kind of Doomsday scenario. She pulled her eyes from the horizon and glanced around. A Bhuaci family picnicked together on a blanket spread under a large maple tree just north of where she sat.

They must've arranged their schedules so everyone got the day off.

Unlike archaic OldEarth customs, where the work week was set at five days and most workers only got "weekends" off, the Newearth system of personal time management made a great deal more sense. *Certainly, makes it easier for family get-togethers.*

The dad held a sleeping baby against his shoulder and crouched between two elderly figures, probably his father and mother, and passed along a plate of dainties. The dignified elders grinned good-naturedly. Being shape-shifting Bhuaci, they weren't as susceptible to the frailties of physical nature the way humans were, but their kind often adopted the customs of their host planet. In this case, in their petite perfection, they appeared as idealized versions of ancient story folks—leprechauns and fairies, creating a charming family scene.

A flutter of joy widened Clare's smile. *They're happy; that's what makes it really work.*

Jerking motions caught the corner of Clare's eye.

Saran practically fidgeted his way across the grassy expanse, his head swiveling and his eyes shifting nervously.

What's he afraid of? The trees and birds going to attack or something?

Clare scooted over on the long green bench, offering him plenty of room to sit on the other end, giving them a chance to talk without being overheard but not close enough so as to appear to be pals or anything disgusting like that. He was a tool. Nothing more. She shrugged off the rising tightness in her chest as he drew near.

Saran stopped before her, not a hint of a smile on his flabby lips. His helm conformed perfectly to his head without obscuring his face. The rest of his Ingot body armor had been tailored to such amazing detail that it was clear he had no muscle mass of his own but depended entirely on technological enhancements to move—probably even to think.

Like a whole-body drug... Clare shrugged off a shiver of horror.

Saran's hands twitched at his sides as he stopped before her. "So, what 'cha call me here for? You could've come to my place of business like any other customer."

"Except that I am not *any other* customer. I'm a Human Services Detective, and my partner wants to see you shut down as soon as possible."

Saran seemed to mull this over a moment, his eyes squinting, as if he was trying to peer through her words to a distant truth.

Clare pushed ahead. "I'm not a fan of your work, but I do see its necessary function in our world. Progress isn't as neat and clean as some people wish."

A burst of laughter from the picnickers grabbed Saran's attention. He looked over, his mouth puckering in distaste.

Irritated and fighting growing impatience, Clare stood and hurried her words. "Look, Ingot, I want to adopt one of your rejects. Some poor kid who might be dismissed to a trash heap if someone doesn't save him. You got anyone I might have?"

His eyes widening, Saran drew back. "You think I'm a fool, don't you? I can see a trap when it's laid before my feet, can't I?"

Clare shook her head, her discomfort rising to full-blown fury. She practically hissed. "No, you idiot. This isn't a trap. Against my partner's better judgment, I don't want to shut you down or even slow your pace. I just want to adopt a kid."

Sneering, Saran expressed his disdain eloquently. "Have your own offspring, why don't you? Even if you can't find an interested male, there are plenty of sperm bank options. Or better yet, we have specially designed fetuses ready-made." His expression brightened as the salesman in him swung into action. "For a very reasonable price, I can sell you a high-functioning green-eyed girl, and we can have it implanted on-site—with our designer pain suppressants, you won't feel a thing."

A strange stench assaulted Clare's nose as if she was suddenly standing in the muck of a decomposing trash heap. Nausea gripped her innards and squeezed painfully. "No! I'm not one of your sicko customers who wants to buy a baby like trading for ship parts. I just want to help some kid who might be disposed of otherwise. A humanitarian gesture where everyone gets what they want. I get a child, you get business, and a kid gets a loving home."

His chuckle sounded more like the grating of gears as they wound down from a long day of service. "No, you're not *one of us*…I get it." Shaking his head and grinning, he tapped his datapad and sent off a quick message. "I got just the thing for you, Human. I was saving her for export at the Newearth Docking Bay gift shop, but I'm willing to accommodate a new customer." His superior expression took the edge off any hint of pity.

Startled by the swiftness of this maneuver, Clare turned and tried to think through her options. She stared over the nearly empty park. The picnickers had gone, their place under the tree as undisturbed as if they had never been there. Two human children ran along the fading garden border with a barking dog in tow, while a large Cresta in a modified bio-suit hunched wearily on a distant bench, pouring a murky snack into his breather helm.

Saran paced to the nearest tree and leaned against it, his arms crossed, his gaze fixed ahead. Just an ordinary Ingot relaxing in the park.

Clare snorted at the ridiculous image. She had a few specifications for the child that she might like, if it was possible. A boy perhaps, with dark eyes maybe, no serious health conditions… She scrolled through her datapad for the list she'd hastily created.

The distinct whine of an autoskimmer caught her ear, and

she turned around in time to see a bulky Ingot yank a tiny child off the passenger seat onto the sidewalk.

The little girl, not more than three or four, tumbled along at the Ingot's side in wide-eyed confusion.

The pair stopped before Saran, an understanding passing between the two Ingots, though not a word was spoken.

With a pleased smile, Saran stepped forward and turned his charm on full blast. He faced Clare. "We've got holding centers all over the city, so I can meet my customers' needs at a moment's notice." He pointed to the child. "Here you go. An imperfect specimen, exactly as you wish. Her mismatched eyes and mottled skin bother people, so she's unwanted, friendless, and soon to be dispatched to service in the outer quadrant. Save her. At a reasonable price, of course."

Without ever looking fully upon the child, Clare took out her Taser and dropped the two Ingots where they stood.

—Rural Vandi—

Friday, August 26th

Kendra loved her brilliant husband, Bala, her adorable seven children, and her country home on the outskirts of Vandi, but an afternoon on an unexpected adventure to help Clare with some mystery or other exhilarated her weary spirit. She relaxed her grip on the autoskimmer as she hummed along the tree line bordering a tawny field, her favorite path from home to town.

Despite a few broken limbs from last night's unexpected storm, waving branches from oak, walnut, hickory, maples, cottonwoods, and a few ash trees encouraged her on her way as she drove under the warm sun. She swerved to avoid a murder of crows settled near her neighbor's pond and gazed longingly at a copse of stately white pines rustling their heavy branches like women sashaying in a country dance. *Bet you gals never trip over laundry hampers after you've asked that they be carried to their proper bedrooms about a million times...*

She shook her head and laughed as the crows rose in a glorious array of bird power, cawing commands to each other. *Oh, ignore me; I'm just being silly. You all, just go on being glorious and majestic.*

Following their own unhurried destiny, they winged their way deeper into the woodlands, away from town. Kendra could still hear them even as she saw the outline of Vandi township rise in the distance.

She refocused her attention on the matter at hand: Clare had messaged, begging for a meetup at the local Human Services branch. *Lord knows, I'll do what I can, but what does she want? There're no big events planned until autumn, and Bala is already working on the new case. Where does an overworked mom with laundry issues fit in?*

Entering town, traffic increased, and it took all of Kendra's concentration to thread her way through the darting autoskimmers as city folks hurried about in their frenzied state. She finally spied an opening, slipped in, and found a spot to park. Once she had paid the auto-attendant, she checked her datapad for any messages from Faye, who was keeping watch over her brood.

Since Seth and Barnabas, mature teenagers if ever there were any, attended Scholars' Classical Private School, and Rachel, a smart ten-year-old, and Veronica, an over-achieving eight-year-old, shared the services of a young and energetic tutor who offered in-home lessons five mornings a week, that left only the younger three kids, David, Martha, and Alexa, six, four, and two to keep any able-bodied person well occupied.

No messages. Kendra exhaled a relieved breath. All was well. She placed her children—as well as Faye—in the hands of the Almighty and stood on the corner of Newearth Avenue and Luxonian Boulevard.

Kendra squinted against the glaring light and tried to remember if the new Human Service entrance was on the right or left side of the building.

Clare's not-so-subtle gesturing from the shaded sidewalk by the three-story brick structure finally caught her attention. Doubt and a hint of dread seeped into Kendra's consciousness.

She trotted across the street, her tummy bag swinging at each step. The fact that, without her kids present, she shouldn't need a face wiped, hair combed, or antiseptic applied, hardly deterred Kendra from coming prepared for any eventuality. She tried to offer a smile but was fully aware that she was now squinting to a new purpose. "What 'cha doing waving at me out here like some school girl trying to avoid the teacher's eye?"

Without further ado, Clare grabbed her friend's arm and yanked her down the vacant alleyway between the Human Services building and the Vandi Public Library and Art Gallery.

Kendra shook her head in bewilderment.

On the back lot, passengers disembarked from sky busses, local folks parked their autoskimmers, and the circular entrance to Aram County Subterrain Tube announced destinations all across the Central Basin.

Clare's grip tightened.

Kendra's heart flip-flopped. She halted dead in her tracks and refused to be budged another centimeter. "Okay, Gal, you've got approximately sixty seconds to explain why you're dragging me across this lot toward Lord only knows what."

Her face flushed, Clare crossed her arms, widened her

stance, and took on an authoritative posture. "You have to help me get to Cerulean's place without being seen, and if I am caught, then you've got to help me get out of trouble before I destroy my entire career."

Something in Kendra's DNA allowed her to deal with emergencies calmly and more efficiently than the average person. She was quite proud of the fact that her husband's near-death experiences, her kids' hyper-hijinks, and her own astonishing ability to take on more projects than was good for a single human being had not left her a withered rag of a woman. But the look in Clare's eyes made her pause.

"I'm not going anywhere until you tell me what's going on. Bala mumbled something about human trafficking and how you dragged in an Ingot trader yesterday. But rather than being pleased, he seemed irritated. Now I'm confused, and with seven kids between us, baffled parents can lead to all sorts of trouble. So, tell all, and don't leave out any details."

"Just come along!" Clare's eyes pleaded even harder than her voice.

If the woman had gotten on her knees and begged, she could not have made her desperation clearer.

Kendra relented. "I can't be gone too long, since I need to be back to save Faye's sanity, interrogate my kids, and figure out if education is all it's cracked up to be. Besides, Bala is planning on making dinner, and he'll need me to remind him of the exact location of the pots and pans."

"Okay, fine. Cerulean's place isn't that far. If we take the tube, we'll be there in just under an hour." Clare glanced over her shoulder, her eyes searching the lot.

"If you're looking for enemies, Newearth is full of 'em."

Clare grabbed Kendra's hand and started towing her away. "No, I'm trying to avoid my co-workers and friends. Right now, they probably want to kill me."

—Wisconsin Territories, North Central Aram County—

Clare sat on the very back seat of the tube, hunched next to Kendra, and gripped the handrail for dear life. "I thought the new governor was going to make these rides smoother! I feel like we're flying around mountain roots the ways this thing veers."

Kendra casually wrapped one arm around a vertical pole and swayed with the vehicle. "If you'd spent any amount of time with Bala at the helm of an autoskimmer, you'd have learned to move with the groove. Now"—she nudged Clare—"get talking. I don't have all day. And I want to know what to say to Cerulean when we show up at his door. He's been laying low since he got back from Mirage-Reborn. Never seen a guy so altered. He may be Luxonian and choose his physique and all, but he's sure not the man he was. Person, I mean. Thanks to the Eternals, he found out what it was like to be a mere human on Mirage and that seems to have nearly done him in."

A shrug and Clare's gaze turned inward. "He went through a lot, soul-searching stuff, I guess. Didn't bother me until…" She shook her head. "Never mind that. I've got a real problem on my hands, and I need you to help me sort things out."

Kendra grinned. "You may dip into the font of my wisdom, ever-confused one."

Clare rolled her eyes and took a deep breath. "Okay, it's like this. I wanted to adopt an innocent kid, someone like Wendell. He told me how he was a reject that some woman saved, and I thought I could do the same. Not open an orphanage or anything but take care of one measly Ingot kid who might be dropped off at the nearest recycling center otherwise."

Kendra's jaw tightened. Never a good sign.

Undaunted, Clare forged ahead. "As fortune would have it, Bala called me over to the Spare Parts shop, and I met the proprietor, an Ingot named Saran. After I talked Bala off the cliff—he wanted to close the place down and shoot the guy—I was able to arrange a meeting with Saran at Vandi Park. You would've thought he'd never seen a tree before, the way he acted. I told him what I wanted, but the idiot called up one of his sidekicks and tried to sell me a little girl. A human child!" Clare's stomach clenched at the memory of those wide, confused mismatched eyes.

Kendra wasn't saying anything, but her whole body had grown stiff, and she was sitting ramrod straight. No moving with the groove now.

The high-pitched drone of the tube slowed, and Newton's first law pulled them forward. Once at a standstill, a group of passengers rose and tugged bags and parcels from side compartments. The overhead flashing red light turned solid green, doors swept open, and a general hustle ensued.

Clare raised her voice over the din. "Next stop is near Cerulean's place. Anyway, I zapped the idiot where he stood and took him and the child to Human Services right there in Vandi. Saran was whisked off for questioning, and the girl was taken to the Child Care Department."

Her jaw clenched, Kendra merely nodded.

Clare huffed. She sure wasn't getting the encouragement she had hoped for. "So, then things started to get weird. I filled in a report, and Bala should've been thrilled. He got his wish, right? But no, he avoided me the whole afternoon and acted like I was the bad guy. Then I got called into the captain's office, and he wasn't alone. I didn't know half the people in there. And most weren't even human. It was like some kind of

Inter-alien Alliance symposium. They were as loud as a nest of rattlers when I walked in, and then suddenly, they all shut up. Captain Walt—I've told you about him—thinks he's an empath and feels for everyone, 'Law from the heart,' he says, but clearly, he's got a personal angle. Loves his wine and women, they say."

As if she had a headache, Kendra closed her eyes and rubbed her forehead.

The tube lurched forward again.

A momentary flash of concern scattered Clare's thoughts, but Kendra rotated her hand in a hurry-up motion.

"Well, you won't believe it, but I got a sharp warning! I was told that Saran's Spare Parts shop was known far and wide and considered a perfectly legal endeavor. If I didn't leave the matter be, I'd face prosecution for defamation and bodily injury. That weasel had filed a report that I'd used undue force and never gave him a chance to come in on his own volition to answer any questions I might have." Clare winced. "That part is true, I guess. But when I saw that little girl being dragged along and offered like wares at a shop, it made me so mad; I just couldn't think straight."

Her eyes now at half-mast, Kendra's deadpanned expression masked the danger in her tone. "Unlike Bala who wanted to take Saran in for questioning right off. The partner whom you had to *talk off a cliff*?"

It hit Clare like a punch to the gut that Kendra was mad, furious even. "Hey, neither of us knew he was selling kids at that point. It had just seemed like a disgusting spare parts shop."

Kendra's expression had not changed. "That's why you met Saran, to buy an Ingot kid?"

"I wasn't going to buy anyone!" Tears stung Clare's eyes. "I was just trying to save some innocent Ingot reject. Is that so bad? I know how they are—they don't consider children as real people. It's not until they have all their implants attached and adaptions fully formed that they are given an actual name. They're just numbers up to that point." Clare rubbed her eyes and set her jaw. "I'm not the enemy, Kendra!"

Kendra's shoulders relaxed just a tad. "So, what happened to the little girl?"

Steadying herself, Clare forced her emotions off a hysterical ledge. "That's another oddity. She disappeared. I thought that maybe I could adopt her, but when I asked, they said that she had already been claimed."

Kendra's eyes narrowed. "Claimed? By family or adopted by someone?"

Clare exhaled a long, straggling breath. "I have no idea. They wouldn't say. I was just given notice that I was to report to Inter-Alien sensitivity training for the next three months and that if I ever brought another complaint against Saran, I would be charged with insubordination and dereliction of duty since I must be neglecting real cases that needed my attention." Clare hung her head. "Bala was right, Kendra. I see why he was mad at me and why you might be too, but really, I didn't think I was doing anything wrong. Not in my heart, anyway. I thought Saran was running a legitimate, though distasteful, shop, and I just wanted to save an innocent life. That's all."

Kendra squeezed her hand. Relieved at Kendra's forgiveness, Clare tried to take a relieved breath, but her chest still felt tight, and she wasn't at all sure what was going on with her heart.

Chapter Four

A Close Relation

—Cerulean's Cabin—

Cerulean lifted a boiling kettle from his OldEarth-styled stovetop and then poured hot water into a thick brown mug, the spicy chai teabag all ready and waiting.

Thoughts of his first introduction to human food, ages ago on OldEarth, brought a smile to his face. It was such a surprise, how much variety humans experienced—wonderful and terrible. Faces floated in his mind along with dramatic events that had frightened him as a child under his father's care. *Teal loved humanity so much.* Cerulean's chest heaved with overwhelming emotions. *Stop it! He's gone…as are so many. But I still have friends…plenty to keep me busy.*

He paced barefoot across the wood floor, his loose cotton shirt and pants fluttering with each movement, nudged open the front screen door, then stepped onto the wide porch. Three steps led down to a dirt path, which descended into the wooded acreage that surrounded his cabin.

Instead of going down, he carried his tea around to the east side of the house, overlooking the lake, and leaned on the railing, a deep sigh of contentment rising from his soul.

Noon sunshine had radiated heat, but now a pleasant hilltop chill was descending. Since the summer sun elongated hot humid days beyond reason, he loved to watch the evening fade with all the glory of vibrant colors parading across the blue-gray lake.

Luxonian by nature, he was a light being of vast experience, but one who had fallen just as deeply in love with humanity as his father the first time he had come to OldEarth.

Cupping the warm mug between his hands, Cerulean contemplated the exquisite interplay of water and sky framed by ancient forests.

Where are you now, Father? You and Mother must be together…truly happy.

Ever since experiencing a true human body—not the approximation of form and perception that Luxonians created—by the power of Abbas, a being known as an Eternal, he had appreciated the gift of his Luxonian nature more than ever. He chuckled, even as he stared across the rippling waves. *Though I'm not the same Luxonian I once was, am I?*

He wondered if Abbas had laughed when he did it, knowing that at some point, Cerulean would figure it out. His Luxonian nature had been returned to him, yes, but his human nature was still within him, too. He now experienced the joys and travails of both natures, offering him the tragedies and wonders of two worlds.

His friend and fellow Guardian, Roux, had noticed the difference when Cerulean had been convalescing on Lux. "You seem wiser, more dignified but relaxed and happy as well." An astute observation from someone who had trouble hitting the broadside of a moral question in the old days. *Glad Roux took the Supreme Judgeship and not me. There's a mess for you. And now he's got to sort out the most recent Ingot overstep—practically invading an unprepared world…*

In an effort to let that matter go, Cerulean took a tentative sip of his tea. He had learned that a burned tongue could mess with his sense of taste for days. Savoring the spicy flavor, he luxuriated in peace and quiet, making a mental note to ask his neighbors, a community of Amens members—humans who lived in simplicity close to nature—if he could trade some of his abundant peaches for another box of spicy tea.

Loud puffing caught his ear. A snappish comment broke the evening stillness.

Cerulean ran his fingers through his hair and tried to brace himself. *It must be Clare. It's always Clare.*

He retraced his steps to the front porch and, sure enough, it was Clare. Kendra huffed at her side and neither one of them looked particularly pleased.

With one foot on the first porch step, Clare glared up at him. "So, aren't you going to invite us in? We've had a blasted hard time finding you. I swear the trees have been moving about, and all the landmarks I knew have been stolen."

Kendra waved a limp hand. "Just water and a chance to call Bala; let him know that he's got full rein of the homestead till tomorrow. It's getting dark, and there's no way I'm navigating my way through those vine-infested woods at night."

Cerulean stepped aside and ushered his guests into his spacious kitchen-living room.

Clare plunked down on a stool at the counter while Kendra dragged herself to the white couch on one side of the large bay window and plopped down with an elongated sigh.

After filling the kettle brim full, Cerulean replaced it on the stovetop and set it to heating. He then went about the business of preparing a simple supper for his guests, to go with the tea.

Propping her head on one hand, Clare watched in glum sobriety. "Aren't you even going to ask what we're doing here?"

Cerulean gazed at the half loaf of oat bread on the counter. Making a mental note to bake a couple of new loaves tomorrow, he sliced it into sandwich sizes and then placed the pieces neatly on a plate. Startlingly, a pleasant sensation warmed his spirits as he worked. He glanced at Clare. "I figured that you'd tell me when you were ready." He pointed across the room. "Besides, Kendra needs to settle her family business. You don't want to start without her, do you?"

Clare yawned and stretched. "I only brought her along to help me get here safely and to keep you from getting mad. Except for a few scratches, I arrived safely, and you seem in a pretty good mood, so she can relax now."

"Her purpose in existence is satisfied for the moment? She'll be so pleased." Cerulean smiled to take the edge off his tone.

Clare's gloomy expression bloomed into a full-blown pout. "You're as bad as everyone else! If you're going to act like that, then I won't bother to tell you how much trouble I'm in and why I think that there's a conspiracy to cover up human trafficking and that I've decided to quit my job and move in with your Amens neighbors."

Laughter fought concern as Cerulean tried to mentally maneuver between Clare's absurd revelations. He grabbed a plate of cheese from his cooler and set it beside the bread. "I don't think the Amens would accept you and quitting has never been your style." He poured a mixture of nuts and dried fruit into a bowl and set it by the cheese.

Kendra ambled in, tucking her datapad into her bag. "I gave him the bad news, and he took it better than I expected. He'd already ordered pizza, and he and the kids are attempting to make cider from the apples that fell off our tree in that ridiculous storm last night." She shrugged good-naturedly as she flopped down on the stool next to Clare. "I wished them the best of luck. With all the holes in those things, they'll end up with cider-worms as much as anything."

Clare squished her face in a decidedly displeased fashion.

Cerulean snorted and finished pouring hot water into the tea cups. "It's not much, but I wasn't expecting company. Eat up and, in between bites, start talking." He glanced at the window as night settled in. *Good thing I have a couple of guest rooms.*

Kendra didn't waste any time building herself a thick cheese sandwich. Clare nibbled a peanut.

Leaning on the counter, Cerulean cleared his throat and poured himself another cup of tea.

Clare sat up. "Okay, it's like this: I wanted to save some poor unwanted Ingot kid like Wendell, and when Bala called me to investigate the Spare Parts shop in Vandi, I couldn't find anything illegal to complain about, but I did arrange to meet the proprietor and asked him if I could adopt an unwanted Ingot, but the fool tried to sell me a little girl, so I dropped him with my Taser, and then my captain and a bunch of higher-ups got on my case and threatened that if I ever interfered in the Spare Parts Shop again, I'd be charged. Now I have to take sensitivity classes, and Bala and Kendra are mad at me, and I don't know what I did wrong. I just wanted to help out a kid—Is that so bad?"

Cerulean and Kendra exchanged a long, commiserating look.

A series of melodic chimes sounded from the front door.

What now? Tromping across the room, Cerulean huffed. *I'm getting old! This human body has some definite limitations.* Dismissing that alarming thought, he stopped dead in his tracks when he saw Roux standing on the other side of the screen door.

He opened it cautiously, terror striking him to the core. "Roux? Has something happened…" He couldn't say Sterling's name but it screamed in his mind. *Why did he use the door instead of just appearing out of thin air like he usually does?* Sensitivity to his new human physiology seemed highly unlikely.

Roux stepped forward and clasped Cerulean's arm with his you-have-no-idea-how-glad-I-am-to-see-you expression.

Uh-oh. He's trying to be nice. Cerulean's stomach clenched. Another informative human sensation he could do without.

"Sterling sent me. He's close to fading, so he asked me to come in person and straighten out this Krowe situation. He seems to think it's important."

Cerulean tried to process the gut-wrenching image of Sterling fading. "He's the oldest Luxonian in history. He'll be remembered forever."

As if he didn't hear the comment, Roux directed his no-nonsense steps to the kitchen and stopped short. He offered a quick wave to Clare and Kendra, whispering from the corner of his mouth. "I didn't realize you had company."

Cerulean brushed past, put the kettle back on the stove, and grabbed another mug. "No worries. They're just here to tell me about a human trafficking case and why Bala has more sense than most, but we might as well catch everyone up on all the latest Ingot idiocy."

Clare jumped off her stool and stared hard at Roux. "Ingots? It's an Ingot that runs the Spare Parts shop, and there were Ingots in the group that tried to shut me up. You know anything about human trafficking running through Newearth?"

Roux lifted his hands in immediate surrender. "Hey, that's not why I came. But if you have proof of such a thing, I can take the case to the Supreme Council."

Kendra swallowed the last bit of her sandwich and dibbed her mouth with a pink cloth from her tummy bag. "So, why'd you come? What have the Ingots been doing that made Sterling send you?"

His eyebrows rising, Roux's expression asked Cerulean's permission to speak.

Cerulean waved to the couch and chairs. "Let's take our tea into the living room and get comfortable. It may be a long night."

Everyone got settled: Roux taking the plush chair by the

bay window and the two women settling on the black couch, while Cerulean stretched out on the white couch. He nodded at Roux. "Go ahead and give them a run-down of what's happened and catch me up on recent events."

Roux took a quick sip and then leaned back. "Well, it turns out that an Ingot trading ship landed on a previously unexplored planet. Somewhere deep in the Sinsinawa District. They expected to find raw materials for export, but instead, they ran into a primitive race of men."

Clare lifted her hand. "Hold on a minute. Are you using the term *men* figuratively or what?"

Roux shook his head impatiently. "No, their DNA proves that they are a close relation of yours—Neanderthals, in fact. On OldEarth they went extinct, but apparently, they've thrived on Tabun. That's the name of the planet, at least that's what they call it. The Ingots call it 967F-Sin."

Kendra reared back. "Neanderthals? You mean the cavemen of ancient OldEarth? From what I learned in history, and I'll admit that's stored in dim memory banks, they were like an underappreciated step-brother. Some humans still carry Neanderthal DNA, but as a race, they couldn't adapt and faded out in ages long past." She shrugged. "Must not have been as smart as the rest of us."

With a quick eye roll, Clare huffed. "Who's being idiotic now? Just because someone dies, doesn't mean that they were stupid. Could be that our ancestors were more ruthless and, when they felt threatened, they killed off the competition. Or the poor Neanderthals might've gotten sick or something."

Cerulean sighed and slugged back the last of his tea.

Playing referee to an out-of-control team, Roux waved his hand. "Not so fast. We could spend all night speculating about what happened on OldEarth. But that's not helping the Krowe family."

Cerulean straightened. "You've met them?"

Grimacing—at an unpleasant memory perhaps—Roux sipped his tea. He then set his cup on the ornate tea table and clasped his hands in a meditative posture. "The Ingot diplomat, Cobalt, decided to 'adopt' a family and brought them to the Newearth Docking Bay to introduce them to their long-lost relatives. He's also hosting a welcome banquet."

Her brow scrunched; Clare fidgeted with her cup. "Well, that's nice, I guess."

"One entry ticket only costs 500 units. A thousand if you want a formal introduction."

Kendra snorted in disgust. "Never put it past an Ingot to make a profit."

Straightening with his perfectly aligned pant leg, Roux shrugged. "I made an appointment for us to meet with them tomorrow, before the dinner. Sterling wants to appear on the holopad."

Clare shook her head. "Just wait till the Cresta hear about this. They'll be ready to leap from their pools to run experiments on these poor newcomers." She glanced up. "How many are there—in the Krowe family?"

Roux pulled out his datapad, scrolled through, then turned it to face the women. "Here's a picture. The older male is Rey, the woman next to him is his wife, Ava, and standing behind them is their son, Gavin. They didn't understand the concept of taking pictures, though I tried to ask their permission."

Doubt hampered Cerulean's relaxed mood. "But you took it anyway?"

Roux shrugged. "I wanted to show you. Look, see? There's just something in their faces that begs for understanding. Childlike even. I'm not saying that they're stupid, but they have some undefinable quality…"

Her voice low, Kendra leaned in, her gaze soft. "Innocence. That's what they have."

His previous feelings of joy in renewed friendships

cringed in the face of grim reality. Cerulean mulled over the Krowe family's future. "And they're about to lose theirs, aren't they? Here on Newearth."

Chapter Five

I'm Just an Android

—Newearth Docking Bay—

Thursday Noon, September 8th

Justine stood back in her form-fitting dark blue uniform and eyed the **"Welcome to Newearth, Krowe Family"** swag that Riko's always-want-to-be-helpful Uncle Clem had designed for the formal reception in the Newearth Docking Bay Great Hall.

As one of only two human-androids on the planet and the docking bay's Chief of Security, she had never considered the idea that she would be arranging decorations for alien introduction to Newearth society.

Another learning experience for the databanks. Thanks, Cerulean. She never rolled her eyes, but she understood the motivation behind the act well enough.

As she stepped back from a row of tables, rubbing what she suspected might be a smudge of yesterday's luncheon selection off her fingers, she ignored humans' inability to keep their meals on their plates and considered the swag with a discerning eye. Logistically, it fit perfectly above the dais where the head table was set, and it would be the first thing the Krowe family would see upon entering the hall. Still…something seemed off. *Just don't know what.* To gain a better perspective, she stepped outside the room and then reentered.

After passing through the double-door entryway, the wonderfully draped deep purple cloth with the glowing green letters practically leaped off the back wall, demanding immediate attention. A large octagonal table, able to comfortably seat twelve, dominated the dais. Before that, four smaller versions of the great table, with chairs for six people at each, surrounded an undistinguished holopad in the center of the room.

Crouching near the holopad, Max focused on the mini-console embedded on the right side. He scratched his head, a clear indication of bafflement which he had practiced to perfection.

He'll figure it out. He always does. Justine continued her appraisal.

On the left, two large windows viewed the swirling universe, while on the right, framed openings peered into the bustling interior world of the Newearth Docking Bay. A snack bar, a well-stocked kitchen, digital wall maps of the complex interior, and a small display case of OldEarth artifacts, completed the scene.

Justine folded her arms. *It's perfect. So why am I irritated by the whole setup?* She surveyed the environment once more.

Clare and Kendra, doing a fair imitation of best friends, meandered the perimeter of the room. They stopped at the display case and entered a quiet discussion. Suddenly, their voices grew louder, and their faces flushed. In the middle of a gigantic eye roll, Kendra turned and locked onto Justine. She began speed walking in Justine's direction with Clare marching angry-faced alongside.

Oh, great, a chance to referee two irate humans. My day is complete.

Kendra came to a halt in front of Justine, her eyes flashing. "Tell Clare that adoption is not *exactly* the same thing as having a natural child. You know the difference. Love may be the same, but DNA is not. No matter how much an adoptive mother loves her kid, that child still has a right to understand where she comes from."

Her hands on her hips, Clare glowered at Kendra, rudely ignoring Justine's presence. "It's not fair asking her! She's not even capable of having a natural child, so she can't say anything."

Kendra's voice rose in exultation. "Exactly! She can't be biased in my favor, so she's completely objective."

A spark igniting in her middle, Justine resisted the urge to catapult the two women across the room.

Luckily, Cerulean and Roux entered the hall at just that moment, sparing Justine murder charges.

Max lifted his head, swiveled his gaze from the newcomers to Justine, and smiled sheepishly, a man not used to "being in love" and clearly abashed by the sensation.

Abruptly, Roux split off from Cerulean and headed toward Max.

Putting on his professional face, Max prepared to receive the Luxonian.

Justine fixed a smile on Cerulean as he neared but snapped her words aside at the two women standing next to her. "No two relationships are exactly alike, idiots. DNA connections matter, but they don't define our complete identity. Parenting is a mystery to everyone. Now shut up and let me talk to someone with sense."

Kendra appeared to wilt as she wandered to one of the tables and plunked down. She pulled a datapad out of her tummy pouch.

Frowning, her arms folded, Clare stayed put, a monument to pure stubbornness.

When he reached them, a flicker of understanding passed between Cerulean and Justine. With a grin, he lifted his gaze and swept one hand through the air. "You've done a great job. The Krowe family should be honored."

Clare huffed. "If they can read."

Justine slapped her thigh. "That's it! I knew there was

something wrong. What a stupid oversight. Cobalt told me that they're picture-people."

Cerulean nodded, but Clare raised an eyebrow.

Exhaling a long, exasperated breath, Justine tromped across the room to the swag and started pulling it down. "They don't have a written, phonetic language; they use symbolic pictures to record information. It's part of the way they talk, too. Apparently, they're really good at similes and metaphors. Brush up on your poetry muscles if you ever hope to communicate with them."

Trailing along behind, Clare sighed. "I wish Omega was here. Or Abbas. One of the Mystery Race, anyway. They'd probably—"

Justine spluttered. "Now you want them! And they're not the Mystery Race! Will you ever get over your ignorance? Eternals, that's their real name. At least that's how it's translated so little minds can comprehend them. Omega rejoined the Communion, and Abbas has enough to do, keeping one eye on Mirage Reborn and the other on his own people. We can't *always* go running to them for help."

Something between a snort and a laugh clarified Cerulean's opinion on the subject. Smothering his humor by swiping his hand over his mouth, he glanced over Justine's shoulder.

Justine glanced back. Max and Roux ambled in their direction. Bundling the useless swag in her arms, she sighed. "I'll ask Uncle Clem to try again and get rid of this. There are collection chutes all over this place. Simms sure had a passion for recycling. Kind of like Bothmal prison. 'Waste not, want not.'"

As usual, Clare had to add her opinion. "Better than the Spare Parts Shop. At least it's not recycling people."

Max shot a glare at Clare. "Some of us hybrids need spare parts as a matter of course. No shame in it."

Impatiently, Roux intervened. "We'll talk about that later. One problem at a time." He nodded to the center of the room. "The holopad isn't working, and Sterling insists that he must be here when the Krowe family arrives."

Cerulean rubbed his forehead and sounded tired. "Sterling is Luxonian. He doesn't need a holopad."

Startled pity filled Roux's eyes. "You haven't seen him, Cerulean. He's… almost gone. He can't do anything for himself anymore. Only with the holopad is there any hope that he can appear, however faintly, before the Krowe family." Tears filled his eyes. "This'll be the last time you see him, Cerulean."

A dreadful ache filled Justine at the image of Abbas leading his son, Omega, into the twilight on their last night together.

Zara, her Human-Luxonian daughter, also designed by Omega, had pleaded for a picnic in the park, and Abbas, acting as the indulgent great-grandfather, had acquiesced. A mere shadow of his former self, Omega had played on the swings in the evening glow, laughing like a boy. Justine would never be able to reconcile the once brilliant Omega who sent her out into the universe, with the idiot-child he'd become.

She dropped the swag and clasped Cerulean's hand. "Go, now, before it's too late. Give Sterling some of your strength, and he can appear through you."

His eyes wide with amazement, Cerulean held her gaze, tears pooling.

A sweet sensation ran over Justine, not the least of which was seeing the jealous pout on Clare's face.

Roux cleared his throat and faced Cerulean. "That might work. Wish I'd have thought of it. But you'd better hurry if you want to make arrangements on Lux and still have time with Sterling."

A quick nod and Cerulean blinked away.

Controlling her startled reaction, Justine stared at where he had been. *With a human body, he shouldn't still be able to do that.* She shrugged the thought off and refocused.

With a satisfied expression, Roux clasped Max's shoulder. "We'll meet the Krowe family and find out exactly what their welcome sign should look like. Then Uncle Clem can get it ready."

Darting a glance aside, Roux marched toward the door. "Clare, you and Kendra let Bala know that we need tight security in place tonight. I don't want an inter-alien disaster to be Sterling's last memory of Newearth."

With a shake of her head, Justine watched everyone scatter to their appointed tasks. She gathered the swag and shoved it into the nearest recycling chute.

—Ingot Diplomat Suite—

Max never thought of himself as slow but compared to Roux's speedy light-nature, his android stamina was pitiful. He had shown Roux the main body of the Newearth Docking Bay in just under two hours, a feat that would have prostrated the average human, but Roux didn't show the slightest sign of fatigue.

Ignoring the propensities of Luxonians to do the unexpected, Max headed for Diplomat Row, a magnificent range of apartments suited for each race that had established residency on the Newearth Docking Bay.

With pardonable pride, he led the way, pointing out the extra-sensitive security bots Justine had installed along each corridor and at every exit and entrance and the colorfully detailed maps he had posted at convenient locations. "I am now the official Newearth Docking Bay Manager, while

Justine is, of course, better suited to her role as Head of Security. Since we're getting married next month, we're considered a match made in Newearth Heaven. I like to think that we're starting our own human-android dynasty. Though we have deeply embedded human sympathies, we remain on the outside, android, and therefore, completely objective. So far, we have met with seamless cooperation from every race—alien and native—that does business here." For a fleeting moment, Max wondered if he was babbling like an insecure fool.

Roux nodded, but his gaze stayed focused inward as he increased his pace.

A large gray door at the end of the well-lit passageway announced the entrance to the Ingot department.

Max waved his hand before the keypad but stopped before entering. "I just want to warn you that Ingots have very different tastes than humans, and some people find it a bit of a shock."

Roux snorted. "I've been to Ingilium numerous times. I know all about their style or lack thereof."

With an air of unruffled dignity, Max crossed the threshold.

Inside the suite, a low hum and stark whiteness contrasted with the general quiet and soft colors of the rest of the Newearth Docking Bay.

To the right, a seven-meter square wall was covered with data-screens, computer consoles, adaptable plug-ins, and minor technology repair tools, with a bold red first-aid kit on the shelf above.

Near at hand, color-coded maps to all known sectors of the universe astonished the inexperienced eye.

On the left, an unadorned Food & Drink dispenser met the daily nutritional needs of Ingots with menus organized by the size, physical workload, and mental activity of the consumer. A rectangular table surrounded by hard, flat stools offered a gathering space for those Ingots who wished to collaborate with others while consuming the necessary ingredients of life.

A medium-sized holopad took a central location, while further down, modest curtains designated a line of Cleansing and Decontamination Stalls.

Directly across, which necessitated a few moments of breezy immodesty, stood racks for formal and informal attire required for specific situations—an introductory dinner or a casual game attendance—were offered in every imaginable size.

Plank bunks lined the last section, framing a view of the universe that couldn't have left even the most practical Ingot heart untouched.

Or so I hope.

Max sighed. The dark irony of humanoids becoming one with technological machines, while he delighted in the slightest hint of his own innate humanity, always left him moderately depressed.

Roux's eyes widened as he surveyed the setting.

Pleased, Max couldn't help gloating. "It's everything an Ingot could wish for. Simms knew what he was doing when he planned this docking bay."

Roux chuckled. "From what little I knew of the man; he was a genius. A very disturbed genius with evil tendencies, don't get me wrong, but a really smart man, nonetheless."

A figure stepped out from behind a clothing rack, perfectly attired in formal bio-ware and far better looking than the average Ingot. His high oxygen breathing tube had been reduced to a mere nostril slit which was camouflaged by an inset of beautiful stones, looking more like artistic jewelry than a technological adaption. His helm was so well sculptured to his head that it fit like a cap, and his entire face was plain to see. Bright blue eyes stared like lasers.

Max stepped forward to make the introductions. "Good afternoon, Cobalt." He motioned to the Luxonian. "This is Roux, a Luxonian, who would like to become better apprised of the Krowe situation before the formal reception this evening."

Cobalt grinned good-naturedly at Roux.

A friendly welcome? A shiver ran over Max. Cobalt had always appeared to look through him, never once attempting to meet his gaze. *Because I'm an android?*

Indicating the solid table with hard chairs, Cobalt invited them to sit. "Let's get comfortable, shall we?"

Roux laughed. Apparently, irony tickled him.

Max waited for them to sit across the table from each other, and then he positioned himself at the end, a referee between two alien combatants.

Roux folded his hands on the tabletop. "So, Cobalt, could you color in some of the details concerning how it is that an unsophisticated, previously untouched population of humanoids suddenly became Ingot treasures to be shown off like national prizes?"

Alarm filled Max. His hands conveniently hidden under the table; he tapped a hurried message to Justine on the datapad embedded in his right forearm. "Ingot Suite. Come. Now."

Cobalt smiled disarmingly and leaned back, appearing quite comfortable on the hard stool. "What began as an accident grew into a mutually beneficial experience for both Ingots and the Krowe family. Though they didn't know about us, per se, their planet has been visited before. Both Rey and Ava insisted that they had heard rumors of strange ships coming from the sky. Our appearance was 'welcome rain cascading over parched land after a long drought.' Or something like that."

Roux leaned forward; his hands clasped much too tightly. "So, you didn't have to convince them to leave their home world and come here? No grand promises of personal fortune or threats to their people?"

"Threats and promises? What do you take us for—Luxonians?" Cobalt sniffed. "Initially, we didn't have anything particular in mind other than to introduce ourselves and offer any assistance they might need. It's a beautiful planet, though very cold in winter, and vegetation is hard to grow in most of the regions because the soil is severely limited."

"But it has incredible mining potential?"

Cobalt shrugged noncommittally.

Max decided to jump in with a safer line of questioning. "Justine had arranged for a sign to hang in the great hall to welcome the Krowe family, only to realize that they don't understand language the way we do. Can you give us particulars on their communication style, their level of development, and what they hope to gain by coming to Newearth?"

Looking bored and after a prolonged stretch, Cobalt rose and gestured to the Food Dispenser. "Would you like something? I'm in need of some high-energy nutrition after all the formal arrangements I've had to make recently."

Max stayed focused while Roux merely rolled his eyes.

Cobalt tapped the dispenser console, talking over his shoulder in the most leisurely manner Max had ever seen in an Ingot.

"They talk pretty. Lots of colorful expressions fill their language with something beyond the preciseness of typical conversation."

Three rectangular bars textured like pie crusts formed on a serving tray.

Greedily, Cobalt snatched them up.

To his horror, Max felt his mouth begin to salivate. *Love them as I might, my human synapses compromise me at times like this.*

Cobalt ambled back to the table and perched on his stool. "As for their development level"—he tipped his hand in the air in a so-so manner. "It's hard to say what they could do given the chance. Survival was the order of their day on Tabun. Family size seemed to be limited with a high infant mortality rate. That's why Rey and Ava have only one son." He chomped on one bar, breaking it in half with his teeth, then chewed reflexively. His gaze seemed to turn inward, ruminating. "I couldn't believe it when Ava said that only about half the population is able to reproduce at all." He shoved the rest of the bar into his mouth and fingered the second, chewing around his words. "To be honest, that's why they've come to Newearth. They're dying out there, alone on that cold, cruel planet. They need a home where they can thrive."

Roux shook his head. "But what about the others? Was Rey and his family sent as scouts or representatives? Are other Tabunites hoping to join them here?"

Cobalt gulped down the second bar and wiped his mouth with the back of his hand. "Not my concern. I was just told to make them welcome on Newearth and then back off." His gaze hardened. "Luxonians specialize in assisting newcomers, so we'll gladly allow you to do what you are so good at."

Roux's edges glowed, in anger or excitement, Max couldn't discern.

With exaggerated politeness, Roux enunciated his words with precision. "So, once the population has been resettled, you'll have the planet to yourselves. Your miners are waiting with bated breath, I'm sure."

A blazing desert could not have shriveled Max's hopes any faster.

With surprising calmness, Cobalt leisurely crunched his last bar, rose, and gestured to the door. He swallowed and smiled. "The formal reception will begin in just a couple of hours. I'd suggest that you prepare yourselves with due modesty and put on your best charm. The Krowe family is a treasure, indeed, as you will soon discover. And you wouldn't want to embarrass Newearth with anything less than a perfect reception. Flowers, some food, and a few musical instruments—drums or flutes—would be appropriate gifts. Don't bother hanging a sign. Kind treatment will be all the welcome they need." He tapped the door console, and the door slid open.

Without even a hint of a respectful goodbye, Roux practically flew down the corridor.

Max bowed in polite courtesy to Cobalt and then hurried to keep pace with Roux.

Raging in a red aura, Roux didn't slow his steps. "Am I a child to be instructed by an Ingot diplomat? What does that fool think? That we were only going to offer them a swag!"

With growing wisdom, Max realized that not all questions should be answered.

They turned the first corner and nearly ran into Justine.

She scowled at Max. "I thought you were in trouble. The message implied something serious, but I had to solve a Clare and Kendra crisis. I sent them home, and Bala is assisting with security." She crossed her arms. "So, what's the problem?"

Still fuming, Roux shoved past Justine. "I'm going to find out what is happening with Cerulean and Sterling." He talked fast as he stopped in the middle of the corridor and looked over his shoulder. "Make sure that you get the flowers, food, and the rest of the stuff Cobalt mentioned. I don't think I could stand it if an Ingot turns out to be more culturally sensitive than the rest of us."

The Luxonian blinked away. Justine turned and stared at Max.

Max shrugged. “It’s pretty simple, really. No one understands anyone.”

Chapter Six

Overwhelming Honesty

—Newearth Docking Bay Great Hall—

Thursday Evening

Gavin, a long-lost relation to the human race, who considered himself a Tabunite first and foremost, blinked at the strong light as he followed his mother and father into the cold, barren space of the Newearth Great Hall. *Winter sleep brings forth future life?* Dressed in a long white tunic and brown leggings, he looked around, uncomprehending, fear rising from deep within. *What lives here?* Murky creatures in the Great Green Sea were more familiar.

Black and white battled against red, green, and yellow all over the room. Hard shapes pointed themselves at every angle while slight, tender cloths rippled at each pass. A large table dominated, demanding attention. Small tables, subservient, bowed low in their designated places. The whole room was stiff and unfriendly, even the floor did not respond to his touch. He rolled his shoulders in an effort to relax the tension tightening his body and resisted the urge to rub the irritating translator embedded in his ear.

His father, Rey, also in a tunic and leggings, though his colors were tan and white, strode forward, his head high and his chest puffed out. Always a bold front. A hum emanated from deep within, resonating with his mother's, who strode at his elbow. Smaller and dressed in cyan, she remained unbowed, though her head swiveled side to side, like a leaf caught in the wind.

As rear guard, Gavin, taller and far more muscular than his parents, protected them with his vigilance and presence.

A line before the largest table formed a waiting assembly, while others watched with focused attention from behind chairs at tables placed around a circular pad. The pad, silent and unadorned, appeared insignificant, but Gavin's heart warned him that it held a secret meaning. *Central position demands great attention.*

Everyone, except his father and mother, maintained perfect silence. No one dared to join their courteous hum. These people did not understand even elementary traditions.

Once before the assembly, his father came to a halt. His hum silenced. His mother stood close but did not touch him. As a leader, Rey must stand alone.

A tall, smooth-faced man with no scent, dressed in a form-fitting bodysuit, stepped forward. A string of undulating sounds came forth, but the transmitter affected an almost instantaneous translation. "Welcome to Newearth, Rey, Ava, and Gavin. We are honored by the gift of your presence."

The man stepped aside, and a woman, also carrying no scent, stepped forward and held out two objects: a beautiful flute with delicate carvings along the edge and a fine drum with an ornate base. "We wish to show gratitude with our humble gifts. Please accept them in the spirit of friendship in which they are offered."

Rey took the drum, and Ava accepted the flute, their hums rising again in a gentle response that Gavin could only hope would be understood as pleasure.

Smooth-face placed his hand on his chest and bowed low. "I am Max, Android-Human, and the Newearth Docking Bay Manager." He gestured to the woman. "This is my partner and soon-to-be wife, Justine, also an Android-Human, who serves as Head of Security. We are here to assist you during your stay." He glanced aside as a familiar form stepped forward.

Unexpectedly, relief flowed over Gavin like spring rain. He nearly smiled at the Ingot.

As if reading his mind, Cobalt grinned. "I'm sure you already know of my devotion to you and your people. Please, feel free to ask for Ingot assistance at any time."

Without further delay, Max gestured to another member of the assembly.

A dark-skinned, muscular man in a sleeveless calf-length, celadon tunic stepped forward and offered a formal bow.

Max continued his introduction. "Here is another guest, Roux, a Luxonian, a light being, who assisted in the formation of Newearth. You will soon meet Sterling, one of the most revered members of the Luxonian Supreme Council, and Cerulean, Newearth's most devoted friend, after dinner. They will appear on the holopad." He gestured to the mysterious circle in the center of the room.

Gavin suppressed a foreboding shudder. It was hard enough to comprehend the distance they traveled on the ship, which had sailed across immeasurable space, bringing them here. What greater realms of the unknown would be revealed by that unassuming ring? He wasn't sure he wanted to know. *Not yet.*

His mother elbowed him. Gavin returned his gaze to the host.

This time Max wore a stern face to beckon the next assembly member forward. A woman. Not as tall as himself but shapely and fascinatingly hesitant. Was she afraid of them? Her gaze darted around the room, looking for protection or escape?

At her side appeared another human, also small and thin, twiggy even, but with the most comical face Gavin had ever seen. A bubble of laughter struggled to erupt. His mother jabbed him harder.

His stern face still in place, Max cleared his throat and

gestured to the two humans. "Clare is one of our best Human Services Detectives. She helps to keep Newearth safe and the human population thriving. Her partner, Bala, is a worthy friend and a powerful defender of Human rights."

Completely beyond his control, a snort of derision erupted from Gavin.

His father glared at him out of the corner of his eye, and his mother grabbed his hand and squeezed. She still seemed to think that such childish maneuvers would keep him in line.

To the twig-man's credit, he smirked at Gavin. "You're my DNA cousin, you know. So that makes us allies. I'll take you anywhere you want to go on Newearth, and you beat up any bullies who get in our way, okay?"

It took a moment for the translation to clarify in his mind, but once he understood, Gavin reached over and gave the little man a solid thwap of approval.

A gasp rang through the entire assembly. Everyone waited in hushed expectancy.

Bala grinned and patted Gavin's forearm, the only part of his anatomy that he could safely reach—a deer approving of a lion—but Gavin could accept that. He nodded.

As one, the assembly exhaled and started chattering in relief.

Once the two humans stepped back, two very odd creatures stepped up. First, a repulsively fat and pulpy figure with little natural coloring, wearing some kind of padded clothing, stared through huge bulbous eyes. It spoke before Max had time to make the proper introduction.

"My name is Taug, a Cresta from the planet Crestar. We are the most scientifically innovative and forward-thinking race in this part of the universe. You will find that we have much to offer your people as you enter into the larger universe."

His mother and father appeared stunned, frozen in place

by this imposing alien. Neither moved a muscle.

Frowning, Gavin did the needful and nodded stiff approval once again.

The other creature seemed more like something out of a dream than a real person. Female, certainly, but with a lithe figure, coy eyes, and a bright dress made of delicate webs woven in intricate patterns, she appeared to be a child-flower but with sensitivity hovering in the depths of her eyes. She did not need to smile. Her whole being beamed.

Gavin swallowed his uncertainty.

His father pressed his hands to his chest and then cupped them together and reached out—it was the gesture one makes to the gods. A beseeching prayer of humility. His heart was his only offering since his hands were empty before such splendor.

Clearly unaware of the identity crisis at hand, Max continued with his speech. "This is Faye, a Bhuaci from the planet Helm. Her people are shapeshifters. They can assume any form they wish—even as liquid or gas. But they prefer figures that charm."

Charm? Or bewitch? There is power hidden in that dainty form. Gavin's gaze returned to Clare, the woman who was closest kin to his kind. Familiar yet tantalizingly different. Powerful but afraid…of something. A thrill raced through him. Suddenly the room did not seem so cold after all.

Max's direction to ascend to the dais and take their places at the main table murmured like background noise to the pounding of Gavin's heart.

Clare was supposed to sit between Roux and Rey, but unexpectedly Gavin switched places with Roux and took the position left of center, leaving Justine to manage dinner conversation between a Luxonian she had little interest in and her hybrid daughter, who was already antagonizing the nearest Ingot with a flurry of questions.

Staring at the child, Clare shook her head.

Zara had gone through so many transformations in her brief human-Luxonian existence that Clare couldn't stop being suspicious of the child. She had been another of Omega's experiments, one that had gone surprisingly right. For a time. Then the child went berserk and almost killed Kendra. Soon after, while the whole planet feared destruction by the planet-eating monster, Cosmos, the child was abducted by the Newearth Docking Bay creator, Simms, who had promptly handed her over to Cresta scientists. After a few simple "adjustments," the child calmed down. When Cosmos was destroyed, so did the entire Newearth population.

Loud throat clearing dragged Clare's attention from the bewitching child to Gavin. *Handsome in a caveman sort of way. Muscled. Piercing eyes.* And he was staring at her!

Gavin smiled, his gaze darting across the table. He spoke a stream of sounds that resembled a tune more than a conversation.

Tapping the translator in her ear as if to make it work faster, Clare hunched forward in concentration.

Gavin's voice clarified from singsong to meaningful words. "You care for that child. A family member, perhaps?"

Clare glanced at Zara. The child was leaning on Cobalt's arm, peering with utter fascination at one of his implants. Surprisingly, Cobalt didn't seem to mind terribly much. He actually appeared pleased. Clare tried not to gag. *How can she charm an Ingot?* Suppressing a shudder, she focused on Gavin. "That's Zara, Justine's little girl. A hybrid, Human-Luxonian. I'm not sure what to make of her. I once believed that the one who created her was a devil." She shrugged. "I'm not so sure now."

Gavin's face swirled with emotions, as if he couldn't

decide on a reaction. Bewilderment won. “Hybrid? I don’t understand the word. Max spoke of himself and Justine as hybrids. Is everyone here hybrid?”

Clare let the question hang in the air while servers, wearing colorful bodysuits, streamed into the room, weaving among the tables, and placing ornate trays in front of each member of the assembly. It was so seamlessly done that it appeared as if everyone was served at the same moment.

The main course consisted of a savory stew with a side of crusty bread and a crunchy salad doused with a creamy topping. The meals were served in accordance with the needs of each race. Clare didn’t need to look across the table to see that Taug’s dinner had already been poured into his breathing helm.

She glanced back at Gavin and quickly decided that overwhelming honesty would be her best policy. “No, hybrids are quite rare. There was a being named Omega, one of the Eternals, who managed to successfully implant embryonic humans inside android bodies. Max and Justine are the result of his early work. I don’t think even he expected them to become so *human*. Somehow or another, he created Zara, the little girl you see over there, and no one, not even his father, Abbas, knows how he did it. There was one other hybrid, Derik, created by Taug’s father, but he died. A long, dramatic story you probably don’t want to hear.” She shrugged and dug into her stew. “Most of us are rather boring.”

Gavin snorted. But, at least, he was still smiling. He grabbed his spoon and got to work on his stew. Clearly, the meal pleased him. He scarfed the entire thing down in a matter of moments, sending the servers into nervous jitters.

Roux leaned over and spoke quietly in Gavin’s ear.

Annoyed, Clare continued to work her way through her dinner, pretending that she wasn’t trying to lip-read Roux’s words.

Soon, all became clear as Roux spoke to one of the servers, and, in a matter of moments, another dinner was placed before Gavin.

Gavin grinned and thwacked Roux on the shoulder.

Barely turning aside, Roux shared a brief eye-roll with Justine.

Gavin made quick work of the second offering and then pushed the tray aside. He leaned on his elbows and peered at Clare. "You are not boring. Veiled like a stormy sea, you hide much under the cover of darkness."

Clare choked. A hot flush worked over her cheeks. She coughed and scraped her throat like a sailor trying to dislodge a tough wad of tobacco. Sweat broke over her forehead. Finally, she gained control of herself.

Roux had rushed to her side, ready to turn her inside out, if necessary, but Gavin barred the way. The caveman did what he knew best and pounded her on the back.

Surrendering to near hysteria, Clare started to laugh. "I'm okay. If everyone will stop saving me, I might live to see another day."

She leaned back in her chair and met the alarmed eyes of the entire room. Hot embarrassment sizzled over her entire body. She lifted her hands. "I'm fine. Go back to your meals. Dessert will be served soon."

On cue, the servers bustled into action, and the dinner trays were swished away. New trays with an assortment of small cakes, pie slices, puddings, and ice cream were set in place.

Clare couldn't help but notice that Faye beamed as she dug into her chocolate cake topped with fudge. Bala's eyes had rounded to saucer size at the swirled topping on his pie, and even the newcomers, Rey and Ava, grinned like children at the sweet confections. Dessert needed no translation.

Unwilling to face another choking episode, Clare nibbled

her way through her dessert. The room bubbled with happy chatter, though Gavin now seemed a smidge discontented. Suppressing a sigh, Clare waded into polite conversation. "So, what do you think of Newearth? How does it compare to your home world?"

His expression serious, Gavin leaned back in his chair, his feet firmly placed, his hands clasped on the table. "Except for this excellent meal, all is in darkness. I do not understand how I got here. I do not understand this place or these people. I do not understand hybrid. I do not understand *you*. I want the sun to shine so that I may see again."

For some unaccountable reason, Clare felt tears rush to her eyes. Part of her wanted to hug this man, and part of her wanted him to hug her. She looked into his eyes and realized with horror that she felt something powerful and totally out of her control.

Cerulean did not want Sterling to die, and this realization amazed him. Since the first time he was forced to work with the all-too-often arrogant Supreme Councilor on Newearth, their relationship had been adversarial. Sterling had never understood humans. He had never honestly cared for them. Through all the generations from Aram, Ishtar, Neb, Georgios, Melchior, and into the last OldEarth age with Anne Smith, Sterling had merely tolerated humanity. But somewhere along the way, Sterling had changed. He had left off underestimating humanity, as well as Cerulean's father, Teal, and after Teal's death, had even attempted to guide and protect Cerulean. When he finally came to terms with Cerulean's independence, he was forced to admit his own dependence. Their odd, begrudging friendship was rooted in ancient but rocky soil. *Or was it the humus of humility*?

After traveling from Lux to Newearth, they were in the correct position now, and they could appear in the Docking

Bay Great Hall immediately. He had no choice but to firmly grip the failing Luxonian at his side and keep him upright.

Sterling leaned heavily on Cerulean as they materialized on the holopad. They could have appeared anywhere in the room, but the holopad was central and a perfect stage. Pale, his elderly, white-robed human form shimmering, Sterling offered a nod and a beseeching expression.

Cerulean understood and propped Sterling in such a way that he seemed to be standing alone, just as the central light in the room brightened, announcing their presence to the entire assembly.

Chattering ceased, and all eyes fixed on them.

Sterling bowed in a formal salute.

Roux and Max jumped to their feet, and the rest of the room rose as if on command. The air tingled with expectation.

Rey wiped his mouth with the back of his hand, clearing off a last bit of cake, while three seats away, his wife blinked, her forehead tying in knots of confusion.

Gavin stared straight ahead through unwavering eyes.

Meeting Gavin's penetrating eyes, surprise sparked within Cerulean. There was more to this newcomer than Roux had led him to believe.

Sterling gathered the last of his feeble strength and spoke loud enough for the whole room to hear. "I am Sterling, a very old Luxonian from the elder days. I have seen so much. But as I had to live to learn, so must you experience the trials of your time. Still, I must warn you against the one curse that haunts us all." A smile trembled and his form wavered, but his voice held firm. "Despair."

Suddenly, he slumped, a wick losing its last breath of light.

Without thought or concern for appearances, Cerulean gathered the slim figure and cradled him in his arms, willing his own strength into Sterling.

For a moment, Sterling brightened, and his gaze

wandered the assembly.

Barely maintaining dual control, Cerulean toured the room with him.

Tears flowed down Roux's face as he stood with one fist clenched against his heart, a loyal soldier before his beloved commander. Justine had taken Zara's hand, and they stood together, their stoic expressions belying the intensity of their feelings. Impassive, Cobalt seemed to be taking mental notes. Bala's compassionate expression spoke of faith that few could see. Tears brimmed Faye's eyes. Like Justine, Max stood at attention, his concern would manifest itself later in kindness. Distracted, Taug fiddled with his breather helm. Clare focused on Cerulean; her concern evident not for the Luxonian slipping to the other side but for the only Luxonian she had ever really loved.

Gavin locked his steady gaze on Sterling, somehow aware of the momentousness of the situation…

Cerulean solidified his form. *Is this why Sterling had to come? To speak to Gavin?*

Using Cerulean's strength, Sterling lifted his voice once again. "This world…like the wider universe…is slipping into an abyss. You must fight." Sterling lifted a wavering hand and admonished. "Never give up. Never give in. Offer the one thing no one else can!"

Swoosh.

Sterling vanished.

Emptiness.

Falling forward, Cerulean realized that he was alone in a way he had never known before. Staring at the empty holopad, he could have screamed in terror.

But, instead, he looked up. Gavin's honest eyes were there to meet his.

Chapter Seven

Is this How They Had Felt?

—Taug's Laboratory—

Wednesday Morning, October 26th

Taug pottered about his laboratory, arranging his instrument panels just so and adjusting the larger dissecting table to a lower height for his slimmer bio-suit and thin boots, which had made him appear nearly trim, though not quite so imposing. He wasn't sure which his vanity needed more, attractiveness or the power to subdue.

He had taken a refreshing dip in the pool earlier, and his body still tingled with the exhilaration of catching fresh food in a murky environment. *Always good to slip into my natural state for a few hours.*

Though the room was supposed to be soundproof, he could still hear a muted version of the myriad conversations from the Breakfastnook Café just on the other side of the shelving wall. Riko's customers always sounded like they were having a fun time. *He's doing good business, at least.*

He padded between the smaller dissecting table and the "Procedure Chair" and surveyed his comfortable visitors' corner. A large overstuffed couch and four padded chairs surrounded a solid oak table, with a small holopad tucked into the far end. His personal doorway to The Breakfastnook Café was on the west wall, while a stocked fish tank, actually a food storage unit, sat comfortably against the north wall.

A glance at the high elongated windows assured him that though the chilly wind had bit right through his bio-suit this morning, there was no chance for snow as the sun still shone through an azure sky.

The sound of approaching footsteps sent a thrill through him. Clare was coming for a visit, and he had plans she never suspected.

A quick series of raps on the back door.

With his slimmer suit, Taug was able to cross the room in no time and open the door wide.

Clare didn't wait for pleasantries. She barged right in. "You sent word, so I'm here. But make it quick. I've got a load of cases piling up, and Bala's kids have all come down with some mystery flu, so he's been helping Kendra at home, leaving me more bogged down than ever."

Concern washed swiftly over Taug. Then professional interest rose to the occasion. "Mystery flu, you say? Hmm. I'll have to investigate. I mean, I'll have to offer my services as a friend and—"

Clare sank down on the nearest chair and dropped her head back, closing her eyes. "Just get on with it. What do you want?"

Flummoxed by Clare's complete lack of manners, so different from Faye, who practically oozed charm on every occasion, Taug considered his options. *I don't have to tell her. It's not like he would do anything terrible to me if I neglected to fulfill his request…Or would he?*

A mental image of Omega getting furiously angry formed all too quickly in his mind. He cleared his throat, padded to the chair next to Clare, and perched on the edge. He clasped two of his tentacles in his lap meditatively. "I have been asked to relay a message to you."

Clare murmured indistinctly. "Hmm?"

"From Omega."

That got her attention. Clare's eyes snapped open, and she sat up. "Omega's gone dotty. He can hardly speak much less ask for messages to be conveyed."

Chiding her with just a hint of disdain, Taug wiggled a free tentacle at her. "You forget who you are dealing with. The Eternals have powers we can only imagine. Even time is subject to them. It is best never to underestimate an Eternal."

Clare rubbed her eyes and yawned. "Oh, get on with it, then. What does our monster friend have to say?"

Scandalized, Taug clamped all his tentacles into an agitated bundle. This fool woman had no idea of her position. *Protected her whole life through and never had a clue!*

A deep sigh and Clare rose to her feet. "Sorry, Taug. I know you mean well, but I've had a long history with Omega and though I know he wasn't really as rotten as I thought, his name still leaves a bad taste in my mouth. But that has nothing to do with you. So out with it. What's he commissioned you to tell me? I sure hope you're getting paid well."

Taug rose, paced across the room, and flung a curtain aside, revealing a small holopad. A snap and a figure appeared.

Omega.

Clare blinked. This was like no Omega she had ever seen. This person appeared sane, happy, and healthy. Dressed in casual clothes, his sleek black hair shoulder-length, and his amber eyes bright with calm intelligence. She swallowed and glanced at Taug. "He sort of looks like Abbas. And a better version of himself."

Taug nodded. "Perceptive of you. Yes. He is much better. Healed beyond description. Renewed, you might say. In any case, he left this message especially for you. So, I suggest that you listen with both ears."

Clare stared as the holopad Omega appeared to come to life.

"Clare, finally! I have wanted to speak to you on so many occasions—through dreams, nightmares, and even on my sickbed. But it was never the right time, and I was never certain what to say. But finally, I have the words. And I must tell you—and so many others—that I am truly sorry. I was a child in mind and soul, playing with people's lives as if they were mere toys. I did not understand our connection. But now I see. I have shared terrible grief. Cried inconsolable tears. Agonized through endless guilt. And come to see my part to play in the destruction of so much good that might have been. Though time is Eternal, evil either grows or shrinks with the current of our wills. I have let it grow to a monstrous size, but I did not work alone. My only hope is to repair the damage I have done. With your forgiveness, we may right wrongs, and remake the entire universe." He stared at Clare, his piercing gaze seemingly seeing her as she stood there.

Taug wasn't sure that he couldn't.

Clare shivered.

Omega pressed his hands together in beseeching prayer. "Forgive me, Clare!" In a blink, the figure vanished.

Clare stumbled backward and bumped against a chair.

Taug bustled over and helped her to sit down. He eyed her, uncertain, though hopeful.

Clare sat stone still a moment. Then she snorted and shook her head. "It can't be true."

With unnamed grief at a missed opportunity, bubbles sizzled as Taug sighed through his breather helm. Omega's effort was wasted. *It's up to me now.*

—Cerulean's Cabin—

Tuesday, Noon, November 1st

Cerulean's nerves were a jumble. He hadn't felt this nervous since…he couldn't think when. *Have I ever been this nervous before? Maybe...* The time he returned to Anne Smith on OldEarth, knowing that she'd been hurt when he'd left without an explanation...

Crash!

The ceramic mug he had been holding now lay in splintered pieces across his kitchen floor. What was wrong with him? Growling under his breath, he pounded to the closet, yanked out the broom and dustpan, and hurriedly swept up the shards. He dropped the mess into the trash with a sickening clatter. In a near frenzy, he replaced the broken cup with a new one and arranged two settings on the kitchen table. His stomach in tight knots, lightheaded, and jittery, he wondered briefly if one of his Amens friends had slipped something unfortunate into last month's tea rations.

A creak on the porch step froze every muscle in his body.

Stop! I am not a child. I've welcomed a great many aliens to my home before. Heavens, pretty much everyone on this planet is an alien!

"Hello?"

Cerulean started for the kitchen door and then halted. He had forgotten his translator. He rushed across the room, swiped the earbud off the large rectangular table, jogged to the screen door, and stared wide-eyed at his smiling guest.

Gavin stood with his chest puffed out, lifted one hand, and patted the air like a toddler proudly waving for the first time. "Hello."

Flummoxed, Cerulean tapped his ear. "Wait, I don't have my translator—"

The smile stayed plastered on Gavin's face as Cerulean shoved the door open, heat rushing over his cheeks. "You've learned a little human speech? I'm impressed." He pressed the bud into his ear. "Unfortunately, I'm not such a quick study with your language." He led the way into the kitchen and pointed to the central oak table. "Please, sit down and relax. I was just getting things ready for a noon repast. Would you care to join me?"

Gavin offered a polite bow of acceptance, then proceeded to sit on the tabletop. Uncertain what to do with his feet, he soon propped them on the matching bench. He tapped his ear and garbled his next words. "I need now. My human words run dry."

Rather surprised at how natural Gavin looked, perched *on* his table, Cerulean refocused on the task at hand. Flatbread, wheat crackers, three kinds of cheese, an assortment of mixed nuts and dried fruit, carrot sticks, the last of the cherry tomatoes, and pepper slices were arranged on an engraved metal tray. He swiped it from the counter and laid it beside his guest. "Tea in a moment. Do you have a preference? Here's a variety. Pick what you like. The water is almost hot." He nudged a bowl stuffed with a variety of tea packets toward Gavin.

To his credit, Gavin wasn't taking any chances. He sniffed everything. Apparently satisfied with Chamomile, he ripped open the soft bag and poured the shredded leaves into his mouth. Then he chewed. And chewed.

Cerulean hurried over carrying the steaming kettle by its wooden handle. "Oh, sorry; I should've explained first. The tea bag goes into the cup of hot water, where it seeps, making the water more flavorful." He grabbed another cup, filled it with cold water, and handed it over. "Drink this to wash that down. We can try again, if you like?"

Gavin grinned. "I play with you—like a brother." He stepped down from the table and took a seat on the bench. Then he dropped a mint teabag into the waiting cup.

Fighting annoyance heavily doused with relief, Cerulean poured the hot water into the two cups. Though he wished he had something stronger, he settled for spicy Chai. He pulled out the heavy ladder-back chair at the head of the table and planted himself, good and solid, his feet flat on the floor. "So, you want to tell me what this is all about? And where does *brother* come in? I didn't know you had any siblings."

After a sip, his gaze roaming the room, Gavin savored his tea. He nodded with a smile. "Good. Like it better this way." He propped his elbows on the table and cupped the mug in both hands, relaxed, but on the edge of something. "I had a baby brother, but he died. Like so many." He met Cerulean's gaze. "Ingots do this. They ruin women, so we need *them* to help us."

Horror raced over Cerulean. Suddenly his anxiety made sense. Sterling had been trying to tell them something. He knew that the Ingots were natural deceivers. They deceived themselves into thinking that they liked becoming one with machines, after all.

The memory of falling, right after Sterling's dissolution, made Cerulean dizzy. He tightened his grip on his mug, heat penetrating his cold hands. Grateful that he was sitting down, he met Gavin's gaze. "Explain."

Gavin plucked bread and cheese from the tray, popped them into his mouth, and then chewed meditatively. He seemed to have all the time in the world to tell his awful tale.

The urge to kick his guest nearly overwhelmed Cerulean. He snatched a couple of baby carrots and crunched down hard.

A shadow fell over the room, and a chill wind swept through.

Gavin shivered and rose from the bench. He strode to the large bay window overlooking the open field facing west. He lifted the lacy curtain and peered out.

A bank of dark clouds covered the sun, and wild grass waved in undulations across the expanse. Trees bordering a creek swayed to the rhythm of a rising wind.

As if speaking to someone outside the window, Gavin broke the silence. "Long generations ago, our people were blessed with children, always born in pairs or as triplets. Those gifted with triplets were favored by the Almighty. The third child born as a triplet would always marry another third child. And thus, those most favored were elected as rulers. We were a healthy, free-roaming people, who lived in ever-widening clans and thrived across the land. The Almighty loved us."

Cerulean blinked back an ache behind his eyes. He could still feel the empty swoosh, the vacancy, where Sterling had been. *How can I miss someone who annoyed me my entire life?* He swallowed a lump in his throat and refocused on Gavin. He pressed his translator tighter into his ear. "And then…?"

Gavin turned and folded his arms across his chest. "Then there were no more triplets. Even twins didn't always survive." He shook his head as if considering a bewildering puzzle. "One renowned elder, one of the last triplets, spoke of a recurring nightmare: Jellyfish appeared hanging in the sky, stretching to the land, and plucking babies from their mothers, gulping them whole.

Nausea roiled in Cerulean's stomach. *My human body tells me too much. I've lived this horror before.* He stood and carried his mug to the stovetop, refilled it with hot water, and lifted it in Gavin's direction as an offering.

Gavin shook his head.

Cerulean placed the kettle back on the stovetop. "Humanity suffered a loss of fertility, as did Luxonians. It seems that renewal is not always assured." He strolled to the matching bay window. A storm was brewing. *Well, it is autumn.*

Rubbing his chin, Gavin didn't seem satisfied. "Our tribulation did not last. Frightened and humbled, Tabunites across the lands offered songs and prayers of repentance. Our rulers had become proud, and many twins had been forced into servitude. As the tide of arrogance had carried triplets into power, the current of repentance swept them away." He stared at the table and frowned. "Do you have any chicken?"

Caught off guard by this abrupt change in topic, Cerulean tapped his translator, convinced that it had malfunctioned.

Gavin strode over to the ornate tray and gobbled a series of cheese cubes and the rest of the crackers. Then he picked through the mixed nuts. "Yesterday, my parents and I visited the home of your friend Bala. His wife Kendra made a delicious stew, which my parents enjoyed very much. Bala and his children were polite, but it was clear that their happiness was submerged under the lake of tranquility. Taking my funny-faced host aside, I asked him what the children would rather eat, and he brought forth Old-World engravings, on thin sheaves, called cookbooks. He became especially excited about roast chicken, which, I understood was something like our field birds—flightless but fat and tender."

Cerulean spluttered. "Bala made you roast chicken!"

Gavin smiled. "No, but he wanted to. He said that Newearth meat was grown in special laboratories, and animals were no longer sacrificed for food. Though he believes that there are some who still cling to the old ways. He suggested that you might have had roast chicken with your neighbors."

The image of the Amens' flock of hens flashed through Cerulean's mind. He shoved it away and ambled back to the table. "That's a topic for another time. If it is any comfort, I'll invite you and Bala to dinner with my neighbors—the Amens community—next week sometime. They do many things in the OldEarth way. Might amuse you. Or make you feel more at home, perhaps." Wrapping three cherry tomatoes and a couple of pepper slices in a piece of flatbread, Cerulean got back to the topic at hand. "So, what happened after the triplets were all gone? Who rules your people now?"

Gavin dug through the tea offerings and snatched up a bag

of vanilla chai. He plunked it into his cup and, making himself rather at home, paced to the stove. "The Almighty took pity on us and gave our women triplets again. My parents are each the third-born of triplets." He poured hot water into his cup and sighed. "But, by then, favor for triplets had evaporated in the heat of suffering. Today, family clans rule small farms, and few want great leaders. I was born a twin, but my younger brother, born almost a day later, arrived deformed and died soon after."

Cerulean wiped his mouth and forced himself into professional mode. "What has this to do with Ingots? That was a serious accusation you made earlier."

"I was one of the first to see the Ingots arrive at our planet. But I do not believe that they told all truth. They enjoy trade with the fat-ones, who, when they are in water, look very much like jellyfish."

"Crestas? You think the Ingots are working with the Crestas to destroy your population? Why?" The whole notion was ludicrous. *Maybe.*

The afternoon sun had all but faded as the autumn season gave way to shortened days.

A knock on the kitchen door turned both their attention. Cerulean frowned.

With a grin, Gavin practically galloped to the screen door. "My funny friend!"

His arms wrapped about his waist, his cheeks pink as bright balloons, Bala shivered at the door. "Let a poor, skinny man inside, won't you?"

Suppressing a groan, Cerulean waved Bala into the sheltered kitchen. "What brings you by this late in the day?"

Bala hopped across the threshold; a sparrow happy to find a safe haven. "Happy All Saint's Day to you, too!"

Tapping his translator, Gavin shook his head.

Bala expounded his meaning, "We remember those good

folks who have gone onto new shores, leaving the light of their faithfulness to shine on those of us left behind." Bala grinned at Cerulean and inched his way to the mixed nuts.

Apparently, Bala made perfect sense in Tabunite. Gavin's "Ahhh!" spoke volumes.

Around happy crunches, Bala explained himself. "You see, Big Gav here told me how he had some concerns about the Ingots and Crestas working together to depopulate his planet…for some reason, he can't quite explain. After a wonderful discussion about OldEarth delicacies, I informed him that he needed to have a chat with you. Hence, the garbled message last night, which was actually me trying to fend off three kids and explain, impersonating Gavin, his need to meet with you. I dropped him off at the base of the hill, and now I'm here to collect my charge, reunite him with his parents tonight at the Docking Bay, and then bring him and his folks over to Faye's place tomorrow. She's got a big feast and some kind of game planned." Bala clasped his chest and inhaled.

Cerulean plopped down on the kitchen stool by the counter and rubbed his eyes. "All I've got so far are a lot of questions and no answers. Where have you been for the last hour?"

Sifting through the salty dust at the bottom of the mixed nuts bowl, Bala shrugged noncommittally. "I stopped by to visit your neighbors. I had an important question to ask."

Cerulean's jaw clenched. *I'll bet you did.* Imagining Bala's entire conversation with his neighbors hijacked by OldEarth recipes, he counted to five and exhaled a long, cleansing breath. "So, what is your opinion of Gavin's accusation?"

Bala shook his head. "I dunno." He set the empty nut bowl back on the table and seemed to be considering the scanty remains on the tray.

Gavin stepped out the door and then returned a moment

later, his face and shoulders wet and a big smile on his face. “The sky is alive! Let’s go and see what rain has to say.”

A streak of lightning flashed. Thunder crashed in quick succession.

Cerulean caught a look of terror ripple across Bala’s face. He closed his eyes and prayed that he could do his duty. “Once a big storm sets in, it’s not safe to travel through the woods. You’ll both stay here tonight, and I’ll take you to Faye’s tomorrow.”

It took a moment for the translation to register on Gavin’s face, but once it did, his grin told all.

Bala didn’t seem perturbed in the least. He sauntered over to the couch and flopped down. “I wouldn’t mind a bowl of popcorn and a movie.” He patted the seat next to him. “Come on, Gav. It’s man’s night out. We’ll talk recipes, and”—His eyebrows danced—“I might even have a lead on a roast chicken!”

For the first time in his life, that he could remember anyway, Cerulean missed Sterling. And his father. *Is this how they had felt?* Discombobulated yet strangely comforted, the air didn’t feel so empty now.

Chapter Eight

Mysteries

—Faye's Apartment—

Wednesday, November 2nd

Faye surveyed the furniture arrangement in her apartment and shook her head. She needed more seating! How had she ever thought this would work without making everyone shrink to miniature sizes? What had been a form of entertainment on Helm—adjusting physical form to fit with the environment—was fast becoming a nightmare on a planet where practically *no one* could downsize on command.

She sighed.

On the left, she had a large mauve couch that could possibly seat three bulky bodies, which meant that Taug, Max, and Cobalt would have to get cozy. Directly across, a tan couch could hold three slim figures: Clare, Bala, and Justine. They always got along. Sort of…

Kendra would help serve, so she'd be bouncing around with Faye. Riko could take one of the plush chairs near her work desk, while Cerulean could take the next one over. Ava and Rey could sit on opposite chairs, and Roux would perch on a stool pulled in from the kitchen island. He was always accommodating. Well, usually.

Luckily, Wendell was helping Jayla at the café while Kendra's oldest could manage the little ones for a few hours. Faye had convinced Justine to let Zara join Kendra's family for the evening, now that she wasn't likely to morph into anything dangerous. *She's gotten over that by now, surely!*

Sterling couldn't come, of course. Faye grimaced, still uneasy with the idea that he had faded. *Into what? Where?*

Eleven deep tones warned the passing hour. *Already? I must focus!*

Who was left? *Gavin.* Where would he sit? Not on a stool! He'd be perplexed. Maybe even insulted. *Oh, why did I ever get myself into this? What was I thinking? I'm not good at hosting parties. I was better as a threatening shadow keeping wayward politicians in—*

The doorbell chimed.

Frozen in place, Faye raced through her daily itinerary. No, she had made sure that her schedule was clear until the first guests would arrive. It couldn't be noon yet; the bells had just tolled eleven.

Ding-dong! Ring-ring!

A familiar voice rose from the other side of the door. "Let me and my helpful tentacles in, Faye!"

Taug?

Rushing forward, Faye's flowing tunic caught the edge of the game table and snagged. The board tipped, sliding the carefully arranged pieces to the carpeted floor. "Arg!" She rushed to the door, slapped the enter button, and then returned to the mess in the middle of the room.

Taug waddled in, cradling a wicker basket, a pleased smile lighting up his face. Then his gaze fell on the figures scattered across the floor. "Not a good omen, Faye. You'd better pick those up before anyone gets here and sees their avatars sprawled across the ground like battle dead."

Grumbling, Faye picked up the pieces and smacked them back on the board. Annoyed, she refused to ask what was in the basket.

Taug didn't need to be asked. He sauntered to the open kitchen on the right and set it on the counter. Then he began to unpack as Faye continued to set the pieces in approximately the right places. "I brought goodies for everyone. Some of Riko's best Green for you and me. Fruity beverages, vegetable slices with a hint of ginger and cumin, soft breadsticks so you won't have crumbs all over your nice clean, well, your floor, and honey cakes for dessert." He beamed.

With an anguished huff, Faye plunked the last piece on the board and wrung her hands. "Food is great, but where will everyone sit? I don't know where to put Gavin, and he's the one I really want to impress."

A flurry of bubbles rippled through Taug's breather helm. "Why Gavin? He's of no consequence. Just a silly alien from an underdeveloped planet."

Faye stared at Taug, bewilderment halting all speech. Then she remembered. "Oh, gosh, I haven't told you my dream, have I?" She scurried over to the counter, spread the dainties from Taug's basket across the large kitchen table, and spoke over her shoulder. "Get the wrapped items in the cooler and help me arrange them here."

In his best butler imitation, Taug snapped a towel off the rack and tossed it over his shoulder, looking as much like a dinner host as he could ever hope. "Dream? I don't dream, so I find the whole concept rather mysterious, but there's no denying that, historically speaking, some dreams portend great events." He lugged a large bowl of pasta from the cooler and waddled over to Faye's side. "Do tell."

Faye plucked the towel from his shoulder and wiped her hands. "Well, I think the creator of this game,"—she pointed to the board—"the holy hermit I told you about, was trying to tell me something. I don't know what it means yet, but Gavin plays an important part in saving Newearth." Her mind clouded and her neck began to ache. "Oh, I don't know. Maybe I am making the whole thing up. It's just that the game came up at the same time that the Krowe family showed up…and it's really strange…but in my dream, Clare became a monster, and Gavin was the only one who could manage her."

Flapping his tentacles, Taug returned to the cooler. "I'll admit that Clare can be a tad sharp-tongued, but I wouldn't call her a monster. Granted, she didn't listen to a thing I had to say about—" Bubbles erupted from his breathing helm, and Taug flushed a bright shade of pink.

Faye frowned. "What?"

"Nothing. Some things are private, and I shouldn't be a tattletale." He lugged another pasta dish to the counter. As he surveyed the offerings, his voice rose, "How much pasta do you think we can eat in one day?"

"They are completely different kinds of pasta, one sweet and the other cheesy." The pain in her neck crawled behind her eyes. A flash of her dream brightened before her eyes. Taug slithering like a snake across his laboratory, a clear, curved box in the background, tilted at a strange angle, and a little girl with mismatched eyes… Pain blinded her. Faye grabbed her head, dropped to her knees, and rocked in mute agony.

Taug didn't enjoy surprises, especially when they involved taking over a party involving a game he didn't understand for a large assembly of people, some of whom he didn't know and others he didn't particularly like. The idea that Faye wasn't feeling well only added to his jitters.

She had insisted that she just needed to lay down for a moment and she'd be fine, but Taug didn't like the haunted look in her eyes. A frightened expression that portended a serious internal disturbance. His own organs squiggled in sympathetic discomfort.

It was nearly noon, and guests would arrive momentarily. He must check on Faye once more. Since tiptoeing was out of the question, he attempted a soft tread and crept into her bedroom. She was lying on her back, her hands folded over her stomach, still and quiet, almost as if she were...

Fear shot through Taug. He padded forward and nudged her shoulder.

Faye stirred but did not awaken.

Taug frowned. All his diagnostic tools were in his laboratory. And everyone he trusted was coming here for a party. *Blast!*

The doorbell chimed.

He scuttled back to the living room, yelling, "Open!"

Nothing happened.

Thoroughly annoyed, he slapped the enter button.

Cerulean stood shoulder to shoulder with Bala, the two grinning like silly fools.

Taug harumphed. "Normally, I would be amused. But Faye had to lay down, strange guests are about to descend, and a holy hermit has sent a game that I don't know how to play!"

Undeterred, Bala slipped around Taug's rotund figure, a bee honing in on savory scents.

All joy fled from Cerulean's eyes as he stepped into the living room. Stopping at the black couch, he faced Taug and rubbed his jaw. "Faye is lying down? That seems odd..." He exhaled a long breath. "I'm still not at peace with what happened to Sterling. We don't just fade *like that.*" He shrugged. "But Bala messaged that Kendra had decided to stay with the kids, and Clare was escorting the Crow family, so *being naturally* shy, he wanted company."

Pausing in thought, Cerulean glanced at the ceiling. *Or somewhere higher?* "The whole way over, he gloried about some saint he read about, mysticism, dark nights, repentance, purification, and enlightenment." He grimaced. "Now you tell me that Faye—who hasn't been sick a day in her life—isn't well?" He shook his head.

Ignoring the superfluous information, Taug pointed to the back of the apartment. "Her bedroom is on the left. Would you take a look at her? I'll admit, I'm worried. Despite being her friend for so long, I know little about Bhuaci ailments—or cures."

Pacing by the kitchen, where Bala made a pretense of arranging the dishes, Cerulean spoke up, "We're going to check on Faye. Keep an eye on things and answer the door, won't you?"

Bala wiped a speck of sauce from his lips and offered a smart salute. "When guests arrive, I'll make sure they are made comfortable and offer a little something to hold them over."

Taug snorted. "If there's anything left!"

With a suppressed chuckle, Cerulean stepped into the large bedroom suite.

Taug hurried after him.

Faye hadn't moved a millimeter. Still as stone.

Cold fear raced over Taug. "Is she—"

Cerulean sat on the edge of the bed, placed his hands on her forehead, and closed his eyes.

Two long minutes dragged by.

Sweat dribbled down Taug's back.

With a sudden intake of breath, Cerulean jumped to his feet. "Holy Hermit? By the Divide, it's Sterling!"

Taug blinked rapidly. "That's not Faye?"

Cerulean paced across the room. "No, *that* is Faye, but the Holy Hermit who gave her this game was not Bhuaci, it was Sterling. What he's playing at, I can't imagine, but I'd recognize him anywhere. He's holding Faye in some kind of stasis."

"He is making her ill?"

"Probably not intentionally." Cerulean clapped his hands together and bellowed, "Bala, get in here!"

Quick pattering of feet and Bala scampered into the room, a hint of cherry cream on his cheek. “Y-Yes?”

Beckoning him closer, Cerulean returned to Faye’s bedside. “She can’t be left alone. I know that Kendra has her hands full, and Justine is covering for Max at the docking bay, so that leaves Clare. Get her over here and tell her that she can’t leave Faye’s side for a moment.”

A dashed-off salute and Bala was on the job.

Taug squared his shoulders, well as best as a Cresta can square any part of his anatomy. “I still don’t understand what Sterling has to do with—

A doorbell chimed.

Cerulean didn’t move.

“I’d better get that.” Taug glanced at Faye, his innards tightening into hard knots. “So, there’s more to this game than meets the eye?”

Cerulean nodded and pulled up a chair. He sat down, clasped Faye’s hand in both of his, and appeared to be praying.

Baffled beyond comprehension, Taug made for the door, calling out, “Open!”

Nothing.

Vexed beyond words, his breather helm at full steam, he scuttled ahead and slapped the open button.

With a soft hiss, the door slid aside.

Max stood ramrod straight, clutching a white box tied with a bright red ribbon. He peered around Taug’s full figure. “I expected Faye.”

Lie or not to lie? Taug met Max’s honest stare and waved toward the kitchen. “She’s lying down. Not feeling well. Bala is calling Clare for assistance.”

Striding into the kitchen, Max frowned. He placed the box on the counter and started to unpack gooey treats. “Does Clare have medical training? With the Bhuaci, I mean.”

Impressed by Max’s culinary delights, as well as his

direct reasoning, Taug stepped closer. "Cerulean believes that Sterling is holding Faye in stasis, and he merely wants Clare to watch over her while he figures out what is going on." He blinked rapidly, trying to hold off sudden dizziness. "At least, I hope he figures it out. I don't understand Luxonian or Bhuaci physiology in the least."

Max straightened, his frown deepening. "But Sterling faded away, correct? Why would he, or anyone for that matter, want to hold Faye in stasis?"

Taug squinted, trying to see through the murky reality before him. "It has something to do with—"

The doorbell chimed.

Bala yelled, "I'll get it. Probably Clare, she said she was just on the corner when I called." He ran forward and slapped the open button.

Riko stood in the doorway, clasping two oversized, colorful bottles. "I bought the best Green I could buy, and a little bubbly for those who prefer something more sedate." He stepped in and surveyed the large suite. "Nice place!"

The desire for a large glass of Green nearly overmastered Taug, but he forced himself to stay calm.

Bala took one bottle and lugged it to the table.

Riko followed close behind.

The sound of voices wafted nearer.

Unable to hold back any longer, Taug ran forward and peered down the long white corridor.

Around the corner, Clare appeared with Gavin at her side. They were strolling along, laughing but came to a sudden halt when they saw him.

Taug couldn't even rouse a smile. Serling's words echoed too loudly in his mind...*trials of your time... Despair.*

Max considered the game pieces one at a time. They were

certainly unique representations of real people. He picked up his replica and considered the miniature android. *Hardly captures my true personality. Only a glimmer of intelligence in the eyes. Not really me at all.*

Riko stepped up and plucked his piece from the board. "I don't get it. Not all of us can be here, and it's not like we should arrange our lives to play designated game roles anyway. So, what's the point?" He dropped his piece on the board, accidentally knocking Bala's figure on its side.

"Hey, I could charge you with figure abuse." Bala grinned as he drew near. Making twirling motions with his fingers, he zeroed in on his piece, straightened it, and then nudged it to the southwest corner. Then he found Kendra's and set her next to him. "We like our privacy, if you don't mind. Hardly ever get a moment to ourselves these days."

Without hesitation, Max found Justine's figure and placed her next to him in an opposite corner.

Riko did the same with Jayla, placing her in the southeast corner.

They all stared at each other, as if daring someone to make another move.

Gavin sauntered over and nodded. He tapped his ear and spoke. "You understand?"

Everyone nodded.

With a sweep of his hand, Max motioned to the board. "Did Clare explain about the game?"

Bending forward, Gavin narrowed his eyes as he peered at each figure in turn. He looked up, stared at Max, then his matching figure, and soon matched each figure with everyone in the room. He pointed to the figures of his mother, father, and himself. "May I?"

Max nodded. "They belong to you as much as anyone." Horror filled him as recorded data concerning ancient human witchcraft practices, involving voodoo dolls, raced through his mind. "They aren't being used for anything bad. No one even understands the purpose of the game." Aware of how idiotic he sounded, he blundered on. "Apparently, we're all just pieces on a board, standing around."

Riko rubbed his hands down his face, clearly exasperated. "I've got better things to do than admire a facsimile of myself."

While turning his parents' figures in his hand, Gavin shot an inquiring glance at Max. "Who knew we were coming to Newearth?"

No answer in his databank, Max wished Justine were present. She had a quick wit and could skirt the truth with exquisite proficiency.

Bala dragged a stool over and perched on the edge. He clasped his hands together, ready to impart human wisdom.

A collective sigh.

Undeterred, Bala forged ahead. "It happens to be All Soul's Day, so I've been reading about this OldEarth guy, John Something-or-other, who wrote a powerful reflection called *Dark Night of the Soul*. Ever heard of him?" A split-second pause and he continued. "Thought not. Anyway, he understood what we humans are so keen to forget, that there is more to our existence than the material world. We were created by a mysterious Being who speaks to us in a mystical manner. All we have to do is—"

Taug toddled over, his tentacles fluttering in all directions. "Cerulean has returned to Lux to determine what has happened to Sterling. Surely, if there's a secret plan, Roux is in on it. I am taking Faye to my laboratory. Medics are expected at any moment, and they will transport her there. Clare will assist with that. Cobalt messaged that he is running late, but he expects to arrive soon." Puffing with the momentousness of the situation, Taug glared at the small assembly. "I am leaving you four with the commission to discover the purpose of this blasted game and how we are supposed to play it. It was the last thing Faye said, something about a dream she had related to this charade. Clare becomes a monster…or maybe she said mobster…and Gavin has to manage her. Though that hardly makes sense. Clare is doing everything she can to save Faye's life and Gavin—" He looked over and met Gavin's intense stare. "Well, you're new here. You don't have any big part to play. Not yet, anyway."

The doorbell chimed, and Clare called, "Taug! Get over here and help me."

An abrupt turnabout and Taug hurried off.

His hands flapping like an anxious mother, Bala followed close behind. "Did you pack her things? She'll want personal stuff, be sure of that! Better let me toss some things in a bag. I've helped Kendra more than a few times, it's practically instinct by now."

With nothing better to do, Max began to arrange the figures on the board according to height.

Gavin shook his head. "No, they go together by relationship." He started putting them into groups. "Me, my father, and my mother. You and Justine and your daughter, Zara." He smiled. "See?"

Taking over, Riko grinned in agreement. "Me, Jayla, and Wendell." He placed them aside. "Faye and Taug here. Bala and Kendra over there."

Max placed Cerulean next to Sterling.

Clare stood by herself. The infant figure lay on its side, and the mismatched-eyed girl seemed to glare from across the room.

Large clattering wheels rolled into the apartment, and a few somber moments later, a paramedic bed wheeled Faye out the front door with Taug and Clare hustling right behind.

Before the door closed, Cobalt snuck into the apartment, frowning as he rubbed his cheeks. "It's getting cold outside!"

He shrugged off any attempted commentary. “I know, everyone thinks that our gear is all-weather, but my face still gets blasted by the cold.” His scowl deepened as his gaze scoured the nearly empty room. “I was expecting a crowd.”

Riko snapped his words, “Did you miss the paramedics wheeling our host out the door?”

“Oh, that.” Cobalt chuckled as he strode forward. “I saw and heard. Clare filled me in on all the dreadful news. I’ve come to appraise the situation and help you figure out this bizarre game. Sounds like we have a puzzle on our hands, and, though I hate to be immodest, I’m actually quite good at solving mysteries.”

Riko snorted.

Bala rolled his eyes.

Like a gentleman, Gavin motioned toward the figures.

Cobalt’s whole face lit up, and his smile widened.

Crossing his arms over his chest, Max shifted his gaze from the board to the living characters before him. *Am I looking at the wrong game?*

Chapter Nine

Chilled to the Bone

—Taug's Laboratory—

Saturday, November 5th

Clare peered into the Breakfastnook Café window, hunger pangs rising at the sight of happy customers gobbling delicious breakfasts on the other side of the lacy curtain. With a whimper, she hugged an oversized datapad against her stomach.

A chill wind breezed past, while above, storm clouds threatened a downpour.

She didn't want to see Faye in her helpless state again, but her friend's sudden coma had caught the attention of influential Newearth authorities who wanted the matter evaluated through *official* channels. She glanced at the moody sky again. *Penance for my sins, right?* The fact that Bhuaci representatives had been informed of possible foul play certainly didn't help. With a deep sigh and promising herself a good meal once her duty was done, she circled around to Taug's laboratory.

You better have some good news, Cresta.

She stood in full view of the surveillance camera, aware that lights were flashing inside, alerting Taug to her presence. *Come on, you old tub. I'll miss the Saturday special if you don't hurry up.*

It didn't take long, and the door slid open.

Taug's rotund form had deflated alarmingly. His eyes red and sunken and his tentacles mere loose ends screamed of a creature in terrible need.

Amazed at herself, Clare leaped forward and clasped Taug's limp shoulder. "Taug! What's happened? Are you ill?"

His head wagging in forlorn grief, he hardly seemed capable of speech. He led the way between the procedure chair on the left and a guest lounge on the right. He stopped at a wide, plush bed laid out before a large wall screen, displaying underwater ocean scenes accompanied by melodious Bhuaci chants. "I thought maybe she would respond to something calming and familiar. She always loved the ocean, and music is good for the soul, they say."

Using every analytical tool at her disposal, Clare considered Faye. The Bhuac was lying on her back as she had been while in her own home. Her face appeared calm, not a hint of a grimace, while her clasped hands rested on her stomach over a light coverlet. Honey-colored hair had been brushed to the side and lay in a soft braid over her left shoulder. Everything was white—the bed, the coverlet, her gown. Only a faint pink hue suggested life still harbored deep within the still form.

Flushing at her need to intrude, Clare lifted her datapad and took a series of photos. She tapped out quick notes and hit the send button. Feeling guilty for simply doing her job, she glanced over her shoulder.

Before the coffee table, Taug sat forlornly on a plush chair, his tentacles draped over his middle.

Clare stepped over and sat on the chair at his right. "You've done your best, Taug. I had to send a report to headquarters. Rumors have been floating around that Ingot or Crestas are behind a subtle attempt to infiltrate Bhuaci leadership, so I had to show that, despite your inability to bring her to consciousness, she is being well taken care of. She appears perfectly at peace. Considering the fact that we have no idea what caused this, no one can ask for more."

Taug's face crumpled. "I can! I want Faye walking

around—dancing the way she used to. She suffered so much after the decimation of her planet and the demise of so many of her people; it has been my greatest joy to see her happy. But now… I'm useless."

Clare retreated into the recesses of her chair, a sense of deflation all too familiar. "I know what you mean. I don't even know why I exist."

A grunted response did nothing to pull Clare from her deepening depression.

Finally, Taug huffed. "You have a job, respect among your own kind, friends, and you live on your home world. You hardly know the meaning of suffering."

Jerking up, Clare snapped, "You know nothing, Cresta! I lost my parents as a child; I've been lonely all my life. My friends, as you call them, put up with me, but they don't love me. Not like family." Sickening anger bubbled like lava. "I may live on my home world, but thanks to all the dominating, deceiving aliens here, I've never felt at home!"

One tentacle rose slowly, and Taug stroked his chin. Bubbles frizzled in his breathing helm. "I see…You need family…your own flesh and blood." He hummed low.

Tortured by naked pain, Clare fought down tears and a desire to rush out the door.

His shoulders straightening, Taug sat upright. "I may not be able to help Faye, but at least, I can help you."

Jumping to her feet, Clare nearly tripped over the coffee table. She caught herself, dizziness blurring her vision. When had she ever been so angry before? Part of her mind whirled at the realization that she didn't know herself. "What are you talking about, Cresta?" She flung herself over to Faye's bedside. "I didn't ask for your help. I've never trusted you…" But as she stared down at Faye's serene countenance, she knew her words were a lie. She dropped one hand on top of Faye's and was immediately startled. Faye's hands were warm. Clare glanced aside. "Sorry. I didn't mean…"

Taug climbed to his feet and padded to her side. He placed a tentacle on top of Clare's hand, over Faye's. "We're *all* lonely." He sighed. "But we're not all liars. I meant what I said. I can help you have a baby, create a little family of your own." He cleared his throat and drew Clare away from the bedside toward his laboratory. "I heard about that sad incident with Saran." Tsk, tsking, Taug wagged his head. "Never ask an Ingot to handle a delicate matter. They aren't capable of the least sensitivity or even a modicum of true genius in dealing with such issues."

Infuriated by the spark of hope welling up inside of her, Clare looked away. She stared at the clear back wall: a Cresta pool swirling with iridescent vegetation and Cresta sea life. "I could get pregnant, if I wanted. But I have my work, and I don't know anyone I want to have a baby with…if you know what I mean. I like my life well enough, so I can't change it too much, but yet…" Her heart pounded. "I can't explain it. I want to do some good in the world, but I feel incomplete somehow. As if I'm on the outside looking in while everyone else around me really lives."

Astonishingly, Taug nodded with an expression of deep understanding. "I, too, want to do some good. Though I have been accepted back onto my home world, despite all the leadership scandals, too much has happened for me to ever truly feel at home there. Like you, my work has become my family." He peered into the pool, his tentacles wiggling free at his side. "It comes to me that we are not alone in our suffering. Perhaps, we can work together and bring new meaning to the word family?"

Ignoring a faint sound in the background, *probably a fish flopping in the tank,* Clare faced Taug and appraised his studious expression. "What do you have in mind?"

A glimmer in his eyes, Taug waddled across the room to

the large shelving unit. He searched high and low and then patted a middle shelf and suddenly snatched up a clear, bean-shaped pod. He cradled it in his tentacles, and his smile widened. "It's called a biomb. When your cycle is ripe, return here, and I'll extract the perfect egg to grow you a beautiful child. You won't have to worry about a thing. He can be grown right here in the lab. You can visit as often as you like. When it's time, you can give him a name and take him home and raise him however you like. You'll have a son; he'll have a mother, and I'll have done some good in the world."

In Clare's mind, "You'll have a son, and he'll have a mother" were more than words, they were magic. Suddenly, Taug wasn't an ugly, misshapen alien with uncertain motives, he was a knight in shining armor from an ancient OldEarth legend. She couldn't kiss him, but she could press his shoulder with the gentleness of sincere gratitude. "You have no idea what this means to me, Taug."

Taug's smile softened. "Perhaps I do."

For once in her life, Clare believed him.

—Planet Lux—

Cerulean marched right past the multi-colored fountain spraying luminescent water twenty meters high and headed for the park bench on the edge of the mossy path. He wanted to feel happy at his homecoming after being away so long, but his heart constricted with conflicting feelings, and his mind felt bogged down with strange foreboding.

Sitting on the bench with his back to him and wearing the Supreme Judge robes, his oldest friend in the universe, Roux, almost looked like Sterling. Only the dark head of hair and slouch gave him away. *He may be a Supreme Judge, but he'll never be a leader. Never did have enough confidence in himself.*

Straightening his own back, Cerulean made a beeline for his companion of old. He tapped Roux's shoulder as he passed and then rounded the bench and faced him. "I want the truth. All of it."

A slow smile spreading across his face, Roux leaned back and threw one arm over the back of the green bench. "Good to see you, Cerulean. I knew you'd be along soon enough. No fooling you for long."

With a shake of his head, Cerulean plunked down on the bench. "Why did you lie to me? *Me,* of all people! I've always been honest and above board with you."

Roux tipped his head. He had let his hair grow out and now curly locks fell to his shoulders. "Except when you weren't. Like with Anne Smith. OldEarth remnant, remember? You never seriously planned to return to Lux. Left the whole experiment to fall on my lap. Where it fell to pieces and nearly destroyed humanity's last hope and Luxonian's moral integrity. What was left of it anyway."

A quick flush of anger and Cerulean bolted from the bench. He ran his fingers through his hair and pounded the ground as he paced before the bench. "Don't deflect this! You knew I would stay with Anne, and you knew perfectly well why. It was the right thing to do. Besides, it didn't fall to pieces; it came together. Which is why"—he glared at Roux—"we are now able to serve Newearth so well! But I can't do anything right if I am being fed lies. Would you be so good as to explain to me why Sterling faked his death, why you went along with it, and why on Newearth you allowed him to put Faye into a coma?" His voice had skyrocketed and ended in a shout.

Roux crunched his brows together, his eyes narrowing. "You think I did all that? Haven't got an ounce of faith in me, do you?"

For a heated moment, Cerulean doubted himself. "Tell me then! What really happened?"

"Sit back down and calm yourself. The whole thing is not nearly as malignant as you suppose."

With a huff, Cerulean dropped onto the bench.

A relaxed pose as he faced Cerulean, his hands clasped just so, Roux launched into his story. "I had no idea that Sterling had arranged his death scene there at the great hall. I was just as bewildered by it as you were."

Bewildered? I was heartbroken. Cerulean shoved the memory away.

"I'd heard rumors of Ingot incursions, which is why I came to see you in the first place, to tell you about the Krowe family. But then Clare had her issues to deal with, and I never got around to explaining what we feared. Sterling didn't tell me everything because he had this wild idea that people need to learn from their own mistakes. Or maybe that was Omega's big concept. Now there's someone who has had a lot to learn! Anyway, like you, I really believed Sterling was fading, that he desperately wanted to offer his final words of wisdom to a much-beloved people. I was certain that if there was any underlying plan, I would have been told."

"So, you returned to Lux to get to the truth? I hope you threatened someone with a long-term visit to Bothmal."

A voice rumbled from behind the bench. "He tried. For a moment or two, anyway."

Chills ran down Cerulean's spine. He couldn't get to his feet and spin around fast enough. His eyes took in what his mind could hardly grasp. "Sterling?"

Looking much the same as always, though he had faded a degree or two, still, his voice was as sardonic as ever. "Sorry for the dramatics. I am fading, but it's a long, slow process, and I plan to leave this realm in full pomp and glory. No last gasp on a holopad." He snorted. "But I did make a good show of it; didn't I?"

His own edges glowing with a warning hint of yellow and orange, Cerulean tried to keep his voice steady. "Would you be at all interested in telling me what is going on?"

Amazingly, Sterling's eyes softened to a humorous twinkle. Almost loving. He gestured to a large, round structure approximately four hundred meters away. "Let's take a stroll, shall we? I'd like to visit the arboretum. The firebirds are in full plumage and quite a lovely sight this time of year."

The three Luxonians in full human form, Roux's white robes barely constrained against his muscular body, Cerulean casual in Newearth wear, and Sterling in his blue tunic, maintained amiable silence as they ambled along the mossy path.

Once they neared the glowing glass enclosure, Sterling cleared his throat and halted. "The Ingots have lost over half of their DNA lineage and will soon lose more. They are facing extinction in the not-so-distant future."

Cerulean froze.

When a distant sun exploded in a supernova, everyone oohed and ahhed for a few days and then moved on. But an entire race going extinct—now, that was disturbing.

Exchanging a glance with Roux, whose eyes widened in surprise by the news, Cerulean understood that anger no longer had a place in their discussion. "Explain."

"Inside. There's a beautiful spot between two glory trees where the birds love to perch and sing their hearts out. It's a pleasant spot to consider the many follies of life."

One by one, they entered the exquisite structure. Luxurious plant life of all hues and textures draped themselves across the walls, ceiling, and even flounced around the perimeter of the floor. Birds flew across the bright arched ceiling, while others alighted on branches and plucked ripe fruit or sashayed a love dance to an alluring mate.

Comfortable chairs, a sturdy bench, and three low stools around a bamboo table made for a cozy corner. Sterling took the largest chair, Roux dropped down on the bench, and Cerulean leaned with his back against an exotic fruit tree.

A waitress appeared out of nowhere and asked what they might like.

Cerulean shook his head, but Roux and Sterling ordered cool drinks.

Within minutes, Sterling had identified nearly twenty birds, and the drinks were arranged on the table.

With a deep sigh, Sterling quaffed his drink and then leaned back comfortably.

Bridling his impatience, Cerulean was not sure if he would spontaneously combust or commit murder in front of a flock of innocent birds.

His gaze shifting nervously, Roux seemed to realize that it was time to tell all. He shifted forward in his seat. "I knew that the Ingots had purposefully landed on Tabun. But everyone assumed it was for the usual reason—mining. Now you are telling us that they are going extinct? So why do they care about a backward planet with no technology or advanced medical opportunities?"

Sterling shrugged. "For the same reason that these birds show off their plumage and sing their pretty songs. They are hoping to find good DNA." He harrumphed. "Centuries of technological invasions into their biological systems have finally reached a breaking point. Either they are biological beings with natural functions or they are programmed data machines with hardwired armature. They tried being both. But there are limits to everything. Except the Almighty, of course. And no one asked Him."

His mind muddled with too many sensations crashing into each other, Cerulean rubbed his forehead. "So, what happened? Their women became infertile?"

"And their men. Poor little sperm can't find an elephant in a closet these days. Their women had become so far removed from the reproductive process that their bodies simply stopped producing eggs." He sighed and took another draught. "Then the disaster happened."

Roux spluttered his drink, nearly choking. "Infertility wasn't disaster enough?"

A sad look and true grief filled Sterling's eyes. "In three years, three generations of their offspring died from an undiagnosed cause. Some debilitating strain they must have picked up and carried home without realizing it. All those dead babies. They never even had a chance."

Bile rose in Cerulean's throat. "The *discarded* ones never did."

Roux's eyebrows rose.

Sterling nodded. "You're right, of course. They created this mess. They've been creating it for ages untold. But still, it's tragic. I saw the remains, flushed into space like so much garbage."

"Into space! Why?" Finally, Roux appeared angry, his face darkening to a fine shade of purple.

"They were afraid of contamination. Wanted to get them off the planet. They killed millions, and now only a few are left. Not a prime one among them. The whole Ingot race depends on fresh DNA." He met Cerulean's clear-eyed gaze. "Something the people from Tabun have in abundance. A hearty stock, they say."

Cold with fury, Cerulean shoved off the tree and paced away. "Surprising they didn't try to steal human DNA. It wouldn't have been hard, what with shopkeepers like Saran around."

Sterling rose to his feet. "Yes. Well, they did try, but turns out that human DNA doesn't do well when attached to too much technology. The results were most disappointing."

Cerulean grabbed Sterling's arm. "You knew about this and said nothing?" He glared at Roux. "What are you and the Supreme Judges doing? Knitting?"

Sterling waved off the comment. "Don't taunt me with that. It was a troubling period in my life."

Roux shook his head. "*I* certainly didn't know!" He pounded over to Sterling. "You'll have a lot to answer for, illustrious history or not. No one on the Supreme Council was aware of any of this; I would stake my life on it."

With surprising strength, Sterling pulled his arm free, his expression sour. He straightened his tunic. "There are other sources of information in the universe. Omega, for one. Abbas, for another." Sterling looked at each in turn. "You should be grateful that I have maintained friendships where few others dare."

The waitress reappeared with fresh drinks, but Roux waved her away. He glanced back at Sterling. "I thought Abbas had passed on."

Sterling chuckled. "You need to brush up on your vocabulary skills, Roux. They aren't named Eternals for nothing."

"So why the death scene? Why put Faye into a coma?" Cerulean clapped his hands together in impotent fury. "Why not just face the Ingal with the facts? Make them stand before an Inter-Alien Alliance board of inquiry!"

Sterling rounded on Cerulean. "And what would they learn? Nothing. They'd just find another race to manipulate. Other DNA to harvest. The Ingots won't change unless they learn the cost of their choices."

A mad chuckle escaping him, despair lashed out at Cerulean. "Will they? Have the Cresta ever learned? Has humanity learned? *We* have liars and manipulators among us. There is no perfect race. The only way to stop evil is to fight it out in the open."

With a deep sigh, Sterling took Cerulean's arm and led him toward the door.

In turn, the three broke upon the noontime suns, a glaring spectacle that brightened everything with shafts of colored light.

Sterling waved his arms in a wide arc. "Look all around you and see what has been given to us. An entire world. Abundant life. What we do with our gifts is our free choice. The consequences are ours, too." His gaze swung wearily from Cerulean to Roux. "I probably broke several laws by putting Faye into stasis, but she is too perceptive for her own good. She started to see things that would have unveiled the mystery. I sent her the game under the guise of one of her wise elders so that she could present it to you and your friends as a warning to watch each other carefully. You wouldn't have understood, but eyes would have seen what hearts refused to believe. Some may have chosen caution and considered their actions more carefully."

Cerulean closed his eyes and lifted his face to the brilliant sun rays, letting them pour vitality into his exhausted soul. "I still don't see how any of this would have stopped Cobalt from stealing Tabunite DNA."

Sterling chuckled. "Stopping it was never the point. In fact, the future is already set in motion. But now, we have a chance. If you two will stay out of the way, disaster will strike, and—with help—invaluable lessons will be learned."

Roux choked. "We just stand back and watch a disaster unfold?"

"Yes. As Omega assured me, we will grow no other way."

Despite the sun's searing rays, Cerulean felt chilled to the bone.

Chapter Ten

Until Now

—Bala's House—

Wednesday, February 22nd

Bala flopped down onto the couch next to his wife and threw his arm around her shoulders.

A fierce wind smacked icy raindrops against the window.

Opposite the couch, a couple of logs crackled merrily in the open fireplace, filling the living room with comforting warmth and a piney scent.

Still dressed in her oversized woolen sweater and thick woven leggings, Kendra snuggled in with a happy sigh. "Glad everyone got home safe and sound. The kids are all settled under their covers, heading off to dreamland." She tapped Bala's chest. "But Seth is getting so big; we really have got to get him a new bed. He sleeps at an angle, but his feet still dangle off the edge."

A yawn nearly split Bala's head in two. "Once we get the second story refurbished, he can move up there. The three boys will love having their own space. Barni wants to decorate it like a medieval fortress with pallets stuffed with straw, bear skins tacked to the walls, and a trestle table for warrior feasts." The last bit of energy seeped from Bala's bones. "I told him we'd think about it."

Kendra shook her head. "No straw. That would be the last straw for me, certainly. You know how hard it is to keep the mud from getting knee-deep in the kitchen. And how rough those boys get. Straw would be absolutely everywhere. Hair, clothes, stuck to furniture…and every rodent in the territory would feel personally invited to make an abode here. Nope. No straw. All the *faux* bear skins, tapestries, and trestle tables they want. Heck, they can sleep on the table, if they'd like."

A snore fluttered from Bala's lips.

Kendra nudged him in the ribs.

Jerking back to full consciousness, Bala stretched and exhaled a long yawn. "Yeah, that's what I told them. No straw. Or I'd get turned into stuffing." Pleased with his little joke, he reached out, ever so slowly, and tickled Kendra's middle. "Course, we can always try out a few new mattresses and see if the stuffing will stay in place. Purely for good housekeeping purposes, don't you know?"

Kendra laughed and retaliated in fine form with a few tickling moves of her own.

A voice, eerily similar to sixteen-year-old Seth's, grumbled from the bedroom across the hallway, "Hey, keep it down, you two. Some of us have school and work in the morning."

Bala slapped both hands over his mouth to keep his laughter contained.

Like a woman trying to hold down a bubbling cauldron, Kendra's shoulders shook.

Eventually, they regained control of themselves.

Kendra rubbed her eyes and lay her head on Bala's chest, her tone suddenly serious. "How on Newearth are we ever going to raise these kids to adulthood when *we* don't act like adults half the time?"

Keeping his voice to a rumbling whisper, Bala restrained a chuckle. "I don't know. Perhaps that's the best recipe. If adulthood isn't all drudgery and grief, perhaps they'll be more inclined to take a stab at it." He grimaced as an image of Clare darting furtively out of the office flittered before his eyes. "Some people are too adult for their own good if you know what I mean."

Kendra lifted her head a fraction and stared at her husband. "What'd ya mean?"

"Clare."

"Oh. What's she up to these days? I haven't seen hide or hair of that gal since the incident with Faye. She go into hiding or something?"

Nervous anxiety started Bala's foot jiggling. His stomach began to tighten. "She's got some kind of secret project going on with Taug. I don't know what they're up to, but it doesn't have anything to do with work; I've asked around. Even Cerulean doesn't know. Or, at least, he doesn't let on. Cerulean has been holed up in that cabin of his for the last couple of months like a bear in hibernation."

Kendra sat up and let her head fall back against the couch, her gaze rolling to the ceiling. "Last we talked, Clare was upset at Saran and his Spare Parts Shop."

Bala's foot jiggled faster. "No, not upset at him as she should have been, upset because she made a mistake trusting an Ingot. What got into her head, I still can't imagine. Everyone knows that you can't trust Ingots."

Her head swiveling, Kendra offered Bala her standard puzzled expression. "You don't trust Wendell?"

Bala waved off her comment. "He's not an Ingot. Not on the inside. They rejected him, and he returned the favor. Actually, despite his limitations, he's more human than most people I know."

Kendra pushed herself forward, faced him with one eyebrow arched, and started her interrogation. "So, the fact that he has Ingot DNA and was tied to technology since birth doesn't mean *anything*?"

His heart sinking to his socks, Bala dropped his feet to the floor. "How did a conversation about Clare become a debate about the merits, or lack thereof, of Ingots? I see the victims of Ingot ruthlessness every day, Kendra. Perhaps there are a few good ones out there, but their biotech systems raise hellions, I assure you."

A snort proclaimed Kendra's thoughts on the subject.

Irritated, Bala padded across the room to the woodstove and threw a couple of split logs onto the dwindling fire.

Kendra ambled up behind him and slipped her arm around his waist. "Sorry. I wasn't trying to micromanage your thinking; I know you deal with a lot. But I just don't want you to topple into the generalities that divide this planet. We must do better if we ever want a decent world for our kids."

Bala caressed his wife's cheek, relief calming his anxieties. "You may be the genetic descendant of the founders of Newearth, but you choose your lineage every day when you demand that we find decency in others. Still, it's hard…when you see kids warped by drugs, business magnets sporting gaudy replacement parts that only make them a laughingstock, relationships torn apart by exotic schemes which turn people into products." He flapped his arms helplessly. "It's not just Ingots. I know that. Cresta have committed their share of crimes; we all have. But…"

Her hand resting on his chest and her gaze peering into his face, Kendra whispered, "But what?"

"Something is going on with Clare that scares me. She's never acted like this before. I tried to talk to Taug about their project, but he only grinned and said that she was making a surprise. A beautiful surprise, and we'd all be very proud of her."

Kendra tilted her head, her profile lit by the firelight. "That doesn't sound so bad."

Bala could barely force out his words, even as he tightened his grip on his wife, and a fresh onslaught of icy rain slashed against the window. "But, Kendra, he's a Cresta. And Crestas love science experiments, not beautiful surprises."

—Newearth Docking Bay—

Thursday, February 23rd

Max entered his daughter's schoolroom and tried to view his wife and child as he had seen them hundreds of times previously.

He failed.

For some reason he could not fathom, the recorded image in his mind did not hold true. He only knew that he now saw them in a completely new light. Justine was now *his wife*. Zara, *his daughter*. Beyond all explanation, those facts made a spectacular difference. Though they didn't exactly glow in a rosy hue as he had read described in OldEarth poetry, his internal temperature did seem to rise every time he looked at them.

How do humans stand it?

Leaning over Zara at a bean-shaped table with inserts for three screens and several keyboards, Justine's brow puckered. She glanced his way.

Suddenly remembering his important mission, Max jerked into professional mode. Rosy hues would have to wait. "Omega just came to see me."

Confusion and then hurt spread over Justine's face as she straightened. "He's come…and gone?"

Like a crazed ballerina, Zara sprang from her seat and fluttered madly across the well-lit room. "He's coming back soon, right?"

Flummoxed, Max looked from his wife to his daughter. This was not what he had expected at all. He had actually whistled as he made his way to deliver this important message, positively certain that he would have an eager audience. Clearly, from the look on their faces, they didn't care about the message at all.

I thought humans were unpredictable. Ha!

His internal laugh seemed hollow, even to him.

Max pulled himself together. "I'm sure that Omega will return at some point. I can't say if it will be soon. I'm not even sure how you define soon."

Zara stomped her foot, appearing much younger than her recorded age of sixteen.

Though it was hard to define a hybrid's age under the best of circumstances. *What measurement does one use?* Being a one-of-a-kind Luxonian-Human created by an Eternal in one of his fits of fancy, there was no precedent for such a situation.

Nevertheless, Max found the command, "Act your age!" tumbling from his lips like a schoolmaster in a dreadful OldEarth drama.

Zara spluttered and plopped down on her chair like a piece of ripe fruit hitting the hard ground.

Justine squinted at him.

Flummoxed, Max realized that he must assert himself or march stiffly out the door in defeat. "Omega informed me that the Ingot race is facing extinction." *There, that should make them listen.*

Justine's eyes widened, and she stepped closer, her whole body bristling with what could very well have been potential hostility. "And he didn't think to let me—the head of Newearth Docking Bay Security—know about this?"

Now she's just being unreasonable. Max placed one hand on his daughter's shoulder. He'd seen this done dozens of times. A simple ploy to gain an ally without actually declaring war. "I am here—telling you—now. He *sent me* to tell you."

Zara shrugged off his hand and smacked the end button on her workstation. Her voice dropped to a plaintive cry. "I'm tired of studying. I want to see Abbas and Omega. I miss them."

Max racked his brain for a response.

Justine, as always, seemed to know just what to do. She stepped to her daughter's side, placed her hands on the girl's shoulders, and looked down into her eyes. "I miss them too. Omega must have had a good reason for sending the message through Max rather than telling us directly. But I know this, he would have visited with us if he could."

Light broke upon the confused, murky mess of Max's mind. He scratched his head. "I can't think why I didn't put his message in the correct order. But you're right, Justine. Omega stated first that he wished he could stop and see you both, but he was afraid that if he did, he would not want to leave. There are important matters that he must attend to, so he dared not put temptation in his way. Then he told me that the Ingots have suffered a series of reproductive failures and they are facing extinction. He warned me that they may become desperate, and we must keep a close eye on Zara."

Zara's head snapped up. "Me? Why?"

Justine's expression hardened as she looked from her daughter to her husband. "Because you prove the impossible, that hybrids between humans and other races can happen. Ingots were very human-like, once upon a time. Perhaps they are desperate enough to attempt creating hybrids of their own."

Max nodded. "Yes, that's what Omega fears. That's why I rushed here with the news." Justified now, he straightened and met Justine's gaze. *Why is she still frowning?* Then it hit him. "Oh, don't worry, Justine. You are the best security any child could ever have, and I am the manager of this docking bay. Nothing slips past me. Zara is perfectly safe." He smiled. Case closed. The situation well in hand.

With a compassionate smile, Justine strode across the

room and wrapped Max in a tight hug.

Surprised but pleased, Max embraced his wife and wished that he knew what the term "turned on" really meant.

Justine murmured against his shoulder. "He didn't mean it. Just a thoughtless moment. He trusts you. That's why."

Max pulled away, more baffled than ever. He gazed into Justine's eyes, looking for enlightenment.

"Omega said he didn't want to be tempted, so he just talked with you."

Though Max might never actually know what it felt like to be turned on, suddenly, he knew how it felt to be crushed.

Then Zara paced over and hugged him from the other side, just over waist level.

Though not turned on and perhaps a bit crushed, Max wasn't too disturbed, because he knew what it meant to be loved.

—Departure Station—

Friday, February 24th

Gavin stood by the wall in the docking bay departure station number seven and hugged his mother goodbye.

Ava squeezed with all her might; her thick arms wrapped around him as if to meld their two hearts into one.

Rey cleared his throat. "It's time. The ship waits. Home awaits."

Despite relief from the suffocating grip, Gavin felt the life-giving wave of his mother's love receding.

She and Father must return to Tabun. He must stay.

The bustling of departing passengers shouting their last goodbyes, parcels bundled into arms, bags slung over shoulders, the warning bells from gate seven-four-seven, created a maelstrom of noisy activity.

Slick cherry red walls denoted the seventh floor, while a wavy blue stripe led from sections one to four, and seven green dots denoted the gateway to a medium-sized shuttle, heading into 967-Sinsinawa District, with a short stop at Tabun. Thirty-six passengers of various races with offers of everything from commercial contracts to official Newearth diplomatic representation hurried onboard.

Rey nudged his wife, ready to go.

Gavin nodded to his father, their gazes meeting.

A meaningful exchange, and Rey communicated his commitment to everything they had discussed the previous evening.

Accepting his fate, Gavin handed his mother over to his father.

His parents clasped hands, turned with bowed heads, and entered the departing throng.

After the last passenger made it through the gate, all that was left of forlorn family and friends sighed, wiped away any traces of tears, and headed off to whatever life still awaited them on Newearth.

As he paced over to the oval viewing window, a gut-wrenching sense of loss assaulted Gavin's equilibrium. He had never felt the like before. Even when they had left Tabun, heading they knew not where, he had known the strength and comfort of his family. Now, he was truly alone, a wolf without a pack.

The ship broke free of its mooring, backing away in a slow arc. The captain had not lied when he said that they would leave immediately after the last warning bell.

I will watch until they are lost among the—

A hand gripped his shoulder.

Startled and not a little afraid, Gavin swung around, his

hands clenched.

Cerulean's blue eyes caught him, and he offered a depreciating grin. "Sorry. I should have announced my presence."

Relief flooded through Gavin. For some reason, he had assumed it would be Cobalt. And he most definitely did not want to meet the Ingot just yet. He lifted his hand to tap his ear, denoting the universal translator, but halted in mid-motion. He sucked in a deep breath and then poured forth the fruit of his studious efforts. "I speak Newearth now. Friend to friend. No interloper."

His grin widening, Cerulean scratched his head. "Well, that's good. I think. It's always better to talk without a translator, if possible."

"I speak; you hear. You speak; I hear. We trust one another."

A spasm that looked a lot like a grimace raced over Cerulean's face.

Gavin's stomach tightened. "You no trust me?"

Distant bells warned of shuttle seven-four-eight's imminent departure.

Cerulean glanced down the long corridor, shaking his head. "It's not you." He thrust one hand against his chest like a hunter pledging the next kill. "I don't trust myself."

Bewildered, Gavin wondered if he had made a mistake in staying behind.

With a soft chuckle, Cerulean nudged his arm and started forward. "Let's go. You can stay with me while we get things sorted out."

Gavin stood rooted to the spot. "Cobalt say I stay with him."

Stopping, Cerulean turned and folded his arms over his chest, his blue eyes as clear as a midday sky. "It's your choice. You can stay with Cobalt in the Ingot quarters on the docking bay if you'd like. Or you can accept the guest room in my cabin. Whatever works for you."

Works? Was he expected to assume some Newearth position and work for his living? It was not an unjust expectation, but the image of a fish flopping on desert sand rose in his mind. The air felt hot and stale. *How can I work here?*

A chime sounded eighteen times, a notice of the passing day. The sun would set soon.

Almost as if reading his mind, Cerulean clapped him on the shoulder. "Come on. Let's stop at Riko's café and get you something to eat. You can decide where you want to stay after a good meal and a little peace and quiet."

Suddenly ravenous, Gavin nodded in agreement.

The two threaded their way through the busy corridor to the elevator. Even as the floors slipped past him on his way to the ground, Gavin realized, with a sinking feeling, that home had never been the soil where he was born and raised, but rather, the embrace of love that had succored him all his life.

Until now.

—The Breakfastnook Café—

Cerulean chose a quiet booth near an unobtrusive door, back by the kitchen in the bustling café. He glanced around as he slid into his seat, glad that Gavin quickly made himself comfortable on the opposite side.

Across the room, Riko looked over and smiled. It didn't take him long to disengage from a conversation at a table of chattering Bhuaci customers and amble closer, calling out, "It's been eons since you shone your face here, Cerulean. What's Newearth's most famous, or should I say infamous,

Luxonian doing in *our* humble establishment?" He swiveled his gaze to Gavin.

Unable to restrain an eye roll or the pleased feeling he always had when Riko engaged in a personal conversation, Cerulean sank back in the plush booth and felt his muscles relax, definitely a plus in human physiology. He stared at his friend's glowing face. Had Riko's charm grown over the years? His Uncle Clem's influence, perhaps?

A pretty Uanyi stepped over, a full carafe in one hand. With her other hand, she patted Riko's side in a decidedly familiar manner.

Cerulean's eyebrows rose in astonishment. Never, in all his years on Newearth, had Riko ever strayed from his professional demeanor around his staff.

With a laugh, Riko wrapped a free hand around the server's waist. "You've met Jayla before, haven't you? My intended." In unison, they both thrust out blunt-fingered hands. The sparkling stones on each of their rings would have blinded a lesser man.

Gavin exhaled a low whistle and leaned in for a closer look.

Jayla's face turned pink while Riko beamed.

Cerulean slapped his forehead. "Clare told me, but I completely forgot. Too much going on." He pretended severity. "I hope you'll do better than Max and Justine. They went off planet and had a formal ceremony with only Zara as their Newearth witness."

Riko eyed his intended a little nervously. "Oh, no. I can't talk her into a quick getaway. She's got half the invitations sent out already. It's not going to be secret or small."

An innocent grin spread over Jayla's face, like the surprised joy of a child on Christmas morning who discovers a gift with her name on it.

I see Jayla's charm... A faint pang shot through Cerulean.

Jealousy? Never! Well, maybe... A little.

By the time he pulled his gaze from Jayla, Cerulean realized with shock that the conversation had slid into unfriendly territory.

"A Neanderthal? Like the black sheep of the family, eh?" Riko was chuckling, but Jayla bit her lip, her gaze darting in uncertainty.

Gavin's expression darkened. "We eat black sheep."

Horror sped over Jayla's face. "You eat *animals*!"

A glint of revenge shone in Gavin's eyes. "As do you. I smell meat cooking."

Drawing himself to his full height, Riko assumed his most formal tone. "We serve the best eco-beef, eco-pork, and eco-chicken ever grown on Newearth. We are civilized. Animals haven't been sacrificed for generations."

Seeing the pink indignation on Jayla's face and annoyed perplexity filling Gavin's eyes, Cerulean clapped his hands together, desperate to keep a feud from erupting. "It's been a very busy day, and Gavin hasn't had a decent meal since…I don't know when. How about you whip up that creamed spinach pasta that made Taug nearly cry the last time we were here, and grill a couple of barbecue patties with your famous seasoned garnish? Some chips and a hot drink to take the evening chill out of our bones would also be welcome." He eyed Riko with meaningful intent and prayed that the message would get through.

Clairvoyant as always, Riko winked and directed Jayla to the next table. "See if the Morolake family want some dessert, would you? They like their sweets, but nothing too sticky. Every doorknob in the place was hazardous after they left last time."

Forgetting her earlier dismay, Jayla bounded away to her next duty.

Cerulean leaned back with a relieved sigh.

Riko propped one muscled arm on the table, getting up close and personal with Gavin. "You want to meet Taug? He's the one who designed my special eco-meat variety, making my little establishment the best café this side of The Divide. He's a Cresta, but once you get over that, he's not actually so bad. Very helpful in a pinch and more generous than most I could name."

Flabbergasted, Cerulean sat in suspense, waiting for Gavin's response. He had spent the last week trying to think up plausible scenarios to get Gavin to meet Taug in his lab, intending to discover what Taug and Clare had been up to. A Cresta was naturally wary of revealing sensitive information, but an opportunity to show a newcomer his latest work? Well, Cerulean had high hopes that he would be in the dark no longer. Without knowing it, Riko had just set the needful in motion. *He can't possibly be clairvoyant, could he?*

His lips turned down and a ridge on his brow, Gavin tapped his fingers on the table. "Cresta be ugly fish."

Riko smothered a snort. "Yes. True. But then to most humans, Uanyi are unsightly. As far as I'm concerned, humans would lose any honest beauty contest. So, you see, you can't judge a person on their looks." He shrugged as he straightened. "Do what you want. Clare has been spending a lot of time over there. Can't see her interest in Taug's experiments, but maybe it has to do with her work." He glanced over his shoulder at Jayla practically dancing from table to table. "She's a charmer, that one. Everybody loves her." He smiled. "Especially me." He started toward the kitchen. "I'll have your order ready by the time you pick out a dessert." He loped away.

After the heavily spiced drinks had been enjoyed, and Gavin got a little food in him, his face relaxed and his mood softened. He stirred the apple pie and vanilla ice cream into a soft mush, and his gaze wandered the room.

Cerulean shoved his empty dishes away and leaned back. He appraised Gavin with cool honesty. *A good heart but not very clever. Though, his language skills are better than—*

"I agree, pie is best blended with ice cream."

Cerulean's gaze snapped up.

Cobalt stood smirking before them.

How did he do that? You can usually hear an Ingot approach twenty meters away.

Gavin started to slide out of the booth, but Cobalt lifted his hand. "No, please. Don't get up. May I join you instead?"

This could prove interesting. Cerulean nodded.

Moving closer to the wall, Gavin made room for Cobalt next to him.

Dexterously angling himself onto the booth without knocking the table askew, Cobalt glanced around, his eyes alight, like a happy kid just released from school.

Jayla pranced over. "What can I get you, sir?"

Without a hint of self-consciousness, Cobalt grinned. "A whole apple pie and two liters of vanilla ice cream."

No order was impossible for Jayla. With a nod, she accepted the commission and bounded away.

Gavin frowned. "I speak. You understand. You speak…but I no understand."

The table of happy Bhuaci customers started clapping as a birthday cake glowing with colorful candles was carried to their table. A spritely song followed and then more clapping. An elderly Bhuac turned bright red, though a smile engulfed his face.

Surprisingly, both Gavin and Cobalt stared in fascination.

Across the room, a woman standing at the counter lifted a tray carrying a tall Green, another bubbly drink, and what looked like a basket of fries. She then edged her way toward the kitchen. With a furtive glance around, she darted through the doorway.

Clare? What's she…? Oh, yes. Taug's secret entrance.

He glanced from Gavin to Cobalt and knew that he wouldn't be getting any answers from Taug today.

Once the commotion at the Bhuaci table died down, Cobalt offered Gavin a brotherly shoulder nudge. "Ingot quarters can be dull at the best of times. Since nearly everyone has returned home or gone to Tabun to assist with formal diplomacy matters, I have been left by my lonesome. A little pie and ice cream will enliven our evenings. Right, my friend?"

Gavin stiffened.

Cerulean was grateful that Cobalt had missed the look of horror in Gavin's eyes. Shuddering, he knew what he must do. Quickly shifting from Gavin to Cobalt, he leaned back, clasped his hands, and took the lead. "You must stay with us, then, Cobalt. I invited Gavin to my cabin in the woods before I realized that he had made arrangements with you. But I have *two* guest rooms. It would be a shame if you had to rattle around the docking bay when the Central Basin offers Newearth's most scenic locations. I could even introduce you to the Amens community. They have some of the best cooks on the planet."

Faint hope rose in Gavin's eyes.

A shield dropped from Cobalt's face, though his fixed smile stayed in place. "That sounds wonderful." He offered a strangely humble shrug. "I was dreading staying in that awful hole one more day."

Gavin's gaze softened as he stared at the Ingot. "No holes. Even Ingots need fresh air."

Cerulean nodded. *Ingots needed a lot more than fresh air.* He knew it. Cobalt knew it. And before long, Gavin would know it, too.

The elderly Bhuaci rose and, while the table of well-wishers bowed their heads, he blessed them.

Cerulean's heart ached. He could use a blessing about now.

Chapter Eleven

Once You Begin to Care

—Taug's Laboratory—

Thursday, March 2nd

Clare stood over the blue-hued biomb in Taug's laboratory, her hands hanging limply at her sides, her heart strangely unmoved, as if the newest member of the local zoo lay before her. She stared at the developing infant. *Her* developing infant.

Taug stood nearby, his tentacles clasped over his rotund middle, a complacent father, charmed by his progeny.

Though the tiny form was only about the size of a lemon and distinctly pink and white, he looked far more human than at any time in his previous thirteen weeks. His head appeared to be about half his entire length, but the umbilical cord, tying him to a perfectly balanced nutrition and waste removal system, pulsated with well-organized life processes.

Overdressed in a heavy sweater and her winter pants, Clare rolled her shoulders as if trying to relieve herself of a heavy weight.

"Herson's intestines are now completely nestled inside his belly, his fingernails are forming, and you can see faint wisps of hair taking shape on his head. Beautiful bones are gaining strength and dimension, and the first signs of vocal cords are present. Believe it or not, but in a few months, he will let us know his pleasure or displeasure by the sound of his voice."

As if waking from a stupor, Clare swung her gaze to the

large Cresta at her side. "Herson?"

Rearing back, his eyes widening in innocence, Taug blathered. "Well, I had to call him something. And"—he pointed significantly to a young Cresta on the other side of the lab— "my intern wanted to know what to call it." A ruddy blush and Taug corrected himself. "Him." His face crinkled into a smile. "I said he was 'her son,' meaning your son, of course. He took it to mean that was the official name and added it to all the reports. 'Herson Taug.' Rather clever, don't you think?"

Speechless, Clare felt her body flush with rage from her toes to the roots of her hair. "Herson is fine, but Herson Taug? You aren't the father!"

A pout and Taug made it quite clear that his feelings were hurt. He harrumphed. "I did help to create him. Granted, not my DNA, but still, it was my skills that put him together, so to speak." He bent over and tapped the biomb, his voice dropping to a croon. "We've become attached, Herson and I. Bonded in our own manner of speaking, haven't we, little one?"

Fear shot through Clare as an image of Derik, a Cresta-Human hybrid who suffered in life and died horribly, ran through her mind. *I can't let him take control.* "It's my baby, and I should be the one to name him!"

The intern turned and stared at her.

Taug straightened, motioned to the intern, and spoke in his most officious tone. "You may go now. But be back first thing in the morning. We have a lot of work ahead."

After a proper bow, the intern accepted his newest order and turned off his workstation. He toddled toward the east wall, whipped a thick cape with a hood that looked suspiciously like a disguise over his bio-suit, and then headed out the door.

Taug locked his gaze on Clare.

Unexpectedly cowed by Taug's intense stare, Clare retreated across the room to the empty bed where Faye used to lie. She ran her hand along the coverlet absentmindedly. "We can compromise. I'll call him Herson T. Clare. How does that sound? If anyone asks, I'll just say the T stands for some heroic ancestor." She shrugged. "But you can feel smug knowing that a human is named after you."

Happy again, Taug practically bounced across the room. "A perfect solution! Now, I want to put Herson's figure between us, to commemorate our understanding." He plucked three game figures off a shelf near the wall screen. "I brought them over from Faye's place." He reached out. "Here!" He handed Clare the woman figure that had been a part of the game set. "That's you, and this is me." He lifted a Cresta-shaped figure. "And here is Herson." He pinched a tiny figure in a surprisingly dexterous tentacle. His gaze roamed the room, searching.

A headache building behind her eyes, Clare examined her miniature self. "Who made these anyway?"

Taug toddled across the room to the sitting area. He placed his two figures on the low table. "Faye said they were presented to her by an elder Bhuaci who wanted to relate some mysterious warning. But I've heard rumors that it was really Sterling who set the whole thing up." He shrugged. "Still a bit of a mystery." Waving Clare nearer, he beamed. "She's recovering beautifully on Helm, by the way. I talked with her yesterday." He pointed to the table. "Come, come. Put yourself here, next to Herson."

Reluctant and feeling out of sorts, Clare trudged closer. She plunked her figure next to the tiny shape, a sour taste in her mouth. "It doesn't look like a baby. Not a human one, anyway."

Taug chuckled as he glowed at the small assembly on the table. "That's only because you don't love it yet. I assure you, once you begin to care, your motherly feelings will—"

A chime rang.

Taug frowned and Clare's heart jumped to her throat. She hissed at him. "Who can that be?"

Pointing, Taug directed Clare's gaze to a screen in the corner of the room revealing three distinctly unique figures standing in Riko's kitchen, just outside the laboratory doorway. "I have surveillance cameras everywhere. Can't be too careful."

Her heart falling an immeasurable distance, Clare thought she might faint.

Cerulean, Cobalt, and Gavin stood right outside the door, waiting.

"Oh, Lord in Heaven. No!" She gripped one of Taug's tentacles in desperation. "They can't see me here. They can't know about this." She pointed wildly at the biomb. "Not ever! It's our little secret, right?"

A few yanks and Taug freed his appendage. He peered down at Clare, a haughty look in his eyes. "What do you take me for—an Ingot? I am perfectly well aware of your discomfort with the artificial aspects of our baby-growing transaction, though I hardly agree with your hyper-sensitivity." He frowned and waved toward the wall behind the sitting area. "There's a walk space behind my pool there. It's so I can strip off my bio-suit in privacy. Go along and hide yourself back there."

The chime repeated.

Fidgeting, Cerulean appeared distinctly uncomfortable. He glared directly at the camera as if aware that eyes could see him.

Her heart pounding, Clare hurried across the room and snuck into the vestibule.

The sound of a door sliding open and steps moving into the lab kept her apprised of events. She stepped over to the pool and realized that, though it was murky, it was clear enough to see through. She leaned in cupping her hands around her eyes. Fear rising, her whole body trembled. Where was Herson's biomb? She swallowed down a scream and looked again.

The space was empty.

A charming host, Taug welcomed the Luxonian, the Ingot, and the Tabunite with the flourish of a thriving businessman who wants to impress his guests. "Come into my humble establishment, gentlemen. May I get you anything?"

Gavin hesitated just inside the doorway, while Cobalt ventured right in and started a private tour.

Only Cerulean, soul of kindness that he was, stopped and addressed the Cresta personally. "Thank you, Taug. We were in the neighborhood and thought that we might take a look at your latest experiments." He leaned in, a brittle smile stiff on his face. "Cobalt and Gavin have been staying with me for nearly a week, and though we have been well entertained by the Amens community, toured the Docking Bay facility twice, taken three sightseeing trips, and even spent a delightful evening with Kendra, Bala, and the kids, we thought it was about time to do something productive." Cerulean's eyes swept from Cobalt to Gavin. "Certainly, you have something interesting to show us?"

Clare's heart pounded in her ears.

A light entered Taug's eyes. "Well, as a matter of fact, I do." He glanced at Cobalt, who had stopped at the place where the biomb had stood.

An open space with loose tubes and technology clearly exclaimed that something was missing.

Practically preening himself, Taug swept back the cilia on the top of his head. He grinned and then wrapped his tentacles around his body, hugging himself like an excited child. "But it's a great secret. You can't tell!"

Gavin stepped forward, his expression bewildered, as he continued to let his gaze roll over the shelving units, dissecting tables lined with an assortment of knives, white machines with screens and tubes, and a procedure chair with numerous straps attached.

Cobalt ambled over to Taug and rubbed his hands together, clearly enjoying himself. "A secret? I love secrets!"

Alarm swept over Cerulean's features and were corralled in a tight grimace almost instantly. He dropped his gaze.

Prickly heat rushed over Clare's body.

Taug didn't need much encouragement. He scurried over to a shelving unit near where the intern had worked and pulled out—*a red-hued biomb?*

Dizziness engulfed Clare. She gripped the edge of the pool and held on for dear life.

Taug waddled into the middle of the room and placed the biomb in the empty space. He attached the tubes and technology with amazing alacrity. "I call him Relevance. My baby!"

Cobalt jumped forward.

Cerulean's head snapped up.

Disgust filled Gavin's face as he edged closer.

Clare closed her eyes and slid to the ground. She didn't want to see anymore. She knew enough. Taug had tricked her. Herson was her son, indeed. But Taug wanted his own baby. Someone to— *What?* She hardly knew. She feared her imagination. And his.

Nausea rippled through her middle, and, wrapping her arms around her knees, she rocked forward and back. Visions of the Spare Parts Shop wavered before her: body parts grown in labs, organs harvested from who knew where, blood bags, genetics charts, price lists, and sales. Products created for a demanding market.

Oh, Almighty. What have I done?

Trying not to make a sound, she laid her head on her knees and hid her sobs.

Gavin stood in the odorless, white interior of Taug's laboratory and could not understand what he was seeing. It appeared to be a baby inside a reddish container. A violent upheaval threatened to discharge breakfast from his stomach. He gripped Cerulean's arm.

Alarm spread over Cerulean's face. "Cobalt! Help me get him to a chair."

Between the two figures, Gavin staggered to the sitting area and dropped down on the couch. He groaned. "Don't know…what happened."

Standing at his side, Cerulean pressed his shoulder. "I do."

Cobalt plopped down on the chair to the right of Gavin. "Oh, come now! Don't be so sensitive. It's a humanoid fetus with not an ounce of sense." He swiveled his gaze to Taug who was still fiddling with the biomb attachments. "I call it a marvelous surprise." He leaned in. "I don't mean to divulge secrets myself, but Ingots are in need of new technology at the moment. We've had an awful scare."

At the sound of sincerity in the Ingot's tone, Gavin lifted his head, his mind clearing.

Cobalt leaned back and tented his fingers together. "Oh, yes. I might as well be honest with you." He lowered his voice. "Taug may be in on it, for all I know, but the Ingots have suffered a great loss—several of our best lines were infected with a disease and perished. We've been having a hard time creating replacements fast enough." He shifted and leaned forward, tapping Gavin's knee. "It's a good thing you have such healthy DNA. You're safe from what nearly destroyed us."

Gavin shook his head, bile in his throat. "You do that"—he pointed to the biomb— "to your children?"

"Refreshments, anyone?" Taug ambled over, a cloth draped over one tentacle, servant fashion. "I've got a number of potent drinks and even a snack pack for visitors."

Cerulean groaned. "Taug, this really isn't the time."

Cobalt laughed and clapped his hands together. "Don't be ridiculous, Cerulean. Just because your Luxonian physiology allows you to eat sunlight, doesn't mean that the rest of us don't have definite nutritional needs." He glanced aside, grinning. "Look at Gavin. Why the man is nearly starved."

Happy to oblige, Taug fluttered his tentacles. "No worries! I have just what you need. Let me get a few things settled, and I will return with a delicious and healthy repast."

Gavin leaned back. "I can't eat. Ever again."

Cerulean sat on the chair on the other side of the couch. His eyes narrowed as he picked up the small figures arranged in a small huddle. "This is Clare and…Taug…and…" He glanced across the room at the biomb.

A shudder worked over Gavin as he considered the figures that Cerulean held in his hands. *Images have power…to encourage…or drive men mad.* The ocean's depths during a storm swirled in his mind. Almost as if drawn by an unseen force, he looked up and stared at the murky Cresta pool. He thought he heard a distant sob. Most definitely, he felt a wave of terror engulf him.

Chapter Twelve

Healing Found His Heart

—Clare's House—

Wednesday, March 8th

Kendra gripped the handrail of her autoskimmer, trying not to crash on account of her growing fury. She was going to have it out with Clare, come Bothmal or bloodbath. There was no way she would watch her darling husband succumb to the madness of imagined scenarios, fearing the worst, and never certain of the truth.

If only Bala would stand up to her!

Kendra sighed. Not the man she married. He might complain, pout, scheme a thousand plots, but he would never confront anyone about anything. Unless it involved the safety of his kids. Then watch out! But this wasn't about the kids, or her, or anything that he could pin down. That's what was driving him crazy. Clare insisted that everything was fine. All the while, Bala's warning sirens were blaring full blast. Well, Kendra had had enough.

Her long skirt flapping in the blustery late winter wind, she directed her autoskimmer to the quiet rural street where Clare lived. The Newearth Human Services Detective hadn't come in to work today, though Bala had tried every means possible of contacting her. No response. He feared she might be dead. Kendra didn't think so. But she planned to find out for sure.

It was mid-afternoon, and the sky remained cloud-covered, a dull gray over a dreary landscape. Snow had been averted for the time being, and only drizzly rain had spat a chill over the dead fields. Even the evergreen trees on the edge of the property seemed cowed and disgruntled.

Not a welcoming environment to be sure.

A single pedestrian crossed from the "Plant Yourself Here" flower shop to the "You Want It—We Got It" variety store on the other side of the street. An undulating Bhuaci melody from the neighbor's house mingled with the complaining winds, creating a distinctly moody atmosphere.

Kendra shook herself as she disembarked from her autoskimmer. She set it into a proper niche and transferred a quarter unit from her datapad to lock it in place. Normally, she wouldn't bother, but today, nothing seemed safe.

Shoulders back, a confident poise, and Kendra pounded up the porch steps. The house felt deserted. No life stirred, even though the wind scuttled dead leaves across the small, barren yard.

She pressed the doorbell.

A razz-razz sounded from the depths of the house.

Kendra waited.

Nothing.

Stifled unease began to crawl out of her internal container and her knees shook. Kendra shoved open the screen door and grabbed the round brass doorknob on the heavy, oak door. To her amazement, it turned and unclicked. The door swung open.

Stifling a gasp and barely controlling the same kind of fear she had experienced when Zara had showed her dark side, Kendra stepped into the dark living room.

"Hello? Cla-are?"

Hazy afternoon light illuminated the large table directly ahead. Similar to Cerulean's kitchen table, solid wood and polished to a high gleam, it could sit ten comfortably, though Kendra was fairly certain that Clare had never had more than half a dozen friends visit in her lifetime.

Had this been her parent's home? Surprised by the question and the fact that she honestly didn't know the answer, Kendra inched forward and stopped between the simply furnished kitchen and the overcrowded living room.

To her left, a curved counter offered plenty of space for cutting boards, pots, pans, and other culinary accessories. Little of which Clare needed, as she rarely seemed to do any home cooking. She usually ate out and raged against poor service and ridiculous prices. Though, Kendra remembered, she was fond of the Breakfastnook Café and often stopped there for a quick meal.

Kendra shook her head. No offense to Riko, but *she* could feed her entire family a delicious, nutritious meal for the price of one of his dinner platters.

Feeling distinctly uncomfortable, Kendra called out again. "Hey, Clare! Where are you, woman? I know you must be home. Never known you to leave your door un—"

If an apparition of the dead showed itself in a pale aura hanging raggedly on a limp form, then Kendra was facing a ghost. A tremor galloped over her, and she wasn't completely sure if she had just screamed.

Wearing striped pajama pants and a loose top, Clare lifted her hand. "Don't. I can't stand dramatics."

Kendra grabbed her wits and forced them to behave. Only the shakiness in her voice belied the casual pose she struck. "Oh, so you are alive. Good to know. Bala wondered. So, I just came to see for myself."

As if sleepwalking, Clare padded on bare feet across the room to the couch placed before the dead fireplace. She flopped down, crossing her arms over her chest as she pulled her legs up and propped her feet on the edge, looking like a miserable little girl.

Much as she didn't want it to, Kendra's heart melted. She

dragged a heavy overstuffed chair close to Clare and perched on the edge. The idea of switching on a lamp rippled over her mind and was swiftly dismissed. No, this was not a time for bright lights. This was the time to let monsters out of the closet.

She leaned in close and placed her hands on Clare. A prayer was not out of the question.

Clare didn't move a muscle.

Almighty, give me wisdom. Kendra cleared her throat. "What's happened, Clare? Tell me."

Her head held straight; Clare seemed to be looking across the room at the big bay window directly opposite her.

By now, the light had faded to a somber slate gray. The bare trees stood like wispy black fingers pointing to the colorless sky.

When she finally spoke, Clare's voice seemed as toneless as the winter evening. "I made a baby. But I don't love it." She swallowed and then picked at a loose thread.

Stunned, Kendra wasn't sure where to go, where to look, what to think. "You-you made…a…baby? You're pregnant, Clare?"

A simple shake of the head. "No. I didn't want to get pregnant. Too much bother and the whole mess would have interfered with my work. But I did want a baby. Someone of my very own."

Adoption? Bala's description of Saran and the Spare Parts Shop filled Kendra's imagination. "You…what? Made a deal with Saran, who found a kid for you?"

For the first time, Clare turned and met Kendra's direct gaze. Her face wrinkled in angry distaste. "No! I wouldn't ask Saran for a fingernail, much less a child."

Kendra rubbed the back of her neck and sat up. "That's not what you told me earlier."

Spitting her words, Clare's face contorted. "That was a

mistake!"

Cold detachment sluiced Kendra. She leaned back in the chair. *This is going to take time.*

Hunching forward, Clare wrapped her arms around her legs, making herself as small as possible. "Taug helped me. I told him that I wanted a child of my own, but I didn't want to get pregnant, so he harvested an egg…or two, and made a baby." She lifted her head defiantly and sniffed. "It was simple, really. Embarrassing as detention in Bothmal when he harvested the eggs, though…"

Oh-my-Lord-Oh-my-Lord-Oh-my-Lord! Fearing the possibility that she might spontaneously combust, Kendra jumped to her feet and hurried across the room.

An art table was stationed in front of Clare's work desk, and various projects perched, leaned, and lay strewn across its dusty surface: one watercolor drawing, a couple of small ceramic figures, and what looked very much like a half-carved piece of driftwood.

Tears blurred Kendra's vision.

Clare's voice rose like a petulant child behind her. "I didn't know what else to do. It was driving me mad! The need for something—someone! I don't have a family. Not like you. I wanted a child to love, to raise as my very own, someone who would understand me because he was a part of me."

A heaving sob clawed up Kendra's throat. She smashed it down. "A baby isn't *yours*, Clare. No one owns a child."

Small and weak, Clare squeaked her next words. "I just wanted someone to love."

Burning anger filled Kendra from head to toe. She swung around and faced Clare. "Love? Is that what you call it? Forming a human being in a dish and planting it—" She froze as a dozen thoughts crashed in her mind. "Where is it, Clare? Where is your baby?"

After unfolding herself, Clare shifted off the couch. She

padded to the art station and lifted one of the ceramic figures. With a puzzled expression, she stared at it, as if trying to remember what it was supposed to be. Then she dropped it carelessly back on the table. One edge chipped and flew to the edge of the table. "Taug has a biomb…a blue biomb for Herson. He's fourteen weeks now. Bigger than a lemon and he has bones, intestines, wisps of hair, and everything." She sighed. "I should love him. Taug does. At least he acts like he does. Even sings to it. But I don't feel anything."

The desire to whip out her datapad and call Bala nearly overpowered Kendra. *But wait.* "There's more, isn't there?" She didn't know how she knew, but she was certain of it; this story was only going to get worse.

Clare nodded. She padded over to the window and stared at the evening blackness. "When I was visiting last week, Cerulean, the Ingot Cobalt, and that Neanderthal guy, Gavin, showed up unexpectedly. Taug had to let them in, but I hid in the back. Taug must have lost his head, or he was trying to cover up the bare spot where Herson's biomb had been." She scrunched her face in perplexity. "He must have hidden him the second my back was turned. Anyway, he brought out a biomb to show off, but it was red, not blue. And there was a different baby in it. Taug calls it Relevance. It's his, he says."

Kendra couldn't think which question to ask next, so many pounded in her brain. She merely spluttered, "But…he used *your* eggs…"

Clare nodded sympathetically, as if the same thought had troubled her. "Yes. He admits as much. But Relevance is unique. Somehow, he's human, Tabun, and"—her face scrunched with distaste—"Ingot."

Her mind nearly short-circuiting, Kendra could only manage one word. "H-how?"

Clare shook her head. "Don't know." She lifted her head and stared right into Kendra's eyes. "Cobalt had something to do with it. He was clearly delighted. He and Taug are best buddies now. I think even Cerulean was surprised."

Backing up like a train that simply had nowhere else to go, Kendra found a chair and then plopped down. "I can hardly take this all in." She looked over at Clare. "You called your baby Herson?"

"Herson T. Clare." She sucked in a deep breath. "Her…Son. Get it? I won't tell you what the T stands for. You couldn't take it."

Kendra muttered, "Probably not. Though I can guess." Bitterness seeped into the very pores of her skin. "How could you let this happen, Clare?"

Clare leaned against the art table and folded her arms over her chest. "It seemed like a good idea at the time. I just felt so needy. And I have a right to be happy, don't I? Taug isn't terribly evil. He just takes advantage of every situation." She shrugged. "Besides, maybe this is a good thing. The Ingots are in trouble. Perhaps the Tabun won't mind sharing their seed, so to speak, and saving a whole race of innocent Ingots."

Kendra shook her head wondering what warped dimension she had slipped into. "Do you even hear yourself, Clare?" A new thought struck her. "Wait! What about Gavin? Does he understand what's happened—who this baby Relevance is?"

Clare flapped her hands against her sides, a picture of helpless dejection. "Don't know. He ran out of the lab when Taug told Cobalt about his experiment and showed off the baby. No one has seen him since."

Kendra closed her eyes for a long moment, praying for strength. Finally, she opened them again. She stared at Clare, a limp doll with the stuffing knocked out of it. She rose to her feet, paced across the room, and spoke in the most commanding voice she could muster. "Go get dressed and pack a bag. You are coming home with me."

Uncertainty wavered in Clare's eyes. "You want me to stay with you and your kids?"

"Yeah, if I can keep Bala from killing you, that's how it's going to be."

Clare pushed off the table and stood on her own two feet. "But why? You probably hate me right now. Why be nice?"

Kendra sucked in a bracing breath. "Because, idiot child, it's who I am…and we all have to do penance for our sins. Now hurry up. You've got reparation to make to two little babies and at least one alien nation."

—Wisconsin Territories, North Central Aram County—

Friday, March 9th

Gavin crouched by the dim cave entrance and peered in. All quiet. With a sigh, he retreated to a boulder half buried in the hillside and sat down. How many days had passed since he first found this cave? He counted on his fingers. A handful and one.

He closed his eyes against the blind horror that had driven him from Taug's laboratory. A mad rush out the door, then weaving through the crowded café into the evening light. Nausea threatened his every step.

He blundered he knew not where, found a quiet spot, crawled under a bench in a grassy spot, and slept. Before he knew it, in blurry weariness, he was hurried on by angry voices. Time passed in a fuzzy confusion. He climbed on board a transport and was thrown out when it was discovered that he had no units.

Finally, a shaft of a memory led him to the central tube

that would take him to Cerulean's home. Cerulean's face rose like a beacon of light. He managed to sneak inside, fell asleep, but miraculously awoke in time to get off at the familiar station.

He had started to climb the hillside when exhaustion and despair overwhelmed him. If this was a world where babies were grown in hard shells, with less consideration than his people offered plants, then it was altogether evil. He rejected it utterly! Even Cerulean could not change his mind.

He turned aside and found another path leading into the thick woodlands.

Wandering aimlessly, he cursed his decision to stay on Newearth, and bellowed at the gray, stormy sky. Darkness and heavy drops fell over the rough path, and only by slivers of moonlight did he discover a low cave. In relief, he crawled in and curled up against a dry wall, falling asleep instantly.

Until a low growl and hot breath brought him to his senses.

The ensuing fight for his life awoke the fury he had suppressed ever since coming to this strange planet. Here was a foe he could fight! And fight he did.

Only after he had choked the life out of the lone wolf and thrown its body aside did he hear the whimpering yips behind him.

He crawled into the back of the cave and discovered, to his shame, three small pups. Sobs welled up as he wrapped them in his shirt and carried them outside to the breaking dawn.

The broken body of their mother lay sprawled in the dirt.

He held the pups and cried like he had never done so before in his life.

It was there that Cerulean found him.

Instead of taking him home, Cerulean had called for help from his friends, the Amens Community, living nearby.

Gavin was half-carried, clutching the squirming bundles, to a wood and stone home built in a sheltered valley, surrounded by the sweet scent of spring ready to bloom.

In a darkened room, he lay on a simple bed, and food was brought to him on a tray. An Elder woman came and spoke kind words, a youth played a gentle tune on a stringed instrument, and soothing teas settled his irritated nerves. In response to his pleas, the wolf pups were finally brought forth, fat with fresh milk. They tumbled like naughty children across the coverlet on his bed. Laughing, he cuddled them in his arms as they licked his face. Healing found his heart.

Kindness replaced torturous memories.

But he could not wholly forget.

Finally, Cerulean came and said it was time to face Taug, Cobalt, and even Clare. They must learn the truth, for there was no other way to set Newearth free of future tyranny. After settling the pups in the warm embrace of a young man with ruddy cheeks and a glad smile, Gavin set out.

Once in the middle of the woods, he had asked to stop at the cave once more. Cerulean had understood and stepped away.

His vision blurring, Gavin sucked in a deep breath. He looked from the cave to the bright blue sky and spoke to the Creator of all. "I know now. Why I live. Despite our failings, I must find a home for the pups."

Chapter Thirteen

Overriding a Few Sensibilities

—Newearth Docking Bay, Reconciliation Room—

Sunday, March 12th

Max was absolutely sure that he was the wrong man for this particular job. *I'm not a diplomat! What was the inter-Alien Alliance Committee thinking, putting me in charge of such an impossible inquiry?*

Though he was a hybrid himself and, as the manager of the largest intergalactic docking bay this side of the Divide, he assisted in maintaining the welfare of aliens from all over the universe, *and* he was the father to Zara, also a hybrid, yet he could not see how he was going to reconcile some of the most divergent personalities on the planet in this monotonously boring room.

Wearing his most impeccable blue suit coat over a starched-to-perfection light blue shirt and black pants, he stood before a round white table centered in a round white room and stared at his round white chair. Clare would sit on his right with Cobalt on his left. Cerulean, Gavin, and Taug would complete the circle. Bala, dressed all in black, was already standing by the door, his gaze shifting nervously as if he expected the walls to cave in.

Max glared at the gleaming walls. No, they weren't guilty of anything worse than a lack of color and perspective.

As the doors swished open, Faye stepped over the threshold and strolled over to Bala, a hesitant smile wavered on her face. Looking much the same as always in her pixie form, wearing a flowing skirt and yellow blouse, it was difficult to comprehend that she had spent months on Helm recovering her peace of mind. Apparently, for Bhuaci, being held in stasis was much like being locked in solitary confinement. *Sterling sure has a lot of explaining to do.*

Images of the sterile holding cells on Bothmal rampaged through Max's mind. Dejected, dispirited prisoners sat slump-shouldered, whimpering in corners, or raging behind remorseless walls. During the years he served there, he could never understand their reaction. It was just a holding cell, after all. But now, glancing around, he realized that if these walls blocked him from Justine and Zara, he would rage, too. And after raging long enough, he might just start to whimper.

He glanced aside at Justine's perfectly calm demeanor in her form-fitting bodysuit and felt a horrifying desire to pinch her arm. It wouldn't hurt her, but in her surprise, she might possibly share his unease. Almost as good. He shook himself and exclaimed in an undertone, "Blewy!" Zara's newest expression of blusterous frustration suddenly made perfect sense to him.

The door opened again, and Cerulean, stern-faced, in a brown tunic over dark pants, stepped in with Gavin, wearing a sleeveless shirt and baggy pants, looking just as grim. In mismatched sweatpants and a sweater, Clare clearly didn't care how she looked as she trailed in behind.

Justine scowled. "You'd better watch your language, Max. Sterling is expected any minute, and *no one* is in a jocular mood."

Jocular mood? What did Justine take him for? A clown? That was more Omega's line than his! Blewy was a legitimate expression of frustration, was it not?

Justine stepped back to her observer position and crossed her arms, looking deceptively harmless.

With a steadying breath that he, technically, didn't need,

Max motioned to the placards on the table. "Clare, your place is here on my left. Cobalt will be on my right. Cerulean and Gavin, you two centered there, just so." He forced a grin. We're just waiting for Taug and—"

The door swished open to startled silence.

Sterling, nearly translucent now, stepped into the room with Taug and Cobalt. Laughing!

If I had innards to squirm, they would be their squirmiest about now. What does that Luxonian think he's doing?

Dropping all pretense of formality, Clare jerked her chair from the table and plunked down with a disgusted snort.

Cerulean and Gavin still stood, glaring at Taug and Cobalt.

Unperturbed, Sterling accompanied the last two table guests to their appointed places and then stepped over to the curved wall, just across from Justine. He had asked to "simply observe."

Ready for anything, Max used his most formal tone. "Please, let's be seated." He motioned for everyone at the table to sit down.

Aside, Justine and Bala remained standing, ramrod straight, like honor guards.

Faye propped her hands on her hips. Though she was not directly involved in the hybrid issue, she had demanded the right to witness the proceedings.

Max looked at the expectant group and gripped the edge of his chair. *What now?* There was protocol… *But it's all made up!* He and Justine had copied and pasted the formal "Newearth Reconciliation Service" together over the last few days, using every resource available on Newearth. OldEarth religious and Bhuaci spiritual traditions were the most helpful, though Justine had insisted that he leave out the formal penance part. He disagreed. Penance was the only part that made any sense to him.

He forced his jaws to unclench and took a metaphorical flying leap. "Welcome, everyone." He nodded to each representative in turn. "Clare as a Human Services Detective, Cobalt as an Ingot Diplomat, Taug as a representative Cresta scientist, Gavin as our Tabun guest, and Cerulean as a Luxonian arbitrator of good standing, we are glad to have an opportunity to heal the divisions that have crept into our community."

Clare rolled her eyes, and Cobalt chuckled, knocking askew Max's fragile confidence.

Sterling clapped his hands and wavered forward. "I had intended to let this assembly manage things in its own way, but it's quite clear that—"

Despite her petite form, Faye shot forward, her pale pink skin shimmering and her eyes flashing. "You dare to suggest that you haven't interfered in Newearth's most private affairs numerous times, taking matters into your own hands? Did you, or did you not, deceive us all with your fake death and then brutally assault me by holding me in stasis simply because I might have seen the truth?"

Stunned, Sterling froze, his protestations becoming nothing more than incoherent babbles, "But I didn't, couldn't! It wasn't—"

Alarmed, Max shot to his feet.

Taug waved a laconic tentacle. "Please, no hysterics from the sidelines. We are here to solve problems, not create new ones."

Suddenly Justine was standing behind Max, nudging him between the shoulder blades.

Max took the hint. "Excuse me, but I must insist that everyone take turns speaking." He lifted his hand and put on his most commanding face. He had practiced this expression at home, and Zara had nodded sagely, saying that it was, indeed, quite intimidating. The fact that she had smiled at

Justine as she said it had not registered as a problem. Until this moment.

He took a more aggressive stance. "I will now review the accusations made by Gavin as the formal representative of Tabun. Also, Clare has asked to address the assembly—not with a complaint—for she acknowledges her part to play in this unfortunate situation, but to ask that new safeguards be put into place for the protection of other Newearth citizens."

A tip of his head and Sterling lifted his hands in acquiescence.

Still glowering, Faye backed up and stood beside Bala once again.

Max dutifully cleared his throat. "On the second day of this month, Gavin discovered that Taug, in a private arrangement with Clare, harvested several of her eggs with the express intention of fertilizing one to create her son. Unknown to Clare, Taug had also made arrangements with Cobalt to attempt an Ingot-Tabun hybrid. Cobalt had somehow"—he shot a scowl at Cobalt— "managed to procure seed from both Ingot and Tabun men."

Cobalt grinned. "It wasn't hard, really. We Ingots have vials full of the stuff, and it is amazing what primitive men will do if given the right inducement."

Gavin jumped to his feet. "Lie! Tabun men do not give seeds to make babies in boxes! Never!"

The smug expression on Cobalt's face was enough to make any sentient being angry. It was certainly enough to push a Neanderthal over the edge.

Both Justine and Bala intervened just in time to keep Gavin's hands from Cobalt's throat.

Cobalt hardly appeared worried; he merely laughed. "Your men didn't mind! Trust me. They were having an exceptionally good time. Seems that Ingot woman when properly attired—or unattired—can arouse their interest with ease." He sighed. "Unfortunately, doing it the old-fashioned way would severely hinder our national interest." He swept his hand toward Taug. "Hence the kindness of the Cresta to discover if a more efficient means of reproduction between our people could be arranged."

Before Gavin could splutter his next words, Max lifted his hand. "We must clarify one point. Clare's baby, the one named Herson, is a Human-Tabunite hybrid. So, what is the one named Relevance?"

Taug rose to his booted feet and attempted a humble posture. "I meant no disrespect to Clare or anyone on Tabun. Rest assured, that my motives were most pure. Clare wanted a child to love. I fertilized one of her eggs so that she would have a baby of her very own. She never specified where the seed should come from. I only used a Tabunite seed because they are a hardy race, and I was nearly certain that it would be compatible. Gavin and Clare appeared to be friends. What could be more acceptable?"

His brows rose in honest supplication as he continued. "Now, as we all know, the Ingot race has suffered a terrible setback with the decimation of several of their best lines. Since I had harvested several eggs, in case one was unfit in some way, I hated to see them go to waste, so I fertilized another. But I decided to make the most of my opportunity. I used aspects of both the Tabun and Ingot seeds and managed to fertilize the first of its kind—a tribrid— Human-Tabun-Ingot." His eyes gleamed as his gaze rolled around the room. "You can see why I named him Relevance!"

With alarming reverberations, Sterling groaned.

All gazes swept to his wavering form.

"Omega warned me of this! He said that you would learn no other way, but I had hoped we could avoid this horror."

His face darkening into an angry scowl, Taug faced Sterling. "A new life form is not a horror! Just because it is different from those you have known before hardly means that it is without inherent dignity or shouldn't be accorded the same respect as all sentient life."

Sterling wavered. "You miss my meaning. And you've bypassed Omega's cautionary tale." He faced Faye and held her stern gaze. "I was guilty of a dramatic trick, though, in truth, my end *is* near, and my concern is real. I should not have pulled you into stasis. Instead, I should have asked for your help." He shook his head. "I apologize for my grave mistake. But, too often, we do not know the consequences of our actions until much later, when all other options are beyond recall." He lifted his hands as if in benediction, his gaze straying to Cerulean. "I will return to Lux for my last days. I can be of no further service here. You have passed a point of no return." He shook his head. "I only hope that you will survive your future and rise higher than you have fallen."

He blinked away.

A babble of voices rose as Clare, Gavin, Cobalt, Faye, and Bala all spoke at once.

Max wished he had brought a gavel to pound. He had to use his voice instead. "Stop!"

The arguing voices rose a decibel.

Justine stepped forward and drew her dustbuster. She lifted it high.

Instantaneously, the room dropped into silence.

With a wave, Justine gave the floor to her husband, holstered her gun, and stepped back.

Surprised at the fury flooding his system, Max spoke with the first real tone of authority he had ever used. He meant every word he spat at the assembly. "There will be no more outbursts, or each of you will be escorted to holding cells and kept there until I deem you ready to rejoin society. The Inter-Alien Alliance asked *me* to manage this docking bay. You will only speak when given permission! Do you understand?"

Everyone, including Cobalt, appeared abashed. Except for Cerulean. He had paced to the other side of the room and seemed to be studying his datapad.

Max had to make sure that the Luxonian was in agreement. Cerulean was too key a figure to leave out of this reconciliation process. "Cerulean?"

Cerulean returned to his place at the table. He nodded. "Yes. Of course. I agree with everything you said." He looked around with something akin to sympathy on his face. "Why don't we all sit back down."

Well aware that he did not have blood pressure which needed to return to normal, still Max felt that a breather was called for. He wanted a fresh start. "Since Clare was the one who began this process, I would like her to explain her thinking and her request. Then we will allow for responses in turn." He gestured to Clare.

Her shoulders stooped; Clare climbed wearily to her feet. "I acted like a child myself. I wanted a baby to love and didn't think the whole thing through. I guess no one really can. But I did ask Taug for help." She frowned. "Or rather, he offered his assistance, and I took it." She shrugged. "I didn't think to ask for details. I just wanted him to get the job done. Somehow…I just figured he'd use a seed from a public bank. Never occurred to me that he'd turn the whole thing into an experiment." Her gaze focused on the curved wall across the room, far from Bala and Faye. "I should've known better." She shook herself and refocused on the assembly. "I only ask that, from now on, whenever a woman's eggs are being used for reproduction purposes, or any experiment, really, that she be informed of all the details, very clearly, beforehand, step-by-step." Clare swallowed hard. "If I had known what was really happening, I would have rethought the whole thing." She plunked down on her chair.

Taug lifted a tentacle as if beseeching his chance to speak.

Max nodded to him.

Taug rose to his feet. He made a formal bow toward Clare. "I sincerely apologize for any hard feelings you have experienced in the reproduction process, Clare." He sighed, and bubbles rose through his breather helm. "I will dare to be as honest as you have been and state that I did not reveal the details of the reproduction process for fear of this very thing. Humans do not take well to the scientific process when applied to living beings. They want the results of scientific procedure but are disgusted by the process." He sighed. "The greater good of creating tribrids for the salvation of the Ingot race, and the possible cure of interspecies hatred through crossbreeding was, I believe, worth overriding a few sensibilities." He clasped his tentacles like a benevolent schoolmaster with nothing else to say. He sat down.

Overriding a few sensibilities? Max stifled an automatic grimace.

Cobalt jumped to his feet; his hands lifted with a "my turn" gesture.

Frowning, Max assented.

"I must support Taug. He has done nothing wrong. He was asked by that woman"—he pointed at Clare—"and did just want she wanted. Without any recompense, I might add! So what if he used old eggs that would have been wasted in the natural process? There's no crime in being thrifty. He knew of our need because I explained it to him and asked for his help over a year ago. The fact that he managed to splice both Ingot and Tabun seeds, creating the first tribrid being is to be praised, not censured!" With a look of righteous indignation, he plunked back down on his chair.

Dead silence filled the air.

Max considered the faces before him. Clare, sullen and unhappy, Taug, a bit smug, Gavin inscrutable, Faye pouted, but Cerulean merely glanced at the door.

Bala cleared his throat and raised his hand.

Max gestured for him to step nearer.

Pacing to the table, Bala's face appeared a mask of controlled fury. He stopped next to Gavin and glanced around at the assembly. "I realize that I don't have an official role in this reconciliation process, but I really think that you have skipped over the one person most offended here. Gavin is a Tabun representative, and his people never gave consent to this reproductive process in any form. They wouldn't have understood it!" Bala laid his hand on Gavin's shoulder and leaned in. "Don't you have something to say?"

Gavin nodded and climbed wearily to his feet; his hands tightly clasped. He looked around and his gaze stopped on Clare. "Wailing mothers will not be comforted. All children gone. Death is better." His eyes narrowed into angry slits as they turned on Cobalt and Taug. "A mother wolf fights for her cubs. What have you done to your woman? They offer eggs, seeds forced into them, and babies grown like plants in a box!" He shook his head. "You must hate women very much."

Clare's head snapped up; her jaw clenched. She stared at Gavin, her voice low and dangerous. "It is not them who hate us. It is us who hate us."

The door swished open. While everyone turned to see, Cerulean hurried to the entrance.

Taug's assistant stood there with two rolling tables. On one table was a blue biomb. On the other, a red biomb.

With a beckoning gesture, Cerulean led him forward, pushing the two tables alongside.

Taug jumped to his feet, nearly falling backward.

Cobalt caught him and stood at his side. "What's the meaning of this?"

Clare and Gavin rose, their eyes wide with shock.

Max bustled around the table and intercepted Cerulean and the assistant. "No one gave permission for…presentations!"

Justine called out. "Bring them forward, Cerulean. We all want to see."

Faye and Bala scampered in close.

In a moment, the assistant had retreated to the doorway while the whole assembly circled the two biombs.

At nearly sixteen weeks, the babies had grown to over ten centimeters and looked more humanoid, their translucent skin showed tiny blood vessels and beating hearts. Herson sucked his thumb, while Relevance crouched into a tight ball, like a person in pain.

Taug rushed up, a worried father with his tentacles flailing. "What are you doing? They must stay connected to their proper units!"

Alarm filled the assistant's face, but Cerulean stepped up and reassured Taug. "I made sure that everything was according to protocol. Herson"—he pointed to the blue biomb—"and Relevance"—he pointed to the red biomb—"are perfectly safe. I just thought…given that they are the ones most involved in our discussion…that they should be present." He stared down at the tiny forms and shook his head somberly. "Though they can't speak for themselves, they do have rights, which must be considered."

Peering at the two infants, a rush of pity filled Max. The human fetus that Omega had used to create him would have been as young, probably much younger. His baby self never had a chance to experience life as a human infant naturally would. Now these—

He wasn't sure what was happening, but it wasn't good. His whole body felt disconnected, weak, at a distance from itself. Could *he* faint?

From far away, Justine's voice called to him, "Max? Max!"

The last image in his mind was the scowl etched deep on baby Relevance's face.

Chapter Fourteen

Truth Is a Mercy

—Newearth Docking Bay, Ingot Suite—

Saturday, April 8th

Cobalt stood before the hologram of his Unit Commander in the center of the depressingly bland Ingot suite on the fourth tier of the docking bay and tried to keep a straight face.

Commander Scoria, bulky in his armored bio-suit, glared, as usual, his thin brows permanently knit into a frown, and boomed from the distant planet of Ingilium, "I want to know when we can have it! We need replacements now."

Never one to voluntarily put his life on the line, Cobalt tried appeasement first. "Taug is growing the thing as fast as he can. It's a complicated process, raising a tribrid. But once he has complete success, he will share the entire process with us. We no longer have to worry. Our future is assured."

In an oddly human manner, Scoria snorted. "You don't understand our predicament, do you? Those seeds we gave you were all that we had. The last of our line. We are out of options. If Taug fails, our whole civilization fails."

Bemused, Cobalt wanted to laugh, but he had never known many other Ingots who could comprehend laughter, much less laugh with him. He restrained himself. Clearly, Scoria was not the exception.

Would reason work?

"We are advanced well beyond mere biology. I see no reason for us to continue the humanoid façade. Perhaps we should transition to full techno-units." He shrugged disarmingly. "Then we'd never have to concern ourselves with eggs and seeds again."

The bafflement on Scoria's face was priceless. If only the image could be preserved. Taug would appreciate it, most certainly.

Unfortunately, bafflement soon turned to rage. "Have you no mind? Do you know nothing of our history—the utter failure of the Born-Again cult since they had no real shield, just their pathetic desire to return to their honest origins? Even the Cresta warned us that we were devolving—" Scoria rubbed his temples and sighed. "I forgot; they replaced history with progressive intelligence." He leaned in, almost as if he thought he could grab ahold of Cobalt.

Just to be on the safe side, Cobalt took a step back and attempted a conciliatory smile. "Yes. We are progressive beings. Our humanoid heritage has always been a weakness. It's time we were done with it. I suggest that losing our lineage may have been the best thing to happen to us. Now we can move on."

Scoria's eyes narrowed. "You are a fool among fools. The Born-Agains were right on that point—our sentience does depend upon our humanoid origin. If we lose all contact with that, we lose sentience!"

Belief rarely came into an Ingot equation, but for a split second, Cobalt felt the need to defy his commander and insist that he knew what he believed: Ingots were not humanoids anymore; they had evolved beyond their heritage.

Not one to leave the point half-made, Scoria pounded the facts home. "Our humanoid ancestors adapted technology to assist our physiology. Except for a few rare "return-to-our-origin" types, our entire race has grown completely dependent on technology. But at the same time, technology depends on our sentient nature. Techno-bots merely reproduce themselves, and, at most, add variations, but no bot can create.

More to the point, no bot *cares* to create."

Cobalt's mind tried to wiggle out of the knot tying up his thinking. "But how about Max and Justine? They are sentient androids."

A grimace advised Cobalt to be more careful.

"They are not and never were pure androids. Even the Eternals used human fetuses to create such unique life forms. We can dream of such ends, but we have not come close. And we never will, if we don't have our human, sentient core!"

A weight like he had never felt before landed on Cobalt's chest. "Relevance is our only hope, now?"

"Relevance or someone much like him. We may dislike our humanoid origin, but we need it. That's why our seeds are failing, our eggs are barren: We lost the fruit of our existence."

"We can't reproduce it?"

Scoria snarled his words. "We don't even know what it is."

For the first time in his existence, Cobalt understood why he could laugh. And, now, why he wanted to cry. Absurdity made both.

—Faye's Apartment—

Tuesday, May 23rd

Faye liked visuals. Perhaps it had something to do with the way her mother had always fluttered her hands when she spoke, practically drawing pictures in the air. Or maybe it had something to do with Bhuaci's love for physical adornments, small traits like almond eyes, radiant hair color, exquisite clothing, and sensitive expressions, which added meaning to their chosen form, notifying even the most unobservant that they were unique in a universe filled with self-important beings.

She stood before her full-length mirror in her pink and yellow bedroom and considered her pixie-like reflection. She had chosen her sky-blue pastel dress carefully and added the small broach, depicting a line of children holding hands, with trepidation lest Taug think it gaudy. But, surely, the peacock feather belt with the all-seeing central eye would make him pause, if nothing else.

Tucking a stray lock of golden hair behind her ear, she smiled at the mirror image. She had never chosen to be a beauty in the traditional sense. For so long, she had remained hidden that after her true identity was revealed, she felt forever shy, like a country child who could never get used to big-city life. Still, she was proud of the reflected Faye. A face and form crafted over long, difficult years, trying to find just the right look to match how she felt inside without exposing her weakness to the world.

A chime rang in the living room. Taug had arrived. It was time. She lighted one lilac-scented candle on the shelf in her bedroom, bowed, and clasped her hands. *Help me, Supreme Spirit. I know what I must do, but it's so hard when it involves a friend.* She waited, listening.

Truth is a mercy.

Peace filled her. She bowed her head.

When the chime repeated, she rushed from the room, praying that she had the wisdom to discern the truth and strength enough to show mercy.

After being let in, Taug practically bounced into the open kitchen on the left, his tentacles clutching gifts. His beaming eyes manifested perfect happiness. He thrust out a bottle of Green and placed it with his assortment of treats on the kitchen table. "I have been waiting so long for our first private day together. I thought you'd never return, and then there was the whole reconciliation hullabaloo, and I must be honest and say that it has been a definite challenge to raise the babies with everyone interfering the way they do. Cobalt has become downright obnoxious. He wants to know every detail of my day, and last month, he practically demanded that I give him my recipe." Taug thrust his tentacles over his protruding middle in an attitude of haughty martyrdom.

Faye sighed. *This will be harder than I thought.*

A bell chimed. *Good thing I'm not doing this alone.*

Before Taug could protest, she scurried to the door.

When the door opened, Kendra stood there holding Zara's hand. They both offered brave smiles.

Relief flooded over Faye. She hugged Kendra and then took Zara's free hand and led the two new guests to her kitchen table.

A pout puckered Taug's mouth, and bubbles rose quarrelsomely from his breathing helm. He spread his tentacles wide. "I thought we were going to have a *private* gathering."

At his tone, Zara hung back, and Kendra stopped in her tracks.

Faye slapped on her most charming smile and retreated to the freezer. With a few deft movements, she retrieved an ornate ice cream cake with fourteen decorative candles arranged around the edge. She glanced from Zara to Taug. "Since we didn't actually know the true date, we chose today as Zara's birthday, and I asked Kendra to bring her over for a little celebration. With your kind generosity, I knew you wouldn't mind a small interruption."

Initial perplexity passed quickly over Taug's face, and then he smiled in benevolence. "Well, I always enjoy a party." He toddled closer and inspected the colorful confection. It looks beautiful. Must have taken you an age to get all the layers arranged."

Faye glanced aside. “Kendra helped.”

Still standing by the cabinets, Zara simply peered ahead, her expression revealing none of her thoughts.

Kendra made herself at home and began retrieving plates, a cutting knife, and spoons.

Faye bustled about, preparing tea for her guests. She shot a meaningful glance at Taug.

Fully committed to enjoying himself once again, Taug gently led Zara to the table. Uncertainly, he glanced around. The game figures—having been returned to Faye—now stood on the cabinet to his left, a shaft of morning light pooling them in a warm glow. A gleam entered his eyes. “Oh, say, you might enjoy playing with these wonderful little figures.” He bustled over, retrieved as many as he could hold, and placed them on the table.” Here we go!” He pointed to one and then others. “This is me and that’s Faye. Here is Max and Justine…and—look! Here’s you!” He chuckled as he plucked up one figure and examined it closely. “Must be Kendra, though she looks more well-rounded in real life.” He returned to the other figures. “And no one can mistake Bala! Here’s—” He babbled on happily.

Faye placed sugar and creamer on the table.

Kendra arranged the place settings, her fingers working mechanically but her gaze flashing from Faye to Zara, a hint of fear in her eyes.

A frown building, Zara lifted the figure of herself and stared at it. Then she grabbed the infant. She held them, one in each hand, and glanced from one to the other. “This is me.” She raised the infant figure in her hand. “And this is me.” She scowled at the fully formed figure.”

Chuckling, Taug laughed and snatched the infant from her fingers. “No, you silly child. This is my son, Relevance. He’s nearly six months prenatal now and growing fast. I’m sure this must be him, since Sterling made such a fuss about his coming into existence."

Faye hurriedly finished placing the tea things, grabbed a lighter, and started lighting the candles.

Her eyes stormy, Zara held her position. "How was I grown?"

Faye sucked in a breath and placed a hand on Zara's shoulder. "Let's sing Happy Birthday, so you can make a wish. Then we'll have some cake, and Uncle Taug, since he is an expert, can tell you all about it."

Momentarily flustered, Taug appeared to choke on a massive release of bubbles from his breathing helm. Once he regained control of himself, the song was sung, Zara made a silent wish, blew out the candles, and everyone was presented with a portion of the beautiful cake.

They all sat down at the table.

Faye poured the tea and sat back on her padded chair. She nodded to Taug in silent command.

Hunched forward, Kendra shoved a piece of cake in her mouth, either focused on doing the dessert justice or trying to keep her mouth too full to interrupt.

Taug shoved the sweet treat aside and poured the tea into his breathing helm. A momentary savoring expression rippled over his face, and then he crossed his tentacles over his ample lap. He peered congenially at Zara. "Yes, well, I suppose this will be good practice for when Relevance grows up and wants to know where he came from."

After wiping a smear from her lips with the back of her hand, Zara stared at Taug. "Omega made me. Abbas didn't know about it, but once he learned of me, he accepted my existence."

Taug tilted his head. "Yes. It's sad that your creator was so emotionally motivated. He hardly knew what he was doing. I suspect that he never even took notes!" A smug smile. "I retraced his process as best as I was able." He leaned forward.

"I have to thank you, Zara, for much of what I learned came from helping you, after that unfortunate incident…"

Kendra's head snapped up, her eyes flashing. "She was just a child, abandoned by Omega, without understanding!"

A formidable frown and Taug attempted to put Kendra in her proper place. "The very reason that I chose to help her." He shrugged. "Never could expect much from such an unscientific being. Though it is true, he has learned to be sorry for his mistakes."

Zara shoved her empty plate forward and propped her elbows on the table, her gaze never leaving Taug's face. "Are you sorry?"

Taug blinked innocently. "For what, my dear?"

"For pretending to be a real Creator."

This time, Taug's choking took a full minute to subside.

Faye attempted to adjust his breathing helm while Kendra took Zara's hand and led her toward the front door. "It's my fault. When she asked me where babies came from, I told her that the Creator makes them and gives them to mothers." She sighed. "We best be going now."

Halting in her tracks, Zara scowled at Taug. "Who is Relevance's mother? I have Justine because Omega gave me to her. But who will you give Relevance to?"

With a mighty effort, Taug rasped his swords. "He is mine! I made him for me."

Her face churning in fury, Zara yanked out of Kendra's grasp, ran over, and snatched the infant figure off the table. She threw it at Taug. "There! That's *your* Relevance." She hissed her last words, "Real babies want real mothers."

After they had gone, Taug glowered silently on the couch.

Faye cleared the dishes off the table and then placed the figures back on the shelf. She considered the infant figure, the little girl figure with mismatched eyes and marbled skin, and realized that they were one infant figure short. *Was this figure supposed to be Herson? No one saw Relevance coming...* With anxiety filling her, she glanced over her shoulder at Taug. He looked miserable: angry and affronted. She sighed. What a mess. *Truth may be a mercy, but how it hurts.*

Chapter Fifteen

With Lilies O'er Spread.

—Shopping Center Courtyard—

Friday Morning, June 2nd

Justine weaved through the open courtyard of the crowded shopping center with Zara keeping pace on her right. The shop she wanted was just up ahead. There! The picture on the plate-glass window—dancing birds dressed in colorful garments—with the words dangling above, "Birds with fine feathers flock together."

Zara huffed and stopped just outside the door with her hands propped on her hips, a petulant expression on her face. "Why couldn't we have done our shopping at home? We always pick out my clothes from Newearth Holopad Fashions. Why get mixed up with all of this?" She spread her arms wide as if encompassing the entire, bustling seventeen-story shopping extravaganza.

Justine looked around. It was a bit of a madhouse with myriad shoppers darting in every direction, hustling for everything from the finest OldEarth ale to a well-tuned zither.

A food station stood to the left, tables and benches arranged a comfortable distance apart. Justine stepped to the closest table and dropped down on a chair. "Sit; I'll order a snack. Then we can discuss the importance of mingling and why I want you to see more of the world."

With a long-suffering sigh, Zara perched on the edge of the chair and shook her head, her gaze drifting upward to a band of Uanyi youths racing along the third-story balcony, calling for someone up ahead. She wrinkled her nose. "They certainly know nothing about style. Unless they are trying to look ugly. Then, I'd say they hit the mark."

Justine pulled out her datapad, tapped in a few snack options for their location, took a selfie, hit the pay button, and slid the thing back into her sleeve pocket.

Zara's eyes followed a Bhuaci couple holding hands and then latched on to an Ingot who passed by with a metal beam in one hand and a pair of hard-soled boots in the other.

Myriad scents wafted through the courtyard: sweet drinks and spicy entrees, fruity blossoms from the flower shop, sweaty humans hustling through, salty Cresta breathing helms bubbling at maximum capacity as sales personnel tried to convince one of their scientific minds to buy a new product.

At least I'm not adding to the smelly universe. Justine sighed as she eyed a perfume shop directly opposite her.

A serving bot zoomed in, checked Justine's face for ID, and then placed a tray laden with two tall drinks, a plate of Nutra-cheese, Vita-crackers, and a bowl brimful of cubed fruit on the table.

Without a word, Zara started in on the cheese.

A tall man, perfectly formed with squared shoulders and an innocent expression, sped by in front of them.

Zara froze. Then she jumped to her feet and called out, "Max?"

As if deaf, the man didn't break his momentum and entered a jewelry store.

Her eyes wide, Zara faced Justine. "I thought that was—"

"Yeah. I know. Easy mistake to make." Justine closed her eyes, trying to gather her scattered thoughts. *Why did we come here?* The images of Max's blank stare and his apathetic efforts the last couple of months rolled through her mind like a tragic silent movie. What had happened to the Max Wheeler that she had come to know and trust? To love?

"He's got a virus, hasn't he?"

Justine opened her eyes and stared at the child of uncertain age. She took a sip of her drink, stalling for time. *Sit straight, face my daughter, compose myself.* "It's not a virus. It's…I don't know how to explain exactly. But I need to tell you something: Max and I are different."

Returning to her seat, Zara squinted as if the light streaming down from an overhead skylight was too bright. "You're both human-androids created by Omega. You are the same."

Justine shook her head. "Perhaps we were created the same, but we've had very different life experiences. I was tried for war crimes and turned off for seventy years. Max lived his whole existence working for traders and, despite a brief stint working as a guard at Bothmal, he never had to deal with the dark side of—"

"What are you talking about? He had to go to Mirage-Reborn and help deal with a civil war. He's overseen the management of the largest docking bay this side of the Divide. He has dealt with all sorts of things!"

Forcing her overactive mind to slow down, Justine clipped her words. "Not inside himself. Not really. He's always been innocent of interior evil. He has just barely begun to comprehend some of his human manifestations, but always like a little child discovering how to walk and talk. Never how to hit and bite."

Zara's eyes narrowed to slits. "You want Max to learn how to hit and bite? That's what got me into trouble, why Simms and the Cresta did what they did—fixing me so I'm not so wild now."

Amazed, Justine stared at her daughter. "You know about that?"

"Cerulean told me. He said that I had better know the

truth before someone told me a twisted tale."

Something beautiful rippled through Justine, and she grinned. *So like Cerulean.* "I'm glad he did. I was waiting till you were older to say anything. But I want you to understand that Omega may not have known exactly what he was doing when he created you, but he did act with love. He wanted me to experience motherhood, trying to right an old wrong."

Zara scrunched her nose as if at a bad smell. "Omega can't do anything wrong. He's an Eternal. They're perfect."

Justine shook her head. This was getting much too complicated. She had only wanted to discuss Max, not delve into the murky depths of immortal though imperfect beings created by something beyond understanding. She nibbled a Vita-cracker. Gathered her courage. And dove in.

"The Eternals were created by a force that we don't understand. Not yet anyway. Maybe we never will. But though they are immortal, they have free will and are capable of making choices, sometimes bad choices. Omega made an uninformed choice when he made Max and me."

Zara's expression remained a cross between distaste and fascination.

"He wanted to experience the act of creating a new life form, but at that time, he had no notion of suffering." She sipped her water and steadied the images flashing through her mind. "He didn't know what pain was. Not until he was forced to endure torment did he comprehend what he had done in unloosing me in a strange world and sending Max off to manage by himself." She swiped tangled thoughts away. "But that's not what concerns us now."

"Max is in trouble; isn't he?"

Justine offered a quick nod. "I came to understand suffering and guilt years ago when I had Cerulean to help me and an old friend named Derik to love me. Max originally thought, with good reason perhaps, that he was the best of

Omega's creations. He honestly believed that he could do no wrong."

Leaning in, Zara squinted at Justine, as if that might help her understand. "*Max* is doing something wrong?"

Her fist hit the table before Justine realized the power of her reaction.

Zara jumped, alarmed.

The table leaned to one side.

A desire to tug Zara onto her lap and rock her like a baby filled Justine with maddening need. With heroic effort, she forced herself to appear calm. "Sorry. I didn't mean to slap the table."

"Slap? You broke the table!" Zara's eyebrows knit into angry knots. "Max isn't guilty of anything!" With a stomp of her foot, she was off, racing across the tiled floor.

In a flash, Justine ran after her, gripped her shoulder, and stopped the girl in her tracks. "Wait! You must understand. Max isn't doing anything wrong, but he realizes now that Omega did wrong when he created him. He ought to have had a chance to be a fully human baby and develop in his own family. Cheated out of a significant part of his life experience bothers him. Justly so. But he doesn't know how to deal with deep hurt. How to be angry. Not safely."

Her gaze appearing to turn inward, Zara stood as still as stone. Emotions flowed over her face like ripples over a pond.

In silent hesitation, Justine prayed they would not rise into a storm.

"It's because of Herson and Relevance. They're growing in biombs." She shrugged. "But Max knows about Ingots…"

"He never made a personal connection before. Now, he has experienced Bala's family, and he compares that to the biomb, and he knows what he missed…what Herson and Relevance are missing. Sometimes we realize just how bad something is when it is done to another person. Then we understand; we were innocent and should have been protected by those who knew better."

Suddenly Zara stared hard into Justine's face. "Was I ever a baby?"

Horror sizzled like fire through Justine. "I assume so."

"I'll never know my parents…or my brothers or sisters…if I had any."

Justine squeezed out her words. "You have Max and me."

Zara leaned against Justine and closed her eyes. "Can I *not* care?"

Sorrow filled Justine to the depth of her being. "You can try."

—Breakfastnook Café—

Mid-Day

Gavin ignored the chattering lunch crowd seated in booths and perched on stools throughout the café and drummed his fingers on the cream-colored tabletop. He practiced slow breaths to keep his anger in check and glanced up when the door chimes rang.

Four Uanyi youths scuffled into the dining room, talking in loud voices, clearly excited about something.

Not interested in the least, Gavin scanned the room again. Cobalt couldn't have snuck in without his noticing, could he? He rotated in the chair, checking all angles. No. Not one Ingot in the whole place.

With a pleased expression and wearing a colorful apron over his immaculate white uniform, Riko sauntered up. "You looking for someone? I can get you something while you wait. How about a dish of my spicy salsa and a side of corn chips?"

Aware that he had enough units to pay for countless meals, thanks to Cerulean, Gavin seriously considered the idea. He had enjoyed the Amens' salsa and chips and figured that "spicy" wouldn't make much difference. He nodded agreeably.

Just as Riko traipsed off to fulfill his latest culinary delight, Cobalt sidled into the café, a strange expression on his face. *Hunted?* The idea was ludicrous enough to shove to the side while the Ingot made his way to the table.

Stiff with controlled anger, Gavin nodded.

A thin-lipped smile and Cobalt slid onto the seat opposite him. "I wasn't sure you'd be here."

Processing the words carefully, Gavin decided that he had misunderstood. "You ask to meet. I come." He lifted his hands in supplication, clipping his words. "What. Do. You. Want?"

Cobalt dropped his gaze and rubbed his forehead, wincing, as if he had a pain between his eyes.

Ingots feel pain? Gavin stored this new possibility in the back of his mind. His disgust for Ingot reproduction systems had not lessened one grain. *Perhaps suffering would be good for him.*

Riko trotted forward and laid a tray with chips, salsa, and two tall glasses of water on the table. He stood back and grinned. "Can I get you anything else?"

Cobalt waved Riko off, clearly trying to get rid of an irritant.

Stiff-faced, Riko turned and left them to their business.

Gavin shoved the chips aside and leaned in. "Why meet, Ingot? I leave tomorrow. Newearth is a trap. Not a home."

Cobalt lifted his gaze and, shockingly, tears swam in his eyes. "I'm dead. My people are dead. No one can save us now."

His stomach tightening, the image of the dead mother wolf flashed through Cobalt's mind. This creature before him was not acting on instinct. It was not innocent! *Still…*

With a shudder, Cobalt clasped his hands beseechingly. "You must help us, Gavin. You have the power to make your people understand that we will die without your assistance. We aren't asking you to become like us. We just want a few DNA strands to repopulate our species. We will never be pure again, but our race will at least survive in some form." His soft gaze bespoke sincere need and honest humility. "Please?"

Begrudgingly, Gavin felt his anger melting away.

A young Ingot that Gavin didn't know, though Cerulean had mentioned him in passing a couple of times, drew near. *Wedel? Wendy?*

Cobalt propped his head on his hands and stared vacantly ahead.

The young Ingot stopped beside the table and waited patiently.

Glancing over, Gavin considered the youthful figure only partially garbed in Ingot gear. And odd sight, like a half-done drawing or partially full moon. He spoke to the youth, "You want something?"

Rather than addressing Gavin, the young Ingot addressed Cobalt. "I am Wendell. From Ingilium but not like you." He pointed to his head with no headgear and his incomplete Ingot bio-ware. "I was reject. But useful now. Have what you need to save Ingots."

Slowly, Cobalt's eyes focused on Wendell. His tears dried, and his expression changed from desperate pleading to slippery cunning.

Fear ripped through Gavin. "No!" He rose and gripped Wendell's arm. "Come with me, boy. I go home; my family accept you…love you." He spat his words at Cobalt. "Not like him. He only wants pieces of you."

Faster than seemed possible, Cobalt rose and forced Gavin's arm off Wendell. He gripped the youth by the shoulder and shoved him toward the door. “Let’s go. If you’re right, boy, you’ll never be a reject again. You’ll be a savior.”

Cold fury lashed Gavin to the spot as the two figures tromped to the door.

The bell chime clanged as Gavin swung it open.

Sauntering in from the kitchen, Riko frowned at Wendell’s back as the Ingots reached the front door. “Hey, you’ve still got another hour before your break. Where do you think you’re going?”

Gavin raced over to Riko. “Stop him! Cobalt steals your boy!”

Wendell looked over his shoulder, even as Cobalt drew him across the threshold. A sad certainty in his eyes and a shake of the head halted Gavin and Riko in their tracks. He lifted his hands beseechingly. “I am Ingot. Go now. Come back later.” He followed Cobalt into the bright noonday sun.

Riko ran to the door and watched them hurry to a Skybus ready for liftoff.

Gavin stood beside him, a groan rising from his gut. “Metal man will kill pups. Not innocent, like me.”

Slapping his hands together in impotent fury, Riko rounded on Gavin. “I don’t know what you just said, but I’m not letting that kid off this planet. I may not be able to challenge an Ingot Representative, but I know someone who can.” He glared at Gavin and wagged his finger accusingly. “You know what’s going on! Are you coming?”

Gavin remembered the ship that was to take him home to his parents and those who knew and loved him. With a grieving heart, he wished it a safe journey. He refocused and met Riko’s hard gaze. “We save your son.”

Shouting directions to his kitchen staff, Riko swiped off his apron. Then shaking his head ominously, he started for the door. “He’s not my son. He’s just a kid who…” With a startled expression, Riko stopped and swallowed hard. His eyes widened. "Yeah. Let's go save my son."

As they trotted toward the Central Basin Tube leading to Cerulean's home, Gavin thought of the babies in the hard shells. He, too, had a son.

—Department of Human Services—

Late Afternoon

Clare yawned, closed her computer file, and stretched back in her office chair. She glanced around.

The Human Services official meeting space—centered on the main holopad with four curved screens hanging around the perimeter—stood empty. In the morning, they had had a formal conference with Deputy Chief Lowman and Chief Benz descending from the upper echelons of the four-story building. Poor Captain Walt looked like he might melt into the floor, his sensitive heart breaking under the pressure of Human Services' worthy purpose.

She sighed. They spoke in deep impressive tones, but, ultimately, it was the same old, same old: Ingot drug counterfeits, Bhuaci newcomers dancing au naturel in the local park upsetting conservative members of the city, a Cresta mishap at the community pool involving live sea creatures and three taunting Uanyi youths, and a half dozen domestic disputes in human homes. What was so significant about a multi-race world where beings didn't understand each other?

Across the room, Bala sat perched on the edge of his chair, his back straight and his eyes focused on his screen. A man of intense concentration.

When he feels like it.

She rose and strolled over to his desk. "Please tell me that you're working on something interesting, something we can sink our teeth into."

Deadpanned, Bala looked at her. "Well, yes, this case does involve the possibility of teeth sinking into something but not quite the way you imagine."

Holding her heart in check, Clare maintained her casual pose.

Bala turned his screen toward Clare.

Before her eyes appeared, what looked like a small dog about fifty centimeters high but with three-inch curved fangs, large almond eyes, long curly fur, and three-toed feet that resembled talons. She squinted as she read the caption. "A domesticated Arturian Yipper?"

His arms folded over his chest; Bala assumed the role of pedagogue. "It was originally brought in by an Ingot trader as a pet, but it has been used for years as home protection."

Clare nodded. "Those talons and fangs certainly look dangerous."

"They *appear* ferocious, but they are actually just ornate weapons, practically useless in a fight. It's their long series of ear-splitting yips that make them good protection. So sensitive to the slightest unusual sound or movement that they are the best alarm system a family could have."

Smirking, Clare shrugged. "With Kendra around, I hardly think your family needs more security."

Bala returned a fake smile. "This one got loose from the home of an eccentric Bhuaci family and hid itself under their neighbor's front porch."

Suddenly exhausted, Clare rubbed her forehead. "So why do we care?"

"The neighbor shot it with a dustbuster, and then the Bhuaci family vowed to shoot their neighbor."

A spark of excitement lit Clare's bored brain cells. "I can go over there with you right now and settle things if you like."

A real grin this time and Bala tapped his screen. It blinked to black. "No, thanks. I sent over a replacement Yipper with sincere apologies from the neighbor."

"You think that will work?"

"Already has. I chatted with the Bhuaci family a few minutes ago, and they've invited their neighbor over for dinner tonight. Best buddies now. Just took a little forgiveness and a free course on how to train Yippers to stay in their own yard." He scrunched up his nose. "I thought about getting one for the kids but changed my mind. I'd rather have a penguin." He shrugged through a sigh. "But no icebergs within three thousand kilometers, so that idea is out."

Bala stood and flung his suit jacket over his shoulders. "Well, I'd better get going. Kendra warned me that I'm cooking dinner tonight, and I better not be late. She woke up tired and hungry this morning."

Looking much too chipper for a guy who had to concoct a meal for nine people, Bala sauntered across the office, saluting the last of the day shift and offering condolences to the night shift as they passed in.

Clare sighed. There was nothing more to accomplish, as the few cases she had were waiting on forensics results. She might as well head home too. The thought of her empty house sent a shudder through her whole body.

After closing her files and leaving her desk neat and tidy, Clare wandered outside. The sun was still high enough to make a stop at VR Vista Entertainment worth her while. She was a third of the way through her tour of St. Basil's Cathedral, OldEarth, Moscow, Russia. She could hardly get enough of the brilliant color design. Though going in person was not out of the question, the VR option allowed her to pause the tour and go home whenever she wanted. Plus, she liked the feel of "being there" without the expense and sweat. Her mood picked up as she considered dining options near VR

Vista. Just as she drew out her datapad to make a reservation, it pinged a reminder message: Time to visit Herson.

Gloom filled Clare, ruining her momentary good mood. Then guilt chased her gloom into a dark corner and screamed at it.

With trudging steps, she crossed the street and headed toward the Breakfastnook Café and Taug's lab. With any luck, he wouldn't be there, and she could grab a bite to eat before heading home.

Would motherhood always be this hard?

A heavy weight pressed on her chest, heightening the fear that this might only be the beginning.

Once inside the bustling café, she looked around for Riko. Nowhere in sight. How about Wendell? He was always helpful and knew her dinner favorites better than anyone. She stopped at the counter and leaned against the last empty stool, glancing about. Nope. He wasn't around either. Odd. Usually, one of them was on hand for the dinner rush.

Finally, Jayla flew by, heading into the throng, two loaded trays balanced on her arms.

"Hey, Jayla, where's everyone?"

Jayla continued forward, heading toward a table packed with hungry Uanyi customers. "If you mean Riko and Wendell, they went out earlier, and I haven't seen either for hours. It's been a madhouse all afternoon, and I'm going to wring their scrawny necks for leaving me short-staffed." Once at the table, she got down to business and unloaded the tray, while snapping witty comebacks to keep the rambunctious Uanyi teens from getting out of hand.

Not wanting to get in Jayla's way, Clare decided that she'd do her motherly duty first and hoped that the crowd had thinned out by the time she was ready to eat.

Use the private side door, or go through the kitchen and figure that no one cared that she was visiting a Taug's lab?

Again.

Oh, let's just get this over with.

She sidled to the door, rang the bell, waited, then grew impatient and used her eye scan to get inside. Taug understood that, as a mother, she should have access to her baby whenever she felt the need. Though he had asked her politely to always ring first. Just in case.

In case of what, he never clarified. And Clare didn't want to know.

Once inside, she realized how late in the day it was getting as the skylight had dimmed to a mute gray.

She looked around for the biombs, which were usually centered in the middle of the room in plain sight. Dissecting tables, trays, vats, the bulky procedure chair, scanners, and other assorted instruments of a well-stocked laboratory. But no biombs, no babies. *Where are they?*

Alarm filled Clare. What if Taug had stolen her baby? Taken him back to Crestar to experiment on! Her whole body heated in a rush of fear and fury. "Almighty have mercy, what if—"

A tiny sound caught her ear. With a gulp, she raced across the room, bumped into the procedure chair, swiveled, and headed toward the reception area, what Taug had recently started calling his "Family Room."

There, nestled in front of matching cushioned chairs, stood the blue and red biombs. Exhaling a long breath, Clare tried to calm her heart rate back to something close to normal.

The chairs were pulled up close to the biombs in the snug space. Apparently, Taug wanted to sit in comfort as he prattled away at the six-month-old developing infants.

Dropping onto the chair before Herson, she gathered her scattered wits. Why had she panicked? What was *that* all about? Then, like a tidal wave roaring over her, tumbling her under the current of daily life, she faced the truth hidden deep inside. She cared. Though she didn't get all sentimental and talk in a cooing voice as moms sometimes did, still, Herson mattered to her.

She stared at the biomb and an image of a large wooden door filled her mind. Strangely, this same image had haunted her dreams for weeks, but she usually forgot about it soon after waking. Only at odd moments did flashes remind her of some sequence, which usually did not make sense but filled her with dread. The door was unlike anything she had encountered in real life so she could not think where it came from. It had seemed to be closing a bit more each day…or rather each night. In her last dream, she had thought for sure that she would hear the muffled clunk of the wood hitting the metal lock. But no…not yet.

A sound made her look up. Squinting, she crept nearer her son's biomb. His fist was smashed against his mouth…*sucking his thumb?*

Herson was still as could be, peaceful even.

A sharp movement and a click.

She glanced aside. Relevance twitched so powerfully, his red biomb jerked.

Her gut clenched; she wasn't sure what to do. Leaning in, she peered at the tribrid infant. Well-formed, good proportions, a solid build, the baby seemed perfect. Handsome even.

Twitch. The biomb jerked again.

Clare rubbed her face. Relevance was Taug's baby—not hers. She lifted her hands and stepped aside to the blue biomb.

Herson wasn't handsome. His scrawny body seemed weak and underdeveloped compared to Relevance. Her heart thudded as she considered how difficult his life would be in a world where might often made right. A hybrid, even as close as Human and Tabun genetics might be, still meant that he would be set apart in a way few people could ever understand.

Her vision blurred as tears filled her eyes. A choking sob rose from her chest. "I'm so sorry I messed this whole thing up, Herson. I should never have let Taug take control. If I wanted a baby, I should have…Well, *I* should have paid the price. Not you."

Herson stretched, sliding his fist off his face. Though his eyes were closed, his mouth turned up in what looked very much like a smile.

Hiccupping through her tears, Clare pressed her hands against the biomb and cried. "I will make things right, baby. Promise. I'll…take care of you…act like a real mother from now on."

As the last of the light leaked from the skylight and thunder rumbled in the distance, Clare stayed with her son, alternating between choking sobs and snatches of a lullaby her mother used to sing to her…

Lullaby and good night.
With roses bedight.
With lilies o'er spread.
Is baby's wee bed.

Lay you down, now and rest.
May your slumber be blest…

Chapter Sixteen

Worthy of Existence

—Ingot Trading Vessel—

Sunday, June 4th

Cobalt loved to fly. He had spent many years as a deep space trader and knew the directional console better than the back of his metallic hand. The mere sight of the instrument panel before him sent an electric current through his system.

Forty-eight hours with Wendell was enough to convince him that he wasn't weighed down by an overabundance of human sensibilities. He could hardly understand the youth, no matter how related they may be. *He's more human than Ingot, perhaps even tainted by that sly Uanyi he worked for.*

After pulling away from the Newearth Docking Bay and clearing the orbital debris left from OldEarth days, he set the cruise control for Ingilium. There were asteroid pockets that he had to navigate personally, but that only added excitement to the otherwise ordinary two-Newearth Day excursion. Space flow from Newearth to Ingilium was so routine now that most ships were managed with autopilots and a first-year student.

A groan caught his ear, and he glanced aside.

Distinctively off-color, Wendell held his head in his hands, leaning forward in the assistant's bucket seat.

Cobalt had to suppress a grunt. He'd invited the reject to sit in front of the directional bay window, facing the universe as they traversed across limitless space, and all the infant could do was moan and squirm. *What next? Regurgitate his breakfast onto the floor mat?*

“What is the matter with you? Besides the obvious.”

Lifting his head, Wendell stared at Cobalt through wide, anxious eyes. “I never travel. Don’t know how.”

The absurdity of this notion caught Cobalt off guard. “You’ve taken a Skybus, right? Driven autoskimmers? Ridden the tube?” He shrugged. “This isn’t so different than those.”

Wendell shook his head. “I walk.”

“Walk!” Cobalt knew the distance from Wendell’s apartment to the café, the nearest grocer, repair clinic, or any store for that matter, or to any of his friends’ homes. The distance was enough to make walking the least desirable option. “Surely you don’t walk everywhere you go.”

A brief attempt to look up at the screen, and immediately, Wendell squeezed his eyes shut again, crouching forward. “I walk. Or jog.”

The term “ludicrous” suddenly made sense to Cobalt. In the Ingot world, any word referring to unusual behavior would simply be encompassed by the term “malfunctioning.” But human speech contained odd subtleties which he was only now beginning to appreciate. He tapped his ear reflexively, as if he was still using a translator to communicate to Gavin. Realizing his mistake, he dropped his hands to his lap and stared at the streaks of stars as they sped through vast space. A question pounded inside his mind until he had to let it free. “Why walk?”

With his hands wrapped over his head, still leaning forward, Wendell spoke in muffled tones, “I like the ground…air…sky…world. Not want to miss it.”

Suddenly hot and irritated beyond any feigned kindness, Cobalt gripped Wendell’s collar and pulled him to a straight position. “Get ahold of yourself, reject! You can’t arrive on Ingilium quivering like an electrocuted Cresta.”

His shoulders still slumped but now upright, Wendell

seemed to gain firmer footing. Wordlessly, he stared at Cobalt.

Disconcerted by the intensity of the reject's expression, Cobalt waved his hand at the screen and turned the conversation. "Look! See what you've been missing all your life? The universe. As an Ingot specializing in trading in every quadrant this side of The Divide, I know the marvels of deep space." He sneered. "You can't even imagine it. If you'd get over your weak stomach for a moment, consider that—because of our fortuitous meeting—you will not only return to your home world, but you now experience space flight as it was meant to be—fast and productive."

As Wendell stared at the streaks of stars rushing past, tears filled his eyes. "Stomach not weak. Heart hurts."

Disgust filled Cobalt. *Blast! He'll expire before the first round of tests.* Fury rising, Cobalt smacked a fist into his hand. "You never told me that you had a weak heart! We could have gotten a replacement while on Newearth. This will delay everything!"

Leaning back, Wendell eyed Cobalt as if he had never actually seen him before, a strange, knowing look in his eyes. "Not weak. Alive. My heart beats with Newearth. Space empty…no beat…no heart."

For a hundredth of a second that stretched into an eternity, Cobalt could not avoid the flash of understanding that exploded inside his mind. He knew exactly what Wendell meant. But he didn't want to.

A red light flashed on the panel. An asteroid belt was directly ahead. Cobalt had to take manual control to keep them from splintering into countless pieces.

Even though his hands did what they had been trained to do, automatically grasping the directional controls, Cobalt knew…it was too late. His heart was no longer in it.

—Ingot Command Chamber—

Tuesday, June 6th

Cobalt rose from the metal bench attached to the stark wall in the tan and brown room and offered his most officious smile to Commander Scoria.

Some enterprising Ingot had given each Command Chamber its own theme. With its brown floor, off-white ceiling, tan walls, and assorted cactus plants in each corner, an Ingot would have early exposure to the desert lands of over a dozen planets, most uninhabited but useful for mining expeditions. Though Cobalt preferred the jungle room, he had been calmed by the sheer banality of the environment. It certainly did nothing to stir his imagination, and at that moment in his life, automation and obedience were the better option.

Commander Scoria plunked down at a narrow table with a wide central screen and peered, from the medical room interior, back to Cobalt. "The specimen you brought is a perfect idiot. I doubt there's much that we can use off of him." He frowned at the screen. "Even his seed is probably useless. For low-grade workers, maybe, but that'll be about it."

An odd sense that Cobalt had never felt before began to worm its way through his mind. A desire to leave the room…hide even…nearly overmastered him. *Embarrassment?* He swallowed a metallic taste in his mouth. He had done nothing wrong. Followed orders, even been creative in seeing this opportunity through to its fullest conclusion. A hot flush worked over his body, making his skin itch. Alarmed, Cobalt recognized what a human might call shame and hurried across the small space to the repair unit.

"What are you doing?"

Cobalt glanced over his shoulder. "A quick repair. I've been so busy, I couldn't—"

"On your own time, 676III!"

Being called by his ID tag rather than his name wiped out any sense of warmth on Cobalt's person or in the room. He dropped his hands to his sides and turned around.

Scoria scowled darkly. "We still need the Cresta solution, so I want you to get back to Newearth and watch over Taug. Make sure that he's taking excellent notes on that tribrid he created. I want to start replicating his procedure as soon as possible."

The relief that filled Cobalt defied any words in his lexicon. "Back to Newearth? Certainly, Sir." Audaciously, he circled around Commander Scoria's desk and looked at the screen showing the medical procedure room where he had left Wendell. "As soon as the boy is ready, I will take him back with me."

His eyes narrowing, a hard line along his jaw, Commander Scoria rose to his feet and leaned into Cobalt's personal space. "Boy? The reject doesn't even have a proper tag. Once we're done with him, we'll harvest whatever is usable and compost the rest. Get ready now and return to Newearth immediately. No need to wait."

The illusion of being welcomed home by a grateful people, graciously offered a good meal, and some token of respect crumpled in the face of reality. What had Cobalt been thinking? Was he a human? A Luxonian? Even Gavin's people had treated him with greater kindness. But kindness was not what Ingots were known for. *Why did I ever think...*

"What are you waiting for? Stop looking like you've short-circuited and get moving. I don't trust that Cresta to keep us informed."

The refusal was out of his mouth before he could rephrase it into deferential form. "No, sir."

Scoria stretched to his full height, flexing his metallic arms. He had replaced nearly his entire body, part by part, until there was precious little of his original biology left. Part of the reason he was so powerful. Not everyone could survive such drastic transitions.

Scanning the figure before him, Cobalt could clearly see that only Scoria's face, brain, and a section of his trunk were still biological. Contempt filled him. *No wonder he doesn't care.*

"Are you refusing a direct order?"

Cobalt hardly knew where his words came from, but he suddenly understood that he could not give up on Wendell. Not without a fight. "He's a member of Newearth…has a job…and is known by many influential people. If he were to suddenly disappear, questions would be asked, and it would create hostilities. We need to maintain cordial relations." The metallic taste had turned sour. He swallowed it down. "I must take him back with me. Unharmed."

Tapping his hard fingers against his hard leg, Scoria appeared indecisive for a moment. Then his face cleared. "Yes. You are being logical. The reject is worthless as spare parts. But a spy working close to Taug's laboratory could be useful. I'll make sure that one of his eyes is replaced with an implant that records everything. You can give him specific directions on the return flight." A strange, benevolent smile cracked across Commander Scoria's face. "Good thinking, Cobalt. Despite appearances, you might rise in the ranks someday."

With that, Scoria turned to the screen, called an attendant to attention, and started giving new instructions. "Get the reject ready…"

Relief washed over Cobalt at the thought of Wendell's release, though, as he stared at the person inhabiting the metallic shell in front of him, a new feeling filled him: hate.

Even during battles, he had never actually hated anyone.

He turned away as a new thought struck him. Probably because he had never actually cared.

—Breakfastnook Café—

10:00 PM

Cerulean helped Riko shove two square tables together at the far end of the café's back dining room. Then they positioned chairs to accommodate six people, though they only needed room for five. He scratched his head. Riko must have miscounted.

Before he could say anything, Riko ambled back to the kitchen, humming to himself.

A spider hung from a silvery thread right above the table. Cerulean swiped at it, but it scurried up the line, out of harm's way.

Annoyed, he considered the cutlery on a nearby table but realized that it would be hard to explain why he was throwing forks and knives at Riko's ceiling.

He huffed his irritation. Their meetings up to this point had not solved problems but only deflected the deeper issue: personal rights vs. the good of the larger community. How could he ever get his friends, much less Newearth citizens and the Inter-Alien Alliance Committee, to realize that if personal rights were sacrificed for national interests, the nation itself would dissolve in the miasma of heartless survival? Turn people into objects and you reject everyone.

Cerulean considered the empty restaurant and decided that he preferred it bustling with happy patrons. A sigh escaped before he could stop it.

Riko returned with a grim expression. "I sent Jayla home with instructions to stay out of sight and talk to no one. I don't want her getting mixed up in all of this. Remember what happened to Bala a few years back, his house got torn apart, and his family was terrorized? Poor guy had a black eye for weeks after that."

Cerulean rubbed his neck. When had he ever felt so stiff before? He rolled his shoulders. "I'll never forget—"

The front door chime tinkled, and Bala sauntered into the room, a startling glint in his eyes. "Hey, Gang, ready for the next level of madness and mayhem? I'm here early and that doesn't happen often." He glanced about, his nose sniffing appraisingly. "There are refreshments, right? Cause I had to miss Kendra's pasta spinach salad for this, and you all know how much I adore spinach salad." He couldn't have appeared more serious.

Riko controlled a grin.

Before Cerulean could say anything, the chime rang again, and Justine stepped inside. Her direct gaze met Cerulean's and held him a moment. *Something is wrong.* He glanced up as if asking the ceiling—or the spider—to explain things. *Now what?* He tried not to tense up. His headache would only get worse.

Riko waved Bala toward the kitchen. "Skinny guy, help me carry things out. You honestly think that I, a reputable restaurant owner, would hold an important meeting without snacks? Don't know when I've been so insulted."

In puppy-like obedience, Bala hurried along at Riko's side chattering his commentary right through the doorway, while Justine met Cerulean in the middle of the diner.

Justine's gaze never wavered. "We need to talk."

The warmth of Justine's calm presence amazed Cerulean. *How does she do that?* His own body relaxed in return. "I'm always here for you, Justine. You know that." He gazed deeply into her eyes, trying to read their depths.

Before he could formulate another question, Justine changed the equation entirely. "It's not me. It's Max. He wants to kill himself."

All warmth instantly evaporated; Cerulean froze in place. He finally understood the strange human expression. He simply could not move.

It was just as well that Justine took his arm and towed him to the back corner near Taug's lab. She leaned against the wall, ignoring the security camera in the upper corners, and dropped her gaze to the floor. "I can't help him, Cerulean. He's depressed and doesn't know how to deal with it. I've never seen him like this."

Trying to formulate the image of a depressed android, Cerulean came up blank. "What do you mean depressed? Is he sullen? Unable to work?"

Justine nodded. "He refuses to recharge himself. Won't do any normal maintenance on his system, and he refuses to speak to anyone. He just said that he should never have been created. He even looks at me as if I'm a—" Her jaw clenched. "In his mind, Omega made a mistake in creating us, and all sentient races are now doomed because of it."

Irritation flared, igniting a new heat inside Cerulean. "And what does he want you—and Zara, by the way—to do with yourselves? What about the babies? We should condemn all hybrids to death in some kind of sacrificial apology? That won't unmake the past, Justine! It will only murder five innocent futures!"

"I'm not the judge or jury, Cerulean. You don't have to shout at me. I'm the defendant, remember?"

Completely deflated, Cerulean could hardly believe how fast he leaped backward when the intrusive spider suddenly dropped from the ceiling and morphed into the figure of Faye.

She tugged at her pink skirt and then glanced up

winningly. "Sorry, but I've been feeling a bit paranoid of late, so I decided to listen in before I joined your party."

After scraping the barest glance possible over Cerulean, Justine gave her full attention to the Bhuaci. "I should be the paranoid one. It's half-breeds like me who are being judged here. Are we worthy of existence?" She sighed. "Always the same old question, isn't it?"

The door chime rang again, and Riko bustled forward with Bala trailing behind, balancing three loaded trays in his arms.

Gavin stood in the doorway, hesitating.

Riko waved him in, and Bala happily arranged the food on the two tables.

Without any further ceremony, Cerulean gestured to the table and indicated the chairs.

Faye slipped onto her seat, waving apologetically. "I know you didn't officially invite me, but I do think that as a shapeshifter from a race that has been persecuted by both Ingots and Crestas for most of our existence, I might have a useful perspective."

Cerulean sighed. "I didn't purposefully leave you out, Faye. I was just in a hurry, and you were nowhere to be found." He shrugged. "And we have a decided interest in keeping this meeting separate from Taug."

Gavin nudged Riko as the Uanyi plunked down next to him. "News?"

Riko held up his hands. "Let me just say this before we start: Cerulean has informed both the Luxonian Supreme Council and the Inter-Alien Alliance of Cobalt's high-handed abduction of one of my employees. Upon investigation, it was discovered that Wendell signed an agreement to go to Ingilium for an unspecified time in order to ascertain his role in Ingot lineage reestablishment. Both organizations insist that their hands are tied, and we have no legal or even moral authority to take action against Cobalt or his Commander Scoria, who I hear is a real charmer." He dropped his hands onto his lap. "That said, I want to know what we are going to do about it. I want Wendell back home alive. Soon!"

Gavin's shoulders swelled as he heaved a deep breath. "Ingots need Tabunites. I give myself. They return Wendell."

Faye shivered. "No! There must be another way. We can't give them what they want! That would reward them for this whole mess. A mess they got themselves into by the way. Ingots should have learned long ago that they were living on borrowed time."

Bala wiped his sticky fingers on a napkin and leaned forward. "Faye is right. How about if Ingots create a super race? Or the Cresta? It's what they've always wanted, dominance over everyone else. Well, if they harvest the best of each of us and create new hybrids or tribrids, whatever you want to call them, what's to stop them from turning every sentient race into a Spare Parts Shop? Not only will they be powerful, they will be unstoppable."

Riko swiped his hand through the air. "Every race is stoppable, if you're willing to pay the price. War is hell, but it's been the price paid to stop evil from conquering. My people paid it for generations."

Gavin nodded. "Killing is bloody work, but sometimes, it is the only way."

Cerulean lifted his voice. "First things first. We need to know if Wendell is even still alive. Then we can decide—"

A voice filtered in from the back. "He's not only alive, he's on his way home."

Faye jumped out of her chair. "Taug! You can't join us unless you promise that you're not working as a spy for the enemy."

Waddling forward, Taug's slumped shoulders and limp tentacles spoke volumes. "I am not a spy, and Cobalt is not the enemy. He is simply trying to save his race from extinction. But you'll be glad to know that he talked Commander Scoria out of harvesting Wendell for parts and then composting his remains." Taug stopped before the group, a chastened Cresta if ever there was one. "No, if we have an enemy, it's our friends we need to watch from now on, friends and family." He focused on Bala, a new light of respect in his golden eyes. "You're right, human. Since we have broken the old barriers, mixing races and combining technology with biology, we have to admit what we should have known all along."

Bala shook his head, his gaze dropping. "We are all capable of good…and evil."

Taug nodded. "I can hardly believe I am saying this, but perhaps, even in science, there are boundaries that should not be crossed."

Cerulean met Justine's gaze. He pictured Max, an android-human extraordinaire who wanted to self-destruct rather than cost anyone their freedom. And he knew with a clarity he rarely experienced who he needed to call upon next.

—Cerulean's Cabin—

Friday, Mid-Morning, June 9th

Max didn't have the slightest interest in drinking tea but he'd have to accept the offer. His efforts at work had been lackluster at best, but Justine continued in her efficient style and Zara merely watched him out of the corner of her eyes, so he defaulted to standard routines that made life appear meaningful, even when it no longer felt so. Still polite habits were hard to break, especially when someone like Cerulean was asking if you wanted lemon or creamer.

"Neither. Thank you."

Placing a steaming cup of bright yellow liquid on the kitchen island, Cerulean continued his gentle murmurings. "I appreciate your willingness to come all this way. I realize that my message seemed unreasonably urgent, but I really am in a fix."

In a fix? Max ran the expression through his data banks and retrieved such an odd array of possibilities that he glanced up at Cerulean for clarification.

Scraping a stool across the wooden floor, Cerulean positioned himself on the other side of the island across from Max. "Yes. You see, there's been a rumor that you were considering a drastic solution to the hybrid-tribrid problem. When I mentioned it to Sterling, he became so concerned that—"

Mild curiosity undulated over Max's brain. "Why would a Luxonian Supreme Judge who is near fading be concerned with anything about me? I pose no threat. He gains nothing from my existence or my demise."

Cerulean clasped his hands and nodded toward the tea. "That's where you'd be wrong." He furrowed his brow as Max took a sip of the brew, a question in his eyes.

Max couldn't help himself. Politeness was the last bastion of humanity even in despair. "It's good. Thank you."

A cat meowed at the door, and Cerulean dashed over and let the feline inside. He placed a prepared dish on the floor and watched as the animal scarfed the food down with a combination purr-growl. Cerulean smiled.

Max wanted to smile. But what was the point? Cats get eaten by wolves, after all. *And wolves kill each other...*

As if reading his dark thoughts, Cerulean clapped him on the shoulder and told him to drink up and come outside. He glanced around the kitchen as they headed out the door, an oddly expectant expression on his face.

He went down the porch steps and around to the west side of the cabin where a bright sunny patch of earth had been cultivated into a neat garden. Tomato, pepper, cucumber, peas, green beans, zucchini, potatoes, onions, and a line of herbs were bordered by a bright array of flowers. Not a weed in sight. Is this what Cerulean did when he wasn't saving Newearth from the latest disaster? How quaint! *Sarcasm? Where did that come from?*

Flapping his arms like a bird ready to take flight, Cerulean seemed to be stalling for time.

For what? Max had even less interest in gardening than in tea. "You said it was urgent that I come. I'm here. What do you want from me, Cerulean?"

As Cerulean blinked in the bright noon-day sun, Max was startled by his friend's humanity. A Luxonian tied to a human body. A hybrid of sorts? And a tongue-tied one at that. Was there no room for pity within his depressed soul? He shook his head. What did it matter? No one was safe anymore.

A muscular figure dressed in sandals, long pants, and a sleeveless tunic ambled from the woods on the south end. There was a steep ravine on that side. Must have been a hard climb, but the figure didn't seem to be out of breath. One of the Amens Community perhaps?

The man stopped on the south end of the garden.

Cerulean stared at him and mouthed the word, "Finally!"

As if Max couldn't read lips. He almost smiled. What was this? A friend who would boost his morale with homespun tales of moral goodness? If his spirit wasn't already dead, he would laugh at the sheer audacity of a simple man thinking that he could direct a superior being. *Human-Android Extraordinaire!* A hollow laugh sounded like a death knell deep within Max's mind.

The man offered only the briefest nod to Cerulean and then marched forward, his robust frame and direct gaze growing in power with every step.

Max stood his ground even as he forced down something he could not name. *Fear?* He knew this person. *But how?*

The man with black eyes searched Max's soul as he stopped before him. He lifted his hands and placed them gently but firmly on Max's shoulders. "It's me, Max. Omega. Your father. I've come to take you home."

—Clare's House—

Late Afternoon

Kendra propped her hands on her hips as she watched Clare stenciling flowers, birds, and butterflies across the freshly painted nursery walls. She could hardly believe her eyes. Had she ever seen Clare *happy* before? There had been times when Clare was less moody, certainly. Even a few moments when she had edged up close to copasetic. But happy—definitely not. She wasn't exactly delighted now but, rather, sincerely enthusiastic. Despite the obvious fact that decorating a baby's room didn't involve threats, handcuffs, or possible prison time.

Kendra shook her head in bafflement. Perhaps the time Clare had spent with Bala and the kids after her meltdown had done some good after all. The woman had moped on the couch most of the weekend, true, and had hardly seemed interested in the children at the time, but perhaps this was a delayed reaction. Maybe Clare finally discovered the true beauty of parenting, even in the ridiculously challenging situation she found herself in.

"Get me that buzzing bee stencil on the dresser, would you?"

From the second step on the ladder, clutching a handful of detail brushes in her left hand, a pallet of assorted paints on the top cap of the ladder, her right hand outstretched, fingers wiggling impatiently, Clare looked the spitting image of an artist intent on her newest masterpiece.

Kendra hated to burst her friend's bubble, but even as she handed the bee stencil over, she had to ask, "You do know that this is a *boy's* room, right?"

Clare stashed all but one of the brushes in her overalls' side pocket, slapped the bee stencil strategically above a hydrangea blossom, dabbed the tip of the brush in paint, and added busy bees to the mural taking shape on the south wall of the nursery. She grunted as she worked. "I'm happy as a clam that Herson is a boy. This way I can introduce his developing mind to the feminine beauty of nature while he's little, and then enjoy rough and tumble sports with him when he gets older."

"Uh, huh." Kendra figured that Herson would make up his own mind about flowers and rough games, letting his mama know in no uncertain terms when he was good and ready. The one thing she knew for certain sure was that at some point, pretty much every kid wants to repaint his room.

She took a step back and appraised the cozy space: a plush circular rug dominated the center, making an ideal play area, a huge wooden toy chest set before the south window glowed in golden glory, a rocking horse with a long black mane promised bounce and excitement in later years, while a cradle sat nestled in the southwest corner, not far from a big-boy bed that would come in handy in the not-so-distant future.

The rectangular bay window with a padded window seat brightened the whole room with evening light, while the rocking chair in the northern corner suggested comforting story time before bed. Even the colorful bookshelves on the east wall packed with OldEarth classics—Clare's family favorites "passed down through generations"—bespoke the gentle love of a strong, imaginative inner life. Kendra couldn't think of anything more to add. It was perfect. She only wished her kids could have had half so much. She thought of the attic room that Bala was trying to refurbish into a boy's den and cringed. Though she had forbidden straw, there was more than enough dust…

Clare climbed down the ladder and wiped her paint-sticky fingers on a towel. "Stop daydreaming, would you, and help me clean up so we can go out and eat. I'm starving. And I want to check in on Herson while I'm there."

Kendra lifted her hands in surrender. There was nothing more she could do here. Clare had thought of everything and done most of the hard work. Even Kendra's usual morale-boosting banter wasn't needed. Clare had enough morale to fill an intergalactic stadium. *Wait till he climbs his first tree to the tippy top; she'll need me then.* With that happy thought, Kendra capped all the paints and tried to decide between a protein burger and a seaside salad.

Chapter Seventeen

Dual Nature

—Breakfastnook Café—

Sunday, July 1st

Riko stood in the middle of his festively decorated café and could hardly hold his tears in check. If only Uncle Clem could've come to the wedding. He considered the crowd of happy celebrants and the lovely decorations that Kendra, Faye, and Jayla's friends had arranged: scented floral baskets on each table, festive balloons hanging from the ceiling, hearts, wedding bands, and facsimiles of Uanyi Love Nests arranged all over the diner. The casual OldEarth-styled café had been transformed into a celebration of nuptial bliss.

Uncle Clem would've added orange and yellow streamers and a goofy banner with a ridiculous rhyme…

A curt message had reached Riko right before the ceremony, but he hadn't been able to deal with it then. Besides, it would have ruined the day for Jayla if she'd seen it. She loved Clem. Whenever he had returned from one of his "family tours," they'd be reunited like long-lost buddies. Clem made her laugh, and she made him proud. A great team.

How could it have happened? Interstellar travel had become so safe that any accident sent shock ripples through the entire district. This one, a ship malfunction, killing both crew and passengers, caught everyone off guard. There would be an investigation; someone would be blamed—probably an Ingot for selling poor quality parts—and then the universe would continue as it always had. Just with a few less travelers.

A lump nearly choked Riko. Recovering from a depressed sigh, he squared his shoulders and plastered on a smile. Standing between the last booth and the swinging kitchen doors, he watched Wendell with his mismatched mechanical eye tromp through, carrying two loaded trays. Inexplicably more confident, despite the fact that his biology had clearly been violated: the addition of the artificial eye, case in point. Yet Wendell didn't seem much changed from the kid he had always been. A bit steadier on his feet maybe and unusually self-assured... *Wonder how he'll take the news...*

Thunder rumbled overhead. The rain had started right after the last guest arrived at the café, but it hadn't let up since. Riko glanced at his datapad for a weather report: "Powerful storms throughout the night." Then he searched the room for Jayla. She was standing at table two, laughing and slapping her thigh in exultation. *Must have been a good joke. Hope it's not on me.* Riko squinted.

Bala, Kendra, and all their kids had somehow managed to squeeze around a table intended for six. Smiling big time, Jayla cradled the littlest one while chatting excitedly with Kendra... Her hips swayed to the Bhuaci beat pounding over the speakers. *Uh, oh, she's talking babies with a reproduction expert...*

A crash splintered the air.

Everyone jumped, but just as quickly, nervous giggles were followed by embarrassed glances.

Even Cerulean seated with Faye, Justine, and Zara appeared startled.

Jayla, pointing at the front plate-glass window, announced, "Even the storm gods are congratulating us!"

Laughter and excited conversations rose to new heights.

Suddenly, a tentacle wrapped around Riko's middle. His heart nearly burst through his chest.

Taug's breather helm bubbled in urgency. "Hate to pull

you away, but I have a little situation in the lab that I need you to see."

With a sidelong glance, Riko faced his fear—Taug's bulbous eyes right up close and personal. He considered a distance-affirming shove but decided against it. Taug wasn't usually known for his subtlety, so this attempt at secrecy suggested something important. Riko slipped free from the entwining tentacle, waved to Jayla with an indication that he'd be in the kitchen, and then marched through the doorway.

Taug padded ahead and hurriedly opened the laboratory door.

Once inside the pristine lab, Riko peered around for any sign of intrusion. Why else would Taug be acting this way?

Nope. All the equipment seemed much the same as usual. Tables, shelves, trays, dispensers, all just where they should be.

A horrified shudder streaked over Riko, and he turned to Taug. "The babies? Something happened to them?"

Tentacles flapping, Taug swept that fear away. "No, nothing like that."

"A break-in?"

Taug shook his head, scuttled to one shelving unit, then pulled out a wide-beamed light. He flicked it on and aimed it at the ceiling. "After your wonderful dinner, I came in here to make a few notes…" He stopped short and focused his beam. "Anyway, I heard a strange sound during the storm."

Directly above them, thin black lines had formed like a massive spider web across the ceiling.

"What do you think?"

Riko clucked his tongue much like Uncle Clem used to do when chiding a wayward Uanyi youth. "Ugly is what I think. They don't look deep, so the structure is still sound, but we'll have to get a construction team on this before it spreads. Flakes could fall into your experiments, and I sure as heck don't want any of this spreading into my kitchen."

With bubbles of relief, Taug gestured back to the kitchen. "I didn't mean to take you away from your festivities on your wedding day, of all days, but I just didn't know who else to ask. You're one of the most knowledgeable people on Newearth." He glanced up and sighed. "As long as the ceiling doesn't fall, I won't worry."

Unaccountably pleased by Taug's praise, Riko nodded, looking as intelligent as possible. "An old friend of mine, from the same village I grew up in, moved to Newearth last year. He does stuff like this all the time and can reseal the interior so you don't even see that a repair has been made. I'll have him check the rest of the place as well."

Smiling, Taug hustled to the door. "Well, then. That's settled. Don't let me keep you."

Riko started forward and then stopped. "Hey, can I see the babies?"

Hesitating for a split second, Taug eyed Riko and then led the way toward the small Cresta pool at the back of the room.

Right up against the glass, facing the swirling, murky liquid, the two biombs stood side by side, blue and red.

Larger than he remembered but still thin, Herson lay curled on his side, his head nestled on his chest and his arms crossed over his middle.

Relevance had grown enormously. He was almost too big for his biomb. Laying on his back, the bed tipped up so that he faced the Cresta pool, he seemed to see through his closed eyes, watching the swimming creatures as they dashed about in their watery world. An expression of concentration…or was it pain…formed ridges on his forehead.

Spluttering, Riko could barely find words. "Relevance is…so…muscular! I didn't know that babies could…do that."

Pride glowing in his eyes, Taug's chest swelled. "It must be the Tabun DNA. Surely, Ingots don't have much of their original strength left, and humans never get muscular until they are much older."

Riko stumbled over his next words, "I don't have much experience with babies. Never had the time. Or the interest."

Taug glanced aside and frowned. "You've been around Bala's children. One afternoon at their house is enough experience for a lifetime."

Flummoxed, Riko could hardly believe he was trying to explain himself. "I mean Uanyi babies. There was a war on when I left, and I never saw many of my own kind…you know…get attached and have offspring."

Taug's bulbous eyes rolled toward the ceiling. "Ah! Offspring. Is Jayla…?"

Annoyed, a flush heated Riko's face. "We just got married a few hours ago, Taug. We don't work that fast."

A click and Relevance's biomb jerked.

Startled, Riko leaned in. "He okay?"

Taug shook his head, one tentacle splayed over the biomb. "It's just a quirky habit. Jerking. Don't know if it is peculiar to Tabunites or Ingots. But I've checked him over repeatedly. He's in perfect health. Developing very well." He gestured toward the door. "I shouldn't keep you any longer. Your guests will worry, and Jayla will blame me. I hate causing trouble….a bad habit, really."

Suddenly aware that he was actually a married Uanyi, and he couldn't just do as he pleased anymore, Riko bounded for the door. He glanced back once at the two biombs, a twisted sensation in his gut. Then a final glance at the ceiling. "I'll get my construction guy out here after our honeymoon. I want to be here when he does his inspection."

With a gracious nod, Taug accepted the plan and ushered him out the door with a grateful smile.

Ignoring the kitchen staff's admonishing stares, Riko hurried to his beloved. Mixed feelings fluttered inside his chest. He still had to tell her about Uncle Clem. But no matter the joys or griefs in life, they would face their future together. And, if there were children in their future, he would give them the best he had to offer...without a biomb in sight.

—Ingot Diplomatic Suite—

Saturday, July 14th

Cobalt rubbed his eyes and leaned back on his desk chair in the cold, sterile room. Even with the air screen on high magnification, reviewing ancient records for most of the day strained him. He pinched the bridge of his nose. *Should have had implants put in, like what they did for Wendell.* His stomach clenched.

Then why did I have Taug replace the spy-eye with a mere prosthetic? He couldn't answer his own question. The fact that Scoria had followed his suggestion and set Wendell up as a secret service implant, implying that his own diplomatic skills were lacking, only boiled his brain every time he thought of his commander. But then, Scoria had been right about one thing: Ingots would never be truly free from their human origin. He tapped the surface of his desk and the air screen blinked back to life. With a sigh, he admitted the truth. Reports from the earliest interstellar records had all come to the same conclusion—Technology could only take Ingot society so far. Beyond a certain point, they became weak and tended to succumb to a host of maladies. From what he had surmised, perhaps that wasn't such a bad thing. Perhaps a more robust interface with their biological heritage would be good for them.

Lazily, he scrolled backward through the files until he

located a section relating a case between an Ingot named Zuri who defended an Old-world cult called the Born-Agains. A fanatical sect that had dispossessed themselves of all technology, forming an isolated community where everyone went around nearly naked. The judge at the time had misunderstood Zuri's reference to their natural inheritance, the hearty stock that protected them when not using technology, and assumed that they had invented some kind of invisible shield.

Cobalt huffed. The judge was incompetent, but that didn't stop later generations from persecuting the Born-Again community to extinction. *Now they're only a footnote in the files of life. What a waste! They could've saved us.*

A smile formed on Cobalt's lips as he imagined them trying to tip-toe across the rocky lands of Ingilium. Must have been nearly impossible…unless their feet had grown thick skin. He frowned. He'd seen humans happily run barefoot in parks and on beaches. *How is that even possible?*

Telling himself that it was simply in the line of an experiment, he tugged off his right boot and then peeled off the thick protective sock. His pasty skin glowed white under the stark lighting. Bone thin, his foot appeared unable to bear his massive bio-suit weight. Gingerly, he stood up, gripping the table with one hand. He felt nothing. Just listed to one side as his footing was now uneven. He plopped back down on his chair with a heavy sigh. What had he imagined? That an appendage encased in armor most of his life would help him understand the mysteries of the human race? He considered his foot. *It's pathetic.* Sadness gripped him. *But it's mine…*

A knock caught his attention. He looked up. *Knocking? Who knocks?* Shuffling awkwardly, he made it to the door and hit the unlock button. "Open!"

As it slid aside, Wendell came into view, standing on the landing before the door, a crooked grin on his face and a brown box in his hands. "Want to thank you. Brought cookies. Riko's special, with nuts and chocolate chunks." He extended his arms, the box held lightly, waiting to be accepted.

Stunned, Cobalt tripped over his bootless foot trying to back up.

Slipping the box under one arm, Wendell reached out and steadied him.

Backing into the suite, Cobalt motioned to the conference table. "Come and sit. I'll get something to go with the cookies." He shivered in disbelief. He actually knew that an imitation drink called "milk" went with cookies. *I've been around humans too long.*

Wendell ambled in and stopped by the chair. He placed the box on the table. "Can't stay. Babysit tonight. Bala and Kendra go on date night. I play with kids; eat pizza." Almost involuntarily, his eyes slid to Cobalt's bare foot.

Covering his embarrassment with a bold laugh, Cobalt swung his leg onto the chair, proudly showing off his pallid, emaciated limb. He shrugged. "I was reading about the ancient cult, the Born-Agains, and I wondered if I could walk barefoot."

Wendell nodded. He looked down, seemingly considering his own feet. "Much practice, but in time..." He lifted his gaze. "You could."

Refusing to follow that train of thought, Cobalt snatched two glasses out of the guest cabinet and then realized that all he had to drink was some rather strong Green that Taug had given him in congratulations for their success with the biomb babies.

"Come! Have a glass of Green with me. It'll take me a year to get through a bottle on my own." With a shocked sensation, Cobalt realized that he almost added the word "please." *What has gotten into me?*

As if he understood more than Cobalt's words, Wendell

pulled out a chair and sat down. He opened the box of cookies and slid two in Cobalt's direction. He placed two in front of himself and then closed the box with precise motions.

Never seen anyone move with such deliberate care. Discomforted, Cobalt sloshed the Green into two glasses and passed one to Wendell. "Drink up! You'll need every ounce of courage you can get if you have to manage miniature human hellions." With a snort, he bit into a thick cookie and chewed emphatically.

Wendell took a bite of his cookie, sipped the green, and took another bite, back and forth, in amiable silence, until both cookies and drink were consumed. He wiped his lips with the back of his hand, childlike, and grinned. "Good!" Then he stood and nodded politely. "Thank you for everything."

Cobalt downed the last of his Green, one eye fixed on the bottle, and furrowed his brow. With a grunt, he stood and faced Wendell. "You're the one who came bearing gifts. I should be thanking you."

Wendell headed for the door. "You had Taug replace the eye that Scoria commanded." He pointed to his new, less technologically advanced eye. "I am glad for that."

It had honestly never dawned on Cobalt what Wendell might think about having his eye replaced by Scoria and then replaced again by him. He looked down at his foot. It was still bare and ghastly white. But it was *his.* An incomprehensible urge to cry filled him.

Wendell tapped the door button and, after it opened, he stopped on the threshold. "This eye not work so well, but it matches me. I not work so well. But I try." With a surprisingly sincere smile, he turned away and was gone.

Only after Wendell had left did Cobalt realize that the floor was cold and smooth, and it felt good.

—Planet Mirage-Reborn—

—Omega's Living Room—

Max sat on a bench before a massive fireplace, staring into the flames feeding off enormous logs, and tried not to imagine the great trees chopped down and then dragged from their origin, only to be set alight in a strange house where no one knew their proud history. He dropped his head onto his chest. *So, this is what depression feels like…*

The entire room screamed Medieval OldEarth, which apparently was one of Omega's favorite epochs in human history. Ages ago, a family man named Melchior had caught his attention, a decent, loving man but flawed. A father who wanted to protect his family but, in truth, hardly even knew them… *Must have been like looking into a mirror.*

Omega strode forward bearing a tray laden with brown bread, yellowed cheese chunks, and goblets of wine.

As he lifted his head, a strange sensation gurgled inside Max's middle. His mind felt muddled and his whole body run down, as if he'd not refreshed his system in much too long. *It's true. I haven't.* Watching Omega in his muscular human form place the tray on the wooden table only increased his sense of unreality.

Who is this? This veritable stranger was as unlike the person he had known as anyone could be. The Omega from his earliest memories was a laughing clown, always ready to rush off to a new experience. Too smart to be called a fool yet he had never exuded any real wisdom.

"Eat something, please?" Dressed simply in a loose gray tunic over baggy pants and wearing sandals, Omega could not have appeared more rustic. A mop of brown hair set off his trim reddish beard. Brown eyes revealed a depth of spirit rarely seen; Omega was a new person entirely.

In habitual politeness, Max picked up a chunk of cheese and nibbled it discreetly.

Omega handed him a thick goblet half-filled with dark red wine. “It’ll help the cheese go down.” He scratched his head as if bewildered. “I hired local help, but it’s been the devil’s own time trying to get anyone to understand the concept of cheese.”

Max choked. He looked at Omega’s face and was astonished to see the hint of a smile. A real smile. Max couldn’t stop himself. He grinned back and accepted the wine. After a few sips, he nodded. “It’s quite good. The fruity aroma tickles my nose.” Then he stopped and stared at the wine, puzzled. He ran through his directory of vintages and recognized this one down to the specific grapes used, but, honestly, he could never remember feeling tickled before. Was that a characteristic of this particular variety or was it a trick Omega was playing on him?

Omega stretched on the couch across from Max’s chair, his back leaning on the padded arm and his legs resting comfortably across the length. He chewed on a hunk of brown bread, staring meditatively at the painting above the fireplace. He gestured upward. “This painting fascinates me. You know it?”

Max considered the brilliant artwork. The face and figure of a handsome man holding an ornate book, with one hand lifted in some kind of signature gesture. A halo surrounded his head, suggesting an association with the divine. Max searched his memory banks and almost came up empty. But there was something…way back in OldEarth history… “The Christ Pantocrator of St. Catherine's Monastery at Sinai from the 6th century?”

Omega's contemplative expression softened as his gaze returned to Max. “Yes. Exactly.” He laid his bread back on the tray and clasped his hands together in prayer form. "Do you know what it means?"

"Literally, it means 'Ruler of All' and is supposed to depict the dual nature of Christ as God and man." Max shrugged. He never understood humanity's obsession with the God-man. *Just a hybrid, after all.* Shocked by the sudden revelation, Max stiffened, and his gaze strayed back to his father.

"Do you see?" Sitting up and leaning forward, Omega locked his eyes on Max. "There are different interpretations as to what the gesture and the Bible mean, but after playing a demi-god for so long, I think I understand now. I am *not* your creator, Max. The Eternals are not capable of true creation. We use, manipulate, alter, combine, but we can never honestly make anything.

"I used you, Max. And I repent my actions—taking your human essence and placing it within an android, no matter how perfect. It was an act of sheer pride and awful audacity. I tried to atone to Justine when I gave her Zara, a child to love. Even before suffering imprisonment and torture, I knew I had wronged her. Clare as well. Though that's a different story. But you? I never even tried to make amends to you." He shrugged. "I didn't think you needed it. You accepted your hybrid role so well; it seemed best to leave you alone."

A crushing weight smothered Max. He knew that he didn't breathe, yet he felt a ghastly need for something that wasn't there. *Am I dying?* No words would come. He reached for Omega, but blackness took him as he fell forward.

When Max awoke, he was on the couch, and Omega knelt at his side. He checked his internal systems and realized that only a matter of minutes had passed. But there was something odd. His sensors seemed off. A pulsing beat within his body... He glared at Omega. "What have you done?"

Blinking in the manner of a man about to cry, Omega

clutched Max's hand and squeezed it. Painfully.

I can feel pain?

"I am trying to make amends, Max. I didn't know what else to do! I can't give you the body you should have had or the childhood you'll never know. I can't even offer you another child. Another wrong can't right this." A bitter chuckle and Omega glanced at the painting over the fireplace. "I'm not in the business of creating hybrids anymore."

Max sat up gingerly and tried to run through his entire body… *What has he done to me?*

"You are still an android with all your advanced capabilities, but I grew your biological nature to intertwine within your android system. Like your brain grew over your technology, I simply advanced the process. You are now the most honest human-android hybrid in history."

Max couldn't process what he was hearing. Words did not make sense. He pulled his hands away, stood, and looked down on Omega who was still crouching by the couch, ready to crumble, it seemed. "I have a *human* body? A complete human body?"

"You can feel and do anything a human can now…except reproduce." He shook his head. "That I cannot replicate."

Dizziness, hunger, confusion, panic, and even pain were now his to enjoy. *How ironic!* Cold fury filed Max. "You are too generous, Father." He could not see his own face, but he could feel a sneer crawl over his features. "Now I am neither human nor android. As an absolute hybrid, I am as isolated, locked in the prison of my own uniqueness, as anyone can ever be."

A light entered Omega's eyes, and he climbed gracefully to his feet. He faced Max and shook his head, a smile spreading over his face. "No, don't you understand? This is how humans feel all the time. They are, each and every one, a hybrid—flesh and spirit, animal and divine." He glanced up.

"That's why the painting fascinates me. *He* understood the need to become a hybrid and join us in our duality."

Confused, Max glanced toward the door. The image of Justine's face called to him. "I need to go." Before a dozen steps, he froze and spun on his heel. "Us?"

"The price I had to pay to regain some measure of sanity. I am simply borrowing this physical form. But now I, too, must die and travel to the unknown lands on the other side of the Great Divide."

Shock sent a cold wave over Max's body. "But you are an Eternal."

Sad but meek, Omega opened his hands and spread them wide, embracing the room, perhaps the whole world. "We all are. And I should be on the other side but for this temporary gift. A momentary hybrid experience where I can atone, in some measure, for the harm I've done."

Before he knew what he was doing, Max felt his shoulders slump and his eyes filling with tears. There was nothing he could say except three small words, and these he meant with all of his beating heart, "I forgive you."

Chapter Eighteen

Parenthood

—Taug's Laboratory—

Tuesday, August 1st

Taug enjoyed mysteries when they involved a scientific quest. When it came to building structures and other mundane realities, he liked to leave those matters to the experts—the brawny specimens who plodded into his laboratory with dirty boots and clumped around with knowing looks on their faces. In a matter of hours, they'd have the faucet working, the electric grid operating, or a wobbly shelving unit securely fixed to the wall.

But the construction engineer that Riko had sent over yesterday had merely scratched his head and said he'd never seen anything like it. He stared long and hard at the cracks that had spread along the walls and ceiling and pursed his lips in obvious disdain. A few measurements, a shrug, and a grunt, the burly man plodded out the door, muttering to himself.

Not a good way to start the week.

Taug considered his beautiful laboratory, marred only by the spidery lines rising along the walls and interlacing across the ceiling. There was nothing for it but to continue his work.

Clare planned to come by after work, and he wanted to give her up-to-date information on Herson. At thirty-six weeks both babies were nearly ripe for birthing. Plus, Cobalt had been stopping in and taking copious notes to send back to Ingilium. The Ingots already had a batch of hybrid samples with various percentages of Ingot and Tabunite DNA, but they still had a lot to learn about biomb adjustments. Taug hardly wanted a lecture about the waste of a batch of rejects.

Out the high east windows, he could see clouds drawing into battle formation. He shrugged. With no plans to go outside, the weather was of little concern.

Throughout the morning, he reviewed the biombs' settings, took measurements, and adjusted the configurations to adapt to the needs of the growing babies. It was delicate work and needed focused attention.

Relevance's jerks had grown more pronounced, setting Taug's breather helm into high bubble mode. Something felt off, as if he hadn't done something...but he couldn't think what.

A rattling against the back wall alerted him to the rising wind. One of the seamless gutters had broken free and slapped against the back door when it became the least bit blustery. *Riko was supposed to get that fixed!*

Annoyed, Taug purposefully ignored Riko when the cook hustled in from the kitchen.

"Do you hear that? It's raining Helluphants and Quizors!"

Taug tapped Relevance's oxygen level up a notch. *Perhaps he needs...*

Shaking water from his normally spotless uniform, Riko lifted his voice two notches. "Are you listening to me? I just tried to fix that stupid rain gutter—see if I ever hire a Uanyi gutter guy again—and the thing flew right out of my hands. It's now firmly lodged against—"

His nerves tight from minute calculations and detail adjustments, Taug snapped. "Do I look like I care about gutters at the moment? I am attempting to do very delicate work here. These babies need me."

His brows crunched and pursing his lips, Riko looked very much like an angry prune. "I tried to do you a favor and fix that thing so you wouldn't get smacked going out your back door, which you can't do anyway because it's stuck now, and *you can't even take a moment to listen to me*?" He crossed his arms and huffed.

The image of Jayla standing in the exact position and saying much the same to Riko the other day sprang to Taug's mind. *Huh. Married life. See what it's done to you.*

Relevance's biomb rocked with another violent jerk.

Alarmed, both Taug and Riko stared down at the baby.

Riko's voice dropped to a whisper. "What's wrong with—"

Whomp! Crackling. Humming. Spine-tingling vibrations.

Taug heard the cacophony but could hardly distinguish the unique sounds. *What is—*

A high-pitched whine, metal stretched beyond its breaking point.

While his legs went wobbly, as if he was floating in a strange pool, Taug felt a sharp pain on his left shoulder, then on top of his head…his arm. Trying to register what was happening, he glanced around and could not comprehend why Riko was dancing in the middle of the lab. But then, there did seem to be chunks of rain falling all around.

Not *rain.*

The ceiling was falling to pieces!

Horrified, Taug scrutinized the walls as cracks grew like slithering snakes and widened into deep caverns.

"Help!" Instinctually, he grabbed Relevance's biomb and started to unhook it from every monitor and support tube. "Get Herson!" he screamed at Riko, who had rushed for the door and was madly trying to open it.

"Can't! Don't know a thing about babies!"

Panic set Taug's internals into high gear. His breathing helm bubbled at full capacity while all four tentacles raced to disconnect Relevance's biomb. He couldn't afford to glance aside at Herson, but his attention fractured when he heard a smack that registered as hard plastic cracking.

A quick look aside and his fear spiked to new heights.

Herson's biomb had taken a direct hit. A large chunk of the ceiling was now embedded on the top, pressing down dangerously on the squirming infant. *Oh, Someone… Help.*

The door burst open and an eight-foot muscled monster stood on the threshold.

Riko screamed and leaped backward.

Taug's breakfast rose unnaturally, making sweat break out all over his body.

The creature's face shrank and modified, clarifying Faye's identity but with a body of enormous bulk. "What can I do?"

Riko slipped by and dashed out the door, calling, "Jayla!"

Taug thrust Relevance's biomb in Faye's direction and then started to disconnect Herson's biomb. The ground shook violently, debris falling in a rocky shower all around. Desperate, he grabbed a dissecting knife, hit the birthing button, and as soon as a wedge opened large enough, he slipped the wet infant from the dripping biomb and cut the umbilical cord. A few spasms and Herson opened his mouth and screamed lustily.

Relief sluiced over Taug as he clutched the naked infant to his chest and ran for the doorway where Faye embraced the wildly jerking biomb. Despite her muscled form, she struggled to keep a grip on the container.

Taug ran through first, weaving between the bustling kitchen help and shiny appliances, all of which seemed strangely untouched by the destructive vibrations or the storm.

Close behind him, Faye hustled at his back, urging him forward. "Keep going! We don't know how far this will spread."

Arriving in the main diner, Taug and Faye stopped cold.

The Breakfastnook Café looked much as it usually did,

filled to noontime capacity with customers scarfing down platters of delicious food. The bustling room fell silent as patrons stared at Taug huffing into his breather helm, a screaming baby wrapped in his tentacles, and beside him, a bulky creature with a pixie face clutching a jerking red biomb.

Riko jogged forward, his hands raised. "Relax, folks. Just a storm. Did some damage to my neighbor's place, so he and his…friend…had to evacuate. All is well. I'll take care of everything. Go on and enjoy your meals." He swung a stiff grin around the room and then rotated toward Taug. "Get back into the kitchen, would ya?"

Confused beyond comprehension, Taug backed up. Faye passed the red biomb to Riko and hustled toward the laboratory, yelling "I've got to brace the main wall."

Completely caught off guard, Riko tried to keep a grip on the red biomb, but with a mighty jerk, it crashed to the floor.

Suddenly, the kitchen door swung open once more, and Cobalt rushed in.

—Department of Human Services—

Clare leaned back in her padded office chair and stretched. It was past lunchtime, and she'd been poring over files since early morning. A glance out the window told her that the storm was finally calming down, though rain still pattered from a slate sky. She leaned forward, trying to get a glimpse of Bala at his desk. Ever since the Spare Parts Shop incident, he had been acting cooler toward her. An occasional quip, sure, but certainly not like the bouncy puppy of the past. She'd like to blame it on the heavy weight of fatherhood, but with each new kid, he had seemed to grow younger and happier. Hardly the icon of gloomy parenting she usually saw in her daily routine. She rubbed her chin. It had been a while since they went out to lunch together. Maybe—

A head poked through her open doorway. One of the new communications officers. "Message for you. Upstairs."

Surprise quickly turning to alarm, Clare dashed a glance at her datapad. Nothing blinking there.

Down the hall, the same voice repeated his announcement with new clarity. "Message for you. The boss says now. No games, Bala."

Clare grabbed her datapad and hustled from her chair.

Coming from the mellow interior where his exotic plants, artifacts, and kid artwork made it seem more like a personal museum than a detective's office, Bala blinked like a sleepy cat.

Assuming a confidential tone, Clare sidled up to him. "You know what this is about?"

Bala shook his head, dug his hands into his pockets, and shuffled across the central meeting space.

Up the stairs, to the right, and they arrived at the chief's office. The door was wide open. They both froze.

"Get in here and hurry up. We have a situation on our hands that can't wait."

Once inside, Clare glanced from the wilting form of Captain Walt to the watery eyes of Chief Benz and then swung to the Commander himself. Her spine stiffening, she saw Bala go ramrod straight out of the corner of her eye.

"Yes, sir! What can we do for you?" She glanced uncertainly from one man to another.

Commander Landry left not a smidgen of doubt as to who was in charge. His voice boomed. "Are you a *mother*, Clare?"

Horror filled Clare as her bones seemed to dissolve into quivering noodles. Could her stomach drop any further? She hardly recognized the high-pitched squeak that rose from her throat. "Yes, sir. I am." The sudden realization that she was really a mother now and had a baby to raise and protect emboldened her spirit far more than she would have ever expected. *Motherhood a source of strength? Who would have thought…* "There is nothing illegal about being a mother, is there?"

Bala shifted nervously, though he said nothing.

Did he rat me out? She shot a glare in his direction.

Bala had his gaze fixed ahead, shoulders back and chest out. But genuine fear gleamed in his eyes.

Fear? Why?

"Normal babies are not illegal but hybrids are, as you well know. Raising babies in Cresta laboratories like rats in a cage is illegal. Also, as you know. Being a part of an experimental conspiracy to develop tribrids for the Ingot race without Inter-Alien supervision and guidelines is most definitely illegal." His gaze shifted to Bala. "I expected better of you, Bala." His tone dropped, disgusted. "You're a father, for Newearth's sake!"

Practically throwing herself in front of Bala, her arms spread wide, Clare rushed to his defense. "He didn't know. At least at first. He tried to warn me—"

With a stuttered response, Bala took over. "S-she acted out of love, just wanted a baby of her own. She had no idea that Taug mixed her human DNA with other races or that Cobalt was involved. She just wanted to be a mother."

With misery in his eyes, Captain Walt shook his head, his empath nature at full strength. "Well, you're a mother for sure, now, Clare. Your baby was born just as Taug's laboratory collapsed."

She heard a shriek but didn't realize it was hers.

Bala grabbed her arm and held on like a man offering a life raft. "What happened? Where is Herson? Where's Taug?"

The raspy voice of Chief Benz spoke up. "Looks like sabotage of some kind. We don't know who did it, but Taug got the babies out in time. His Bhuaci friend helped him and carried the tribrid known as Relevance from the scene. The biomb broke open and amazingly, the baby survived."

Clare began running for the steps. "Herson! Is he alive?"

Commander Landry called after her. "Both babies are at Vandi Hospital for proper evaluation." He lifted his voice as Clare started down the steps. "They were lucky, Clare. But their troubles have just begun. And so have yours!"

Clare couldn't see Bala as he raced behind her down the steps and out the main doorway, but she knew he was there, the only comfort she would accept.

—Vandi Hospital-Maternity Room One—

Wednesday, August 2nd

Gavin laid his head back on the padded rocking chair in the first room in the Vandi Maternity Ward and pushed with his toes, setting a slow, gentle rhythm back and forth, the bundle in his arms settling comfortably for the first time since he had taken charge at 1:05 a.m.

Golden dawn light streaked from the hospital window, slanted over the floor, and ran up the far wall.

Cerulean had received news of the disaster at Taug's lab soon after the babies had been taken to the hospital. He had bustled Gavin into the transportation tube with directions to the correct hospital but insisted that he needed to see what happened at the lab before he could join them. He'd pick up Clare and bring her with him.

With images of the dead wolf and the helpless pups swirling in his mind, Gavin steeled himself for whatever awaited him. Once at the hospital, the Inter-Alien Alliance personnel had carefully studied his identification, and then, finally, he was allowed into the maternity room. He ignored the dark irony of the setting.

Inside, rural paintings, a low bed, a large cradle, a rocking chair, and bay windows created a homey scene. In contrast, the oversized baby screamed fitfully, Cobalt paced irritably, and Taug was near despair. The doctors had run every test imaginable, but no medical condition explained Relevance's violent irritability. Finally, they diagnosed "colic" and left Taug to his own devices. The Cresta had rocked and hummed, cajoled, and offered synthetic human milk, wrapped, and unwrapped the baby a dozen times, but the infant had only grown more frenetic. For hours, Relevance squirmed, jerked spasmodically, and agonized in writhing seizures. Finally, Cobalt couldn't stand the fuss and left, snapping his prescription, "Rejects should be contained, not coddled!"

Gavin stepped aside, glad to let him pass.

Taug's terrified demeanor was unexpected. The Cresta, desperate with fear from the laboratory collapse and his growing anxiety over Relevance, helpless in his inability to diagnose the baby's condition, became little more than a blubbering mess.

Though Gavin had little patience with the Cresta and blamed him for much, his heart softened at the sight of the pathetic creature cradling the screaming baby. So, in the middle of the night, he took charge.

Amazingly, Taug let him. He released the writhing infant into Gavin's waiting arms and waddled despondently out of the room. Gavin didn't know where the Cresta went, and he didn't honestly care. All that mattered was calming the child and seeing to his welfare.

Holding the little body, deep memories rose like snatches of songs that his mother had sung when he was small. Acting on instinct, he tore off his shirt, stripped the baby bare, placed the tight little body high over his left shoulder, one hand on his rump, the other firmly on his back, and he strolled around the room, a slight sway to his step, humming the tunes he had loved as a child.

Slowly and incrementally, Relevance's screams faded, his jerks lessened in violence, and his muscles finally began to relax.

Once the sun crested the horizon and a new day had broken, Gavin tucked a light blanket over the naked form, shifted him into a cradle position, sat down on the rocking chair, and began to rock. Slowly. Calmness pervaded his being. He didn't know when he had ever felt so wonderful.

—Maternity Room Two—

Cerulean balanced a breakfast tray with one hand, clutched a bright blue **Congratulations!** balloon string with the other, and hit the open button to room two of the Vandi Hospital Maternity Ward with his elbow. He had no idea how the hostesses at the café made such tricky maneuvers look so easy.

Clare lay flat on her back on the bed where he had left her an hour before, with Herson contentedly sleeping on her chest. Her eyes closed and her breathing regular, he figured she must have fallen asleep as well, so he tiptoed across the room, gingerly placed the tray on a side table, and nearly had a heart attack when a hand tapped his arm.

He glanced over and stared right into Clare's sleepy eyes. She placed a finger to her mouth as if to keep him from talking boisterously, which he had no intention of doing anyway, and shifted her gaze to the rocking chair.

In her usual petite form again, Faye slumped with her

head back on the headrest and her feet sprawled out. She looked more exhausted than the mother and child.

As well she might, Cerulean realized. She managed to brace up the main laboratory wall but nearly killed herself in the process. Shapeshifters had limits, too. They may change their appearance but that didn't give them bulk and strength for any great length of time beyond what they had developed in their daily form. If Faye really wanted the strength of a muscled monster, she would have to eat like one and develop the form longer than a few minutes. The short burst of muscled strength she had acted on had drained everything from her usual pixie frame. Now she must recover her strength. He smiled to himself as he appraised the sunken bags under her eyes. *Good thing I brought a Green, extra-strong.*

He took the large Green drink from Clare's tray and set it on the window sill by the chair. Then he returned to Clare and leaned in for a better look at the sleeping infant.

Herson was out cold, dead to the world. Wrapped tight in a blue and white blanket, his face was turned to the side, squished flat between Clare's breasts, her light shirt wet with stains of spit and drool.

Cerulean looked into her eyes.

She didn't seem to mind.

He smiled at her and mouthed the words, "How are you?"

She tipped her head, attempted a shrug, then whispered. "Good."

Unease filled Cerulean as he dropped his voice to a low rumble. "You don't look good…I mean you seem upset."

Tears filling her eyes, Clare placed both hands on the baby's back and let them rest there, a light embrace, but a signal too. "Can I take my baby home with me, now? He's *mine*, isn't he, Cerulean?"

His head dropping to his chest, Cerulean felt his heart fall unfathomable lengths. How could he tell her? *That's not how parenthood works.*

Chapter Nineteen

There Lies Our Hope

—Newearth Docking Bay—

—Bhuaci Suite—

Friday, August 4th

Faye knew that her planet's preeminent spiritual leader, Song, hated to travel far from Helm and had only come at her request. If the situation were any less dangerous, she would have simply gone home to consult with the "Wisdom of Ages." But as the drama on Newearth unfolded, she realized that with this custody battle, the future of millions would be determined. As a Bhuac, having suffered from repeated invasions, misunderstandings, and untold hardships, she knew only too well that the cost of unbridled ignorance might be the destruction of innocence for ages to come.

The Bhuaci Suite on the Docking Bay was not ideal, being that they were not housed on land in touch with the natural world but rather set on the third floor in a facsimile of nature. Though the central garden was honest enough—a quiet space to stroll through with bright native plants, whirling insects, a small pond, and even the green sand of western Helm shores.

Song had not said much since arriving, just rested in her room for a few hours and then took a light noon repast. She reviewed reports from the Inter-Alien Alliance, which had set a hearing date for early Monday, shook her head, but asked no questions and made no pronouncements.

Faye was ready to burst at the seams. Finally, as the day neared its end, Song announced that she would meet her in the garden. Faye sat on a smooth wooden bench and tried to keep her form intact. Ever since being held in stasis by Sterling, it took her longer to recover from any major shape-shifting. Bracing the laboratory wall had tested her strength beyond anything she had ever experienced before. She could only hope that Song wouldn't keep her in suspense much longer. They needed to do something. Fast. Or the babies would be whisked away to some horrible Ingot lab and experimented on. The very thought twisted her soul and the edges of her pixie figure wavered.

A light touch on her shoulder told her that Song had finally emerged, ready to discuss their future, the babies' futures, perhaps the future of Newearth, and the entire universe as they knew it.

Song slipped onto the bench next to Faye, leaned back, and clasped her hands, an image of prayerful patience incarnate. "Tell me, Faye, why did you risk your life to brace up a laboratory wall?"

Completely flummoxed, Faye shifted to the corner of the bench, her form solidifying and her voice rising. "I didn't want it to fall down, obviously. It was the main wall for Riko's kitchen as well as Taug's lab. If the damage spread, the whole café might have collapsed. There were innocent lives at stake." She frowned. *Why am I being so defensive? She probably has a perfectly good reason for asking...*

A butterfly fluttered near, wavered, and then settled on a yellow flower.

Though staring in that direction, Song's gaze seemed focused on something much further away. "I was in love once."

Shocked, Faye glued her gaze on Song.

A sigh and Song dropped her hands onto her lap absentmindedly. "A Luxonian. We never could have a full relationship, being so different, and he often acted as if he could live just as well without me as with me." She shrugged. "Perhaps that was part of the attraction. He didn't need me absolutely. He cared for me, valued me, even understood me in ways that few others ever did, but—" She shot a glance at Faye. "You probably think less of me for admitting this. Not the perfect Bhuac of resilience and autonomy that I appear, eh?"

An uncomfortable mix of uncertainty and understanding swirled through Faye. *Why is she telling me this?* She shook her head but remained silent.

"In any case, there came a time when he decided that he really must marry. Have a child. Complete his life. But without me. With sincere regret, he chose to end our relationship and asked that I always trust in his devoted love. But from a distance. He returned to Lux, and I never saw him again."

"He had been a guardian on Helm?"

"Not officially since there was no recognized Luxonian presence on Helm at that time, but, yes; some might have called him a spy. He was much too honorable for such a term. Though, as time has passed and I have learned from hard experience, I understand that a person does not need to lie to deceive. One just needs to avoid telling oneself the truth." Song lifted her gaze to Faye's face and locked eyes with her. "What is the truth about your relationship with Taug?"

Horror wiggled through Faye with angry denials ready at the tip of her tongue. *How dare she!* But then, as she stared into those gentle eyes and the compassionate expression on Song's face, a new truth rushed in and pounded on Faye's mind. Tears stung her eyes, and grief tore at her chest. "Taug should have known better… He had no right to create babies!

It wasn't natural, not helpful, not good for anyone—except *him*. Him and that Ingot…horrible Ingots who toss rejects into the trash like so much garbage."

Without words, Song opened her arms, and Faye slipped into her motherly embrace as sobs of repentance and grief poured from her shimmering essence. Murmuring onto Song's shoulder, she cried, "I do love Taug; he has goodness inside of him, I know it, but I hate him now, too. Oh, I wish I were dead."

It had grown dark by the time Song led Faye back into their suite and presented her with a small gift. A painting of a beautiful Bhuaci home on a hill overlooking a frosted lake. The lights were on inside the house while a red bird sat on a snowy branch, looking in the window. She sat beside Faye on the couch with the picture propped on the table before them. "I found this in a small Newearth shop many years ago. It spoke to me then as I hope it will speak to you now." She gestured to the comfortable home, nestled in the wintery scene. "Sometimes, we are inside the house enjoying the comforts of family and loved ones." She pointed aside. "Sometimes we are the bird, sitting in the cold on the outside." Her gaze shifted back to Faye. "And, so, it's true of everyone. No one gets to stay warm and comfortable inside all the time. And there will be a day when even the smallest bird gets to build its own perfect nest."

Bewildered, Faye shook her head. "I don't understand."

"You will, someday, Faye. Your love for Taug was not wrong, but perhaps your expectations were misplaced. He is a Cresta, my dear. And Cresta value science and learning above all else. He'd probably be distressed to know that he has hurt you, but he'll be baffled as to what he did wrong. In his eyes, developing a hybrid baby is an accomplishment not a crime against nature and good sense."

Faye stared at the bird in the wintery landscape, her voice dropped low. "I wasn't trying to kill myself. I really was worried about the wall caving in. Though, there might have been better ways of handling the situation. I realize that now." She sighed and looked at Song. "Are you in the house…or out in the snow?"

A soft smile played on Song's lips. "We are outside together…but I don't feel a bit cold."

—Planet Lux—

Saturday, August 5th

Cerulean couldn't get over how much he liked Sterling's new home on Lux. For someone facing the end of his lifespan on this side of the Great Divide, his father's old friend certainly had invested heavily in landscaping and home décor. Pretty much took Cerulean's breath away. Now that he had a real human body, that was an interesting experience, to say the least.

The three-story stone farmhouse built on a low rise beside a fast-running stream with a churning watermill, which seemed quite busy at the moment as customers lined along a pebble path, struck Cerulean as quaintly provincial. He rubbed his forehead. *What is going on here?*

Sterling stopped on the arched wooden bridge beside him, eyeing the picturesque scene. "It's become all the rage." He shrugged, mystified by his own creation. "I always thought that OldEarth watermills were pretty, so I copied a few designs I discovered from ancient databanks and hired a Bhuaci artist, a Uanyi foreman, and a human architect. Who would have suspected a latent Luxonian desire to grind their own grain for homemade bread?" He scratched his bearded chin. "I suspect that Roux's flamboyant parties, featuring OldEarth cuisine, have something to do with it. Crusty Italian bread dipped in garlicky olive oil is now expected at every gathering."

Pleasantly bewildered, Cerulean followed Sterling across the bridge and under the boughs of two enormous trees with high-arched branches and velvety leaves. Flowers meandered along the pebble path to the dark wooden front door, hung on golden hinges. Sterling led the way inside, entering the cozy front room which elbowed to an open kitchen.

Charming hardly covered it. Cerulean shook his head. A fireplace sat at one end while a woodstove perched on stubby legs along the central wall, massive dark wood beams ran along the ceiling, and every piece of furniture looked comfortable and inviting, with bright, well-padded cushions. Braids of onions hung from one rafter while bunches of herbs hung from another. Jugs, mugs, plates, platters, and ceramic bowls lined a solid shelf. Bay windows let in streams of light, though a corner sheltered a bookshelf stocked with ancient titles.

Turning and facing Cerulean, Sterling rubbed his hands together like a host eager to please his guest. "What can I get you? Tea? Coffee? Juice perhaps?"

More attractive than Cerulean could ever remember, Sterling had managed to maintain his fading shape. Though he no longer stood as straight as in years past, with his shock of white hair, piercing gray eyes, and flowing robes, he remained as imposing as when serving as a Supreme Judge. But now, with softer edges, humor in his eyes, and a glimmer of humility, the figure before him was the same yet completely new. Trust and attraction to someone he had previously found exasperating unsettled Cerulean.

Sterling still waited for an answer.

"Oh, tea, if you have it. Any kind will do. I grow herbs and teas at home." *Am I babbling?* A flush worked over Cerulean's face. Never, in all his years dealing with Sterling had he ever felt this caught off guard. Sterling frequently horrified, disgusted, and amazed him, but never this. *This what?* Cerulean didn't even know where to begin analyzing his own feelings much less Sterling's change of personality.

Sterling began the tea preparations: mugs drawn from a low shelf, a canister of aromatic tea opened, sending a spicy scent through the air, and a kettle placed on the stove. With a sharp snap of his fingers, Sterling had glowing heat radiating heat through the stovetop. "I haven't been abducted and replaced if that's what you are thinking."

Cerulean nearly choked. "I didn't think that…I don't know what to think, to be perfectly honest. This"—he waved his arms—"it just doesn't seem like you. High-rise apartments, clean lines, a few simple luxuries are more your style…though there was that spell with growing houseplants…and the knitting episode…"

Sterling slid a platter of scones out of the oven with mittened hands and placed it on a small table between two chairs set before the fireplace. "Yes, well, people can surprise you, rise above their former selves." He glanced out the window where the sun shone bright and hot. "No need for a fire today, but I thought these would go well with the tea." He shrugged. "Don't think too highly of my culinary abilities. Roux made them before he had to rush off to the emergency Supreme Council meeting. Then he's heading to Ingilium on a fact-finding mission." His tone softened as he returned to the kitchen and began to pour hot water into the waiting mugs. "He's really not a bad sort, Roux. I do wish you'd get over the spy thing, ancient history now, and trust him as he deserves. He admires you so much."

Cerulean thought his head might burst. "I respect Roux…I just know that he tends to value other people's opinions a little too much."

Sterling ambled forward and handed a steaming mug to Cerulean. "He's not *you.* That said, he's a remarkable person with his own unique qualities." His gaze turning inward, Sterling made his way to the chair across from Cerulean and sat down with a soft sigh.

Cerulean placed his tea on the table, sat on the matching chair, and took a scone. It smelled wonderful. He took a small bite and realized that Roux could indeed cook. That really did surprise him. *Have I never eaten Roux's food before?* Certainly. Lots of times…there had been gatherings, parties, even formal settings…*but did I know*… A lump formed in Cerulean's throat. "I suppose I do owe Roux an apology. He's always been kind to me…and I've not always appreciated his efforts."

A fatherly smile and Sterling nodded his acceptance of Cerulean's moment of personal growth. "Now we really must deal with matters at hand. As Song likes to remind me…a Cresta is a Cresta and an Ingot is an Ingot." He grinned, a sparkle in his eye, and leaned back. "Now there's a remarkable person for you. That Bhuac is one in a trillion."

Cerulean took a sip of the spicy tea and relished the opportunity to listen, for he suddenly realized that, in his retirement, Sterling may have become more honest with himself. Now this odd old man in the mystifyingly charming house apparently had a story to tell.

Sterling clasped his hands over his lean stomach and stared across the room with a faraway expression on his face. "Long, long ago, Song used to spend quality time with an important person, a Luxonian of high repute. I didn't know him well, more of an acquaintance really, but everyone was aware of their relationship. Only *she* seemed to think it would go anywhere. The rest of us understood that he just needed company as he made his way through his early years."

A picture of Mauve, Sterling's one-time flamboyant lover, rushed into Cerulean's mind. He closed his eyes to the memory. It had a sad ending, and he didn't want Sterling to become distracted.

In a weirdly mind-reading sort of manner, Sterling waved his hand as if brushing Cerulean's thoughts aside. "Song was never like Mauve. No, Song was always dignified. A beautiful soul with an honest desire to do the right thing no matter the cost. She couldn't imagine that anyone would act like a lover without actually being in love…or knowing what love meant. Blind perhaps but not a fault really. Like all of us, she had a choice to make. Stay the same or grow beyond her past into someone new." He shook his head as if warding off further memories and took a sip of his tea. Then a bite of a scone. He hummed in base pleasure. "A good batch. Though next time, I'll request the jelly-filled ones. Messy but such a treat."

Feeling reckless, Cerulean treated himself to another. He stared at it before he took a bite. *Is this thing drugged? I'm much too relaxed.*

With a sigh, Sterling sat up and slapped his hands on his knees, finally getting down to business. "We have a custody battle on our hands, and Song as well as Omega have warned me that if we do not gain control of this situation, we are facing a future of dark dread."

Cerulean slapped his hands free of crumbs, gulped the last of his tea, and sat up, ready to accept whatever solutions Sterling had to offer. "So, what do we do?"

Sterling seemed to deflate, his shoulders sagging. "I don't know. I tried to keep this from happening. I knew the Ingots were desperate; I realized that they wanted to use the Tabunites for reproductive purposes. When I tried to stop Faye from interfering, I solved nothing, only made her ill and angry.

Even the game I sent as a warning became a ridiculous side note." He shook his head. "No, the only knowledge is what I have always claimed: free will decides our fate."

Shadows falling, Cerulean stood and paced to the window. The Luxonian suns had moved west and now only weak light filtered through the bay window. "I don't know what that means."

Sterling rose and crossed the room. He stopped beside Cerulean. "As Song said, a Cresta is a Cresta and an Ingot is an Ingot. But free will offers…well, they are not chained to their heritage. They can surprise us. And there lies our hope."

Hope? That Taug stops trusting in Cresta science, and Cobalt breaks free from Ingot technology? Cerulean glanced aside and considered the fading figure whom he always thought he knew so well.

Perhaps there is hope.

—Vandi Hospital-Maternity Room One—

Gavin stood in the middle of the maternity room before the imposing figure of Scoria and refused to wilt. The fact that the Ingot commander had come in person to participate in the Inter-Alien Hybrid Custody Hearing suggested a determined interest in Relevance's fate. Yet from where he stood, cradling the baby in his arms, Gavin sensed annoyance rather than sincere concern. "Why are you here?"

Scoria attempted a smile, which appeared twisted even as he stepped closer. "I want to see the thing. Make a personal appraisal. You haven't allowed my technicians to perform tests, take measurements, or anything. Cobalt acts completely helpless in the face of hospital administration, but I know it's fear of offending you, the one claiming to be the baby's father, that really ties the system in knots. Don't you understand what is at stake here?" He scowled as Gavin backed up and then scooted to the side, keeping several lengths between himself and the Ingot.

Relevance began to squirm, his face crunched in serious discomfort.

Gavin adjusted the baby, hoisting him onto his shoulder. "You are disturbing us. The trial is Monday. Make your claim then and demand tests. Until then, Taug left me in charge. I will not release him to anyone." He stared hard at the commander. "Do *you* understand?"

Scoria pounded his gloved fist into his metallic hand. "Your Neanderthal seed has nothing to do with the production of this creature. The fact that he is tribrid means that he is outside normal parameters and belongs to no one until the matter is settled in court. I have as much right to him as you do!"

Wiggling became spasmodic and Relevance started to scream. An ear-splitting cry that rang like alarm bells through the hospital room.

Scoria stepped back, his scowl deepening. "What is wrong with it?"

"Pain!" Gavin stepped forward, a picture of serene mountains alongside a meandering river hung over his right shoulder. "You had Taug experiment with life-generating forces and you are surprised that the result is anguish? I have sent word to my people; they claim all children born from Tabunite seed as their own. No matter the cost, we take care of our own." He paced to another corner, rocking the baby.

Scoria shook his head. "Cobalt will take this…whatever it is…back to Ingilium, and we'll fix it or put it out of its misery. We're not completely heartless as you seem to think. We don't destroy rejects because we have no empathy but because we do have feelings. No one should have to live with pain. You'd allow this creature to suffer and puff your chests out with altruistic pride. But that hardly seems kind or sane in any world."

Stopping momentarily and cradling the calming baby, Gavin faced Scoria and dropped his voice to a husky whisper. "You will experiment on him and get rid of anything that stands in the way."

Apparently deciding to stop chasing his opponent, Scoria leaned against the window frame, morning light framing his tech armor. "I want to save my people from extinction."

Gavin huffed. "People! I do not see people. I see machines wearing the faces of men."

Pushing off the wall Scoria snorted. "You have it backward. We are men, wearing the faces of machines." He started toward the door and then stopped. He looked back and pursed his lips. "You've done well with it. Perhaps you could act as a nanny to keep it calm while we figure out how to improve the process." His lips curled in distaste. "I hardly dream of a future of Ingot hybrids screaming in pain."

Gavin closed his eyes, hearing only the door as it slammed shut and the unsettled breathing of the baby in his arms.

—Maternity Room Two—

Sunday, August 6th

Kendra rubbed her eyes and sat up groggily. The chair may have been padded, but it was not meant to be a bed as her back so eloquently attested. Suppressing a groan, she glanced around. Clare lay sleeping with Herson resting comfortably on her chest. *A perfect picture of mother and baby. If only...*

A knock was followed by a smiling red-headed nurse poking her head in the doorway. "Just wanted to see if anyone was awake and ready for breakfast."

Kendra nodded. "I'm both, but I'll have to roust the sleepyheads. Just give us a few minutes, okay?"

"Sure thing." The happy paragon of good news slipped away.

Her muscles stiff, Kendra climbed to her feet and made her way to the window. She pulled back the curtains and let in a stream of morning light. Rays stretched across the floor, warming the cool interior. Next, she sucked in a deep breath, closed her eyes, clasped her hands, and prayed, "Almighty God, Your will be done. But, if by chance, you'd let me know my part to play before I bumble any further into this mess, I'd mighty appreciate it. And perhaps, You'd keep Bala in one piece while I'm gone. He means well, Lord, as You know, but his housekeeping and kid managing skills are…well, enough to send a distracted mom right over the edge." A deep sigh.

Followed by another sigh from across the room.

Kendra turned around and took in the scene.

Clare managed to scoot to a sitting position while Herson appeared to stay glued to her chest by magic. Once upright, Clare maneuvered the baby onto one arm, sort of slung him into a hip-arm embrace, and reached with the other arm for her datapad on the end table.

Clasping her hands tight, Kendra rolled back on the balls of her feet, holding herself back from any drastic action. *I've never seen anyone so clumsy with a baby before. Didn't know it was possible. I've seen vultures treat their young with more grace.*

Apparently sensing Kendra's stare, Clare squinted at the bright light and whined, "What now?"

Kendra ran her fingers through her hair and kept her voice even. "Nothing. Just breakfast is coming, and we might want to get that baby settled comfortably before he falls to the floor."

Clearly bewildered, Clare looked down at the squirming infant. The tight blanket kept most of his body straight but his head was decidedly off-kilter. "Oh. Here." With surprising swiftness, Clare lifted the bundle and held him out, suspended over the floor.

Panicked, Kendra leaped forward and grabbed ahold of Herson, one hand under his rump, the other holding up his wobbly head. *Four days! And, still, she doesn't know any better?*

Once breakfast trays were delivered and the nurse took Herson to feed him his Nutrabottle, a solution that Taug formulated for his unique hybrid needs, Kendra attacked her breakfast, gulped her juice, added enough creamer to cool her scalding hot coffee, which she promptly tossed down her throat, and then began cleaning up the minuscule leftovers.

Clare chewed her marmalade-covered toast, took a sip of tea, and then stirred her fruit cup, watching Kendra with absorbed fascination. Finally, she sat back against her heap of pillows with a sigh. "I don't know how you do it. I didn't even give birth, and I'm tired just watching you. I can only imagine what you're like at home. Do they give you some kind of superpower after you deliver a baby or something?"

Sensing a teachable moment, Kendra shoved the large padded chair over to the bedside where Clare still resided as if she was actually recovering from something. She plopped down, clasped her hands, and then leaned toward Clare. "It's called love. And it isn't divided up the way some people think…like if you have two kids that means you have less of it to share around. Naw, not like that at all! It really is amazing. Love is the only force in the universe that gets bigger the more you use it."

Clare nodded; her eyes expressionless.

Did she hear me?

Kendra motioned for Clare to finish her breakfast. “Go on and get that inside of you so you’ll have the energy to deal with what’s coming. We need to come up with a game plan before the custody hearing tomorrow. And you need to practice your speech.”

Replacing her teacup, Clare shook her head. “I already have everything covered. Mother’s rights, the benefits to the child in a stable home, stats about government interference, and my own personal decision to become a mom.” She shrugged. “The Inter-Alien Alliance can’t deny that I am Herson’s mother, and we don’t know who the biological father is. In the absence of that information, I am the only known parent. Case closed.”

Kendra felt her chest constrict. She closed her eyes, offered another quick prayer, then opened them and stared right into Clare’s eyes. “And Relevance? You are his mother, too.”

As if someone had just thrown her a hand grenade, Clare jerked back. An instant scowl and she shoved her breakfast tray aside, threw her legs over the side of the bed, and hopped off. After a quick over-the-shoulder glare, Clare started to clean up her minor mess, tossing her breakfast leavings onto the tray and then carrying it to a depository in the wall. Her grumbling eventually worked its way into recognizable speech patterns. “He’s not mine. I never asked for him, and, frankly, I don’t want him.” She swiveled around and faced Kendra, her hands on her hips, anger in her eyes. “He’s part Ingot! I can’t raise a monster like that. Gosh knows what he’ll do when he reaches puberty. Might decide to take over the world, and I’d be stuck trying to use mom guilt to keep him from killing everyone.” With violent hand motions, she refused the whole idea. “Let Taug and that Ingot idiot deal with their mess. Relevance will probably love technology. All that jerking? It's him saying in baby talk, 'Plug me into something!"

Nausea rose in Kendra's stomach. She didn't know when she'd ever felt so sick…and weary. Bringing Clare to compassionate reason wasn't just going to be difficult, it was going to be impossible. There were no words…no understanding. Nothing to connect her to the truth. How could a human being be so completely detached from her own child?

"Stop looking like that. He's not mine!"

Clare's screech focused Kendra's attention. She pulled her gaze from the empty cradle and met Clare's fury dead center. "He is yours. In fact, he is all of ours. And until we accept that reality…"

Clare pounded across the room. "I'm going to get my baby—Herson. The only one I wanted."

Kendra closed her eyes but didn't know what to pray for now.

Chapter Twenty

Heartbroken

—Newearth Docking Bay—

—Great Hall—

Monday Morning, August 7th

Justine stared at the sign posted on the door:

Custody Hearing and Inter-Alien Alliance Ruling on Hybrid Creation

She sniffed at the bland writing. *Surely there is a better way of announcing such a momentous event.* Various titles came to mind: *We Are Hybrid, Truth Unveiled; Who Is My Mother? A Unique Family Reunion…*

Perturbed, she longed to look into Max's eyes and ask him what he thought. She sighed at her helpless ignorance. *Still with Omega…and not a word from either of them.* Clenching her hands, she marched into the Great Hall and down the aisle between the curved rows of seats rising from the floor to the ceiling. Room enough for two thousand if one included the balcony; it would undoubtedly be packed. Memories of her war crimes trial, in which she was found guilty and sentenced to be turned off, flashed through her mind. *If it hadn't been for Cerulean…*

With a shock, she realized that she hadn't thought about him in days. Preoccupied with Max, and Zara's fears that her adopted father might never return, had kept Justine focused on matters at hand. Cerulean had sped off to Lux to discuss matters with Sterling and the Supreme Council, supposedly. Though she had her doubts. A smile crept to her lips despite her shadowed anxiety. *Cerulean is his own man. No worries there. If he can help, he will help.* She bit her lip in a startlingly human habit that she couldn't seem to shake. *If he can't…well, then, it's up to us.*

A noisy throat clearing caught her attention. She looked straight ahead and focused her gaze to clarify a small figure on the judge's high bench.

A human with what appeared to be a hunched back sat on the oversized bench before an enormous table, a gavel in his hand and a bemused expression on his face. He waved her forward. "Come and help me, would you?"

This is unexpected. Justine strode forward and stopped before the table. Standing before a judge without a threat of sentencing was a novelty to be sure. "Can I be of service?"

A wicked twinkle shone in the judge's eyes. "Justine Santana! What a great surprise. My name is Judge Ibzan. I doubt you remember him, but my grandfather, Judge Tola, attended your original trial. The stories he told! One of the reasons I chose this profession, despite the many obstacles in my way." He glanced over his shoulder as if pointing out his misshapen back. "An accident in my youth, a foolish attempt to steal from an eagle's eyrie without the proper equipment. I paid for my stupidity with a broken back. But I refused to pay with my life." He waved the gavel at Justine. "Like you!" His grin widened to an engulfing smile. "You were never defined by your physiology, and so I followed your example and became a judge."

Startled, Justine wasn't sure how to respond. So, she maintained a neutral expression and waited.

The smile faded, and the judge laid his gavel aside. "Well, I best not keep you waiting. I need assistance in two matters:

First, this bench is altogether too low. Though I lost part of my spine, I refused to be put together like a patched-up Ingot. So, you see, I need a more accommodating chair…one that allows me to look down upon the scene." He smiled again, a glimmer building in his eyes. "And I would like you to stand beside me during the hearing to answer questions as they come to mind."

Justine tilted her head, a frown building between her eyes. She didn't know how to respectfully express her uncertainty any more clearly.

"Oh, no worries. I'm not about to ask your opinion of the participants or anything like that. I am well aware that as the Newearth Docking Bay Head of Security your participation in this matter is objectively professional, and you would not want to be discharged from your duty on charges of personal bias." He exhaled a long sigh. "No, I'm afraid, I have already heard enough about this case to make my stomach turn." He peered closely at Justine. "What I need from you are facts. I know all about Crestas, Ingots, Luxonians, and the run-of-the-mill Newearth citizenry." He ran his fingers along the gavel. "What I don't know about is Tabunites from Tabun. Never heard of them till recently; they make no sense to me at all. Long lost Neanderthal relations? A DNA match for desperate Ingots? How is that possible? I'm sadly behind the times on these hybrid creations." A blush tinged his cheeks. "I'm not counting you in that category. As far as I am concerned, you are a human trapped inside a mechanical body. Doesn't change your true worth a bit!" Gloating, he appeared to be watching for some appreciation of his generous assessment.

Justine forced herself to unclench her hands and attempted an appreciative smile. "I am grateful that you can discern my humanity, though my understanding of the term may vary from yours. However that may be, I will be happy to replace the bench with something more accommodating to your needs. As for answering questions concerning the Tabunites, I believe that Gavin would be your best source of information. He is intimately involved in the case, of course, but also the only person who can truly explain the nature of his people and his personal dedication to Relevance."

Judge Ibzan scrolled through a datapad attached to his arm, a scowl forming. "Relevance? Ah, yes, the Tribrid baby. What an odd name." He shook his head and shrugged. "I would have enjoyed meeting with the Tabunite informally, but with the appointed hour drawing near…noon, correct?"

Justine nodded.

A deep sigh. "Alas, this work allows me few personal interactions. I must forever remain aloof, my judgments formed objectively, without even a hint of sentimentality."

"There is such a thing?"

Ibzan nudged his gavel aside and peered directly into Justine's eyes. A long moment passed, and a smile crept over his face. "Yes, Justine. Stand by my side. With your help, we might just tease out the truth of this matter."

Justine couldn't help herself. She had to ask. "Whose truth, sir?"

The smile widened even as Ibzan's eyes hardened. "The babies' truth. Almighty help the rest of us."

For the first time in ages, Justine was satisfied. "I will get you that chair, sir."

Late Morning

Riko huffed up the steps toward the high balcony, trying to keep ahead of the crowd milling around below. Once the first Bhuaci chimes rang, it would be a madhouse with everyone trying to find last-minute seating. "They should make everyone wait outside and file—"

A large Ingot brushed past, halted suddenly, spun around, and grabbed Riko by the shoulders.

Stifling a scream, his gaze frantically searching for an Interventionist or two, Riko tried to shake himself free. "Unhand me, you—"

"Riko!" A loud chuckle and the Ingot smacked Riko on the arm.

Looking into the face, Riko sucked in a gasp. "Lang?"

The Ingot before him, dressed in form-fitting techno-armor, her head free from any helmet though she clearly had an enhanced hearing mechanism in her ear and a mike attached to her stiff collar was grinning at him. Though she appeared much the same as she had years before, her eyes were laughing now. Her brilliant smile changed everything.

"What are you doing here?"

Lang laughed and smacked his arm again. "I could ask you the same thing!" A knowing look entered her eyes as she wagged a gloved finger in his face. "I should've guessed. You're always involved in Newearth drama." She glanced around. "Where's Cerulean? He's usually overseeing these heart-wrenching personal interest stories. I'd love to interview him for Newearth News. You too, if you have the time. I'm sure my audience would love to hear an honest Uanyi—" Her gaze fixed on Riko's hand brightly adorned by the Promise ring with matching wedding band.

Distinctly uneasy, Riko clasped his hands behind his back and rocked on his toes. "Well, Cerulean is a busy guy, been trying to get things settled on Lux. Lots of Inter-Alien Alliance rules have been broken, but he doesn't want anyone to make the situation worse with unnecessary charges."

Lang leaned in and whispered in her husky voice. "I'd rather hear about your wedding. Was it nice?"

Heat working over his body, Riko ducked his head and

nodded. “Yeah. Jayla is a great gal.”

Her expression softening, Lang’s tone gentled. “I’m happy for you, Riko. You deserve the best.”

His heart twisting in ways he had never imagined possible, Riko ignored the first Bhuaci bells. “And you? Are you doing okay?”

Glancing aside, Lang took in the throng jostling for seats below. “Yeah. I’m happy enough. Still at Universal News, obviously, but I foster kids on the side. Love it.” Her brilliant smile told no lies. “That’s why I’m here. A custody case involving babies created in Taug’s laboratory? Heck, you couldn’t have kept me away.” Her jaw hardened. “We’ll get justice for those little ones, no matter what it takes. If not in the legal system, then in the court of public opinion. Taug will be lucky if he walks away from this hearing without a stiff penalty and jail time. He’ll get his, one way or another.”

Alarm sped through Riko. He didn’t normally consider himself Taug’s friend, but images of Faye and Taug sharing meals together in his café created a proprietary interest. They were his customers, after all! And Taug and he shared a wall, nearly destroyed, but still, it was a physical bond between them. “It wasn’t just Taug’s doing. That Ingot, Cobalt and—”

The bells rang again, more insistently.

Lang readied herself to race down the last steps. “Well, in any case, the stage is being set. I better hurry to my station by the judge’s bench. I don’t want to miss anything.”

Riko watched her bound away, his insides a contorting mass of uncertainty. He turned and climbed to the very top tier. Most Newearth citizens wouldn’t see much from this vantage point, but with his large Uanyi eyes, his long-range vision outperformed even Ingots on an average day.

He flopped down, propped his feet on the empty seat directly below, and leaned back. Jayla wanted him to report every detail, as did many of his regular customers. A betting pool arranged the outcomes in order from possible to outrageous.

He pulled his datapad from his sleeve and scrolled through. "Split custody— Clare for humanity, Gavin for the Tabunites, and Cobalt for the Ingots, seemed the most likely. However, there were opinions suggesting that Taug might get visitation rights…or he might be sent to Bothmal. Some insisted that the babies should be raised in the Newearth foster care system. A couple of customers hoped that the Luxonians would take the babies until the age of reason and then let them decide where they wanted to live. One woman, Bhuaci, of course, claimed that Song was going to offer a haven on Helm where they could grow up free from the scrutiny of Universal News, the pressure of Ingot demands, or the unstable parenting skills of Newearth Human Services detective.

Riko shook his head. Of one thing, he was sure. Herson and Relevance would not be treated the same. A memory of an endearing old woman attempting to raise a motley assortment of unwanted children filled his mind, and, as the last bells rang, sadness filled him.

Mid-Afternoon

Clare leaned back on the hard chair, stunned beyond comprehension.

Quiet, Cerulean sat on her right, his hand clasped in his lap. No words of support. No encouragement. Not an ounce of wisdom to make her impossible life manageable.

She swallowed back hurt, fury, and traces of bile. "I don't want Relevance! Herson is mine, no one else's. Taug sure as hell doesn't have any right—"

Cerulean seemed to be speaking to the bright lights overhead. "You were the one who suggested this whole idea…I mean, you wanted to be a mother, Clare. Now you are. The judge recognizes your DNA in both babies and insists that it is each baby's right to know his own mother and each other as DNA half-brothers. A just claim."

"But I don't recognize Relevance as mine! He was Taug's idea. And where does Taug get off claiming visitation rights? His job is finished. I paid him in proper units at the very beginning."

"You can't pay for babies, Clare."

Not the least interested in listening, Clare slapped her hands together and tried to pull the threads of her life into coherent shape. "Relevance can be shipped off to Ingilium twice a year and then visit Tabun as often as they're willing to take him. Fine! I don't even care that Taug wants a hand in his upbringing. He and Cobalt made some kind of secret deal, no doubt. Want to keep running tests is my guess. But why do I have to allow Relevance and Herson to play together? Herson should be free of that tainted mess."

Cerulean dropped his gaze and sat up. Slowly, he climbed to his feet, strode to Clare's side, and propped his hand on the arm of her chair, leaning toward her. "They are brothers, Clare. They need to know who they are, where they come from, even though you don't see that just yet."

Revolted by his know-it-all attitude, Clare clenched her jaw. *He doesn't have kids. He can never understand.*

Cerulean's measured steps paced out of the Great Hall, leaving her within the confines of the echoing chamber. All alone. Tears slid down her cheeks. *Damn it. This isn't what I pictured at all!*

A hand pressed her shoulder, and she nearly jumped out of her skin.

Dressed in a simple gray tunic, like a mendicant of

OldEarth, Omega knelt at her side and reached for her hand.

"Almighty!" Weary to the point of exhaustion, Clare let him take her hand and clasp it within his.

Wincing, Omega stared at her. "You are not alone, Clare. I've made terrible mistakes, definitely not the Almighty. But I do care…that must count for something."

A sneer wiggled its way up from the angry depths of Clare's mind. *Monster.*

A sad sigh.

Perturbed, Clare glanced down.

Omega's hands shook as they held hers. "Please, let me help you. I promise to ask your permission before I do anything. I want to make amends."

Blinking, Clare sat up and exhaled a long breath. She spared a glance Omega's way. "Herson is mine. I didn't choose Relevance, but now I'm stuck with him, part of the year anyway." She shrugged. "I shouldn't feel this way. Perhaps Relevance does need me, too." Irritation bubbled up like lava from an erupting volcano. "But Taug really should have gotten a bigger fine and more community service, no matter how Cobalt made it seem as if the Ingots were indebted to him for saving their entire race." She snorted. "It may be true but at what a cost!"

Omega stood and reached down. "Come have dinner with me. We can make plans for two separate nurseries and even think of ways to allow the boys to grow up together with minimum…inconvenience." He flashed a smile. "Believe it or not, I'm great with scheduling off-world visits. I can make this work, Clare."

Getting to her feet and stretching, bypassing Omega's outstretched hand, Clare nodded. "Oh, all right. I could use some logistics help. And it'll probably take the skills of an Eternal to raise these boys without fuss and drama."

Stuffing his hands into hidden pockets, Omega laughed.

"Oh, there is always fuss and drama. What would life be like without them?"

Hardly believing it possible, Clare quirked a smile at the being she had hated for so long. "Sane, maybe?"

Grief entered Omega's eyes. "Sterling and Song warned me that if I try to help you, my heart will get broken."

Annoyed at the bitter edge in her voice, Clare started toward the door. "Sometimes that's the only way to know if you have one."

Chapter Twenty-One

Parenting Skills

—Bala's Home—

Tuesday, August 8th

Bala stood in the middle of his bathroom, a screaming, naked baby strapped to the changing table, and barely refrained from covering his nose, whacking Gavin, or slugging Cobalt. It took every ounce of his self-control, which was fading fast. "Okay, guys, I know that you hate each other beyond the farthest stars…I get that. But really, Relevance is in serious need here. Diaper changes are a form of life support. Hear me? Life. Support! Babies *can't* change themselves."

Gavin grunted and yanked a fresh diaper from the stack on the left. "I did this many times in the hospital." Head up, shoulders back, Gavin spread the clean diaper with one hand, the other hand resting lightly on Relevance's chest.

A dirty diaper dangled from Cobalt's technologically advanced fingers. The scowl on his face screamed his question.

With a flick, Bala pointed to the sealed trash container. He returned his attention to Gavin, who seemed to understand the mechanical workings of diapers surprisingly well. He tried not to let his own long and messy history in such situations influence his appreciation of Gavin's natural skill.

After beating the trash can into submission, Cobalt dropped in the dirty diaper. Then, with frantic jerks, he wiped his hands front and back on a hanging towel.

A squeal from the kitchen alerted Bala to the fact that

Kendra's patience was nearly as fried as his own. Clare was not an easy woman to teach. And a baby bottle in a baby's mouth could be a tricky affair. He shook himself free from the memory of Clare trying to get Herson to hold his own bottle while propped on the corner of the couch.

Once Relevance was properly diapered, Bala squared his shoulders and did the needful. He peeled off the diaper and handed the now furious baby to Cobalt. "Your turn."

Glowering, Cobalt lifted his hands as if in surrender and shook his head. "We have attendants bred for just this matter. Nanikins. Their sole purpose in existence is to manage infants before they are technologically connected. They take care of such…" His mouth puckered.

A slow shake of the head and Bala made it known to the universe that he was disappointed in Cobalt…in Ingots in general…in everyone who tried to sidestep the messy parts of life. "Judge Ibzan put your name on the birth certificate as "Ingot Parent." You may think that means you can hire someone to take care of Relevance, but that hardly means that you don't have full responsibility for his care during Ingot visitations. Diapers are a part of a parent's life, my friend." Attempting a paternal expression, which was darn hard while peering up at a mechanically armored man, Bala stared into Cobalt's eyes. "You can do this. You *must* do this." He glanced over his shoulder. "Kendra will kill me if you leave here not knowing how to do this."

With a flat stare, Cobalt snatched the diaper, grabbed the baby, and maneuvered him back onto the changing table.

Gavin jumped forward.

His heart thumping like a maniacal woodpecker, Bala shoved himself between Cobalt and Gavin. "Let him try."

"You insane? He kill the child, squeeze him to death with unfeeling hands!"

An odd sound made Bala whip around, fear ripping

through his body.

Peek-a-boo?

Gavin pressed forward, trying to see.

Stepping aside, Bala tried to convince his heart that it was safe to stay in place.

Leaning over the baby thrashing on the changing table, Cobalt pressed his hands over his eyes, then quickly moved them away, while popping the sounds, “Peek-a-boo!”

All crying forgotten, Relevance relaxed and stared up, entranced.

Cobalt repeated his maneuver, this time one-handed, while the other hand slid an unfolded diaper next to the child’s bottom. “Boo-Boo!”

A baby grin slid over Relevance’s face.

Instantly, Gavin slipped the diaper in place, wrapped it, and sealed the ends, his eyes never leaving the baby’s face.

Well, I’ll be hog-tied at the Newearth Fair. Bala snuck a glance at Cobalt’s face.

It glowed. A happy Ingot?

Didn’t know it was possible.

Bala glanced at the third person listed on the birth certificate—Tabunite Parent.

Astonishment fought bewilderment. Huffing, Gavin reached for the baby. “He tired. Needs food and a nap now.”

Cobalt stepped back and let Gavin scoop the satisfied infant into his arms.

Rubbing his forehead in a vague attempt to forestall a headache, Bala muttered as he led the way to the kitchen. “Feeding isn’t hard. Not really. Much easier than diapers, I assure you. We got the worst of it over with.” He led his obedient followers from the master bathroom, down the dim hallway, toward the open kitchen on the right.

Her eyes sparking hellfire, Kendra stood with Herson cradled in one arm, swinging a half-full baby bottle with the other. Clare stood facing her with hands propped on her hips, a deadly glare in her eyes.

Bala had been around women long enough to read the signs of the times. *Danger! Danger!*

Hardly missing a beat, he kept going and strolled to the living room where two cradles were set, one in front of each couch, facing away from each other.

"You two decide who needs the most practice putting Relevance to bed"—he pointedly stared at Cobalt—"while I navigate the landmines in the kitchen and retrieve a nutritionally balanced meal in a bottle. If I don't return in five minutes, consider me dead and follow at your own risk."

Not to speak ill of the dead, but family archives related astonishing stories about Kendra's parentage; apparently none of her ancestors were people to mess with. In life-is-weirder-than-you-expect records, the powerful genealogy strains seemed to have coalesced as they went along, not becoming watered down as one would naturally think, but rather condensing into the soul of the human being now known as Kendra, wife of Bala. Women of OldEarth would have stood back amazed. A little scared, too, if they knew what was good for them.

Bala was no fool. He knew to stick to the shadows as he inched his way toward the refrigerator.

Clare lifted her arms and wiggled her fingers in her own unique form of command. "Give me my baby, Kendra!"

Kendra held her ground. "Happy to. Once you say what you need to say."

Bala shot a glance heavenward, hoping his prayers could blast through the two stories above and nudge the powers that be into sending muscled angels to tread where he dared not.

Grinding her teeth, Clare continued her eye assault. As if glaring Kendra into submission would work.

Ha! Never does.

Bala reached for Relevance's bottle inside the fridge.

"I promise never again to leave Herson alone on a couch, chair, or anywhere except in his proper crib." She rocked her head like a spasmatic bobblehead. "There! You happy now?"

Herson had called it a day and lay slumped in a heap in Kendra's arms. Remaining calm, she stayed focused. "And…"

Clare slapped her hands together. "And I'll never, ever again, prop a bottle in his mouth."

Time to give the troops a breather. Kendra handed the sleeping baby to his mother. "Okay. Now, I hate to wake him, but his diaper is soaked, and if we don't deal with it soon, he'll get a rash and chapped. So, let's go!" Military Commanders had nothing on Kendra when it came to wet baby bottoms. She high-stepped down the hall.

Resistance futile, Clare followed, not marching certainly, more like being tugged along by an invisible tow line. Herson had no idea what was in store for him.

With a quick shake of Relevance's bottle, Bala hustled back to the living room where he could only pray that parents two and three hadn't murdered each other.

—Faye's Apartment—

Monday, August 14th

Faye had gotten an earful from Kendra on the doleful parenting skills poor Relevance had to endure. Insisting that she'd do her part to correct the grievous injustice, she quickly ordered Taug to bring the baby to her apartment for a lesson in proper bathing methods on his visitation day. She had to hold back a shudder at the terrifying image of Taug tossing

Relevance into a Cresta pool, thinking he should swim instinctually.

She leaned against the bathroom counter; a small red bathtub filled with only a few inches of water stood ready. She tried to keep a firm hold of Relevance squirming in her arms and smiled weakly at Taug. "Song said that she'd like to help, but she had to return to Helm. Something about a meeting with Sterling."

Taug stood by, a fluffy red bath towel draped over one tentacle, frowning at the tub. "I hardly call that a fit pool for a Cresta…even a Cresta tribrid." He looked around as if a bucket of water might be hiding nearby. "We need to fill it higher."

Faye waved his efforts off. "No! He can't be fully submerged yet." Carefully cradling the baby, Faye lowered him into the warm water.

Relevance screamed bloody murder.

All his tentacles flying, Taug huffed anxiously. "Are you sure you know what you are doing? Please, please be careful!"

A sidelong glance at the anxious honorary "uncle," and Faye decided that Taug was sincere. He might be an unrepentant scientist who couldn't control himself when it came to experiments, but he seemed to genuinely care about this baby. *Probably.*

She let Relevance slip.

The baby screamed louder, kicking his legs, and swinging his arms.

With unprecedented speed, Taug shoved Faye out of the way and protectively draped his tentacles around Relevance, lifting the wobbly little head, water swirling about the baby's buttocks. "I don't know what I was thinking, letting you teach me bathing techniques. I know far more about water and Relevance than you do!"

Faye stood back and smiled. *He's really not a bad person.*

Just a mixed-up Cresta. I can work with that. She pulled the towel free from his tentacle and held it up, ready and waiting. "You can lift him out and dry him if you want."

Stroking Relevance with two of his tentacles, Taug crooned through his breathing helm. Bubbles rose in a flurry.

Suddenly Relevance stopped crying and locked his gaze on Taug.

Astonished, Faye watched. *Can he see Taug?*

Taug grinned, his large golden eyes beaming in happiness. He cupped water in one tentacle and dribbled it over Relevance's tummy.

Startled, Relevance's eyes started to crinkle in fresh rage.

Taug splashed himself in the face.

Relevance relaxed; his gaze fixed on the Cresta.

Taug slapped the water, splashing himself and the baby.

With unusual intensity for a baby so young, Relevance stared at Taug. Then his gaze moved to Faye.

Transfixed, Faye stared back at the deep black eyes. There was a mind at work within their depths. *Intelligent. Thinking. Processing...*

She cupped water in her hand and flicked it in her own facc.

Relevance's eyes lit up. He smiled, beaming much like his uncle.

Taug chuckled, his rotund stomach shaking like a bowl full of jelly.

Faye stood very still. *This is no ordinary baby. He's much too smart.* Fear rippled over her. But looking at Taug's happy face, she knew she could never tell him.

—Cerulean's Cabin—

Friday, September 22nd

Cerulean placed a knife, napkins, and three mugs of hot cocoa next to a plate of carrot-zucchini cake on a tray and carried it into his living room.

Max and Justine sat together on a white couch, staring at the sleeping babies in their matching cribs.

Herson was dressed in two-piece blue pajamas. Relevance, larger and bulkier, was dressed in a red onesie.

Attempting to cover the awkward moment, Cerulean grinned and set the tray down on an end table, his gaze darting to the babies. "They had their cocoa and cake earlier. Knocked them both out."

An inscrutable stare and Justine waited.

Max grinned and reached for a mug.

Annoyed at Justine but charmed by Max, Cerulean straightened. *So, he really is okay…*

An irritated snort and Justine crossed her arms. "I left Zara playing at Faye's, but I'd like to get back to the Docking Bay as soon as possible. There's a fleet of Ingot trading ships due tonight and a Cresta convention starting tomorrow." She lifted her chin toward the babies. "So, if you'd like to explain what we are doing here, that would be terrific."

Unperturbed, Max sliced the cake, without a word or a sidelong glance.

Anxiety swirling in the depths of his being, Cerulean tried to formulate a concise answer. "Well, to begin with, you wouldn't believe how hard I had to work to bring this about. Clare isn't exactly an easy-going mom, and Gavin and Cobalt fight over Relevance like dogs over home territory."

Justine's jawline tightened as her gaze hardened. "They are parents. They shouldn't feel comfortable letting their babies leave home."

Cerulean tipped his hand in a so-so gesture. "Clare has a string of babysitters to take care of Herson, while she's at work, which often goes into the night. Cobalt hardly sees Relevance. Nanikins take care of everything during visitations. He makes sure that "Uncle" Taug takes weekly measurements and then sends reports back to Ingilium."

Max leaned back, a thick piece of bread in one hand. "And Gavin?"

With a long sigh, Cerulean took a cup of cocoa and sipped it carefully, trying not to singe his lips. A most unpleasant experience. "Gavin is a nervous wreck. He lives for Relevance and can't eat or sleep properly when the baby is with anyone else."

Justine began to tap her fingers together. "You still haven't answered my question."

His own nerves taut, Cerulean snapped. "By the Divide, Justine, you aren't making this any easier."

Max swallowed the last bit of his bread, wiped his lips with the back of his hand, and moved to the edge of the couch, sitting straighter. "What is going on, Cerulean?"

I can't do this. I thought I could but... Cerulean pressed his hands together. "Sterling is all but faded and, as you know, Omega helped Clare get everything settled, and then..."

Max's expression softened. He nodded.

Clearing his throat, Cerulean tried to scrape together a sane way of telling them his fears. "Before Omega passed on, he told me something. It happened to be almost exactly what Sterling warned me about before he...became unable to communicate."

Justine's hard expression turned angry. "Spit it out, Cerulean. Enough drama."

Cerulean stood, paced across the room, and stopped before the bay window facing the late summer fields. "It's the babies. They are going to change the future." He turned around and faced Max and Justine. "But not for the better."

Justine jumped to her feet, a scowl darkening her features dangerously. "What does that mean? Because they have mixed DNA? Bothmal, Cerulean, we are all hybrids here!" She swung a jabbing finger at Max. "He is as human as they come now! Except for the mechanical armature, of course. You're human just with Luxonian abilities." She shrugged. "While I'm still an android with a human personality…charming as always." Her supercilious smirk belied her words. "Are *we* a problem? Dangerous to humankind? What about Zara? Mixed breed and all. She's certainly rough around the edges. Might want to get rid of her, too, while you're cleansing the universe of unwanted elements!"

Dead silence.

Though he knew his heart must still be beating, Cerulean was practically positive it had just broken beyond repair.

With a long sigh, Max rose and paced over to Justine. He placed an arm around her shoulder and drew her into an embrace.

It was the first time Cerulean had ever seen them act like a loving couple…like flesh and blood humans. He swallowed down an ache in his throat. "I'm sorry, Justine. That's not what I—"

Max lifted his hand and peered over Justine's head, which was now buried in his shoulder. His gaze compassionate but commanding. *Wait.*

Startled by this role reversal and uncertain of his part to play, Cerulean paced over to the babies and checked their breathing.

Both fine. Herson lay flat on his back, his arms and legs spread, completely free and relaxed. A peaceful expression on his tiny, pink face.

Relevance had tightened into a ball, like a Roly-Poly Pill bug. The habitual scowl on his face had already created ridges on his forehead. Only when something caught his attention and fascinated him did he offer a smile. Otherwise, he appeared to be generally disgusted with the world and annoyed by personal contact. His skin was thickening in the Cresta manner, while his body style appeared human. *Only the Almighty knows how the Ingot part of his nature will manifest itself...*

A sniff returned his attention to the matter at hand. Justine.

Cerulean turned and faced his guests.

Her head back, wiping her face, as if to erase non-existent tears, Justine still stood within the confines of Max's arms.

Max glanced over at the cribs. "What do you have to say, Cerulean?"

Flabbergasted by the realities being ignored, Cerulean didn't know where to begin. "I can't do this. Not without your help."

Her words, "cleansing the universe" staccato shots, reminded Cerulean of a piece of OldEarth music he had heard long ago…*something so sad...*

Justine stared at Cerulean. "It's not you. Just me. I'm…so…angry!" Her gaze softened. "I was happy when you discovered your human nature. After all you've done for humanity, it was a well-deserved gift. Abbas loved you deeply in that act, and it cost him dearly." She shook her head as if trying to clear her mind. Then she pulled away and met Max's gentle gaze. "And Omega honestly wanted to make up for his mistakes by completing your human development." She shrugged. "Not very original, perhaps, but kindly meant." She broke free and wandered over to the cribs, stopped, and stared down at the sleeping babies. "I have Zara. I know. And I am human-ish." Reaching down, she caressed Herson's forehead.

"But…I'm also trapped in a mechanical body. The only two beings who could have set me free—are gone." She glanced over. "Guess I'm more human than I realized. But not in a good way."

Max stepped forward and placed his hands on Justine's shoulders. An intimate act, courageous, yet sharing vulnerability. Pealing his gaze off the babies, he looked over at Cerulean. "Why do you fear these infants?"

A desire to throw something, scream, and kick the furniture nearly overmastered Cerulean. *How can I possibly explain?*

"I don't fear them…but what we will make of them!" Exasperated, he flung himself down on the couch. "You have to look at the situation objectively…from the vision of an Eternal and a pragmatic Supreme Judge." His gaze fell on the silent cribs. "We failed them before they were even born. Brothers where the mother only cares for one son. Fathers, not their fathers, who hate each other with a passion. An uncle who can hardly see beyond the measurements in his laboratory. Fractured and fragmented, they have no identity beyond their momentary environment. When they are on Newearth, they must at least seem human, but when on Tabun, they must fit in there…and good luck trying to adjust to the sensibilities of Ingot society. No matter where they are, they are in exile, traitors to some aspect of their own nature." Tears welled up in Cerulean's eyes. "When your origin hates parts of itself…"

Silence allowed the thought to complete itself in the minds of those present.

Justine sighed and softly recited a deeper meaning.

"And Melancholy mark'd him for her own.
Large was his bounty, and his soul sincere,
He gave to Mis'ry all he had, a tear…

She shrugged off any pretense of showing off her intelligence. “Elegy Written in a Country Church-Yard by Gray. An OldEarth poet who understood hearts long before I came into existence.”

Max clasped Justine’s hand and stood before the cribs. Together they faced their friend. “How can we help?”

Tears building, Cerulean shrugged in helplessness. “Pray.”

—Clare’s House—

Saturday Morning, March 23rd,

Clare plopped down on the couch in the middle of her living room and stared at her two seven-month-old sons, rolling about on a baby blanket that Kendra had given her.

Squish toys, bells, and mirrors, attached to the edges made the soft coverlet more of an experience than a comfort. Kendra swore that it kept her babies happy for hours, saving her sanity on more than one occasion.

Easing herself into the confines of the enfolding cushions, Clare allowed her thoughts to drift. Spring sunshine streamed through the front windows, lighting the room in a relaxed, golden ambiance. A few unfinished art projects stood aside on a table, and a couple of ferns in large vases by the door were clearly in need of water.

At only seven months, Relevance was already a proficient crawler, making his way from the blanket to the toybox where he reached for a stuffed bear hanging over the side. Herson lay on his back fingering a mirror, staring at his own reflection with a perplexed expression on his face.

Memories of her grandparents' visits, back in the early days, year 24 Newearth reckoning or so, when everyone would gather in this same living room, chatting about personal affairs and how much Clare had grown, filled her mind. She was too young to take part in the adult conversations, but she had understood more than they realized.

The sudden tense atmosphere and strained voices when the topic of aliens arose never failed to catch her attention. Her mom and dad were remarkably tolerant of alien races but not so her grandparents. They had lived through the initial Cresta invasion and felt the betrayal of the Luxonian's retreat, leaving the colonial human remnant to face the swift incursions of the Cresta, Ingots, Uanyi, and even the desperate Bhuaci populations as they staked their claims to the planet. She could never forget her grandmother's shrill imitation of alien slogans including, "We will treat the planet better than humans did!" and her snarled response to that boast. "They are not one of us! How dare they take the moral high road on our planet!" Shivers would run down Clare's spine at the vehemence of the woman's hate.

Lord, if she could see her grandsons…what would she say? She'd probably want to strangle me.

Myriad arguments galloped over Clare's mind, various ways that she could explain how this situation came to be, how it wasn't her fault. *Heck, would anyone force a rape victim to care for a kid she didn't ask for? Isn't that what Taug did to me?*

Logically, she knew it wasn't the exactly same, but her emotions battled in mighty conflict. *Whose rights are primary here? Mine or…*

Herson started to spit up and gagged while at the same moment, Relevance yanked on the stuffed toy hard enough to pull over the entire box, sending an avalanche of fluffy animals over his small body.

In a split-second decision, she ran to Herson first and scooped him into her arms, patting his back to make sure that his airways were clear.

Relevance screamed under the pile of soft toys, his arms flailing.

She stared down at him, a lurch of pity propelling her forward.

But then the screaming stopped.

She froze.

Relevance yanked the largest toy, a stuffed squirrel of all things, off his face, his eyes large with fear. In an astonishingly swift transition, his flailing arm halted and drew the soft brown-eyed squirrel closer. He peered at it; his brows furrowing. Then his whole face beamed. Smiling, he smashed the stuffed animal onto his face and bit down hard.

Shocked, Clare stood stock still, Herson's warm, snuggling body still cradled in her arms. She swallowed back bile. *You're right, grandmother, he's not one of us. I don't know whose he is.*

Chapter Twenty-Two

Half Brothers

—Waukee—

Seven Years Later

Mid-Summer, August 15th,
Year 65 Newearth Reckoning

Herson did not like his brother. Standing in the middle of his mom's backyard dressed in a casual shirt, shorts, and boots in his favorite Interventionist style, he propped his hands on his hips and waited for Relevance to throw the ball back to him. He could see the gleam in the tribrid's eyes. Wicked. Always getting into trouble. He glanced skyward as if in prayer. *If only Taug had taken him for the summer.*

Smack! Flaring pain with bright red lights. The ball had hit him right on the forehead. Falling backward, he struggled to keep his balance and reflexively grabbed for the hard blue ball. It slipped out of his grasp, and he stumbled.

Relevance, large and bulky, without a hint of Ingot techno armor under his pristine white shirt and dark blue shorts, appeared as human as anyone. Except for the thicker skin, of course. Only Clare and Herson knew about the implants—one eye could see better than an eagle, and his ears were more sensitive than the average bat. A handsome kid with straight black hair, black eyes, developing muscles, a strong jaw, and a determined expression. Relevance never failed to attract notice. Even of grown women. And he was only seven.

"What'd ya do that for? I was right here!"

Relevance's expression did not change. He stared, deadpanned, at his brother. *Little* brother, he'd say, though, technically, Herson had been born first. "You weren't paying attention."

"I was, too!"

A squirrel scampered down the maple tree, froze, and waited, ears perked and tail swishing.

Instantly focused, Relevance reached into a pocket, retrieved what looked very much like a stun gun, and fired.

Fury boiled up in Herson, his face flushing. "Stop it! That's my squirrel!"

Striding toward the creature now stretched out on the grass, Relevance spared a glance over his shoulder, a smirk playing on his lips. "Yours? How is it yours?"

Running forward, Herson panted with effort. He'd much prefer to play indoors with the Universal Travel set. He'd racked up nearly a million points and had beaten his mom to three mystery destinations already this week. Still, the squirrel was his, and Relevance, guest or not, had no right to touch him. He sprinted the last few paces and got between Relevance and the frozen critter. "I live here. This is my property. You are just a guest and have no rights here. NONE."

Lowering his gaze so that he locked eyes with Herson, Relevance stopped, the stun gun still in his hand at his side. He smiled and raised the gun.

Suddenly afraid, his body beginning to tremble, Herson stepped back. His foot touched the immobile squirrel. "You hurt me, and Mom will disown you. For good and always."

With a shake of his head, Relevance dismissed the threat. "She disowned me before I was born." He placed his finger over the trigger.

Herson placed his booted foot over the squirrel. "You want it alive?"

Relevance frowned. He stopped, the gun aimed and ready.

Feeling rather smug at such an easy win, Herson decided to play the situation to a fine ending. He lifted his arm, his hand open, demanding.

Relevance didn't move a finger, though his gaze shifted for just a millisecond and then returned to Herson. He did not offer up the gun.

Unable to read his brother's expression, doubt crept over Herson. He screamed, "Give it to me!"

In an unbelievably fast move, Relevance lifted the gun high and shot again.

A second squirrel fell to the ground, stunned and immobile, about a meter away.

The first squirrel started to wiggle.

Herson pressed down harder. *He won't get both of them.* He readied himself for a crushing stomp when Clare stepped out the back door. A much bolder move flashed into his mind. He stared at Relevance, smiled, and then charged, his head in ramming position.

Relevance fired.

It hurt, but not as much as Herson had thought it might. Blackness took him quickly.

—Docking Bay—

August 18th

Relevance felt immensely bored as Justine and Max babbled on about his travel itinerary. On the third tier of the Newearth Docking Bay, they stood before a twirling three-dimensional map of the surrounding universe and pointed out pertinent locations.

It didn't matter if he went to Crestar first, then Ingilium, or the other way around. Or even if he stopped by Tabun for a visit. The Tabunites were afraid of him, though. That was interesting. At least for a while. He glanced at a distant sector. He wouldn't mind seeing Helm, but, apparently, Song had rejected the option. Clare hadn't even wanted to make the request, but just to seem fair, she had done as he had asked. It was a worthy effort. After all, shapeshifters were always entertaining. And he enjoyed entertainment of all kinds. Though he loved learning new skills more. Something his little brother could never understand. A sigh escaped Relevance.

His few possessions had been stowed away already, and he was dressed in a blue sleeveless tunic, black leggings, and suede moccasins. He was a child being sent into the world by his mother in response to a "deadly assault" on his half-brother, though everyone knew it wasn't strictly true. The stun gun was set for small mammals, not for humans. It had rather astonished him that Herson had fallen unconscious. He had assumed that the whole blackout was faked, but Clare's hysterics were real enough.

Max stepped over and clapped Relevance on the shoulder. "Are you going to be all right?"

Clearly the metal-man felt some unease at the thought of sending a little boy into the universe unescorted.

Why waste a good opportunity? Relevance hunched his shoulders, dropped his head onto his chest, and whispered huskily, "I-I suppose so."

Stepping forward, the metal-woman peered down at him and seemed to see through everything.

Annoyed, Relevance straightened but let his lips quiver. "I wish my mom would come with me." He forced a tear. A significant skill that had taken him months to master.

Softening, Justine crouched before him, her hands clasping his forearms. “Cobalt will be at the Ingot gate to meet you. He has a wonderful educational sequence arranged. You’re going to join others your own age and experience lots of interesting activities. And before the year is out, you’ll head for Tabun to visit with Gavin and other Tabunite family members.” She offered a stiff smile. “They are looking forward to seeing you.” Her gaze searched his eyes. “Maybe you can convince them to send ambassadors back to Newearth.”

Family members? Cold swept over Relevance. He didn’t bother with a nod. He looked around, instead. Where was Clare? The least his mother could do was show up for his departure. The one she had insisted on.

In a flurry, Clare hurried down the incline and skidded to a halt in the holographic map room. She glanced around anxiously, though her mouth hung open stupidly, and she had to grab a handrail for balance.

A couple of Cresta travelers were deep in a whispered conversation, a map of the Sinsinawa district rotating before them.

Ingot traders thrust gear over their shoulders and hustled away from their holograph of Sectine. What they wanted with Uanyi was a mystery, but their plans were clearly mapped out and downloaded.

Relevance’s gaze followed them as they marched up the incline, proud and strong, everyone scooting out of their way.

Except Clare, who seemed oblivious to their passing.

The fact that he shared DNA with the unknown Ingots was not lost on Relevance. He would’ve liked to race after them and find a way to take skin samples, then compare them with his own. Probably not a perfect match, but likely something revealing. After all, it was his tribrid nature that managed to recharge the whole Ingot race. In only seven years, their population numbers had risen by ten percent. A fact Cobalt proudly updated every time they met.

Clare wobbled forward, grabbing one handrail after another. When she finally came to the open space around the holograph, she lurched forward, barely maintaining her balance.

Relevance wrinkled his nose. He could smell the sharp alcoholic stink from four paces away. He shook his head. It was odd how she slipped into these stupors during times of stress. She told him that the OldEarth lubricants helped her to think more clearly. Obviously, she was wrong. At the moment, she could hardly walk a straight line. A painful ache pulsed in his chest. He could not breathe properly. What had he expected? Remorse? Guilt?

Stumbling, Clare continued forward.

Justine intercepted her and grabbed her arm, scowling furiously.

Max stepped over and put his arm around Relevance, protectively. A couple of gentle pats, assuring him that everything would be okay.

Relevance knew better. He was only seven, but he knew his mother was a failure. She may have a good position in Human Services, but if she kept up the recent pattern, she would lose it. *Then what will she have? Herson?*

He almost laughed.

"Let me go! I'm going to say goodbye to my son, Justine. Don't be an idiot and think you have some dramatic part to play here. Security guard—that's all you are." Casting herself into the very dramatic role she refused to Justine, Clare fell on her knees before Herson and gripped his hands, her tears pooling.

Oh, good. I'll get some remorse after all.

"Listen to me, Relevance. None of this is your fault. I didn't mean any of it to happen. If I could have been a better mother, I would have been, but the judge insisted that you had to have your fathers in your life, and I had no power to stop it." Her face wrinkled. "Gavin means well, but he couldn't adapt. His people are primitive; they'll need generations to get accustomed to us. And Cobalt—" She searched Relevance's eyes as if trying to discover her next words. "Well, you know what he is." She snorted. "Not human, that's for sure!"

Max's hand tightened on Relevance's shoulder. A tug and soon he would be pulled away.

Clare clawed her fingers up his arms like spiders trying to find safety. "Wait! I want you to remember something. You're human, Relevance. Humans are the best of the lot. Aliens are like failed experiments. You have to put up with the others, but remember, you're not one of them. Not really."

Max's tug became imperative.

Relevance let himself be turned around and led away. Justine flanked him on the left, Max on the right. His mother probably followed. Out the door, down the long corridor, to the departing station. Up the steps. Into the loading tube. Through the hatch. Onto the ship.

A ship's attendant took his hand.

Max patted him on the back.

Justine whispered final directions to the steward.

He was led along another corridor and to a row of seats.

Cresta, Ingots, Uanyi, Bhuaci, and a smattering of humans were already in place. The attendant assured him that it would not be long, and he could move into the recreational room. Food would be available after that.

He was buckled in a seat next to a window.

It was only after the ship broke free of the moorings that he realized. He'd never said goodbye. And probably never would.

—Clare's House—

Midnight

Clare couldn't stop hiccupping. She tossed and turned on her bed, her throat felt dry, and her head ached, but she knew she had to get some sleep before the series of departmental meetings tomorrow. Bala had insisted that no one would cover for her. *Pig. Gotten nasty in his old age.*

She hiccupped again. Loudly. Suddenly her stomach heaved. Scrambling from the bed, she tried to make it to the bathroom, but the laundry hamper tripped her, and she fell.

The heaving would not stop, and she left a mess on the rug.

She was too ill to be disgusted. "Almighty! What're You doing? I deserve this?"

The pattering of feet down the hall sent a chill over Clare. "Wait, Herson! Mommy's not feeling good. Stop." She fell flat on her back and let her arms drop to her sides. One landed in the mess. *Oh, gross!*

"Herson?" Her voice had turned weak and whiny. She couldn't help it. She couldn't take much more. Idiots at work. Bala and Kendra leaving for that stupid trip to enroll Seth in an Off-World Academy. *For what? To be an Environmental Manager of Aram County? Like that's so great.* Their second son, Barni, wanted nothing more than to be a Counselor at the Docking Bay Emergency Treatment Center. *A feel-good position that means nothing!*

"Mom?" Herson dressed in his summer pajamas padded forward. Then he stopped and wrinkled his nose. He put both his hands over his mouth and nose. "Yuck, Mom!"

"I told you to wait!" She squeezed her eyes shut. "Mama is really sick. I need a towel. Get one for me, okay?"

Herson waited.

He had a price. She knew that. "You can have the ice cream I brought for the weekend. It's in the freezer, top shelf. Strawberry. Your favorite."

Sidestepping the splattered mess, Herson paced into the master bedroom, yanked a towel off the rack, and then tossed it her way.

She wiped her face and then pulled herself to her feet, surprisingly clear-headed. *Must've eaten something bad at work. The shrimp probably. Never trust a food service with the word "speedy" in it.*

Herson started down the hall.

Throwing the towel aside, Clare followed. Ice cream might be just what she needed right now.

Once they were seated at the kitchen table, the light set at a dim glow, bowls of strawberry ice cream before them, she sighed and leaned her head on her hand. She snuck a glance at her son. "You know I had to do it, don't you? I mean, he tried to kill you practically. He's dangerous. He had to go away."

Herson scooped a spoonful and stuffed it into his mouth.

It was hard to tell if he understood. "*You* are my son. Really. Like any other normal child. Tabunite DNA isn't really different. It's just older. A variation of human. But Ingots...well...they're not human. Not at all."

Herson swallowed and looked over. "Taug said that Ingots are human by nature but machine by choice. And my teacher said that we share much the same basic biology. We could have sex with one and not know the difference. Until it was hooked up, of course."

Horror sizzled over Clare. Then fury. "Who has been telling you stuff like that? It's a lie! I'll be having a talk with your teacher, believe me. And never listen to Taug. You know better. I've told you that he's unreliable. Tries to be nice with the whole uncle routine but don't believe a word he says. He can't help himself. It's a compulsion."

Herson took another scoop and savored it with his eyes closed.

Clare stabbed into her ice cream; her stomach churned. She lifted the heavy-laden spoon before her face and stared at it.

"Compulsion?"

She looked over.

Herson was staring at her, a quizzical expression marring his face.

"Yes. You know what that means. It's like how Ingots have to have technology. Supposedly they could still live without it, but they are so addicted to it that they would go insane. Taug's the same way. Science rules his mind and soul."

Two more bites and swallows before Herson ventured another question. "And alcohol is your compulsion?"

Her mind blank, Clare didn't know what to say. She hardly realized what she was doing when she slapped the two bowls off the table. They landed with a clatter, splattering ice cream and strawberry bits across the floor and up the wall.

Herson started screaming.

Clare hardly cared as she rose from her seat and started down the hall. She needed sleep and would clean up later. Herson would calm down eventually. He always did.

Tomorrow would be a new day. She'd start over. Herson would understand.

Relevance, hopefully, would never return.

Chapter Twenty-Three

Love Hurts

—Faye's Apartment—

Eight Years Later

September 21st, Year 73 Newearth Reckoning

Taug scooted back on Faye's plush pink couch and tried to get comfortable. Unease filled him. Tapping his tentacles nervously, he glanced around and cocked his head. She was still in the kitchen fixing a treat. Not that he deserved one. His behavior had become quite erratic this past year, and he had some serious explaining to do. But dear Faye was always willing to listen. If only he could get Cobalt out of his mind!

He pulled his slim black datapad out of his sleeve pocket and scrolled to the Universal News announcement. Lang always did have a flair for the dramatic.

Ingilium Ingot Extinguished!

Cobalt, the leading Ingot in the historic hybrid case fifteen years ago, who managed to return his race to population prosperity, was discovered dead this morning. Few details explain the cause of his demise, but the official report states that he suffered organ failure after updating his system with faulty replacement parts. A sad end for any technologically advanced being. Questions rise as this reporter wonders how he could have been so careless. Unless he trusted the wrong

person, perhaps? When we know more, so will you!
~Lang, Universal News

Pushing a rolling tray into the living room, Faye hummed a happy tune, a sparkle dancing in her eyes. "I found a new recipe using water thymes and sea kale. It's delicious! I thought we could enjoy some while I catch you up on all the news." Her expression darkened. "You've been so elusive lately that we hardly ever get to talk."

Chastened, Taug laid his datapad on the table and folded his tentacles on his lap. "You're a patient friend, Faye, and I don't deserve your kindness." He glanced pointedly at the open page on his datapad.

Quick to catch the hint, but duty first, Faye set out the two dishes heaped with her latest culinary delight. Then she scooped up the datapad, scootched back on the chair next to Taug, and scrolled through. Her eyes grew wide, and her body stiffened. A moment later, she glanced over. "Cobalt was murdered?"

Taug lifted two tentacles. "It doesn't say that, exactly."

"Lang seems to think it's possible…"

Taug nodded. "Yes. And she is not alone there." He closed his eyes. "But I can't believe that Relevance would take things this far!"

Rising bolt upright, Faye gripped the arms of her chair. "Relevance! Why would he kill the one person who always wanted him?"

Taug opened his eyes, his anxiety dissolving into exhaustion. "Cobalt never really cared about Relevance. It was…a choice he made. He wanted to be the one to save the Ingot race from extinction. So, he was kind. Kind of…"

"But he always treated Relevance with great respect. I saw that myself."

"Certainly. As one treats a dangerous beast. Talking

softly and moving very carefully."

Faye frowned. The food began to congeal, its colors running together. She ignored it for the moment. "Relevance was offered the best training available, given every Ingot advantage, even sported the newest, most advanced technology. He would be insane to murder the one person who made that all possible."

Taug spread his tentacles wide. "I never claimed that he was sane. I just state for the record that Cobalt never really cared about him personally, and I believe the emotional indifference was mutual."

Regaining a sense of her hostess position, Faye sighed and pointed to the plates. "You'd better eat up or it will get too sticky to pass through your breathing helm."

With alacrity, Taug took up the challenge and started in. Faye was right. It was delicious.

Once they had finished, she leaned back, her hands clasped on her belly, and she looked at Taug, her brows arched. Waiting.

"Ah, yes. I said I would explain my elusiveness. And, so I shall. But would you like me to clear away the mess first?"

Faye shook her head. "Tell me what has been going on, Taug. I am dying to know."

Sudden weariness warring with the need to clarify his position forced Taug to struggle free of the couch cushions and pace across the room. An oak shelf, thick and rustic, dominated the east wall. Figures from the game they had attempted to play so many years ago stood silent and forlorn. A few pine cones, acorns, and dried flowers offered a natural setting, but still, the figures, besides Faye and Taug, not claimed by their owners—the infant figure, the girl with the mismatched eyes and mottled skin, Cobalt and Saran—cast a depressing shadow over his mind. He lifted the infant and the girl figure. "Herson was Clare's idea, though Relevance was my surprise. But, still, no one knows who this is."

Her brow furrowed; Faye ambled forward. "I've long wondered about her." She shook her head. "Perhaps Sterling made a mistake when he sent the figures. He didn't really know the future. Perhaps he added someone who never belonged."

Increasing shadows revolved around Taug, like swirling waters that obscured the view. He turned and faced his friend. "I am being haunted." He shrugged. "Hounded, more accurately. But it was my own actions that set me up for the hunt."

Looking like an innocent pixie, Faye stood before him, her wide-eyed gaze fixed, but hardening by the second.

Bracing himself, Taug exhaled a bubbled breath and began again. "Members of a secret Uanyi organization want my tribrid biotechnology to assist them in a reconstruction plan they have in the works." He paced across the room toward the window where light streamed through. "You know how Uanyi are regarded by most other races—ugly and stupid. They don't deserve it, but their physiology does lend itself to mistaken ideas. Insects have never been highly respected…and they do look…"

Faye followed Taug, her lips pursing as she stopped before the window and stared upon the busy street.

Reorganizing his thoughts, Taug tried again. "In any case, they started with tempting offers of research opportunities, using Sectine as a base of operations. When I resisted, more out of dislike for Sectine geopolitics, quite honestly, they then upped their offers to include monetary bribes." He swallowed. "That only irritated my sensibilities and made me suspect darker motives. My resistance became rather rude, I'm afraid. So, now, they threaten me and Crestar's planetary security."

Her voice rising, Faye turned to him, horror in her eyes. "They wouldn't! They'd be destroyed by the Alien Alliance."

Grimacing, Taug swiped back unkempt cilia that had fallen into his eyes. "If they were alone in their demands, I would say you are right." He leaned in and dropped his voice. "Things have changed within the Inter-Alien Alliance these past few years. They are not the impartial organization they once were. New players have arrived on the scene, and they want to…how shall we say…they have dubious plans."

Her hands planted on her hips and fire in her eyes, the pixie suddenly developed muscles. "What plans?"

"Social engineering plans."

"What does that mean?"

The sweet treat in Taug's tummy threatened to regurgitate, and he was well aware that it wouldn't taste nice the second time around. He forced it back down. "It's not just Uanyi…Ingots and even some humans are involved." He blinked back tears. "I fear that certain never-to-be-named Cresta scientists are not immune to research opportunities offering fame and fortune. But exposure would ruin the Cresta standing within the Inter-Alien Alliance, perhaps demoting us to third class."

"They've approached you personally?"

Reaching out, Taug gripped Faye with two tentacles, the others flapping uselessly at his sides. "They've done more than that. They threatened the most important person in the world!"

Faye gasped, "Cerulean? They want to hurt him?"

Amazed, Taug pulled back. "No, not Cerulean! You!"

Fear filled Faye's eyes, her pixie form dissolving into a frightened child. "Me?" She looked up, a wordless cry in her expression.

"Because you are what matters most to me, and they know that I won't let anything happen to you."

Pulling away, Faye seemed to be struggling to breathe, her body trembling. "You can't give in to them."

An ache beyond any he could ever remember feeling rose in Taug. "Yes. I know. I have tried to stay out of the way, keep quiet, cease all communication…but it hasn't worked. I must leave Newearth."

Quiet for several moments, Faye crossed her arms over her chest, her form solidifying into the calm, responsible Bhuaci woman that Taug had come to know and love over the years. "No." She shook her head, her gaze wandering back to the busy street below. "Newearth is still the safest place in the universe. Though the Inter-Alien Alliance may be compromised from within, most citizens still profess the core values we have based our lives on here." She faced Taug and rested a gentle hand on his shoulder. "You will hide somewhere on Newearth. I will find you a safe place that no one will ever suspect." She stared deeply into his eyes. "And I'm coming with you."

Taug didn't know what relief felt like until that moment. Jumping into the Cresta sea after wandering a desert for months could hardly have felt so good. He wanted to hug her, but a Cresta embrace was not welcome by anyone other than another Cresta, and only under very specific circumstances. No, this called for a new response, one he had never imagined before but now happened to be true. "I love you, Faye."

She smiled. A fuller truth gleaming in her eyes.

With a glorious sigh, Taug padded back to the table and his datapad. "An Inter-Alien Alliance Convention is planned for next month. And I fear that Relevance is returning. I must escape before then."

Faye hustled to clear away the dishes. "I'll get my search systems coordinated, and we will discuss possibilities. But let me clear away the dishes first. We have a lot of work to do."

Watching her hustle away, Taug's inner being settled into a peaceful rhythm. Anxiety and weariness still weighed on his spirit, but he was not alone. And for once in his life, he was not wrong.

—Tabun—

Gavin stood on the seashore of his Homeworld and watched gentle waves roll in. The sky had softened to pink and lavender; a few dark clouds building in the north hinted at a stormy night.

Roux stood on his right, also facing the boisterous sea, though he remained stiff and clearly was not finished with his business.

The dreadful ache inside Gavin had lessened over the years, but every time a Newearth or Luxonian representative came around, he felt the loss of the boys like a fresh wound. Neither Relevance nor Herson ever responded to his messages. They simply did not care about him or their Tabunite heritage.

When his father, Rey, had passed, the boys were still very young. He had anguished over leaving Newearth, but his primary duty had been to see to the needs of his mother. He was their only son, and his people demanded that he return and take up his position as leader of his clan.

For the first few years, Herson had dutifully arrived on Tabun for his bi-annual visits, but Clare found excuses to resist: school commitments, health issues, dangerous alien forces that might harm the child of a Human Rights Detective. By the time he was six, Herson hardly ever came. At ten, he stopped altogether. It had been five years since he had seen the boy. Considering how unpleasant those visits had become, he should have felt relieved, but disappointment was always foremost in his heart. Why had the boy rejected him?

Relevance was another matter entirely. He had never felt

as inclined to force the tribrid's visits. Though he had received the title of "parent," never for one moment had Gavin felt it to be strictly true. Somehow the very nature of being a tribrid meant that Relevance belonged to no one. He was unique and alone in the universe. He should have pitied the child, but something in Relevance's eyes that had developed at about the age of two had challenged any sense of kinship. The boy was not his personally and did not belong to the Tabunite race, no matter what his DNA might say. Still, it was a pity. A pup that left the pack, never to return.

Roux threw a stone into the crashing waves, still waiting, apparently, for Gavin to respond to his last question.

Gavin braced himself and spoke into the rising wind. "Tabun has no interest in the Inter-Alien Alliance or their latest conference. We will not attend. Newearth is a world apart from us. Our people need time to adjust to our new awareness. The universe is much greater and more dangerous than we had ever imagined. Many are frightened and most want peace without the trials of trying to discern friend from foe. We are simply too ignorant of the wider landscape. We must wait and watch."

Roux scooped up another pebble from the shore and shot it into the sea. It skipped three times and then plunged into the depths. He turned and faced Gavin. "Don't get me wrong, I am sympathetic to your peoples' fears, but isolation is not the protection you think it is. The universe grows dangerous when unwatched and unguarded." His white robe flapped against his human form. "I want you to come, not for your sake but for ours. We need people with good hearts and clear minds. You are not tainted by the desire for conquest or use subterfuge to gain power." He lifted his hands skyward. "By the Divide, Gavin. You and your people are exactly what the universe desperately needs!"

The ache inside Gavin grew into a torment. How could he

leave his people? His mother was nearing her end, and she needed his presence more than ever. Yet, if what Roux suggested was true, did he not have a duty to the larger world? Revulsion filled him at the memory of seeing the babies in their biombs the first time. What kind of beings could do such a thing to little innocents? Rumors of slavery, selling body parts, and the rising fantasy of newly improved races haunted his sleep. He was helpless and perplexed by it all.

A face rose in his memory. He had to ask. "What happened to Clare? After Herson stopped coming, I never heard from her."

Rubbing his face, Roux appeared more befuddled than usual. He finally lifted his face and dropped his hands. "She's had a few setbacks."

Setbacks? Clare was the strongest woman he had ever met. Demanding, imperious, intelligent, and dramatic when the occasion called for it. He could not imagine that anyone could get in her way for long. He cocked his head, folded his arms, and waited for more.

Rolling his eyes skyward, Roux seemed to be speaking to an unseen being. Then he exhaled a forced breath. "She started drinking. Strong stuff. A coping mechanism. It's a part of her heritage. Many humans struggle with addiction. Not completely her fault, though absolutely her responsibility."

Confused, Gavin considered the gathering storm. It was rising faster than he had expected. With a shake of his head, he voiced his confusion. "I don't understand. We have plants used in drinks that make us act silly, but little harm is done…a way to relax." He glanced at Roux's furrowed brow. "Explain this to me. How is Clare set back? Is Herson all right?"

Roux waved all concern for Herson into the crashing waves. "The boy is fine. He plans on becoming a Human Services Detective like his mom. Though"—Roux glanced around as if making sure that no unseen force was listening in—"I suspect he simply took the easiest path. Clare knew how to pull the right strings to get him admitted into the academy; his grades weren't so great."

"How is Clare set back, then? If Herson is well, she must be happy."

Roux tipped his hand, so-so. "She lost control. Almost lost her job. Cerulean intervened and admitted her to a detox center on Helm. He threatened to have Herson taken away if she didn't get help."

Alarm spread through Gavin and immediately turned to anger. "When was this? I never heard of it. I should have been informed!"

Roux shrugged, seemingly refusing any responsibility for a fellow Luxonian's actions. "It was a slow process but came to a head when she sent Relevance away when the boys were seven. Cerulean did the best he could. He was afraid that if you knew, you'd contest the custody arrangement, which, looking at you now, I suspect he was right. Anyway, it worked. Clare got herself cleaned up."

His head swirling, Gavin started to pace along the beach, his feet gouging the pebbly shore. "But I saw Herson during visits, before he stopped coming... He never told me!"

Hurrying to keep pace, Roux called over the wind. "He wouldn't. Not Herson. He knows perfectly well who butters his bread. Clare is not just his mother, she's practically his slave. He could tell her to jump into the sea, and she'd probably do it."

Gavin stopped, his heart pounding. "Not the Clare I knew."

His head level, Roux offered a deadpanned stare. "You didn't know her very well, then. Clare may be smart, but even Cerulean has admitted, on more than one occasion, that she's rarely been wise. You can't trust her judgment, at least, not when it comes to Herson."

Large drops of rain pelted Gavin's head and arms. He looked up. The storm clouds were now directly overhead. He could not escape. He looked at the Luxonian who could blink away at a moment's notice. "Go on. We will talk another time."

Roux stayed on the shore as if planted in the pebbles. "Not till I have a better answer than 'We're not coming.' He placed one hand on Gavin's shoulder. Understand this, my friend—trouble won't stay away. It'll find you eventually. Either you are prepared, or you are not."

Becoming drenched, Gavin realized he would never make it home as free of Newearth as he had hoped. He met Roux's gaze, his heart sinking to a nameless pit. "Give me time. But, yes, I will return."

With an affirming nod, Roux blinked away.

Gavin looked to the sky and hummed supplication for those he did not understand in a future he could not see.

—Bala's House—

Bala shivered as he tiptoed across the cold bedroom floor and then made a dive for his bed and blankets—and Kendra, of course. She would warm him up like nothing else ever could.

A muffled squeal and Kendra let it be known that his frozen feet had made contact with her warm legs. "What did you do—spend quality time in the freezer before coming to bed?"

A "very funny" expression did Bala little good in the dark bedroom. He snorted. "On the contrary, I braved the north wind, took out the trash, let in the demanding cat, patted our sleeping watchdog, and then navigated my way through treacherous hallway territory till I made my way back to you, my love."

Kendra didn't even have to huff, "Uh huh." He knew that's what she was thinking. He flopped on his back, playing hard to get. *It might work...* But instead of romantic moves, images of the next Inter-Alien Alliance Conference itinerary flashed through his mind.

There was no way that Max and Justine could cover everything with their limited staff. Not with so many members of leadership arriving at the same time. Commander Landry had made it quite clear that all available Human Services personnel were expected to do their part. Clare thought this would be a great opportunity for Herson. Bala wasn't so sure. He drummed his fingers on his chest.

Kendra smacked him. Playfully. Sort of. "What's gotten into you? Been scatterbrained all evening. I thought for sure you'd say something to Barni about his counseling service when he asked about the big conference coming up, but you just got that far-away expression in your eyes."

Bala stared at the ceiling. He couldn't really see it, but he was relatively certain that it was still there. "I didn't know what to say. Part of me wanted to ask if his training prepared him to keep a sociopath from acting on his instincts, and another part of me wanted to know if it would be legal to stand back and let two brothers kill each other."

Slowly, Kendra edged to the side of the bed. She reached over, flipped on the light, and sat up. Her arms draped over her legs, she stared at Bala, who had remained in the prone position.

He knew what she expected, so he squiggled to the up position. "Don't dagger-eye me, woman."

"Words like 'sociopath' and 'kill' make me uneasy, so I can make any eyes I want."

Bala huffed, his shoulders sagging as he leaned forward.

"I'm really glad Barni got the job at the docking bay. Don't go misunderstanding me. I know perfectly well that he is an excellent counselor capable of helping troubled travelers deal with the Newearth experience. But this whole Inter-Alien Alliance Conference has me on edge. Clare has set Herson up to be a child wonder who will take over Captain Walt's position before the month is out, get the Chief's job by the end of the year, and become acting Commander before he turns twenty. Her ridiculous expectations make Moses' parting of the Red Sea seem downright frivolous."

A smile and Kendra tossed part of the blanket over her husband protectively. She leaned closer. "What are you really worried about? Barni can handle himself. Max and Justine are happy with him. All the other kids are fine. Heck, Seth is the only one living far away, and he's in Aram County, near Cerulean and those Amens people, doing whatever it is Environmental Managers do."

Bala nodded. "I know. Seth and Barni are fine. It's not the kids…our kids anyway. It's Herson and Relevance meeting again after all these years. I feel as if a bomb is about to explode and the Inter-Alien Alliance Conference, in only three days, is the perfect setting."

Kendra reached out and rubbed Bala's tense shoulder. "We don't know for sure that Relevance is even coming back. It was just a rumor. One that Herson started, I bet. Just to add a little drama. That kid is a glutton for excitement. No spotlight is ever big or bright enough for him."

Bala fixed his gaze on the door. One that had been destroyed years ago when Ingoti drug runners followed instructions from a power-hungry governor. *There's always the danger we don't see*. "What about Zara?"

Kendra blinked; her hand stilled. "What about her? She's going through a stage, I'll admit. A little old for the bratty teen thing but—" She shrugged. "She is half Luxonian and they live for ages untold. Perhaps she's still a baby in their timeline."

"She has been communicating with Relevance secretly."

Kendra frowned. "Now how would you know that, sir? You don't have any spy capabilities that I don't know about, do you?"

A wry smile and Bala shifted his eyes in mock nervousness. "I can't say. Secret spy stuff and all." He felt his chest tighten and all attempts at humor slipped away. "But there are reasons why it behooves the Department of Human Services to keep an eye…and an ear…on Relevance. Especially since he has spent so much time traveling around. That kid has been to every known planet this side of the Divide practically."

Kendra snorted. "I hardly think so."

Bala looked her square in the eye. "Seriously. He's advanced in ways we can't even begin to comprehend."

"The whole point of this Inter-Alien Alliance Conference is to address such issues…advancements that might pose a threat to the universal community. They're supposed to reassert the ban on hybrid technology."

Leaning forward over his knees, Bala rested his head on his clasped hands. "Supposed to. But they might redefine what hybrid or tribrid mean."

"We all know what the words mean, don't be silly."

A sickening twist in his gut, memories of OldEarth files flashed in Bala's mind. Broken bodies thrown into dumpsters, children sold as slaves, images of horrific scientific experiments between humans and animals…" Nausea rose, threatening his composure.

Alarmed, Kendra rose onto her knees and wrapped him in a hug. "Bala!" Her voice strained, she struggled to keep a soothing tone. "Don't worry so much, Man-o-mine. You are a great detective, and we are not alone. Clare may have fallen for a time, but she's back on track now. Even Herson, stupid kid that he can be, knows the difference between right and wrong." Her embrace tightened. "Whatever it is that you're afraid of, it can't be that bad. Just monsters in the closet, darling. Relevance is only fifteen! Gosh, he isn't even fully grown. He can't do any real harm. Not yet anyway. And we'll be prepared if he…or anyone…has any bad ideas. Our kids are grown-ups now. They'll help. Relax, okay?"

Bala laid back on the pillows, glanced at his wife, and forced a smile. He loved her more than anyone in the world and most of what she said was true. Their kids were grown, except for Alexa, and her eighteenth birthday was just around the corner. They were good people, and he was not alone. But trouble was coming, and for the first time since he'd known her, Kendra might not be right.

—Docking Bay Great Hall—

Justine nodded and waved across the room affirmatively at Max. The swags he had hung on each wall, bright with a positive message: "United We Grow," and each one written in a different language, gave the place a universal sophistication. Not that they needed it. They were the largest Docking Bay on Newearth, after all. Still, with so many diplomats, judges, government personnel, and planetary leadership arriving for the most definitive Inter-Alien Alliance Conference in decades, it was important to set the right tone. *Only two days to go…*

Max sauntered in her direction, his whole face smiling.

Out of the corner of her eye, she caught sight of Zara slipping through the doorway with an oversized datapad in her grip. *What is she looking up now? Always on that thing!*

Now blossomed into a fully grown woman, Zara's unique physiology still offered her some Luxonian advantages, but as the Cresta scientists had discovered years ago, she could only use her Luxonian shape-shifting abilities at great risk. Omega may have created the first Luxonian-Human hybrid, but even he could not see all ends. The cost of mixing the two races had been very high. Her abilities were limited, her life span was uncertain, and she was most definitely barren. As time went on and her development slowed, her limitations became more apparent. Only in considering the fate of her daughter did Justine ever feel appreciative of her own identity. She may have a human spirit trapped inside an android body, but she had learned to be grateful for both.

Zara didn't always choose to follow her example.

Max stopped before her, his whole body practically glowing in happiness. *He's like a child sometimes...endearing but...*

"Everything is ready. I love the swags. Guess Riko must have inherited his Uncle Clem's artistic flair."

"It was Jayla who came up with it." Justine wrinkled her nose, a long-familiar way to express bafflement without seeming ignorant. One that even Max in his charming blindness could understand. "How she manages to keep up with Riko, the café, and three offspring is beyond me."

Twirling around, Max appeared to embrace the whole well-decorated room. Handsome tables in a variety of accommodating sizes, comfortable chairs of all kinds, holograph pads centrally located, and banks of communication systems, translators, and even a food stall stocked with everything from fresh Cresta seafood to Ingoti energy bars stood ready and waiting. "It's wonderful! Riko and Jayla make a great design team."

"Good thing they have Wendell to watch the kids and the café."

Suddenly Max peered over Justine's head. His eyes narrowed and his smile fled. "What is she doing?"

Justine turned on her heel.

Her attention focused; Zara sat at one of the communication consoles tapping away.

Her hands clenching, Justine started for her daughter. *Enough was enough.* A hand gripped her shoulder. She looked over.

Max stood stock still, his gaze still fixed on Zara. "Wait. Let her finish and pretend you didn't notice."

Justine rolled her shoulder out from under her husband's grip, seriously annoyed. "Why on Newearth would I do that? I need to know what she's doing! These are secure computers meant for—"

Dropping his voice, Max wrapped an arm around his wife and, using his latent android strength, ushered her in the opposite direction. "I am well aware of the security issues. What I want to know is what she is doing." He glanced over his shoulder and then turned back, tipping his head toward Justine as if they were having a romantic moment. "She's been chatting with Relevance. We need to figure out why."

Justine halted in her tracks. It took every ounce of her self-control to refrain from turning around and marching over to her daughter and confronting the situation head-on. She glared at Max, almost too angry to speak. "How do you know that? And why wasn't I told?"

"I only discovered the pattern recently. She uses different systems every time. At first, I thought it had to do with research she was conducting on hybrids. You know, she told us about the scientific journal that wanted her personal perspective. She thought they were being invasive, but she decided to do her own series on the history and development of hybrid technology."

Justine frowned. Why did she know so little about what

was going on in her daughter's life? Trying to shove anxiety away, she shrugged. "Sounds like a worthy endeavor. Though I don't see why she didn't tell me about it." She narrowed her eyes. "She told you?"

After sucking in a deep breath and exhaling, perhaps to clear his head of human sympathies, he nodded. "Only after I asked her why she was logging onto so many foreign sites."

"You knew this, how?"

Max blinked. "You may be head of security, but I am Zara's father. There are a lot of predators out there. I've been reviewing her communications ever since she was little."

Justine rubbed her head. "Serious breach of privacy rights, Max."

Max's gaze hardened. "Not for a father."

Growing impatient with being on the side of an argument that she wasn't sure she wanted to defend, Justine crossed her arms over her chest. "Yes, Max. Even her father can't—and should be the last person to—invade her personal space!"

A gasp forced Justine and Max to turn around.

Zara stood there staring at them, glowering.

Max swallowed. "You think she heard us?"

Justine wasn't going to indulge in speculation for another second. She plowed across the great hall and came to a halt in front of her furious daughter. "First, tell me why you are using communication systems that are off-limits to you. And second, tell me exactly who you were communicating with."

Zara stared first at Justine and then at Max. The young woman who had come through such a tumultuous childhood most often seemed in perfect control of herself. But there were times when her riotous nature rose to the surface. Her eyes sparking fire, this was one of those times. "I will answer your questions when you answer mine."

Max folded his arms and stood like a mountain that had an eternity to wait. "Sure. What do you want to know?"

Zara's expression flittered from anger to disgust as she glared at her mother. "Were you hired to kill a mixed-breed named Derik?"

The floor did not actually fall out from under her, but Justine did stumble. Her mind froze as the bits of Derik's destroyed body plastered over the walls and floor rose like a choking tsunami in her mind. *I tried to save him—it wasn't my fault!*

Max grabbed her arm, sustaining her, keeping her from slipping to the ground. His voice rose, far away, like someone talking through a hollow tube. "It wasn't like that. It was Taug who tried to use her to kill Derik. But she never agreed…it was Governor Right who—"

Zara's voice rose, nearly hysterical. "Relevance told me, and I didn't believe him! I thought that you'd never really been involved. You'd been nothing but an android during the war, no one could blame you for that…but Derik…he was a hybrid, one of us!"

The stubborn guilt that had never been totally erased rose like a Crestonian Hydrafierce, grabbing her in its tentacles, squeezing the life out of her.

Distantly, Max's voice rose louder, impatient and demanding. "You don't know the truth, Zara. You can't judge."

Zara's fury reached deep into Justine's soul. *The past is never really gone.* She stared into her daughter's eyes.

"I know more than you think." Zara shook her head. "Don't worry about security. I replaced all the systems to their original status and erased all history. No one will ever know your dark past. Except me, of course. But that, I will never forget."

With those parting words, Zara stomped away. Her shoulders back, her head up, toward a doorway that would take her away.

Max gripped Justine's arm, holding her steady.

Justine didn't want to care. *Love hurts too much.* She wished that she were just an android.

—Cerulean's Cabin—

Cerulean stood on the edge of his balcony overlooking the great lake and basked in the crisp autumn coolness. Steam rising as swirling whisps, he took a sip from his favorite mug and savored the subtle flavors of ginger peach-turmeric tea.

Squirrels scampered about the side yard and chased each other up and down massive moss-covered oak trees. Maple branches lay strewn across the lawn on the edge of his property, with pinecones from damaged oaks scattered between them. The storms have grown worse of late, though there was little anyone could do to explain, much less control, the weather patterns. He tried to put the similarity to an experience, ages ago, out of his mind. *OldEarth suffered from toxic weapons then; this is now.*

A bobcat slunk into a honeysuckle bush, its tufted ears and spotted fur disappearing so fast he nearly doubted his senses. *Why are you out so early?* He considered the setting sun and dusky horizon. *Oh, guess it's not so early.*

He shook his head at his own confusion. Spending too much time remembering the past… Youthful days traveling with his father, Teal to OldEarth, observing ancient clans. He knew the lives of Aram, Ishtar, and Neb as well as any Luxonian, probably better than anyone in the universe. Few cared to remember that far back. Georgios and Melchior rounded out the old world, offering him insight into humanity's best and worst moments. Though, he had to admit, for an uncountable time, that though the greater universe may have a wider reach, few races managed the duality of good and evil as dexterously as humans.

Most of the time.

The image of Anne Smith as she knelt in a silent church, praying for what she thought she wanted but did not understand, rose before his eyes. A lump formed in his throat. Still, a disconcerting experience, even after all the years he had inhabited a human body. He forced his eyes to see the rippling waves in the distance and murmured his words aloud, "What do you think of us now, Anne? So many years, so much change… But are we better off? Are we better people?"

There was no audible answer, but his heart lightened just a touch. He considered Justine and all she had endured, the trial and conviction, a wounded soul who had sinned in the eyes of her sentient peers. She had done wrong, and she paid the price. Deactivated for seventy years, she missed out on a lifetime of experiences. Though—Cerulean shrugged off a blast of cold wind—she had gained the data to fill in the blanks eventually, and her human spirit had developed at an unexpected pace.

He took another sip of his tea. It had cooled considerably.

A lovely woman, Anne had lived and died according to her convictions. Few could make such a claim. Justine had to discover her humanity as well as her convictions over time. She was still discovering them. Though trapped inside an android body, Justine managed to bring humanity to the hardest of human trials: motherhood. He grimaced, uncertainty gnawing on the edge of his mind. Zara was also changing but not for the better. Something had gotten into her, but he had no idea what…or who. And he feared what that might mean for two people who had gained a greater sense of their human worth than most who had been granted the gift since birth.

His datapad vibrated. He peered at his arm where he had

strapped it and forgotten it. *Meant to leave it in the kitchen...* He couldn't help himself, he had to look. Clare's ID flashed before his eyes. He shook his head. *Always Clare.*

A rueful smile played on his lips, but the gentle touch of his preceding thoughts receded as new dread filled him. *What does she want at this hour? The conference isn't till the day after tomorrow...*

It vibrated again.

With a sigh, he tapped it. "Yes, Clare. You need something?"

Her voice, high and strained, barely rose above the whipping wind. "You."

Confused, Cerulean set his cup on the railing, hoping that it would stay put and not fall off the balcony and over the wooded cliff edge below. He turned his back to the wind. "Say that again. Me? Why? What's going on?"

"I'm going end this, Cerulean. I should have done it fifteen years ago. The world would be better off if I had. Still, you've always been good to me. I wanted you to know...I am sorry, truly sorry...for everything."

Pounding toward the front door, Cerulean screamed into the phone. "Stop it, Clare! Whatever is the matter, you don't need to do this. We can work it out. Just stay—"

Silence and the communication's light faded to black.

Cerulean froze, horror filling him. He tried to blink away, but with his new human body, his Luxonian abilities didn't always work as they should. Panic rose as he began to shake. He couldn't get to where he must go. Calling out, he prayed, glaring at the angry sky, "Almighty, save her!"

He rushed inside, grabbed his jacket off the back of the kitchen chair, and then scuttled down the porch steps. Ignoring whipping winds, snapping branches, and pounding rain, he raced along the dark path leading to the tube station on the edge of his property.

His phone vibrated again. Clumsily and with a drenched hand, he smacked the on button and leaned in as he continued to hustle along. *Bala?* "Bala! Thank God. You've got to get to—"

Strangely controlled, as if he was eking out each word in a separate breath, Bala's voice rose over every other sound, a pounding drum of doom. "I'm…already…here."

Clutching the datapad like a life raft, Cerulean stopped in his tracks. "At Clare's house?"

"Yes."

"Is she okay?"

"No."

His mind going blank, Cerulean couldn't form the next thought. He opened his mouth once, twice, but no words rescued him.

His voice deadened, Bala whispered, "She's alive. Barely."

Cerulean could see Bala in Clare's house, standing there…*in the living room?* Not her bedroom, surely. *She wouldn't...* Refusing to follow that thought, new words tumbled out. "What happened?"

"A message from Relevance, some argument with Herson…I'm not sure. Kendra saw Herson with some 'Ingot babe' in Vandi, Kendra's words, not mine, and she got worried. Sent me over when Clare wouldn't answer. The Conference is tomorrow…Herson was supposed to be home, and Relevance was coming, but…" Bala sighed; his stumbling efforts punctuated by exhausted sighs.

"Bala, where is Clare now?"

His voice cracked. "They just took her to Vandi hospital. I thought I should let you know…I don't know what to do."

"Meet me there. Bring Kendra if you can."

Silence. Cerulean imagined he was nodding at the phone. "Bala?"

"Yeah. I'll meet you."

The communication light turned dark.

His hands shaking, Cerulean tried to blink away again but failed. Furious with startling inabilities, he raced down the path again. He remembered his mug perched on the railing but then waved that thought away. *It doesn't matter.*

As he hurried, he swiped a branch out of his face and pictured Clare's face. *She matters to me.* He had to save what was not already smashed to pieces.

Chapter Twenty-Four

Amends

—Vandi Hospital—

September 22nd

Clare felt her headache before anything else. A groan rose from the depths of her being. *I'm not supposed to be alive.* She opened her eyes to be absolutely sure, saw the tiled ceiling, and knew the truth. *A hospital.* She had not escaped. Shame and guilt swarmed in and nearly engulfed her. Sobs rose like a tempest.

A gentle touch caressed her shoulder and a soft voice spoke. "You will heal, Clare. And start again. This was not meant to be your end."

It would be Cerulean.

Her words felt thick on her tongue, and she had a hard time making her mouth work properly. *What's wrong with me*? She forced her eyes to focus on the fuzzy figure to her right. "You saved me?"

His head shook from side to side, though he remained blurry. His words, distant, as if spoken from the other end of a tunnel, had to be processed one by one.

"The…doctors…did. Bala's daughter…Rachel… remember…her? Intern…here. She…helped—"

With great effort, Clare lifted one hand an inch or two and forced out a single word, "Stop." She tried to shake her head, sending off spikes of pain. Grimacing, she stared up. She'd rather look at the bland ceiling than those haunting blue eyes. "Go…away."

A white figure maneuvered to her left, doing something…

Cerulean's voice rumbled, as it always did when he was trying to be authoritative. "Not an option…"

Clare closed her eyes, her breathing slowed. She almost felt comfortable.

A new voice rose.

Bala?

"Rachel is giving her something to inhibit further damage. They tried to stop it…but by the time we got here…"

Damage? She'd tried to kill herself but wasn't dead. End of story. She wanted to ask what they were talking about, snap a question, and make them jump, but her mouth wouldn't work. She tried to move, to open her eyes…but nothing happened. Her body, what she could feel of it, weighed her down as if a monster held it in her grip. *Take a deep breath...* But even that wouldn't work.

Am I trapped inside my body?

The murmuring conversation continued. Words floated above her: "Someone has to tell Herson…"

"Relevance…"

"The Conference…"

It didn't make any difference. She had no part to play anymore. Relevance had shown her the truth, and Herson had deceived her. What did another conference matter? *What does anything matter?*

Her eyes, already closed, didn't need to do anything. She'd let sleep take her. Who knew where she would wake up next?

—Vandi Hospital—

October 15th

Clare opened her eyes and blinked in the slanting light. It wasn't that bright, but her eyes felt terribly grainy and dry. Even the dim shafts that slanted through the window stabbed her brain. *Where am I?*

Slowly, agonizingly, memories rose. She struggled to put them into proper order. Her head resting on the pillow, her arms at her sides, and her legs stretched out on the clean white bed, she exhaled very carefully and let memories march through her brain.

A colleague on work break, smirking, had leaned back on the counter, and joked in front of everyone about how Herson was going about town with an Ingot babe, making quite a reputation for himself. "Always a new one and always an Ingot. The guy is red hot for the latest in bio-technology."

Everyone—must've been twenty people in the cafeteria at that point—laughed. Real belly laughs. They all knew about it and would soon excavate every juicy detail. No secrets in the Human Services Department. Except to Clare.

Herson hadn't been coming home for dinner, skipped their usual Sunday picnics, and claimed that he was preparing for the academy. New research. Taking on extra assignments. *Lies.* He only smiled when she finally caught up with him. When he got home late, spluttering some weird Ingot rap to himself.

He faced her, belligerent beyond description. "I'm not a child, Mother!"

When had he stopped calling her mom?

She complained…said something to remind him of his place, what he owed her… A choking sensation interrupted

Clare's breathing. She had to stop. *Calm down.*

She tried to sit up.

Her body did not respond.

She frowned and tried to clench the sheets to lever herself up. *Bothmal! I can't have gotten so weak in just a few hours!*

Her heart began to race, pelting uneven smacks against her chest. A horse galloping over slippery terrain… *What's wrong with me?*

A white-clad figure padded into the room and came to her bedside. A face appeared over her.

Young, smiling, though the eyes harbored concern. "You're awake. Wonderful. I saw your monitor flash, so I informed Doctor Killdeer. He'll be here momentarily. I'm Rachel, by the way. Bala's daughter." Her smile faded a bit. "You probably don't remember me…among so many. Hard to keep us all straight. Anyway, let me just check—"

Clare tried to shake her head, but she could only move it a tiny bit. Panic roared like a spinning tornado. She grunted, forcing words out. "What—is—wrong—with—me?"

Understanding settled into those honest eyes. Sadness flittered over her face. "Dr. Killdeer will explain."

Furious, Clare wanted to smack the bed…anything. "You! Explain. Now."

A slight narrowing of the eyes, and Rachel's charm faded. "You took a potent drug, and it has done significant damage. Your mind may not be dead, but much of your body is insensible."

Horror froze Clare's thoughts, stuck on the word damage. She was damaged? Her body was dead? She stared at the ceiling and started screaming in her mind, *Almighty, how could you? Why so cruel? Haven't I been through enough? Everyone betrayed me!*

Alarms beeped, and Rachel's face receded…a man's voice rose; hands fluttered all around. Finally, sleep dragged her into the deep again.

October 16th

Clare awoke and stared at the plain white tiles, hospital-standard. A faint light off to her right made her turn her head. She tried to lift it and found to her amazement that she could, at least a few inches. A man sat in a chair, reading a book. A real OldEarth novel of some sort with a colorful cover. "Cerulean?"

Cerulean looked over, laid the book down, and scooted his chair closer, right against the bed. He placed his hands on hers, which were folded neatly on her stomach.

She could feel them. Barely. Her words came out as a whisper. "You."

A grief-stricken expression passed over Cerulean's face. "Me."

"I wanted to die."

Cerulean held her gaze, no words. Only sadness.

"Is my body dead forever?"

A hint of surprise and a small head shake, Cerulean straightened, releasing her hands. "Your body is damaged but healing. Very slowly. It may take years before you regain your abilities. Never exactly as you were but well enough that you should be able to get around, even resume your duties…" He grimaced. "If you decide to do that."

Forcing her mind above a raging torrent of grief, she returned her gaze to the ceiling, trying to focus on something clear and obvious. "Where is Herson?"

A throat clearing and Cerulean's voice fell back, as if he had retreated into the confines of his chair. "He came a few times to see you. Find out how you are doing." A breath. "Relevance messaged you, too."

Clare started counting the ceiling tiles. "Relevance hates me."

"Apparently not. He sounded grieved."

Clare clenched the sheets and surprised herself with the feel of the cloth bunched up in her fingers. Stiff and weak, but they worked. Hope flickered in her chest. "He showed me what a monster I really am." She swallowed down an ache rising in her throat. "He was not wrong."

Cerulean scooted forward, his face inches from her own. "I saw the message. Bala found it on your datapad." He huffed. "Listen, Clare, Relevance shouldn't have blamed you. Not everything is your fault."

With a surprisingly quick response, her head turned and faced Cerulean. "He told me about the girl he met…the one with mismatched eyes and mottled skin. The one Saran brought for me when he thought I was willing to buy. The one I forgot about when I stunned the two idiots."

His voice husky, Cerulean squeezed his hands together as if in prayer, pressing against her chest. "You didn't know. You trusted the authorities in charge to take care of her. The fact that she was…" Words failed. He could not voice them.

"Abused? Enslaved?" Tears burned her eyes and began to fall, trailing down the side of her face. She could not wipe them away. "I never checked! The girl slipped out of my mind. Like Relevance said, I didn't want her. I only wanted a child on my terms. I wasn't a mother…only pretending."

Silence.

Cerulean flopped back, his hands falling away.

Clare wanted to sit up, to look at him, see his face, read his mind, know what he was really thinking. But she couldn't move. Imprisoned, she was helpless. She hardly meant to speak her next words aloud, but the astonished look on Cerulean's face made her realize she had. "This is how Justine felt…trapped inside a body?" She choked back another sob.

"How that child felt, trapped by mismatched eyes and mottled skin…at the mercy of those who…?"

Echoing silence.

Clare stared at the ceiling tiles above. No counting, no facts, no distraction, no excuses. "I am guilty, Cerulean. I did wrong to meet with Saran in the first place, to follow up with Taug…to agree to any of it. So busy filling the hole in my life, I never thought how…"

An anguished sob and Cerulean slapped his hands over his eyes, tears flowing. "Stop. Clare."

She could not stop. Not now. Exhaustion wearied her beyond comprehension, but she could clutch the sheets and lift her head an inch off the pillow. That was something. "Omega tried to apologize, and I didn't want to hear it. I wanted to hate him. Hate felt powerful and comfortable."

Cerulean didn't move.

"Is that how Relevance feels?"

Slowly, Cerulean straightened. He stood and paced to the window, his footsteps stopping a few paces away. "Perhaps."

"Herson is a brat. Spoiled and selfish. I gave him everything and…nothing."

A moment of silence and then a whisper. "Perhaps."

"I conceived Relevance and Herson. I forgot about the girl and let evil have its way with her." Clare had to pause and catch her breath. "I tried to escape my punishment."

"Perhaps."

"But I am still a mother."

Padding footsteps and Cerulean appeared above her bed, his grief-lined face peering down on her. He said nothing.

Images flashed before Clare's face. Her living room. A book. "Can you get my family album next time you are in Waukee and bring it to me?"

His gaze perplexed, a frown building, Cerulean looked up and away. "Kendra is coming tomorrow. She'll bring your stuff…whatever you want."

As if standing on firm ground for the first time since she could remember, Clare felt real purpose enlivening her being. "Good. I need to reorganize the photos and make some room."

A shaft of light broke through the window and slanted across Cerulean's face, highlighting the blue in his eyes.

"Room for what?"

"The amends I must make."

Chapter Twenty-Five

My Sons

—Vandi City Park—

June 21st

Bala leaned on the hard park bench and wondered why Cerulean had asked him to meet him there, of all places. The very spot where poor, misunderstood, hybrid Derik had once asked Justine to marry him, and Taug had nearly killed them both. *Should I be suspicious? After all, nothing ever seems to go as expected.* Only the Almighty knew if any part of his life was on the right track. He could only hope.

Using a mental checklist, he reviewed his kids, as if that could somehow keep life's rampaging changes clear in his head.

Seth, thirty-one, still hadn't found the right woman. He preferred open country and wild animals. Bala winced. Working as an environmental manager was great and all, and since Cerulean lived in Aram County, his son wasn't completely alone. It just seemed like it might be a daunting change after a lifetime of dealing with a houseful of people. A nagging suspicion rose in Bala's mind. *Perhaps that's why he wants to be so far away.*

Depressed by the idea, Bala hurried on to his next child, Barni, who, at twenty-eight, was the "success" of the family. At least that's what everyone said, though it rankled. Yes, the kid was doing well as a counselor at the Docking Bay, and he also served in the Emergency Treatment Center when needed, but it wasn't the glorious position people seemed to think. "Spend most of my time trying to help travelers figure out if

Newearth is really where they want to be and, if not, where they should head next." Well, Barni could manage other people's worries. There was no reason for Bala to fret about him.

Hot sun rays beat down across the park. Bala rolled up his sleeves and resisted the desire to take off his shoes and stroll through the grass barefoot.

Rachel's smiling face came to mind. She always laughed at his antics. Twenty-five and she was already an intern at Vandi Hospital and loving it. He shook his head. She even managed to keep Clare in line during her recovery and rehabilitation, all through late autumn, winter, and early spring. His eldest daughter was a young woman with a calm spirit and a get-it-done attitude. He stroked his chin. "No worries there."

Now David was a bit of a handful, though he had picked the perfect job. As a Communications Officer at the Newearth Docking Bay, the boy, just twenty-one, was always relaying messages, streamlining schedules, and updating onboarding and offboarding graphics for message centers around the station. He knew something about everything and had made friends on every level. Literally. A shadow flittered across his mind, tightening Bala's stomach. *The incident with Relevance wasn't exactly...*

A squirrel scampered down an oak tree on his right, snatched up a nut, and bounded across the freshly shorn grass to a maple tree. A husky dog rushed over and nearly clipped the squirrel's tail with his teeth.

Bala jumped up. "Hey! You stupid dog, quick picking on the little guy!" He flushed as two Bhuaci joggers ran past, staring in his direction.

The squirrel made it to the top of the tree and expressed his outrage in vehement chattering.

The dog plunked down near the roots and harrumphed in

doggy depression.

Slumping back down on the bench, Bala tried to remember why he was feeling as depressed as the dog. *Oh, Relevance, yes.* That trick he pulled, showing up at the last Inter-Alien Alliance Conference—when he hadn't been invited—though perhaps he should have been, Bala wasn't sure, and pretending to be owner and manager of some exotic wilderness destination had set a dangerous precedent.

Relevance had declared he was representing a whole new class of beings, and it was impossible to argue the point since he insisted that they were not ready to show themselves yet. A nerve twitched on Bala's face. *David's part to play hadn't been illegal, exactly, though he had definitely colored outside the lines, giving Relevance assistance he shouldn't...*

A man approached in the distance, walking with a determined step, though his gaze flickered about as if surveying the environment closely. *Cerulean acts like he suspects an enemy attack at any moment.* Bala rubbed his face. *That's supposed to be my concern...not his.*

Cerulean arrived at the bench and, without a word, plunked down next to Bala.

Glad to finally get the ball rolling, Bala slapped his hands on his knees and leaned forward. And waited.

Cerulean leaned back and seemed to be taking in the beautiful day, though there was a surprising amount of haze on the horizon, and the storm the night before had left several branches and leaves strewn about the place.

He'll talk when he's ready.

Silence.

Bala peered at the sun directly overhead. Clare's celebration was set for noon sharp. He cleared his throat noisily.

Undaunted and staring at the tree line, Cerulean spoke in the most matter-of-fact voice available to human vocal cords.

"Penguins are disappearing."

A joke? An opening line? Bala smiled and turned so that he could see the glint of humor in Cerulean's eye. "Yeah? Did Luxonians teach them how to blink away?"

Cerulean's blue-eyed gaze crashed into Bala's. Not a hint of a punchline anywhere.

"Relevance has something to do with it; I'm sure of it. But what and how…I have no idea. I need you to figure it out."

The whole idea was so ludicrous that Bala couldn't help a snorted laugh. "I'm a human services detective, not an animal rights activist. You want to ask Seth, maybe he can figure something out."

"Aram County is north. Penguins live on the Antarctic coasts and sub-Antarctic islands."

Bala straightened and tried to wrap his mind around this very weird conversation. "Why should we care about penguins?"

With an irritated grunt, Cerulean snapped to his feet and speed-walked toward the race track on the other side of the park.

"Wait!" Bala scurried along after him. "Clare's party is at noon. Kendra and Jayla put a lot of work into it. They're expecting us both to be there."

Cerulean didn't slacken his pace. "I knew something like this would happen. I tried to warn Justine and Max, but they felt that I wasn't giving hybrids a fair chance. They let the matter drop, even when they saw how Clare spoiled Herson and what was happening to Relevance…" He glared at Bala. "You know!"

Forced to jog to keep up, Bala nodded and tried to breathe through his nose so he could respond without huffing like the middle-aged man he was. "But ever since her…episode…Clare has been a new woman. She put the brakes on Herson; he can't use her to cover for his Ingot exploits anymore. He almost got kicked out of the Academy! For goodness' sake, Clare is doing everything she can. She may never walk without enhanced leggings and her arms will always be a bit wobbly, but she's done well. We can't lose focus and let a little incident with Relevance spoil her achievements."

Cerulean halted and faced Bala. "Clare has been very lucky. She almost died—by her own hand, I might add. You saved her. Your daughter, all the medical staff, and enhanced bio-technology made her new life possible. She wants to make amends. Great. Except the blasted penguins are missing, and I don't think she can fix that!"

His head spinning, and it wasn't for lack of oxygen, Bala reached out and grabbed Cerulean's arm. "Stop. Back up. I don't understand what you're telling me…what you want."

Cerulean started back the way he had come. "We'd better hurry, or we really will be late, and Clare will roll her eyes with that martyred expression, and Kendra will…well, you know."

Hardly believing the cliff-edge audacity of his move, Bala stopped in the middle of the track and folded his arms. "I will talk Kendra out of killing me, but you have got to explain about the penguins. What on Newearth is Relevance doing that's got you so worked up?"

Cerulean rolled his eyes heavenward. "I'm not sure, but I don't think he's working alone." He clasped his hands together. "Look, once long ago, before OldEarth passed into history, there was a crisis. A fertility crisis. Women stopped being able to get pregnant."

Despite the sunshine, a cold sensation worked over Bala. He nodded. "Textbook stuff. Chapter thirteen, if I remember correctly."

Cerulean stared far away. "There are no more penguins. They are almost completely extinct."

“Sometimes animals do go extinct…it’s tragic, but it does happen, Cerulean.”

“Not in one year.”

Startled speechless, Bala stood rooted to the spot. “What do you want me to do?”

“Check it out. Find out where Relevance has been the last few years. Keep a close eye on Herson…he’s trouble, though perhaps of a different kind, and keep your sons, Seth, Barni, and David, as far away from all of this as possible.”

Suddenly weak in the knees, Bala wanted to lie down on the racetrack and think things through, very slowly. Maybe sleep for a couple of hours. He lifted his head instead. “Can I tell Kendra?”

Snorting, Cerulean started toward Main Street. “You’d better. I don’t want her coming after me…I’ve got enough to worry about.” He picked up his pace.

Running alongside, Bala had to ask. “Where are we going now?”

Cerulean stopped on the curb and waited for a couple of autoskimmers to pass. “To Clare’s party where we’ll celebrate an honest victory, small as it might be.”

—The Breakfastnook Café—

Clare rose carefully to her feet in the center of the café, now packed with people ready to celebrate her achievement, and nearly cried. She could walk with stiff steps, using every ounce of her training with technologically enhanced leggings and, though her arms didn’t work perfectly, still, they did work. Finally, she could partner up with Bala again and recommit herself to her role as a Human Services Detective. Commander Landry had reinstated her last week, and she would return to full-time duty tomorrow. *Thank the Almighty.* Now all she had to do was thank all these kind people who had supported her through the hardest days of her life.

She looked over the crowd.

Her sons were not among them.

Clutching a beautifully carved cane, a gift from Cerulean, she smiled warmly at Jayla, to the right of her, who had decorated the café with her favorite colors—blue and green—and placed streamers and "Congratulations!" banners over all the walls.

Riko stood with shining eyes in his crisp white uniform before the swinging kitchen doors, his culinary delights just waiting on side tables to be enjoyed. He had outdone himself with spicy veggie mixes, pasta salads, fruit-nut bread, and drinks of all colors and flavors. *I've never really appreciated him…in all the time I've known him, he's always done his best…*

"Speech! Speech!"

Startled, Clare glanced around the crowd, searching faces.

Kendra's oversized grin gave her away. Wendell's teasing expression as he stood to one side suggested that he had been the one to prompt Kendra. *Though…it wouldn't take much to encourage that woman.*

Tongue-tied, heat flushed Clare's face. These were her friends but…

Suddenly Justine maneuvered her way through the crowd and came to a stop right in front of Clare.

Oh, Bothmal, she's going to say something terribly honest and much too blunt, like, "So, now you know how I feel."

Contrary to expectations, Justine pulled one hand from behind her back and held up a beautiful sculpture of a cat.

It's lovely, so detailed. Clare squinted. Her eyesight, among other things, wasn't what it used to be. *Looks awfully familiar.*

Smiling in a very un-robotic manner, Justine offered the figure to Clare. "If you remember, we once nearly bonded over a cat. We weren't ready then. But I believe we are now."

Tears filling her eyes, Clare nodded and accepted the sculpture.

Justine turned to go but before she could get away, Clare dropped her cane and wrapped the human-android in the best hug she could manage, now that her arms took little direction and had less strength.

Justine hugged back.

Gently, thank goodness.

Once Justine worked her way to a back booth, squeezing between Max and Zara, Clare wiped her eyes with the back of her hand and lifted her voice. "I just want to thank everyone for coming…for—"

The café door opened with a jingle.

Cerulean and Bala tried to sneak in unnoticed.

Hunch-shouldered, Bala looked properly chagrined, especially considering the dagger-eyes Kendra sent his way, but Cerulean barely glanced over.

I will never understand that man…Luxonian…person.

She returned her focus to the expectant crowd. "You all have been so kind. Far more than I deserve." She held up her hand as if to stall any protestations, which there weren't, rather embarrassingly. "I know I messed up, and I have tried to apologize in my own way to everyone."

Uncomfortable, some of her co-workers glanced aside as if wishing they could leave now.

Clare pushed on. "But I just wanted to say that you are more than just supporters, co-workers, and kind friends…" A lump formed in her throat. "You are my family. Really. DNA is biology, but family is spirit." No other words forthcoming, and frankly, none more wanted, she flapped her hand at the crowd, pointing to the loaded sideboards with delicious offerings artfully arranged.

Nothing more needed, the crowd clapped and then surged toward the food and drinks.

Clare edged back to the booth she and Faye always shared, disappointment needling her happy moment. Faye hadn't arrived to share her joy. *Where is she? And Taug? Haven't seen him in an age.* She flopped down on the red cushioned seat and relaxed on the firm back. *Omega is gone now...Abbas, Sterling...so many I've known.* Flashes of memory ran through her mind. She couldn't sort them all. *Probably shouldn't...*

She looked around, her heart softened by the generous spirit of those who had come. *I really am blessed.*

—Clare's Home—

Clare enjoyed the quiet of early morning, when the day softly brightened toward day, slanting shafts of light announcing new possibilities. She leaned back on the rocker on her front porch, letting it sway with a light push. It didn't take much, and with her impaired strength, little was all she had to offer. *But that's all right. At least for now.*

She cupped a mug of hot coffee in her hands and took a tentative sip. The bold flavor tasted good, invigorating her spirits. A quote she had heard Kendra exclaim while balancing a dinner tray in one hand and a baby on her hip, filled her mind: *Do few things but do them well!* Though the irony between Kendra's multitasking life and her mantra made Clare smile, she knew that in her spirit, Kendra was true to herself, and that was what mattered. Peace settled in her soul. *I'm me, Clare Erlandson, a human rights detective, a friend...and a mom. I don't have to save the world. I don't even have to solve all the mysteries of life. I can't. Never could.*

Her own mother's face rose in her mind. *Whatever you'd think of Newearth now, you'd love it—no matter what. Might hate some of the changes, but you'd fight for the best in us, human and alien alike. You and Dad were the best of us. Your death could never kill that.*

A mountain of grief rising from her chest, Clare exhaled a long breath. *Hold onto the good.*

With renewed conviction, she climbed to her feet. Her socks made little sound as she shuffled to the front door and made her way inside. Long hours of cleaning the day before had wearied her body but refreshed her mind. The living room looked perfectly neat with the washed curtains, an organized work station and dusted shelves. A white rectangle lay sprawled on the floor by the couch. She traipsed across the room and managed to snatch it up without falling over.

A picture of Herson and Relevance when they were about three, sitting together on the couch, holding colorfully wrapped birthday presents. Their eyes, so different, yet familiar in a family way, glowed with the innocence of children excited by surprise gifts. A good moment she had forgotten about.

She plodded to the wood shelves and reached out. The OldEarth album fell into her arms heavily, but she managed to carry it back to the couch and plopped down. Her heart wasn't strong enough yet to review the whole catalogue, but she flipped to an early section and found a picture of herself at about the same age as the boys in the picture, sitting on her mother's lap, her father looking over her mom's shoulder, peering down. She set the boys' picture next to hers. Yes, there was a family resemblance. In an odd trick of the lighting, her father's gaze seemed to embrace Herson and Relevance as well as herself.

Do you see them now, wherever they are?

As if to answer her own question, Clare's head nodded. *You would care about your grandsons.* Despite their distrust of aliens and hurt over the loss of their planetary heritage, their enemy wasn't a person, but the hatred that broke humanity apart. No one was lost from the family without losing something dear—irreplaceable.

Forgive me, mom...dad. I didn't understand. Hurt so great turned to hate so blind.

A new sensation pierced her soul, filling her eyes with tears—not with pain but hope. No matter what it would cost or how things might develop in the future, a new reality would lead her forward.

She closed the album with the boy's photo inside, replaced it on the shelf, and faced the brightening day. *Forever and always, I will love my sons.*

Epilogue

Relevance turned from the Breakfastnook café window and strolled away, whistling, down the busy Vandi Street.

He could almost feel a fondness for the city scene. Happy merchants, bustling business people, families with children, and oldsters hustling along, trying to catch the latest tube or make it to some appointment or another. They appeared to find meaning in their petty little lives. Simple beings, uncomplicated, unimportant. A lonely death was their lot. Doomed at birth, but they didn't seem to care.

Must be nice.

He could still hear OldEarth's musical brilliance, Beethoven's 7th, play in his mind. Great music stirred his soul. Assuming he had one. Perhaps it was simply a pleasant aspect of his late breakfast's digestion process. Setting philosophical mysteries aside, he allowed the musical score to play in his mind while he walked to the tube that would take him where he needed to go. A meeting place with very special people who had wonderful plans.

Loneliness and death would not have the final word. Not for him. Not if he had his way. Hybrid reality could be for everyone, and he'd never be alone again.

But first, he had a few changes to make in lowest levels of the Newearth population. They had no idea what was coming. An incredible change they could either accept or refuse. It honestly didn't matter. He could always grow more. And once he had grown enough, Newearth would finally be *his*.

A squirrel scampered across his path.

He smiled, and with innate dexterity, he grabbed it and stuffed it in his pocket. "Oh, no, you don't. I let you out for a little run, but if you ever hope to see your family again, you'd better stay with me."

The squirrel poked his head out of the deep pocket, gripping the edge to steady himself. He opened his mouth as if to speak, but no words came. Only his soulful eyes spoke of sentience and a longing for home.

Do Not Cheer

At the death of your enemy.

For when he falls,

Far from the Kingdom of God,

Some part of Us,

Fails.

What could have been,

What should have been,

Never will be.

Forever blotted out.

Only in forgiveness and love endured

Is hope renewed.

~Unknown Newearth Citizen

A. K. Frailey

A. K. Frailey has written the historical sci-fi *OldEarth Encounter* series, a contemporary first contact novel, *Last of Her Kind*, the *Newearth* sci-fi series, an *OldTown* series, short story collections, a modern parent's reflection on J. R. R. Tolkien's works in *The Road Goes Ever On: A Christian Journey Through The Lord of the Rings*, personal and introspective *My Road* books, children's books, and a poetry collection.

She taught in Milwaukee, WI, Chicago, IL, Los Angeles, CA, and Wood River, IL, as an elementary education teacher.

She also trained teachers in the Philippines for the Peace Corps and later earned a Master of Fine Arts Degree in Creative Writing for Entertainment from Full Sail University.

Ann homeschooled all her children and currently manages her rural homestead with her family and their numerous critters. In her spare time, she serves as an election judge and secretary/treasurer of her small town's cemetery.

A. K. Frailey Books QR CODES

A. K. Frailey Website

Translated Books Page with Links

A. K. Frailey Interviews Page

A. K. Frailey Amazon Author Page

www.ingramcontent.com/pod-product-compliance
Lightning Source LLC
Chambersburg PA
CBHW070613310726
48982CB00001B/69

9798999824110